The Third Thing

A NOVEL

SIRKKA SMITH

TARICHA BOOKS

Excerpts of poems cited in the text are in the public domain. Translation into English is by the author.

Cover illustration: Pradeep Premalal

ISBN: 978-1-954087-01-9 (trade paperback)
ISBN: 978-1-954087-00-2 (ebook)

For more information or to request additional permissions, please visit: sirkkasmith.com

Library of Congress Control Number: 2021906794

Published by TARICHA BOOKS, United States of America

10 9 8 7 6 5 4 3 2

204

To those who love anyway

The Third Thing

1

FALLING OBJECTS

Elliot toggled between almost-identical photos on the computer. Happy people with fresh-baked pies. Blue huckleberry had won the contest, but he still had to narrow a dozen photos down to two—perhaps one if something else newsworthy happened.

A voice from the chatter in the newsroom broke his concentration, though it wasn't directed at him. "It'll be ten years next month."

It was a quarter to noon, so everyone but Elliot had abandoned their computers to talk. Usually it was about where to eat.

"What'll be ten years?" somebody else asked.

Elliot tried to block out the conversation. There would be two photos, for sure.

"Since the outbreak, remember?"

Without looking to see who had brought up the topic, Elliot quietly rose from his desk, looped his camera strap over his head and across his chest, and headed for the door.

Alec broke away from the others, intercepting him. "Want to grab some lunch?"

"Uh...not today." Elliot lifted his camera. "Might get some photos. Something seasonal." Hopefully, Alec wouldn't question the excuse.

"Okay, catch you later," said Alec. Elliot nodded, relieved, and went out.

The day was too bright and empty, all yellow leaves and blue cloudless sky. The only thing moving in Lingen besides Elliot seemed to be the train wending its way through the pass and into town, blowing its lonely harmonica wail.

Ten years since the mountainpox outbreak. Elliot didn't need it put into words. It had crept into his consciousness as it always did near the end of September, with the smell of frosty air mixed with wood smoke. And each year he put it out of his mind again, as he would this year.

Elliot turned downhill, past the visitor center with its faded Job Opening sign still in the window, to watch the train come in. Up close, the smell of sun-warmed creosote on the railroad ties filled his nose, the rumble of the cars shook through him, and the whistle drowned out every other noise and thought.

As the brakes squealed, birds erupted from the Oregon grape bushes beside the station. They quickly resettled on the sidewalk, doubtless used to the comings and goings, remaining even as another whistle blast only too quickly signaled the train's departure.

This was what fall ought to mean: migrating birds and beautiful leaves. Change. Not dwelling on past events that were unchangeable.

Tiptoeing into the empty street, Elliot knelt to steady his camera and brought a bird—small and brown, with a heavy, flattened beak— into focus against a background of reddening foliage. He was about to press the shutter button when the bird startled again and flew off.

"Did you get it?" asked a cheerful voice.

Elliot raised his head. The flock had scattered as a woman emerged from the station. Now she balanced precariously on the edge of the curb, dipping the toes of her hiking boots to the pavement and back up again, apparently on the point of crossing the street. She was tempting fate by wavering there, encumbered as she was by a stack of books in one arm, a large cardboard box in the other, and a backpack slung over her shoulder.

He glanced around. There was no one else present to whom she could be talking.

She hiked up her load. "I meant, did you get a picture of that bird?"

"Uh, yes," said Elliot. "I mean, no. It flew away before I could."

"What kind was it? I didn't get a good look."

"I'm afraid I have no idea." Elliot lowered his camera and stood up.

"I love birds," she said matter-of-factly, scanning the sky. As far as Elliot could tell, the flock had vanished, but she stared over his head as if awestruck. "Wow, just look at this place."

Elliot turned to look in the same direction, at the rest of Lingen spread out on the flanks of snow-capped Mount Arin. It was certainly pretty, but she seemed to see something more, something that he could not. She breathed deeply, as if filling her lungs with everything her eyes touched, gathering it to her. Her gaze did not include Elliot, aiming higher than mere human presence.

Then she fixed her wide brown eyes on him with the same wondering look. Elliot froze, his glasses slipping down his nose. A strange tingling sensation spread through him in a wave, reminding him of times when his leg would fall asleep from reading in an awkward position and then begin to wake up again. Though it ached excruciatingly, he did not want it to stop.

Her load of books slipped, breaking her attention, and Elliot jolted free of the effect. She clutched at them and tipped sideways as she lifted one foot off the ground for balance.

Elliot recovered his manners rather late, still feeling disoriented. "Please, allow me." He stepped forward and reached for the stack of books.

"Oh!" She hesitated, then let him unburden her. "Okay. But not that one." She plucked an open notebook off the top of the stack. "It has my map."

Elliot craned his neck, but only caught a glimpse of the map, as she was several inches taller than he was and had tucked the notebook between her chin and the box she now held with both arms.

"I suppose I could have printed it out," she went on. "But when I've drawn something, then I can picture it better in my mind. You know?"

Elliot nodded. In fact, he could not recall ever having drawn a map, but he must have done so at some point.

"Here, I think I can handle them now." Shifting the box to one hip, she attempted to take back the books.

She was going to leave. In another moment, he would never know who she was or how to find her again. "I would be happy to accompany you to wherever you're going," Elliot protested, without relinquishing the stack. "Are your accommodations nearby?"

"I'm actually going to the…" She paused and read aloud from her map, "'Mount Arin Visitor and Natural Resource Center.' I may have a job there."

"Ah, yes, of course." Elliot beamed, flooded with fresh purpose. Now that he had something to connect her with in the physical world, he was regaining solid footing. "It's this way." He started up the hill in the direction he had come.

"Thanks, that's nice of you. I'm Xiomara, by the way. Most people call me Xo—it's easier."

"Not at all!" Elliot's mind was whirling. He ought to have said who he was, as well. He tried to frame his thoughts into words, but Xo was still talking.

"I haven't nailed down the accommodations part yet. I have a few places to look at after I meet with my new boss—that is, if I get the job. But she wouldn't have asked me to come if she didn't think I could do it, right? That's what I keep telling myself. I'm trying to shut up the voice in my head that keeps saying, 'What makes you think you can start over at thirty-one making a living as an artist?'" Xo laughed breathlessly as they walked uphill. "You must be thinking I'm crazy, telling this to a complete stranger."

"No, I'm not," Elliot said hastily. "I'm…uh…if you don't have somewhere to stay, I know of a place."

Xo looked at him expectantly. "Oh?"

It occurred to Elliot that it might have sounded like he was inappropriately asking her to stay with him. He cleared his throat. "What I mean to say is: there's a studio apartment for rent not far from here." He halted, pointing down the side street. "Over the coffee shop."

Xo smiled, apparently unoffended. "That sounds convenient." She turned to look up at the large wooden sign they were now standing under, which announced the visitor center in carved script. A small wooden bird perched on top of the sign.

Xo thrust her box against the door. The door rattled in protest.

"It's just the other way." Elliot reached around her with difficulty on the narrow doorstep and pulled the door open. She flashed him a brilliant smile and squeezed past.

Neither of them rang the call bell to summon another person into the room. Xo set the box on the desk, and Elliot did the same with the stack of books, then watched her explore the visitor center. He should say something while it was only the two of them; in fact, he should have properly introduced himself much earlier, but his mouth had gone dry and he couldn't get any words in order. While he'd never been particularly loquacious, it wasn't usually this bad.

Xo was examining the objects on the shelves lining the walls and windows, lightly touching each item in turn: rocks, nests, blown eggshells, feathers and artwork. She slowly rotated a stand that held pamphlets about hiking, bird watching, and skiing, then looked up at a shelf of numerous stuffed and mounted birds.

"I have pages of these guys, but they're different in person," said Xo. "Well, more dead, of course." She returned to the counter and removed a spiral-bound book from her stack, flipping it open to show Elliot. It was filled with drawings.

He looked at the bird on the page. "Yes…uh. I've—I've seen this one."

"Yeah, I guess they're supposed to be pretty common around here." Xo turned and started to drift away again, continuing to page through the sketchbook.

Elliot swallowed hard. He was unprepared for how he felt whenever Xo looked his way, and equally unprepared for how much he wanted her to keep doing so. Anything he could say about birds or drawings had flown his mind. As he grasped at shreds of ideas, his eyes fell on a large taxidermy owl staring down from the top of an open-shelved display case, claws and wings outstretched in a hunting posture.

"Ah!" Elliot's voice came out unnaturally loud as he gestured at the bird.

He didn't know exactly how he'd intended to finish the thought, perhaps to note he'd always admired that one, but Xo jumped and spun around at his exclamation. Her backpack collided with the display case, and the owl heaved into space on its last flight.

Elliot watched in horror as Xo stepped back and then froze, apparently too shocked to flee the avian avalanche. With no time to think or say anything, he threw himself into the path of the hurtling bird. For a few gruesome seconds it seemed to gain new life; its wings were everywhere; its talons raked his arm. It was incredibly heavy, much heavier than it looked, and he sprawled sideways under the impact as it ricocheted off his head. Xo ducked and rolled out of the way at the last moment as other bric-a-brac dislodged by the owl's wings came clattering down.

Silence fell at last, after several other knickknacks.

"Are you—" Elliot coughed dust out of his throat, "—all right?"

Xo raised herself on one arm and nodded, looking dazed. Elliot struggled to his feet in hopes of getting up quickly enough to assist her, but she scrambled up even faster, and he was left picking broken bits of bird off his clothing. The owl seemed to have been reconstructed over a core of heavy clay that had come apart spectacularly. A haze of debris clouded Elliot's glasses, but happily, they were not broken, so he fished in his pocket for a handkerchief and cleaned them.

As he put them back on, the door behind the front desk banged open and the owner of the visitor center strode into the room, doubtless drawn by all the commotion. Elliot's relief dissolved at the look on her face. He tried to dust himself off with the handkerchief he was still holding, dislodging feathers from his hair and sideburns.

The owner advanced rapidly to the scene of disaster, gaping first at Elliot, then Xo. "What in the name of heaven and earth has happened here?"

"Sade, I…I'm terribly sorry," said Elliot. "You see, I…" He reached down and picked up an owl wing, aiming to collect the scattered parts.

"Don't you touch a thing! That's quite all right!" Sade's voice made it clear that it was not all right in the least. Elliot hastily dropped the appendage as she bustled forward, herding him towards the door. He stumbled back, unknown detritus crunching underfoot.

At the doorway he tried again. "Please, it was entirely my fault—"

Xo made a protesting noise. Elliot looked at her imploringly and she fell silent, her face uncertain.

"I'm sure it was." Sade pointed to his arm. Blood was soaking through the white sleeve where the owl's talons had gouged him. "You should go get that looked at." Her glare added that he was to leave now, and offered none of the sympathy the words themselves suggested.

"I'm awfully sorry…" Elliot gulped, managing one last look at Xo as he was forced backwards out the door. Sade closed it firmly in his face, cutting off any further chance at reparation.

Elliot waited uncertainly on the sidewalk for a few moments before he came to his senses. Lurking there until Xo exited in dismay from the interview he'd ruined would not be welcomed, nor would any further assistance from him at this point. The important thing was that she hadn't been hurt, at least. If only he hadn't cost her the job…there was still a small chance she might stay on. But what in the world was he thinking? It must just be that he felt awful for the role he'd played in ruining someone's day. Why should it matter to him if she stayed in Lingen?

A couple passing on the sidewalk looked at him curiously as he stood facing the visitor center. Elliot ducked his head and turned to walk briskly away. The possibility of seeing Xo again did matter, somehow. An energy surrounded her, an excitement and wonder that was almost infectious. He'd started to feel a little of that wonder as well—until he'd brought everything crashing down. But the feeling wasn't entirely gone, even now; he felt more aware of everything around him, sights he saw every day. He found himself picturing how Xo would react to them. It had been a long time since he'd felt so alive. His mind started to drift into the past, and he reflexively clutched the cuts on his left forearm, abruptly returning himself to the present.

After putting a good distance between himself and any others out strolling the sidewalk that day, he peeled back his now-red sleeve. The cut was deeper than he'd originally thought, and a wave of nausea washed over him. He pressed the sleeve back down and applied pressure to stop the bleeding. It would be best to deal with this before returning to the office, especially if he wanted to avoid any commentary from his coworkers.

As he passed the intersection that led up the hill to the medical clinic, he slowed momentarily. No, it shouldn't need stitches—it was a minor injury that would just take time away from those with more serious medical issues, especially considering that he would have to explain it. Better to take care of it himself at home. In a few weeks it would blend right in with all his other scars.

Elliot's plan to slip home quietly was interrupted mere steps from his door, when a wave from across the street caught his attention. Kitty-corner from his own house, Mrs. Dupesh sat out on her porch, her year-round afternoon station except in the most inclement weather. At any other time, he would have happily stopped to visit with her; now he tried to get by with a quick return wave, angling his body to hide the blood-soaked sleeve. Her vision had not diminished with age, however, and she responded by beckoning more urgently for him to come over.

With a longing glance at his own door, Elliot resigned himself and cut diagonally across the street.

Mrs. Dupesh rocked her chair thoughtfully as he climbed the porch steps, her forehead creased with a concern that was harder to cope with than the pain in Elliot's forearm.

"It's a nice day today," said Elliot, drifting to a halt. He turned, concealing his arm, to take in the same view that Mrs. Dupesh had from her front porch: the blue-and-white crags of Arin. He tried to call up Xo's awe at the similar sight from the train station, but failed, instead remembering the way he had felt when she looked at him.

Mrs. Dupesh cleared her throat and tapped his good arm. Her expression told him she was not going to be put off by pleasantries.

"Ah, yes." Elliot regarded his left arm as if he had momentarily forgotten it. "It's not serious. A falling…object grazed me. Nothing really, just an unusually large amount of blood for a small scratch."

Mrs. Dupesh regarded him with folded arms and a good-natured but suspicious countenance, as if she didn't quite believe his story. She leaned back and patted the wicker visitor's seat next to her chair. As Elliot settled on the creaky woven stool, she tucked her pink crocheted shawl closer around her, and he noticed that her lap was not occupied by in-progress crochet work today. Instead, she had a small electronic tablet.

Elliot seized the opportunity for a topic change. "Is it new?"

She smiled and with obvious reluctance dropped the question of the injury, for now at least, to show him what she'd been working on. With the careful deliberation of one handling a new device, she pulled up an email she'd been writing to her nephew Francis. On closer examination, it was an email message without any text, with an attachment containing her scanned, handwritten letter.

Elliot smiled in spite of himself. "Still not a typing enthusiast?"

Mrs. Dupesh laughed creakily. While her fingers were agile in her crochet-work, Elliot knew she had always preferred pens to keyboards—how much more personal it was than the quick and convenient typing that governed all communication nowadays. He understood the appeal. While his own handwriting was nothing special, he treasured the few handwritten cards he had from his parents. Lia had understood that, too, he remembered, leaving him little meaningful notes about insignificant things. He'd tried to do the same for her, but he didn't have that gift of words. Elliot sat up straighter and shook his head to clear his thoughts; it was not a good time for her to be on his mind.

"Have you seen him lately?" inquired Elliot, nodding at the letter on the screen. He suspected he already knew the answer, and had no particular interest in Francis's well-being, but it was better than talking about Lia or his arm.

Laying the tablet on her lap again, Mrs. Dupesh counted off ten years on her fingers. Actually, by Elliot's count it was a trifle longer than that since Francis had moved out of town. Elliot did not miss him. But Mrs. Dupesh had no living children, and as far as Elliot knew, no other relatives left besides Francis.

"I'm sorry," said Elliot. "He should visit you."

Mrs. Dupesh turned to Elliot, her keen eyes seeming to probe his thoughts. Then she smiled and patted his cheek affectionately. Taking up the tablet again, she began slowly tapping out a postscript where the body of the email should go.

It was a good opportunity to depart, so Elliot excused himself and returned home to deal with the inconveniently bleeding arm in private. As he put his shirt into cold water to soak, he tried to guess how much time had passed since he'd left the visitor center, and if Xo's interview would still be in progress. That is, if it had happened at all after the mess he'd caused.

A couple of layers of bandages later, he decided it wouldn't hurt to pass by the visitor center again on his way back to the office. He approached cautiously, but the door had a Closed sign on it. There was no discernible activity inside. Elliot was afraid to linger in case Sade came out and yelled at him again, which she'd have a right to do, considering, but he still walked away with great reluctance. A return to the ordinary business of editing the day's photos felt impossible. Despite its irrelevancy to anything else in his life, nothing seemed as pressing as whether he would see Xo again.

2

THE SITUATION OF XO

Sade turned away from the closed door of the visitor center after forcing the bleeding man outside, then paused, shaking her head at the mess on the floor.

Xo shifted from one foot to the other uncomfortably, trying to catch a glimpse through the window of the man who had just left. She ought to make sure he was okay. On the other hand, if she left after this unfortunate beginning, she'd surely lose the job opportunity, which he'd tried to save for her by taking the blame. Guiltily, she took a deep breath and forced down the urge to go after him. She could track him down later and make sure he had not died of sepsis or something. For now, she must act cool and professional, like a real artist.

She removed a few pieces of feathers clinging to her jeans and carefully placed them on the desk. It would be inappropriate according to the standards of interviews to take the employer's chair, and there were no other chairs, so she swept an area of the floor clear with her hands and sat down cross-legged. She smiled politely at Sade.

"Shall we begin the interview? I'm Xo, by the way. I think we talked on the phone?"

Sade now held a broom with which she was attempting to corral the broken bits from the display. "What are you doing down there? I'm going to have to close to deal with this."

A stab of worry went through Xo. She'd been through some bad interviews before, but this was the first time she'd started off by destroying the room.

She got back to her feet and offered one of her sketchbooks to Sade. "I could help clean up the floor, and then we could have the interview," Xo said hopefully.

With apparent reluctance, Sade traded the broom for the sketchbook. Despite her baleful expression at the moment, she had a grandmotherly look, with a natural hairstyle of close-cropped, tight grey curls. Perhaps she was friendlier under less messy circumstances.

Xo set to work vigorously with the broom. "I used to have a specimen kinda like that sparrow you have over there—the one lying on its side by the counter with part of its tail missing? It was in pretty good shape though. I guess yours probably was too, before. Is it a golden-crowned? It's hard to tell now."

"You're a babbler, I see," mused Sade. Xo shut her mouth tightly and went back to sweeping, meeting with resistance as fallen pieces skittered away under the desk and into corners. The mess was actually starting to look worse, or maybe it just seemed that way because she still hadn't admitted to causing it.

Sade paged through the sketchbook, her expression softening as she paused to examine each bird. "You know, Lingen used to be one of the great birding destinations, especially for the seasonal migrations. Of course, the big draw was the rare ones they could only find here on Arin."

"That's why I wanted to move here." Xo poked the broom ineffectually at a smashed eggshell stuck to the floor. It would be a lot easier if she were wielding a shop vac.

"You think they're still out there, then?" asked Sade, turning to the windows that faced Mount Arin. "Not many birders these days, and fewer rare sightings. The tourist trade is dicey. In droves they can be a nuisance, but we can't do without them either. I only hope the new field guide I'm working on will drum up interest again—that and adding illustrations to the weekly newsletter."

"If they are out there, I'd like to find them," said Xo. "The birds, that is, not the tourists."

"Good," said Sade in a satisfied tone. "None of them are going in *Birds of Arin* without proof that they're still here, but I'm getting too old to go traipsing around on the mountain all the time."

"Don't worry, I'm excellent at traipsing," said Xo eagerly.

Sade switched to eyeing Xo's resume. "No work experience in illustration though, I see."

"I did have one piece published! I have the original here." Abandoning the broom, Xo heaved her cardboard box off the desk and onto the floor, ripping off the tape holding it shut. Last-minute random additions of extra socks and scarves erupted as the flaps sprang free. She rummaged in the box, looking for the painting. "It's underneath somewhere…"

Sade winced. "Let's don't add to the rubble."

Guiltily, Xo reversed her process to squish her belongings back down. She compressed the flaps of the box with one knee, but it refused to be contained, her poorly-packed possessions getting away from her just like her chances for a fresh start here in Lingen. Even if she did manage a fresh start, should it really be built on deceiving her employer about who knocked down the display?

"I've been drawing birds for years. I can do this job—I can. I need to do it—" To Xo's horror, her voice started to crack. She took a deep, shuddering breath, forcing her face back to neutral. A serious professional artist would not lose control; she would be calm and collected and let her art speak for itself. That was the only thing she could do. If it was good enough, nothing else should matter. If it wasn't, then nothing else mattered anyway.

Xo tried again more slowly. "You've seen my work now via email and in person. You know what I can do. And you should also know that even though I knocked down this entire shelf and shattered your owl, it has no impact on my capability as an artist. It was a total accident, for which I am sorry, but as far as the job goes it's completely unrelated." She braced herself.

"Don't bother trying to cover for *him*. It's a marvel he's survived this long." Sade shook her head.

"No, it really was me!" said Xo. "I sort of jumped, and forgot I was wearing my pack. It's just not connected to my ability to illustrate your newsletter. Or your *Birds of Arin* guide."

Sade stared at her, then abruptly reclaimed the broom from where it leaned against the desk, as if worried Xo might use it to demolish more of the visitor center. "Is that so? Then I'll have to seriously consider if you're too much of a hazard to have in my building!"

Xo thought rapidly. "I could put the illustrations under the door."

Sade snorted, which almost became a smile. She shook her head again, looking around. "You either just shot yourself in your own foot or you're covering for someone who I can only assume is a complete stranger to you."

"It's the foot one," said Xo. "I just didn't want to get started the wrong way, if you were going to hire me. I guess that's sort of unlikely now." She shoved the top of the box again. The wad of clothes on top refused to flatten back down, but she kept her focus there, afraid she would fall apart if she looked at Sade again. "I really, really want this job."

For a moment, Sade didn't speak. Then she said briskly, "Your drawings and paintings are good. Superb, actually. I think they'll do well for my projects."

"Are you…wait, are you saying I get the job?" Xo swiveled back to face Sade, releasing the box she'd been fighting with. The box flaps opened again, but more slowly this time, like a flower blooming.

Sade gave a quick nod. "If you're satisfied with the conditions, you can sign here."

Xo eagerly scanned the contract Sade had placed on the desk, and her excitement wavered slightly. "You mentioned on the phone that there was a range of pay…"

"Based on experience. I can't go any higher at this point."

Worry flickered within her, but Xo quickly squelched it. She'd known this would be an adjustment. Even at a lower wage, it was something real that she could care about, something that mattered to her, rather than something that just ought to matter to somebody like her. In comparison, money was an easily solvable problem. She signed her name.

"This isn't going to be your sole source of income, is it?" asked Sade, tidying the papers.

"I suppose it shouldn't be," conceded Xo.

Sade glanced up at her with a frown.

"Don't worry, nothing will interfere with my art," Xo assured her. "That's my top priority now and I'll figure out how to make it work. I came here to make a change."

Sade sighed and took up the broom again. "You've done that, all right. You'd better switch the sign to 'Closed' on your way out."

Outside the visitor center, Xo couldn't suppress a wild grin that made her cheeks hurt. She spun around and around delightedly until her armful of belongings unbalanced her. Then she stood still and took a deep breath of the crisp cool air drifting from the blue mountains that ringed Lingen. She was officially an artist! She was actually going to be paid to do what she loved best.

Bursting to tell someone about her success, she scanned the street. The man from before was long gone, unsurprisingly. Now that the interview was no longer at stake, she felt worse about not having checked on him. Lingen was small, though, she might be able to locate him again. First, she needed to find a place to live and now yet another source of income. Xo had little interest in being the starving sort of artist, and she was already getting hungry.

Reorganizing her load, she flipped through her notebook to review her list of potential rentals, then closed it again. Lingen wasn't so small that she was particularly eager to cross it on foot while carrying everything she'd brought with her. The clear choice was to check out the much nearer apartment over the coffee shop that she'd gotten the tip on.

Just a few blocks away, thankfully not uphill, the coffee shop had the same steeply peaked roof and half-timber design she had seen on most of the buildings in Lingen, along with giant windows covering the front and one word on the sign: COFFEE. Once inside, the high-ceilinged main room smelled not only of espresso, but of the sweet yeasty deliciousness of fresh pastries and other treats. A few customers sat at scattered tables to the right of the entrance, in an area dominated by a large brick fireplace.

At a counter that spanned the left side of the room, a short barista with sparkling eyes and a scattering of dark freckles grinned at Xo from behind the espresso machine. Her hair was brown like Xo's, but darker, and luxuriantly curly and glossy where Xo's was straight and tended towards the uncooperative. Xo approached and rested her armload against the counter.

The barista glanced over Xo's supplies. "What brings you to Lingen?" she said brightly. She looked to be in her mid-twenties, with energy to match.

"I've decided to start living the life I want," said Xo.

The other woman laughed delightedly. "And what is it you want? Coffee?"

"I do want that…" Xo inhaled the scent in the air, and let it out again regretfully. "But, first, I'm actually here about something else."

"Ooh! I was hoping you'd say that. You look like you'd be perfect as our newest barista. I'm Megan, by the way. Have you worked in espresso before?"

"What?" said Xo. "No, I don't know a thing about espresso. Except drinking it. Especially breves." Xo's mouth started to water. She shook her head vigorously. "I heard there was an apartment for rent. Is there still?"

"Oh, that." Megan pushed open a swinging door behind the counter and yelled, "Jacqua!"

A few moments later, a large, broad figure loomed through the doorway from the kitchen. Had Xo been Megan, she wouldn't have yelled at him so carelessly. He looked scary, like a roused bear.

"What?" he growled.

"It's about the apartment." Megan cocked her head at Xo.

Jacqua pointed his bushy black eyebrows in Xo's direction. "Mm. Do you want to see it?"

"Yes, please, if I could." Xo pasted on what she hoped was a winning smile.

Jacqua studied her silently. He did not look like the type to be taken in by winning smiles, but he rounded the counter, producing a set of keys.

Xo followed him to a bannister staircase on the other side of the room, which led up to a small landing with a single door. The place was a bit smaller than her previous apartment, with only one large room plus a kitchenette and bathroom, but the main room had plenty of natural light from a bank of windows overlooking the street. With the inclusion of utilities due to its attachment to the café, it was also cheaper than the apartments Xo had previously found online. She signed for it on the spot.

After Jacqua had turned over the keys and departed, Xo sat down on the bed frame and pondered her next step. At least housing was taken care of. Now the delectable odor of espresso seemed to have become even stronger, but there was also unpacking to do.

Before Xo could decide what to tackle next, a knock resounded on the ajar door, and Megan poked her head around. "I come bearing coffee! It's on the house."

"Oh, wow, thank you!" As Xo sipped from the cup Megan had placed in her hand, she started to relax for what seemed like the first time in days. It was a breve. Unexpectedly, Xo's eyes stung at the kindness. She quickly blinked the sensation away before Megan could see her acting so ridiculous over a cup of coffee.

Megan plopped down on the bed frame next to her. "So, moving to Lingen, eh? Are you running away from something or running towards something?"

Xo blinked. "Towards, I guess." There certainly wasn't much to leave behind, just acquaintances and relatives who had all advised her it was an impractical idea to move here.

Megan grinned. "Stupendous! It's usually one or the other, as remote as we are. Sure you're not interested in making coffee? The last barista quit abruptly. Total drama."

"I really don't know how to make espresso," said Xo. "I just started a new job today, actually. Though I was considering maybe adding something part-time, to supplement."

"What do you do?" asked Megan.

"I'm an…" It was still hard to say the word out loud. Was it technically true? She hadn't gotten paid yet; could she call herself an artist before the first paycheck? "I'm going to be painting and researching birds, for the visitor center."

"Oh, right, I heard you were coming." Megan chuckled in response to Xo's stunned expression. "Don't look so surprised! Word gets around in Lingen. Sade and her husband were in here the other day, and she was talking up the pictures you sent her."

If Sade had spoken about Xo even before she was hired, maybe that was a good sign of her employer's confidence in her. "If you heard that, you're gonna hear something else pretty soon," said Xo.

"Ooh!" said Megan. "Do tell!"

Xo recounted the owl-related catastrophe she'd had in the visitor center. As Megan burst into gales of laughter, Xo began to see the funny side of the event herself. It was in the past now, and everything was looking up.

"So, who was this guy who tried to take the blame?" asked Megan, still grinning.

Xo winced. "I don't even know! I think Sade knew him, though."

"I can't believe you didn't ask his name. He probably thought he was saving your life!" Megan giggled.

Xo smiled thinly. Though she desired camaraderie with Megan, it was unfair to make fun of him. She was the one who had collided with the shelf, and he *had* saved her—not her life, but possibly an injury—and he had tried to smooth things with Sade.

"I wish I'd had a chance to…I dunno, make sure he was okay."

"Well, what did he look like?" said Megan, more soberly. "Half the town comes in here."

"About yay high." Xo gestured to around Megan's height. "I think he was a few years older than me. Glasses. Kinda messy blond sideburns, and hair the same. I think it was sort of curly or rumpled even before all the debris fell on his head." Faces were hard to remember, but he'd had enough distinctive features that she thought she could recognize him again.

Megan frowned. "Did he have a lot of scars on his face? Skinny and kind of serious looking?"

"Maybe…" Xo hesitated to apply the unflattering description, since he had helped her. "He had nice eyes. Green, I think."

"Could be Elliot. It's hard for me to picture him trying to save you from the owl, but it would be hilarious!" said Megan.

"Is he from Lingen? This guy had a different accent than the other people I've heard here."

"Elliot's not from around here, no. But he's lived here for a long time. You usually see him with Alec, they're always together—totally different, though. Elliot is…well, he's just Elliot. Now, Alec you would remember. He's a kick!" Megan waved her hand in exasperation. "Though he's impossible, too. I've known him forever. You'll like him, everyone does."

"I dunno, the popular sort usually doesn't have a lot to do with me," said Xo uncomfortably. They seemed to attract their own kind, always in a crowd, and the few times Xo had found herself caught up in their midst it just accentuated the feeling that she was very much alone, never really one of the group. Of course, if Megan had known him forever, perhaps she was one of the popular ones too—and now insulted. A little late to think of that…

Megan, however, didn't seem bothered. "Alec's too popular for his own good, anyway. Now, if the guy from the visitor center was Elliot, you'll probably see him again soon. Especially if you take that barista job I think you should take. He comes in here pretty often." She poked Xo with her elbow. "Also, we baristas get free coffee!"

Free was certainly appealing, but learning a new skill on top of everything else Xo had recently changed in her life might add an unnecessary layer of challenge. "Like I said, espresso isn't really my field."

"It's easy," Megan said cheerfully, with a toss of her head. "I'll show you what to do. And you already drink it! Knowing what it's supposed to taste like is a huge plus to getting it right. The barista that just quit didn't even drink it." She rolled her eyes.

"What are the shifts like? I still need to have time to go out and sketch in the daylight."

"Well, mine begins at five a.m." Megan laughed at Xo's shocked expression. "It's not so bad! I get to start pastries. But the one we're looking to fill is only noon to four."

That sounded more reasonable, though Xo was still uneasy about her lack of knowledge. But it would be convenient, and the extra money would help. She took another sip of the delicious breve, and the warmth of it spread through her.

"Okay," Xo decided. "I think I can do this. Is there a test to take or something?"

"Don't worry, Jacqua will be happy to hire you on my say-so, he hates interviewing. And you can apply for a food handler's permit online. We'll give you a little time to settle in and then you can get started!" Business resolved, Megan jumped up and began poking at Xo's sketchbooks. "Are these for your other job?"

"Yep. Well, technically, these are old sketches. I'll make new ones from life, and then I'll base the paintings on those."

Megan flipped through a couple of sketchbooks. "Just birds? I was hoping for pictures of cute guys."

"Oh, I don't draw people," said Xo.

Megan looked up in surprise. "Not at all?"

"I'm mainly interested in birds. And I'm better at that."

"You don't like people, huh?"

"Well…I mean." Xo felt herself blushing, hopefully not enough to notice. "Some people are okay. I like the concept of people."

"Theoretical people only?" Megan giggled.

"No—you seem very nice, for instance," Xo added quickly. "But drawing people is so personal…and it's hard to get them right. Birds on the other hand don't mind being scrutinized, and they're fascinating to watch. People think they're dumb, but there's always a reason behind their actions, if you study the clues. Even if it's something like trying to drive away their own reflections in a window."

"I'm more of a people watcher," said Megan.

Xo shook her head. "People make less sense."

"Maybe that's what makes them interesting."

Xo considered this. "Interesting, but difficult." Hopefully, learning to make espresso wouldn't be nearly as difficult.

❖   ❖   ❖

A few days later, true to her word, Megan walked Xo through the mysteries of the espresso machine. Xo carefully recorded the steps in her pocket notebook, though it was hard to keep up with everything Megan was saying. The lunch shift was busy, and Megan interspersed plenty of chitchat about the town and the coffee house along with the instructions for different espresso drinks.

Xo attempted to track pertinent facts about Lingen on another page of the notebook, but with the rapid flipping back and forth the pages were starting to get mixed up. *Breve = latte but with half-and-half* had somehow ended up as a bullet point under *Library 4 blocks South.* Xo frowned and began to erase.

"Well, I think you've got the hang of it now!" Megan thumped the metal frothing pitcher down on the counter. Xo looked up, startled.

Megan untied the waist strings on her apron and lifted it over her head. "We'll go over food prep later on, but you can just work espresso today." She reached through the swinging door into the kitchen and hung the apron on a peg.

"You're not leaving already, are you?" Xo frantically flipped through her notes about the different coffee concoctions, which had already begun to blur together in her mind.

Megan laughed. "You'll be fine. If you forget what goes in a particular drink, one of the regulars will tell you, and Jacqua's in the kitchen." She danced breezily to the side door by the bottom of the stairs. "See ya tomorra', Xiomara!"

Xo followed her to the threshold. "Wait! What's the difference between a cappuccino and a latte again?"

Megan surely heard her, but just laughed again and waved, disappearing around the corner. Xo darted outside and leaned against the wall, glancing through the little window in the door to make sure no one noticed her absence. The lunch rush had slowed by now and there were no customers waiting at the counter. She took several deep breaths before reviewing the procedures she had written down. She should have asked for more details from the beginning of the lesson, but she hadn't been expecting Megan to leave—not so soon, her first day on the job.

Xo peered through the window in the door again. Still, nobody was waiting for her. Whew. Bracing herself, she casually strolled back inside. Theoretically, she might have popped out on a short, coffee-related errand.

A moment later, Xo became aware that all conversation in the coffee shop had ceased abruptly.

3

Encounters in the Café

Xo halted in confusion on her way to the counter. A tall man about her age with broad shoulders and neatly trimmed black hair, who must have arrived while she was finding her composure outside, was standing in the middle of the room watching her. His dark eyebrows arched high over his striking eyes, as if he were surprised to see her. Worse, the other customers in the room were following his lead, so now they were all staring at her. She examined herself. There was no coffee spilled down her front to attract such attention.

He stepped forward and took her hand, his face broadening in a handsome smile. "I don't believe we've met before!"

"We haven't." Xo jerked her hand away and used it to assist her other hand in holding her notebook, which was unnecessary since it was very small.

He burst into hearty laughter, and most of the rest of the coffee shop patrons joined in. If only she could sink through the floor and into a deep, dark pit under the building and not come out until everyone had gone home. Xo dodged around him and scurried behind the counter. His laughter was again replaced by a look of surprise.

"I work here," said Xo. Too defensive sounding, but too late. She quickly grabbed an official apron from behind the kitchen door and tied it on. Turning back to the counter, she lined up cups to be ready for the next orders, then vigorously wiped down the steam wand on the espresso machine.

He was still there.

"Did you find everything?" asked Xo. "I mean, do you want to order some coffee? Or possibly a baked good?"

"I was going to ask you to have a coffee with me, but as you're on duty, I can see I'll have to wait." He smiled. "Hey, I didn't mean to embarrass you. It's just that you looked so beautiful coming in with the sun behind you, like you were descending from a beam of light."

Xo had an urge to laugh sarcastically, but suppressed it. It wouldn't be good customer service. On the other hand, if she said "thank you," as if she were acknowledging the compliment, that would sound conceited. Why would he say such a thing? He obviously did mean to embarrass her. She knew quite well that her appearance was average and not prone to turning heads. Until now she hadn't realized what a relief it was to pass unnoticed.

He spoke again. "I won't bother you while you're working, if you let me take you out afterwards. What time do you get off?"

Xo stared at him. "Four o'clock." It came out automatically, before she could stop it.

He grinned. "Perfect. Now, what variety of coffee does the barista recommend?"

"Whatever you like."

"Well, I know what I like…but I can't tell if you're serving it or not."

Xo blinked. She was supposed to get something from that, but what? An explanation was not forthcoming, so finally she blurted, "I dunno what you mean."

He scanned the menu on the wall behind her. "Hmm…let me see…what's the most complicated drink?"

"Alec! Stop tormenting her." She recognized the new speaker's voice. Another man had appeared at the counter, smaller and more slightly built. So the tall one was Alec. She might have known. And the other she did know. His face was pale and angular, and yes, scarred with pockmarks especially on his cheeks, though the fluffy sideburns distracted from the scars. "Please excuse his manners," he said to Xo.

Alec laughed. "I haven't properly introduced myself. I'm Alec, and this is my best friend in the world: Elliot!"

"I'm Xo." Her face was growing warm. Now she was doubly embarrassed because of the circumstances in which she'd last seen Elliot. She definitely hadn't been floating on beams of light when she knocked all that stuff on his head.

"I am delighted to meet you again." Elliot's quieter speech was a contrast to Alec's jubilant tone.

Xo felt her face flush once more, this time from relief. She'd half expected a wisecrack about her clumsiness, considering how they'd parted. Not that she really cared, but prolonging Alec's perception of her a little longer wouldn't hurt, especially since she couldn't recall anyone describing her as beautiful before. Remembering what she was supposed to be doing, she tilted the empty cup she was holding. "Are either of you wanting something to drink...?"

"Just a latte for me, please, if it's not too much trouble," said Elliot. "And Alec will have a mocha. He always does."

Alec chuckled. "It's true, he knows me too well. Go ahead with it."

At last they took their drinks and sat down. Xo tried to look busy to discourage further awkward conversation: rinsing the grounds baskets, picking up each item on the counter to wipe clean and arrange. When these ran out, she decided to clean the espresso machine. Unfortunately, it took longer than expected to put back together after she'd completely disassembled it, causing a short backup of puzzled customers.

Xo served them as quickly as she could and tried to relax. She snuck a peak at Alec from behind the coffee syrup bottles. He was good-looking enough that he couldn't actually be interested in her. She caught him glancing back at her, his expression open and friendly. Was it possible he wasn't just teasing her?

Even though she was here to focus on drawing birds, she couldn't deny a tiny hope of finding human connections as well. Maybe it just took that first change—deciding to come here—to start improving other areas in her life. She'd heard of such things happening, where a person took one authentic step and then everything else just fell into place. It might be something like solving a logic puzzle: the part at the beginning was hardest, but once you got on the right track there came a point when the rest was basically solved. If you got the first part wrong, though, you could work at it forever and still not solve anything. That was what she'd been doing most of her life, it seemed—but perhaps now that she'd taken a step in the right direction, her true self was more visible, making others able to appreciate her.

Unless he was only joking around.

Xo frowned. She was getting way too carried away. Solving puzzles was all well and good, but it was unlikely that she'd brought out magical attractive qualities in herself that nobody had ever picked up on before. If Alec was as popular as Megan said, maybe it was because he made comments like this to everyone. It would require careful evaluation to determine if he was serious in his interest. If she was going to be authentic, then she at least deserved the same.

She turned her attention to the rest of the room, so Alec would not see her looking at him again. Her field experience kicked in as she watched other customers coming and going, and she tuned in to snippets of conversation. Just like observing a flock of birds, they were aware of her presence, but disregarded her to go about their lives: talking and touching familiarly amongst themselves and enjoying each other's company. She was in their midst, but both sides knew she was not one of them.

As time passed, it became evident that many people entering the shop knew Alec well, since he greeted them enthusiastically. Especially the female customers. Xo's breathing constricted. He must have been flirting meaninglessly, as he probably did with everybody, and she'd been foolish enough to be taken in by it. She was smarter than letting herself become flustered by a word of flattery. What she really cared about was her art, and she couldn't afford to be waylaid by a statistically unlikely level of attraction. Alec's game was clear now, and he was sure to leave before her shift was over anyway. Elliot would likely go with him, if he didn't flee beforehand to avoid her pouring coffee on him or something.

But when four o'clock came and the next barista arrived to take over, both Alec and Elliot still inexplicably had nowhere better to be. Xo deliberately untied her apron and hung it behind the kitchen door. Outwardly calm, she proceeded in measured steps towards the stairs. She would go up to her apartment, change clothes, get her sketchbook, and go out to find some birds.

Alec called out loudly as she walked past. "Hey!"

Xo checked out of the corner of her eye to make sure it was directed at her. She'd made the mistake before of enthusiastically answering someone's hail only to find out they were actually talking to another person behind her, and today didn't need any more uncomfortable situations.

"Hi." Her voice was even and noncommittal.

"Is your shift over, Xo?" asked Alec.

Strange to hear this stranger say her name, in such a familiar manner! At the sound of it, her resolve about his ill intentions melted away like it had never existed, before she could catch it and hold on to it.

Xo still tried to keep her voice neutral. "Yes. I was just going up to my room to get some things." At his expression, she realized she'd stupidly given away the fact that she lived there. Oh well, he'd have figured it out eventually.

"Wow, everything about you is a surprise! But you still haven't given me an answer to my earlier question. Will you be joining me?" He smiled teasingly.

Xo studied Alec carefully and for the life of her couldn't detect that he was joking or doing anything other than honestly asking to spend time with her. Maybe she'd been wrong in her earlier evaluation. Maybe. But even if he wasn't serious, one evening talking surely couldn't distract her too much from her object here. She would have more time to go out and sketch tomorrow. Plus, Elliot was here, and she did want a chance to make sure things were okay with him after that business with the owl. She would have preferred that conversation not happen in front of Alec, but there was no choice. He'd probably already told Alec what had happened in the visitor center by now, anyway.

"Well...okay," said Xo. "I've only been here a short time...I don't know any place to go."

"That explains it. I knew I'd remember you if I'd seen you around before," said Alec.

Elliot leaned forward from his seat on the fireplace hearth with a tentative smile. "I hope that your interview went well."

"It did. I hope your arm is feeling better." And thank you for trying to help with Sade, Xo added silently.

Elliot accepted her unspoken thanks with a nod of his head, his lashes fluttering down over his eyes. He seemed slightly embarrassed. A huge load lifted from Xo's shoulders now that the incident was acknowledged. She wouldn't have to dread it coming up again, and he didn't seem to harbor resentment towards her for it.

"I'm glad you weren't too hurt on my account," she added sincerely.

Alec's confused face turned from one to the other, and then broke into a grin. "Well! I didn't realize you two knew each other! I guess I'm the one behind the times."

Apparently, Elliot had not mentioned the incident in the visitor center to Alec. Or he had just left out the part about her. Odd, if they were such good friends. Maybe Elliot had noticed his friend's interest in her and decided not to embarrass her by telling Alec the story. Even though she'd laughed about it herself with Megan, it was a relief to find they hadn't been sitting here snickering over her clumsy start. Giving Elliot a grateful smile, she pulled out a chair next to Alec and sat down.

4

SECOND CHANCE

It had seemed like a miracle when Elliot saw Xo enter the café earlier, after he came in with Alec. He hadn't been sure at first if Xo working here meant she hadn't gotten the other job, but at least she was still in Lingen. Thankfulness for that was coupled with apprehension over whether she would deign to speak to him after the owl incident.

Elliot's discomfort grew as he watched Alec interact with her at the counter, until he was forced to step in regardless of whether she really wanted to talk to him again. Alec's joking behavior was hardly unusual, but it was irking him unexpectedly today, perhaps just from knowing the trouble Xo had already gone through recently at the visitor center.

Finally, he managed to drag Alec away with their drinks. Elliot seated himself on the hearth, giving Alec a sharp look. "Honestly!"

"What's up with you?" Alec sounded genuinely surprised.

Elliot hesitated. Lightening his tone, he said, "It's just…she's still learning how to run this shop, and here you are trying to come up with a confusing order."

"Nah, she knows I'm just messing with her." Alec settled back in his chair. "They like that sort of thing."

Elliot raised an eyebrow. "'They?'"

"You know, the baristas. Women in general." Alec gestured vaguely.

Elliot watched Xo deftly manage the counter, each movement and toss of her head adding to his inner tension. He could not quite fathom the strange grip in which she held him. She didn't seem to fit amongst *women in general.* But how to even begin to explain that to Alec? He wasn't even sure how to explain it to himself.

Alec was looking at him curiously. Elliot busied himself by removing the book he was currently reading from his coat pocket. He opened it to the bookmark and smoothed it on his lap.

"I'm not sure the last barista cared for it," Elliot said in an offhand voice.

Alec tipped back in his chair. "Why do you say that?"

"She's not here anymore, is she?" Elliot nodded towards the counter, where Xo had taken the recently vacated job.

Alec angled his head sideways, a smile on his face. "Come on, now, Elly. She didn't quit because of me."

"Hmm." Elliot turned the page of his book, as if he were only partly invested in the conversation.

Alec sat forward again and leaned his arms on the table, nodding. "No, she...she definitely liked it."

Elliot gave up pretending to read. He wasn't exactly sure how Alec's relationship with the last barista had ended, but it had been rather abrupt. "Xiomara is a different person. They're not inter-changeable just due to working the same shift."

Alec shrugged, laughing. "You're the one who brought her up."

Elliot uneasily returned to watching Xo. The disquieting feeling that had cropped up while Alec and Xo interacted earlier had returned and intensified. Hopefully he hadn't prodded Alec in the wrong direction while trying to discourage him—it might have been better not to say anything at all. He glanced at Alec. Alec was unfortunately also watching Xo, with a bemused expression.

Alec turned back to Elliot. "Let's hope she gets better at the coffee." He tipped his mug to stare forlornly into the remainder of his mocha and sighed exaggeratedly.

Elliot took a sip of his latte. "Mine is excellent." He focused on his book again. Despite Alec's assessment of Xo's espresso skills, he appeared to be planning to continue to wait until her shift ended, and Elliot resolved to be right there as well.

❖   ❖   ❖

Now that Xo had sat down to join them, it was Elliot's chance for a new beginning, this time not associated with taxidermy birds.

Alec was talking, though. "Since you're new here, I'll have to show you around town! I lead tour groups sometimes, you see. Hiking in the summer, skiing in the winter. That sort of thing."

"It would be nice to see where the nearest trails are," said Xo. "I'm on the lookout for good places to sketch birds."

"We'll schedule it in." Alec pushed the plan into the future with a wave of his hand.

Elliot cleared his throat. "How about this coming Saturday? I often like to take a walk on the mountain myself in the morning…" Elliot trailed off as Alec raised his eyebrows quizzically.

"That sounds great," said Xo. "Ten?"

"Sure," said Alec.

Elliot nodded, congratulating himself internally for managing to step in at this moment.

Luckily, Alec didn't seem anything but amused by Elliot's interference. He'd already launched into a new topic with Xo, an explanation of his main job as a reporter for the newspaper. "And Elliot takes pictures for the paper, too."

Elliot had intended to bring up photography on his own, but Alec and Xo were going a mile a minute. As an artist, Xo would probably be more interested in his non-professional photography, or his freelance work outside the newspaper. Of course, photos didn't compare with the pictures he'd seen where Xo seemed to capture the birds' spirits in a few strokes.

Elliot opened his mouth to speak, but trying to insert any observation into the active discussion was like trying to jump onto a moving train. He lapsed into just watching Xo as she explained her illustration job to Alec. The way she gestured and spoke was mesmerizing, continuous as a running stream. But he must say something, or the only remembrance she would have of the evening was talking to Alec.

There was a pause, and Elliot hurled himself into the breach. "I was wondering…uh…that is: if you ever reference photographs for your paintings."

"Sometimes. It's best if I can get several photos of different individuals," said Xo. "If I'm doing a painting for identification, then I don't want it to look like a specific individual. It needs to be more representative of the species as a whole. Imagine if you were doing a field guide about humans. If you used just one human as a reference for the species and gave it to alien sightseers, they'd have a hard time with identification in the field. You'd have to draw generic looking humans instead, based on a variety of male and female subjects, and give a range of possibilities in your description."

Alec grinned. "What do you say, am I a good representative?"

Xo looked at him steadily for a few seconds. "No." Her eyes flicked over to Elliot, but just barely before glancing out into the rest of the room. "You're more generic than Elliot, but neither of you is generic enough."

Elliot wished she'd looked at him a little longer, even though he wasn't sure he wanted to be generic. He said, "It would be hard to come up with a generic human."

"Not really," said Xo. "A lot of people look pretty generic. I would just glom them together for a mixture. The average appearance isn't what any real person looks like, but it's close."

"I've read that generic faces are considered more attractive," put in Alec, with another grin.

"Not to me, they're harder to recognize," said Xo. She ducked her head, looking flustered. "Anyway, this is just a hypothetical example, since I'm not going to be portraying people."

"So you do…uh…use photographs?" said Elliot, to steer the conversation away from wherever Alec was going.

Xo seemed relieved to return to that topic. "Yes, quite a bit actually. I make most of my pencil sketches from life, but photos are handy for getting colors in the right place on the finished paintings and finding small details. Of course, birds are good at camouflaging in photos, so if you use them for identification, they have to be pretty clear and have a good background, and then there's the individual differences I mentioned. I guess that's why paintings are still useful for field guides. Did you know Sade's making one? But I'll need to get sightings for that, too, not just photo references."

"Er, yes. Yes." Elliot nodded along. At first, he had been sure he could be useful; then he was certain that photos would be completely unhelpful, and that he ought never to have suggested it. Or maybe she already had all the photos she needed?

Elliot realized Xo had stopped talking and was idly tracing the wood grain on the table with one finger. Alec had excused himself to get some food from the counter, and Elliot was supposed to be saying something.

"Did you…were you still looking for photos of any particular birds?"

"Oh sure," Xo said, straightening in her chair. "For example, the lesser red-backed alpine finch on Mount Arin may be a completely different subspecies than those in other areas, but there have been so few conclusive sightings, you know. Some people also claim to have seen the flammulated grosbeak here, but they're not even supposed to live in this area, and they're threatened even in their usual range, so…" She shrugged. "There are dozens I need to document."

"Uh, what were those names again? Perhaps I have photos."

Xo produced a small notebook from her pocket and scribbled them down on a blank sheet, then roughed out a picture of a bird. "For the lesser red-backed alpine finch, the possible subspecies is supposed to have a white patch here." She tapped the drawing with the point of the pencil.

Elliot was in way over his head. He pressed forward. "In that case, you are specifically looking for the white-winged lesser red-backed alpine finch?"

Xo laughed merrily. "Yeah, that would be a bit much, wouldn't it? They'll have to give it a shorter name if it turns out to be a different subspecies. Could just be a color variant, though, or leucism."

"Naturally." Elliot smiled dazedly as he took the paper she passed. He barely registered Alec sitting down again with food for them all. Most of these birds he would have to look up. Others were vaguely familiar, but he definitely did not have photos of them. Not yet, anyway. Tomorrow, he knew what he would be doing, with the assistance of an identification book and a tripod.

❖ ❖ ❖

The week was long and full of blurry bird photographs. Elliot found himself torn between stopping at the café to buy coffee—which he now needed to do on a near-daily basis despite caffeine being freely available at the newspaper office—and managing to wrangle birds into the frame of his camera. But each time he parted from Xo, replaying her interactions with him in his mind to sustain him until the next encounter, he was filled with fresh inspiration for the task. She actually seemed to enjoy talking with him, maybe even looked forward to seeing him. Of course, she'd seemed quite chatty with Alec as well, but just in a friendly way, he hoped.

Elliot had wanted to fulfill his commitment to bring her the photos before their walk on Saturday, but the ones he'd assembled by Friday as the end of Xo's shift neared were a poor assortment. He'd found only one of the birds from the list she'd given him, and a lot of others she probably didn't need.

As Elliot approached the counter, all the moisture which should have gone to his mouth to facilitate speaking seemed to re-route to the sweaty hand gripping the envelope of prints.

Xo finished serving the customer in front and beamed at him. "Elliot!"

"Xiomara," he croaked.

She looked at him expectantly. "A latte, then?"

"Yes, thank you." At least these default phrases still worked, even if he couldn't manage to say anything intelligent.

"I—I've brought the prints that I said I would bring. Earlier." Xo looked blankly at him in response. Did she even remember?

Then her eyes went to the envelope he'd managed to detach from his hand onto the counter. "Ohhh, the bird photos. I was gonna say, I didn't remember you promising me royalty!"

"Sorry," said Elliot, after a moment catching up. "No princes, I'm afraid."

"That's okay," said Xo, with one of her brilliant smiles. "I like more down-to-earth guys."

Elliot remained rooted to the spot, trying not to over-interpret whatever Xo had meant in the way he would really like to. Was she referring to him? Or was he being silly?

"I don't have much time to chat today, unfortunately. It's so busy that I'm working late." Xo gestured to the backup of customers behind him, and Elliot quickly stepped out of the way. "But I'll see you tomorrow," she added. "Ten, right?"

She had remembered.

5

THE TOUR

Saturday morning came at last. Elliot arrived at the coffee shop well before ten. He had risen early and spent extra time choosing and ironing one of his many white button-up shirts and even more time pacing his kitchen and imagining how the day might go. Might Xo notice him in a different way, feel a spark from a word? A touch? He gulped. Definitely a word. Or just a look.

If her inclination turned another way, he would of course graciously accept her decision. He could do nothing less. As for Alec…the potential complication that Alec might seriously be interested in her didn't seem likely. Not because of her lack of merit, but because Alec seemed to exist in a constant state of flirtation around women. Naturally, if it did turn out that there was something between Xo and Alec, Elliot's sense of honor would prohibit any further action on his part. Better not to dwell on this possibility— things were currently up in the air and it was yet to be determined where they would fall.

Elliot obtained a coffee from the barista, but neither Xo nor Alec materialized, so he sat down to wait. He'd gone backpacking with Alec up to a fire lookout just a few weeks ago, and it had been quite a pleasant excursion, but he would not be at all disappointed if Alec did not show today. Time spent with Alec or Xo was considerably more enjoyable when the other one was not present.

Xo clomped down the stairs in her usual hiking boots, shoving her sketchbook into a light fabric shoulder bag. She did not appear to see Elliot at first, but he expected this and watched in anticipation of her surprised expression of recognition when she found him. When at last she turned to him and greeted him, a rewarding warmth flowed into him.

Then she was sitting right there on the hearth directly beside him, and the pleasant warmth became a rush of clammy sweat prickling his back. At such close quarters, it was impossible to turn and speak. He focused instead on her nearest knee.

"Where's Alec?" Xo swiveled around.

Elliot managed to clear his throat. "He is not here yet."

"Those photos you brought in the other day will be good for plumage reference." Xo's smile lighted their corner of the room. "I hadn't realized you were such a bird enthusiast."

"I—I'm glad." Elliot hadn't realized it either. "I'm sorry I could not find more of the birds on your list." In fact, some of the species he'd had no idea about, since they weren't in the general field guide he'd picked up at the local bookstore. He guessed Sade's visitor center had a better identification book, but it might be a bit soon to return there.

"Oh, that's okay," said Xo. "I think some of these are gonna be hard to track down."

Alec walked in at that moment, waving lazily in their direction, and Xo sprang up to join him at the counter. After a moment's vacillation, Elliot approached them, still holding his mug of coffee. At every step he almost spilled it. Should he have stayed on the hearth? Their coffee came in to-go cups, so Elliot gulped the rest of the scalding liquid in his mug to finish it, choking as it burned his throat. A series of bad decisions...not an auspicious start.

Outside, Alec said, "I've had the most brilliant idea! And Elliot has his camera with him, so this will work out great."

Elliot looked down at his camera slung across his chest, as it was always, as Alec must surely have known it would be.

"What if—" Alec held up his hands in front of Xo, "—I did an interview with you for the *Mountain Herald*! About your new illustration job here, the upcoming field guide...you know! Elliot could take some pics of 'The Artist at Work.'" Alec framed these in another section of the air with his hands. "What do you think?"

Xo's round face showed blank shock. "I dunno..." She wrinkled her nose. "Are you sure that's a good idea?"

"Are you kidding? It'd be great publicity for you. Get noticed, even get more work commissions?" Alec was all enthusiasm.

She tilted her head thoughtfully. "Well...I suppose that could be useful. But would the newspaper go for an article about just me?"

"Sure! People love this stuff."

"They do?" said Xo.

"Trust me. We do human interest pieces like this all the time. Plus, everybody will want to read about you. I'm sure the locals have seen you around town and are wondering what you're doing here, and if you're planning to stay."

"I guess it's harder to be anonymous in Lingen," said Xo. "I'm not used to anybody caring what I've gotten up to."

"Well, caring and wanting to know are two different things." Alec chuckled.

Xo frowned.

"But I mean, why be anonymous, right?" Alec added. "Publicity is a good thing!"

Xo turned to Elliot. "What do you think? You haven't said."

The idea of photographing Xo was incredibly appealing. Now that it had come up, it was all Elliot could think about, besides the fact that she was actually interested in his opinion. He felt lightheaded. "It could be advantageous to your career."

"Okay," said Xo. "I'll do it. So...how do we start?"

"I'm still going to show you around," Alec patted her shoulder in an overly-familiar way. "We'll do, like, a walking interview. I'll introduce you to the sights, ask you questions about yourself and your work, and so on."

Alec led the way uphill from the coffee house to the high road, which ran along the outskirts of Lingen, as far up the flanks of the mountain as the town went. This gave a nice view of the rest of Lingen below. Alec pointed out features and mentioned historical notes, anecdotes from his own life, where there was once a fire, another place a landslide had occurred—no, not in recent memory but everyone spoke of it anyway as if they'd been there—and so forth.

"Why do they call this mountain just 'Arin?'" asked Xo. "It says 'Mount Arin' on the map and at the visitor center, but everyone says 'Arin' or 'The Mountain.' Like you say, 'The Cat,' if you're talking about the one in the house."

Alec shrugged. "Just how we do!"

"I asked the same question when I first arrived here," put in Elliot. "And got just as unsatisfactory an answer."

"At least I'm not the only outsider around here." Xo threw Elliot a look of gratitude. "Everybody else seems to have lived here forever."

Another warm thread of connection tied them together, though from Elliot's point of view, being an outsider was a positive thing. Not having everyone on the street know his past was one of the main reasons he'd moved here in the first place, all those years ago. Unfortunately, history did tend to repeat itself, and the respite of anonymity had not been a long one.

However, Xo likely knew nothing of that period of Lingen's history, nor Elliot's connection to it, and she wasn't going to learn about it from Alec's tour. Alec probably mentioned the mountainpox epidemic to tourists, but he would not bring it up with Elliot present—in this area of Alec's loyalty, Elliot was confident. Xo could see everything with fresh eyes, and standing beside her, Elliot saw a world refreshed as well. The fall day had all the possibilities of spring.

They had reached the place where the high road curved downhill again, but Alec turned off the road and onto the well-worn footpath that wended its way through the rocks and bushes above the town. It was one of Elliot's favorite places to wander, though it would have been better if it were just him and Xo.

"So, let's talk about you!" said Alec to Xo. "Any husband and kids along for the ride?"

Xo stared at him. "No. I kinda think you already know that."

"Boyfriend?"

"No." Xo spoke lightly, examining some flowers beside the path.

"Readers will want to know!"

"You aren't gonna put that in the article, are you?" Xo's voice went from unconcerned to horrified.

"Not if you don't want me to," Alec reassured her. "How about your work, then? Are you planning to stay here long? Why birds?"

"I dunno, I just got in the habit of drawing them, I guess, from watching them. I draw other things too sometimes. Other animals... well, occasionally. Flowers. Various objects. And yes, I'm planning to stay here—at least, as long as job opportunities last. Are you sure this is worth putting in the article?"

"Sure. Let's get a picture of you here on the hillside, then. Okay, Elliot?"

It was a beautiful day to photograph her: sunny and warm, but not too bright. A gentle cooling breeze blew down Arin from high above, where snow glistened on the upper peaks. The only marring point in the scene was how Xo kept watching Alec, as if seeking a sign from him. When Alec touched her, which he did with bothersome frequency, she did not move away.

A growing sense of despair began to condense within Elliot like dew. He had seen this before. Women were often quite taken with Alec, and he knew Alec was aware of it—possibly even played it to his advantage. It had not troubled Elliot much in the past. He'd never been that type of man himself, and he'd learned it long enough ago that he didn't even wish to be. He wouldn't have known what to do with a collection of admirers always trying to gain his attention. They were always disappointed eventually when Alec failed to reciprocate or lost interest.

Elliot admitted—only to himself—that he was lonely, but if his cure existed at all, it was in complete dedication to one woman. He looked at Xo and a complicated rhythm played in his heart, a song he could feel but not hear.

He raised his camera and framed her profile as she half-squinted into the hazy distance. She turned to retrieve her notebook from her bag and jotted something, then squatted against a rock, and he snapped another photo. When the click sounded this time, she turned to looked up at him wide-eyed, and with another press of the button he recorded the expression that had come to endear her most to him.

That evening, at home, Elliot went through the photographs of Xo for a long time. They seemed raw, true. The best photos always were, but as he examined them it became evident that he could not possibly print them in the newspaper. They were too personal, embodying too exactly the way Elliot saw her.

Until recently, the present had just seemed like the leftover remnants of a painful past, but Xo made it seem like the beginning of the future instead, one that might be as full of life, hope, and possibilities as she was.

He set aside one print that captured her perfectly, that moment she had turned to look up at him. She looked like she did when she heard one of her birds singing and turned towards it excitedly hoping to see it, and he felt honored that she would turn to him with this same anticipation.

When she gazed back at him thus, clear and open, it seemed she concealed nothing, even though he did not see what he longed to see. Still, perhaps one day she might look into his eyes and see written there what he felt. He marveled that she did not sense the strength of it radiating off him, like heat ripples in the sunshine. It seemed so obvious that Elliot half expected everyone to know just by looking at him when he looked at her.

His mind returned to the troubling matter of Xo and Alec. He had earlier hoped the excursion would clear things up, especially whether he should honorably withdraw if the other two seemed to be getting involved. He felt miles away from this position now, but he still wasn't sure if anything was going on between her and Alec. It would be premature to ask Alec if he was pursuing Xo. Plus, Alec might not step back even if Elliot privately confessed his interest. Alec seemed to have different moral boundaries than Elliot in matters of romance.

Of course, he didn't want any type of rivalry with his friend, but it surely wouldn't come to that. The more important question was what Xo thought. Perhaps Elliot's own genuine interest would gradually open Xo's eyes.

Elliot lay back on his bed and switched off the bedside lamp. The only certainty, which was much more pleasant to dwell on, was that he needed to take some new photographs of Xo for her article.

6

PACKAGES AND POSSIBILITIES

On her own today, Xo descended a footpath amongst scattered boulders, rejoining the sidewalk at the upper reaches of Lingen. There was a bounce in her step despite the grey, misty morning and the fact that she hadn't gotten quite as much sketching done as intended.

She'd spent a few hours with her sketchpad near a glacier stream that poured down the side of Mount Arin, a spot she'd noted on an earlier, sunnier day for the shade provided by a footbridge crossing high over the gully. The water collecting in little pools among the rocks was ideal for dippers and other birds in search of an icy bath, as well as attracting insectivores to the clouds of gnats that hovered nearby. As expected, there had been plenty of action this morning, but although she'd managed some good rough sketches, her mind had mostly been on last weekend's walking tour with Elliot and Alec.

There was now little doubt in her mind that Alec was interested in her. He had been most attentive during the tour, and there had been the question about the "boyfriend," who did not exist. At the time, she'd been flustered by how often his hand brushed her shoulder or arm as he pointed something out, but upon reflection, she had to admit it was flattering. The more she mulled over the outing, the more positive it seemed.

Historically, she had not attracted much attention from guys, so a relationship had rarely even been an option. But then, she'd once thought a career as an artist wasn't realistic either. With a practical plan and careful approach, that was working out, so perhaps this could be tackled the same way.

There were potential useful aspects to pursuing a relationship. She would always have someone to talk to, plus studies showed that those in committed relationships were healthier and lived longer. Her romantic needs, long suppressed, would presumably be addressed, and it would be comfortable knowing she could rely on someone being there for her, maybe forever. Now that she'd run into a guy who was—against all odds—actually attracted to her and interested, it seemed like the obvious choice.

However, there was one issue that kept rising up in her mind. Alec had asked her out when they first met, but they'd ended up eating at the coffee shop. They still hadn't gone anywhere and he hadn't spoken of it again, even though it had been several days since the tour. Unless the tour was the date?

The puzzle was still unsolved by the time she reached the coffee shop. Xo pushed open the door to see Megan waving from behind the counter, where a line of people had queued up. It was already noon. Stashing the bag with her sketching supplies behind the counter, Xo quickly washed up. Megan had marked the codes for several espresso drinks on to-go cups, which were piling up, so Xo set to work making them as fast as she could. Luckily, she'd managed to learn the abbreviations and most of the specialty drinks by now.

When there was finally a lull in the lunch rush, Megan pulled a peach-colored slip of paper from her pocket and handed it to Xo. "This came while you were out."

Xo took it curiously. "Oh! My packages are at the post office. It looks like I have to sign for them."

Megan wiped down the counter and leaned against it. "New furniture?"

"No, it's some of my things that were too big to take on the train. When I moved out of my old apartment to come here, I stored them at my mother's house and asked her to send them along." The recollection tempered Xo's excitement somewhat. "She wasn't that keen on me moving out here to be an artist."

Megan shrugged. "At least she stored your stuff."

"That's true." It was best to focus on the positive, and hopefully her success would show in time. "I guess I'll try to pick them up later." She chewed the inside of her cheek thoughtfully, calculating how many trips it would take.

"Need a hand?" asked Megan. "It'll have to be right after you get off work, though. I have evening classes tonight."

"That'd be great!" said Xo. "Do you have a car?"

"Not at the moment," said Megan. "But I can borrow my sister's wagon."

"Are we talking a station wagon or the kind with horses?" asked Xo, picturing the latter.

Megan laughed. "Neither. The little red kind."

"How old is your sister?"

Megan laughed again. "Your age, but she's got kids."

A familiar empty feeling surfaced. The ramifications of not being in a relationship increased as Xo got older, as others of her generation moved on with their lives. Megan was probably either too young to be affected by it yet or wasn't bothered by such things. On the other hand, she was likely knowledgeable about current relationship expectations, which would be helpful in clarifying the Alec situation.

"Do people still 'date' these days, or what's the procedure?" asked Xo.

"Some of them do." Megan looked amused. "Why, what's up?"

"Well…there's this guy. I feel like he's interested, and we've hung out and stuff, but we haven't really gone on a date. Didn't people used to actually ask each other on dates, and then they were 'going out' or whatever?"

"Maybe he's shy," said Megan. "Why don't you ask *him* out?"

Shy didn't really sound like Alec, but Megan did know him better, and Xo had been wrong about people before.

Megan grinned sideways at Xo. "So, are you going to tell me who it is?"

Xo glanced around the coffee house. Alec was often here in the afternoons. It was usually difficult to tell from her vantage point at the counter if he was interviewing people for newspaper articles or just chatting with friends, but he always encouraged her to join him when she got off work. Elliot was typically here by the late afternoon as well, always on the fireplace hearth near Alec's table, and usually reading one book or another which he put away when she sat down. Luckily neither of them was present now.

Megan followed Xo's gaze to the hearth. "Not Elliot?" she whispered gleefully.

"What? No..." said Xo, momentarily derailed by the unexpected suggestion. For some reason, she vividly recalled the moment when she'd met Elliot for the second time, here at the café with Alec, and her face grew warm at the memory. But that was just because the whole situation had been embarrassing due to her recently having knocked a heavy bird on top of him. No...Elliot had been nothing but nice to her, but there was no indication he was attracted to her. The idea gave her a funny feeling, and she quickly pushed it away. It seemed disloyal to Alec.

"I don't think Elliot's interested in me." She hoped he would remain a friend, though, especially since he seemed to share an interest in birds.

Megan elbowed her in the side. "Who, then?"

"It's Alec," said Xo in a low voice.

"Oh!" Megan withdrew from her conspiratorial posture and re-arranged some cups on the counter. "Not shy, then." She laughed shortly.

"I don't think so, but I'm not sure of the best way to move forward with him. You're friends with him, right? Has he said anything?"

Megan turned to Xo and sighed. "Alec...let me put it this way, Xo: in all the time I've known him, he just fades from one woman to the next. At first, he seems interested, then..." She cocked her head to one side. "He kind of disappears. It doesn't seem like he wants to get seriously involved, if you get my drift."

"Maybe he hasn't met the right person yet."

"Yeah." Megan's voice turned sarcastic. "That's probably what they all think."

"You think he's not serious, then?" asked Xo. Megan's lack of endorsement of Alec was somewhat surprising when she'd appeared to heartily recommend him before.

"If he decided to get serious, it would be obvious. You wouldn't have to ask," said Megan firmly.

"I'm not sure I'm good at picking up on the signals," said Xo slowly, beginning to doubt the evidence again. It had seemed so solid.

"How did you know in your last relationship?" pressed Megan.

Xo hesitated.

"You have been in a relationship before, right?" Megan looked at her sideways.

"Of course I have. At least, I think so."

"You think?"

"I'm just not exactly sure how it started." Xo could feel her face heating up. "There was a guy I worked with…I asked him if he'd seen this movie, and he hadn't, so I ended up inviting him over to my apartment to watch it. And he…" Xo paused. "In retrospect, I think he may have thought I meant something else."

"Didn't you?"

"Well…no."

Megan looked at her like she was speaking another language. "Then why did you ask him over?"

Xo shrugged. "It was a good movie. It seemed like a friendly thing to do at the time, but then it sort of turned into more than that. I mean, I was okay with it," she added hastily.

"Sounds thrilling," Megan deadpanned.

"I just could never figure out where I stood with him, or what the nature of our relationship was, even as time went by. One particularly confusing day, I asked. He didn't seem to know either, or have any inkling of where he wanted things to go from there. Under examination, it kinda fell apart. And that was the end of it, as it turned out—we weren't together anymore after that conversation. I didn't exactly intend that, either, but I was relieved when it was over." She was also relieved when telling Megan was over.

Megan did not seem shocked, however. "Probably a good thing it ended, then. What are you looking for in a guy now?"

Xo thought for a moment. "Someone who gets me. And not so confusing."

"And you think that's Alec?" asked Megan doubtfully.

"Well…it takes time, sometimes." Theoretically, at least. "And if a guy is already interested, that's half the battle. It's so difficult when I pick someone first and then I'm trying to gauge their interest level and I can't figure it out. It always turns out to be a wasted effort that goes nowhere. But Alec always seems in a good mood to see me, happy and kinda fun to be around. And he doesn't seem to mind me talking."

With many people, Xo would embark on a topic and then accidentally lose the thread somewhere along the way, and the conversation would subsequently die since the other person didn't know where to pick it up again. This did not happen with Alec. He seized on a new topic as soon as there was a pause and was off and running. Admittedly, sometimes Xo had to wonder if she need be present at all for him to continue, but she supposed she shouldn't be too picky.

"So, do you think Alec would mind if I just ask him out myself?" asked Xo, preferring to revisit Megan's earlier and more positive suggestion. "Then I'd know for sure, at least."

"It's up to you," said Megan. "Just…keep in mind what I said, so you don't get too disappointed."

❖   ❖   ❖

When Xo finished her shift, Megan was waiting with the wagon on the sidewalk outside. "Let's make this quick. I have loads of homework to get to before my evening class."

"Thanks, it shouldn't take long," said Xo, hoping her guess was accurate. The sky, grey all day, had gradually grown darker and the clouds were now a heavy steel blue that threatened to burst.

"Hey!" called a voice behind them. Alec caught up to them, having evidently switched course on his approach to the coffee house. "Where are you girls off to?"

Xo explained. Alec seemed to find the plan hysterical. "You're going to haul all that stuff in the wagon? It'll take forever!"

"We got it covered," said Megan. "Go have your coffee."

"Come on, that can wait," said Alec. "It'll take me two seconds to run back to my house and get the truck. It's crazy to try to do it with the wagon."

"You did say you were in hurry," pointed out Xo to Megan.

Megan frowned. "Then I hauled the wagon over for nothing."

"Wait here!" Alec departed at a brisk walk.

Megan sighed and sat in the parked wagon.

"I can take it back for you after," offered Xo.

"Nah, it's okay," said Megan. They lapsed into silence.

"What classes are you taking?" asked Xo.

"Business."

"I really liked college." Xo smiled. "Especially biology and art—those were my favorites. I spent most of my free time drawing birds." Humans had been a bit of a conundrum even then, but she still remembered the time fondly.

Megan didn't respond, perhaps thinking of the homework she had to get to. That part, Xo did not miss.

A large pickup truck pulled up next to them with the windows down. Alec leaned across to their side. "Hop in!"

Megan stood up. "I can't leave the wagon here."

Xo glanced at her in surprise. "Alec and I can probably get the boxes…" And then Megan could take the wagon back to her sister, she was going to say, but she trailed off at Megan's perturbed expression. She must seem ungrateful for Megan's original offer of assistance, being so ready to ditch her for Alec after Megan had taken time away from her studies to help.

"Why don't we put the wagon in the back of the truck?" Xo said instead.

"Good idea," said Megan, in a more chipper tone. She and Xo picked it up together and put it in upside-down so it wouldn't roll, then both got in the cab with Alec. The wagon clanked as he accelerated, and he eased off the gas.

Xo glanced over at Alec's profile, close on her left, as he continued to talk in a joking manner about how the truck was an improvement over the wagon. It would've been a good opportunity to broach the date question, if Megan weren't pressed quite so closely into her other side. Before a solution came to mind, they were at the post office disembarking. Xo went inside to sign for the packages, the others trailing behind.

"What *is* this?" Megan tugged on one of the large boxes that had been wheeled out from behind the post office counter on a hand truck.

"Part of my easel," said Xo. "I disassembled it into three boxes for shipping. And the big square box is just random stuff."

"You were expecting me to haul all of this back in the wagon?" squeaked Megan disbelievingly, as Alec guffawed.

"I think we could have done it," said Xo defensively. In fact, Megan had insisted they could, earlier.

"You guys are nuts," said Alec, propping a box on his shoulder somewhat carelessly. He pushed the door open with the end of the box.

"Careful with that!" Xo hurried after him with a smaller package. After depositing it over the side of the truck bed, she climbed in the back to arrange the next easel box which Alec brought out. Now was her chance—Megan was still in the post office dealing with the awkwardly-sized box o' randomness.

"So, I was wondering…" Xo began, wedging the wagon against the boxes to keep them from sliding on the downhill. Alec leaned both arms on the side of the truck, watching her, which was distracting and made Xo need to concentrate on the boxes. She went on, "You mentioned a while back that there were some restaurants I should check out, right? I'm thinking of doing so this weekend." She left Alec an opening, in case he preferred to do the asking.

Alec didn't appear to see it. "The Italian place is good, and it's right near the coffee house." He gestured in its general direction. "They have music sometimes."

"Hmm," said Xo. Out of the corner of her eye, she could see Megan emerging from the post office with the last box.

"Do-you-think-you'd-wanna-go-there-Saturday?" Xo blurted out, in the space of a single second.

"Oof…" Alec blew out some air. Apparently, it was a most difficult decision. He switched his position on the truck so his back was against it and stretched his arms, interlocking his fingers and resting them behind his head. Then he looked back at her. "I guess I'd have to see what I'm doing this weekend. Ask me on Friday!"

Xo stared at her own address, upside down, on the box in front of her. "Ask me on Friday?" she repeated under her breath.

When she turned back to him, Alec had taken the box from Megan and was tucking it into the truck bed, acting unaware of any problem. "That's everything! Now aren't you glad you don't have to pull it back?" He and Megan both got in the cab.

Xo swung her feet over the back of the truck onto the bumper and jumped down. *Ask me on Friday.* What kind of a response was that, and what was up with his schedule being so needlessly complex? He was a reporter, after all. It wasn't as if he was going to be called on to fight fires or something at a moment's notice.

Tiny drops of rain began to spatter on the cardboard boxes in the back of the truck. Xo squeezed in between Megan and the door and they zoomed back to the coffee house. The return trip seemed faster, or maybe it was just because Xo's thoughts were jumbled and the drizzle on the windows was obscuring everything passing outside. Alec pulled up at the front door of the café in a no-parking zone, and they all began to unload the packages onto the sidewalk. The eaves overhung enough to make a dry place for the boxes, but at the rate the rain was picking up, it wasn't going to stay dry for long.

Xo picked up one of the boxes again and poked the café door handle with her knee, trying to push the latch that opened it.

"Give me a sec, and I'll help you carry those up," said Alec.

"What about the wagon?" protested Megan. "I need to take it back to my sister's house, and I have class soon."

Alec turned to her. "Don't worry about that. I'll drive it."

Xo managed to get the door open at last.

"I'll come back and give you a hand after I drop Megan off," called Alec from the door of his truck. Megan had already climbed into the cab again.

Xo crossed the coffee shop rapidly and ran up the stairs with the first box. When she returned, the truck was gone. If she worked fast, she should be able to get them all before Alec returned. She didn't need his wishy-washy help anyway.

She grabbed the next box and walked briskly between the tables, her head down. He could have at least parked by the side door, next to the bottom of her stairs, so she wouldn't have to walk through the dining area. Fortunately, there were only a few customers in the shop now, and aside from some curious glances they didn't pay her much attention. Two boxes left. She almost tripped going up the stairs. The last box: losing its shape where she gripped the sides, and smelling of moist cardboard. Alec was not back yet.

At last, sweaty and breathless, Xo collapsed on her bed, all the boxes safely stowed in her apartment. The bank of windows facing the street had fogged up on the inside as her clothes and belongings steamed in the warm indoors. Her heart was pounding even louder than the rain, which had shifted into a downpour. The din of it beating on the roof was strangely satisfying, now that she was inside and Alec was out driving around in it somewhere.

Fine. She would ask him again on Friday, if that was what he wanted.

She would, maybe.

7

MORE PHOTOS

"What do you mean, 'they didn't come out right,' not even one?" Alec sounded unreasonably perplexed.

Elliot's refusal to relinquish the photographs of Xo was not going over as easily as he had hoped, though it had taken Alec a few days to notice and demand an explanation as to why Elliot still hadn't brought forth any pictures to go with his article.

"They won't work." It was impossible to explain without going into too much detail or creating an elaborate deception, neither of which Elliot wanted to do.

"Don't you have anything we can use? I know you're a good photographer, Elliot—you must have something."

"I'll redo the shoot, stop fretting." Elliot tried to make himself sound disappointed, but the excitement at having another reason to meet up with Xo was infecting his voice.

Later, thankfully without Alec, Elliot entered the coffee shop with fast-beating heart and eager smile. He had timed his arrival towards the end of Xo's shift.

"Xiomara, how lovely to see you."

"Oh, hi, Elliot. What would you like today?" Xo's eyes looked tired.

"Just a latte, please. How has your day been?"

"Long, I guess. I've been having trouble focusing on my drawings. I didn't get as much sketching done this morning as I wanted."

"I am so sorry to hear that." He ought to have followed up sooner about the photos. "Is there anything I can do to help?"

"Nah, thanks. I'm gonna be off soon." Xo started heating the milk.

Elliot hesitated. "I was wondering...but perhaps it's not a good time."

"What's that?" Xo glanced up from the espresso machine.

"If you're feeling unwell or too tired, please don't hesitate to say so. It's certainly possible to do it another day," Elliot finished hurriedly.

Xo looked at him for a long moment. "Sorry, what is it exactly that you're asking?"

"You see, the photos the other day...for the newspaper..." Elliot swallowed hard.

Xo paused again in the coffee-making operation, her face worn-out and perplexed.

"Never mind, please forget I said anything. Another day is perfectly fine."

"Elliot!" exclaimed Xo. "Just spit it out!"

Elliot jumped, the sharpness of her tone stabbing him. He was a babbling buffoon, even trying to arrange a business proposition. If he had been trying to say anything more meaningful...it was too horrible to think about.

He spoke in a low voice, as steadily as possible. "The...newspaper photos...for the article. They did not turn out, and I was wondering, if it would be possible..."

Xo leaned in closer, possibly to urge him on, but unfortunately her proximity had the opposite effect. Elliot's words dried up altogether.

He rallied, swallowing again, and finished: "To take some more. Of you." Elliot kicked himself mentally for not having picked a better moment.

"Oh." Xo's shoulders relaxed. "That's all? Sure." She didn't question why they hadn't turned out, unlike Alec. "How about taking them here in my studio?" Xo handed Elliot his coffee. "After all, Alec did say 'the artist at work.' You could do me painting, or photograph my drawings. That'd be more interesting than me standing around outside."

"Excellent idea!" Elliot was immensely relieved at Xo taking over steering the conversation before it completely crashed. "Not that the outdoors isn't also a good setting…" He trailed to a halt. The plan of going up to her apartment was not soothing his nerves.

"Okay, good," said Xo. "We can do it after I get off. I'm almost done for the day."

"I already have my equipment." Elliot patted his camera. "I'll just wait over here." He smiled and gave her a little bow, for reasons he couldn't fathom, and backed away, almost tripping over a nearby chair.

Elliot recovered and found his spot on the hearth near the foot of the stairs, his heartbeat pounding in his ears. He glanced up at the landing. The lone door at the top glanced back, now without its former "For Rent" sign. He had looked inside when it was still up: there was only one main room, with a bed in it—a problem in his own small house as well. Soon he would have to stand with her beside that bed. If he were Alec, it would probably trigger a comment that would alert her to his romantic interest, to see how she responded. Of course, that would be completely inappropriate during a professional photography session. What would one say anyway? The only phrases which came to mind sounded horrifically rude and not at all appealing. Xo would never respond positively to such remarks, regardless of her feelings.

Elliot revised his daydream instead, to where he said nothing at all. He populated the empty room, in his mind, with the two of them and some random painting equipment. Xo stood by the windows, looking out. A bird flew up and perched on the sill. Another joined it. The birds sat fearlessly looking in, while Xo pointed them out to Elliot. As they stood close together, she took his hand, and suddenly they were looking deep into each other's eyes. Words were unnecessary.

"Shift's over." Xo was in front of him, bouncing on the balls of her feet. The imaginary version of her evaporated abruptly. She seemed more energized than before as she headed for the stairs.

Elliot quickly followed, catching up before she reached the top to walk beside her. At the entrance, she started to open the door, but stopped with her hand on the knob. Had she reconsidered, finding the idea of him in her apartment unappealing?

"Thing is, I'd kinda like to change." Xo wrinkled her nose. "I'm sweaty, and I smell like food. I think I spilled some coffee, too." She plucked her shirt away from her body, examining it. "I mean, as long as you're taking pictures, might as well not look like a complete slob, right?" She laughed faintly. "Anyway…be right back." Xo opened the door, ducked through, and closed it again.

Elliot stood on the landing, still facing the door. Obviously, he should not have raced up after her. He could hear Xo thumping around inside, opening drawers. One of those sounds would be her taking off her clothes. He turned away self-consciously, directing his attention over the railing down into the café. Several people looked up at him from their tables. One of them laughed to a companion. Elliot turned again so he was facing the wall rather than the railing or the door, careful not to lean against the railing. It was not particularly stable.

"Just a minute!" came Xo's muffled voice, although he hadn't said anything and had no intention of interrupting her.

The thought of her doing whatever she was doing immediately on the other side of the door was extremely unsettling. Focus: he was here to take pictures. Unfortunately, that made him imagine taking pictures at precisely that moment, if he were on Xo's side of the door.

Elliot ran his hands through his hair and shook his head briskly. Clearly, he had to get hold of himself if he was going to make any kind of favorable impression. How could she ever find an interest in him if he always acted like a nincompoop in front of her? His comparatively normal behavior in front of other people would be immaterial if his common sense and control of his tongue departed nearly every time he tried to talk to her.

"Okay, I'm ready!"

When Elliot hesitated, Xo's voice became louder. "Elliot? Are you coming?"

Mindful of the growing attention of the audience in the café below, Elliot seized the knob and plunged inside.

8

Xo's Room

Elliot closed the door carefully behind him. The room was different than he remembered, and much more personable with her things in it.

"You've quite made this place your own."

"You've been in here before?" Surprise was all over Xo's face.

"Yes. I mean…" Elliot coughed. "Not when it was occupied! Only while it was being shown for rental purposes."

Actually, he'd merely asked Jacqua if he could take a look when the rental sign went up, out of curiosity, and Jacqua had told him to go ahead. It hadn't exactly been a showing, and since he had his own house, he had not been planning to rent it anyway. This was far too complicated to explain, but the implication of him having been a visitor in the room before—when rented by the person before her, or when nobody was home—was one he wanted to steer far away from.

Fortunately, Xo didn't demand further explanation. She had moved to the far end of the room, where an easel now stood. Next to it was a table that Elliot recognized had come with the place, but which was now covered with her paints and pencils. She started arranging them, possibly to look more organized for the photo, though it was all the same to him. The shelves behind the easel and chair now overflowed with books, sketchbooks, and larger drawing pads, while on the windowsills along the right-hand wall, jars of water held individual wildflowers picked from the sides of the mountain.

To the left, the bed and chest of drawers still stood on either side of the doorway that accessed the kitchen and bathroom, but now the bed was covered with a colorful, rumpled quilt. The shirt Xo had been wearing earlier for work had been thrown haphazardly across it. Some of the drawers of the dresser were ajar, and a hairbrush lay on top along with other personal accessories, which Elliot forbore from looking at too closely out of consideration for Xo's personal space.

He moved to join her at the end of the room, but his foot hooked around another article of clothing that had fallen off the bed.

"Elliot, you've got…" Xo advanced on him, knelt at his feet, and grabbed his ankle. She tried to lift his foot. He complied, acutely conscious of her touch. Xo rose again, narrowly avoided banging her head on his dangling camera, and held up one of her bras.

She giggled. "Whoops." In her embarrassment, and now his, her laughter was contagious. He laughed while trying not to, which made her laugh more.

"Well!" Xo stuffed the garment into a drawer. "At least we got the awkward part out of the way!" She plunked down on the chair in front of the easel, rosy-cheeked and smiling.

Elliot grinned back at her. Though he still felt uncomfortable about the underwear entanglement, basking in her warmth was impossible to resist. Gravitating towards her, he examined the books on the shelves behind her chair.

"I have this series." He gestured to the set.

Xo spun halfway around in the chair to see. "Oh, really? I didn't get around to buying them all, and they don't have them at the library here."

"I'd be happy to lend them to you." Elliot pointed to another book. "I have other works by this author as well, if you like."

"That'd be great!" Xo beamed. "My own personal lending library!"

Elliot was delighted at the similarity in their taste in books. He mentally noted a few titles she had on the shelf that he had not read, to investigate later. There was something deeply personal in knowing someone through the books she enjoyed. It might reveal other sides of her. Also, the shared books could be a basis for future conversations. Each time he saw Xo, he felt he must come up with a specific reason to see her again.

"Too many people don't like to read for fun anymore," Xo said wistfully. "Sometimes I read a great book and have nobody to recommend it to! Or I read one that drives me crazy and I want to discuss what's wrong with it, but I can't find anyone who's read it."

It was hard to imagine a sparkling personality like Xo lacking for someone to talk to, but she had just moved to a new area, without friends or family, like Elliot when he first came here. Perhaps she was even telling him she would not be averse to more companionship in her life.

"If you're interested, I could bring over some other books that you might like as well."

"That's so nice of you." Xo smiled.

The conversation fell into a lull. Xo recovered first; evidently her daydream wasn't quite as compelling as what Elliot was busy adding to his. "So, for the photos, do you want to have me here painting, or...?"

Abashed, Elliot quickly replaced the book he was holding on the shelf and stepped back to a more suitable distance for framing a photo. It required some maneuvering in the small apartment.

"Whatever you're comfortable with."

"Should I actually paint or just look like I'm painting? How should I pose?"

Elliot raised the camera. "You can paint, or pretend to, if you like."

Xo stared into space for a moment, considering what to do, and Elliot snapped a picture.

"Don't take that one!" Xo exclaimed.

"Why not?" Elliot looked up from the camera in surprise.

"I dunno, it doesn't seem like the right 'look.' I'm just staring out the window."

"It looked good from over here." Elliot was relaxed enough to be a little amused. At his small smile, Xo gave him a mock reprimanding look.

A pleasant warmth spread through Elliot. He wanted to hold on to this easy camaraderie and prolong it. It felt like they had known each other longer than they actually had.

Even once he had enough newspaper-worthy shots, Elliot kept taking photos. Xo was still talking and posing, and he didn't want the session to be over, though he didn't want to overstay his welcome either. She had seemed tired earlier, and he wanted to end on a good note, if it had to end. It did have to, he reminded himself firmly. He would just continue until Xo herself gave some cue.

Eventually she flopped back in her chair and stretched. "Whew! Do you think we have enough photos now?"

"Most definitely," Elliot replied. "They'll probably only run one or two—one of you, and likely a close-up of one of your paintings."

"Is that all?" Xo pouted.

Elliot was alarmed for a moment, but it appeared she wasn't truly disappointed, just teasing him in a way. This meant they were close enough to do so. He smiled. "No ten-page spread this time. Perhaps in the future."

"When I'm famous!" Xo spun her chair back and forth.

"Is that what you want?"

"Nah, not really." Xo shrugged. "I just like to make the pictures. That's why I moved here. I needed to get back to being me."

Elliot nodded. He understood. Had he, though, achieved "being himself?" He enjoyed living in this beautiful area, and he enjoyed photography, which also paid the bills, but there was something lacking. Something like Xiomara. He allowed his eyes to linger on her face. If only he could communicate telepathically.

In the course of his telepathy attempt, the silence became rather long.

"Well..." said Xo after a while.

Elliot sprang into alertness. "I should let you get to...your painting. Thank you for a charming photography session. I won't keep you any longer." He backed towards the door.

"No problem. Don't forget those books!" Xo's reference to another future meeting between them gave him a thrill of delight.

"I shall certainly remember!" said Elliot. "Until then!"

Elliot closed the door quietly, and floated down the staircase and back to his home to select the volumes he felt would please her most—and one or two to give her other ideas, in case she thought of him while reading them in the coming days.

Xo had been surprised by what a good mood she was in after the photo session. She hadn't been looking forward to it after Elliot said he needed to retake the photos, but it had turned out to be a nice distraction from her other concerns. He hadn't seemed to mind the silly poses she struck for comic effect, and she'd eagerly dived into the books he'd brought her later. Such a comfort—and another happy distraction—to return to the series she'd been reading before she moved.

Several other books he'd brought were piled on the dresser to look forward to: a few authors she already knew plus an unfamiliar novel he'd recommended called *Precipice and Precipitation: A Backcountry Romance*. Reading was a respite into a world of beloved characters who actually made sense, and when she emerged from it again, it seemed like people in the outside world could make sense too.

Alec, in particular. The lack of progress with him bothered her, and the fact that it bothered her also bothered her. It was causing a lack of progress on her artwork as well. Couldn't she just concentrate on that and leave Alec and human problems for the rest of humanity to worry about?

She could not, because Alec did not come into the coffee house at all on Friday—or the rest of the weekend. She hadn't made further reference to the date when he came by as usual earlier in the week, since he'd said to ask Friday. But why would he do that and then not even turn up? Was he avoiding her, or were things just more casual these days than in the stories she enjoyed?

He might have simply forgotten, a thought which did not cheer her. Or maybe there was some bizarre, news-related event that had pulled him away to his reporting duties. This was unlikely, as urgent news in Lingen seemed always to be weather-related, and the days had been clear and sunny.

By the time Alec rolled into the coffee house on the following Monday afternoon, a couple hours into Xo's shift, she was not feeling charitable about whatever his excuse was going to be. He stood near the door talking with friends for interminable seconds, obviously in no hurry. Xo realized she was staring fixedly in his direction and went to the other end of the counter. She felt the pressure building inside, heating her up, and took a deep breath. She should give him time to offer an explanation. Getting all emotional accomplished nothing.

Alec came over and leaned on the counter, grinning. Xo turned slowly, fighting to maintain a neutral expression. He did not look apologetic at all.

"Well?" asked Xo.

Alec raised his eyebrows and looked at her inquiringly, apparently oblivious.

Her voice sharpened. "What do you want to order?"

"You pick a drink for me," said Alec cheerfully.

Xo frowned and tapped the counter impatiently. "That's not how this operates."

"Come on, Xo." Alec draped himself along the counter like a dog wanting to play. "Why are you being so mean to me today?"

Xo started an espresso shot for whatever he was going to order, and began to heat the milk. It was too ridiculous to keep going along with the charade that nothing was wrong; she had to say something. Still, she must not overreact.

"What happened to 'Ask me on Friday?'" It came out more abruptly than intended.

"What?" Alec seemed momentarily taken aback at her harshness. "Oh…I had something going on. With work. Course, if I had my druthers, I'd be in to see you every day."

Doubtful, and he still hadn't addressed the issue. Xo bit her lip. She wanted to ask him again, but another invitation was sure to come out wrong in her current mood, and furthermore, she shouldn't even have to ask again.

Alec glanced at the pitcher she was still frothing. "That milk seems to be getting pretty steamed up." His voice was tinged with amusement.

Xo glared at him, shut the steam wand off sharply, and wiped it down. The espresso shot had now been waiting too long; Megan had told her they would go dead if not quickly tempered with a little milk. She poured it out and started another one.

"Look, sorry I didn't get back to you," said Alec. "I had to go out of town this weekend anyway, there was a game I was covering for the paper."

Xo didn't trust herself to speak in case she snapped again. So he did remember. Why couldn't she keep things cool and casual, like he did? Or was he just acting like that because he didn't really care?

"What are you doing this evening?" asked Alec, who still hadn't told her what drink he wanted.

Xo let out the breath she'd been holding. "Painting. I'm getting behind." Somehow, it seemed like that was Alec's fault, too, though this was completely illogical.

Alec pushed back from the counter, considering her. "You're different, Xo," he said with a half-smile.

Xo looked back blankly. "Different how? Is that good or bad?"

"Just different," said Alec. "Good, but different."

It wasn't the sort of conversation she'd been hoping for, but she wasn't sure what to expect at this point. She poured the plain espresso into a small cup and pushed it towards him. To her surprise, he accepted it and paid.

"See you around, then?"

"All right," said Xo.

It was worse than before he had come in. She still didn't know if he'd forgotten or if he didn't want to go out at all, and now she had no idea who was supposed to go next. The more she interacted with Alec, the more confusing the relationship became—if it even qualified as one. Weren't they supposed to get easier as one got older?

When she returned to her apartment that evening, she looked over her paints and in-progress drawings, uninspired. She picked up the book she had been in the middle of and sank into that consolatory world instead.

9

THE ARTICLE

Later that week, when Xo came downstairs a few minutes before her shift was due to start, Megan pounced on her, full of excitement.

"Guess what, Xo?" Megan grabbed a newspaper off the counter and waved it in the air, grinning. "Your article came out!"

"Yay!" Xo gave a little jump. Megan's enthusiasm was infectious.

Excitement restored, Xo unfolded the proffered newspaper on the counter. Megan pointed to a section titled *Painter Spreads Wings in Lingen* and poured her a breve.

A photo of her at the easel was stretched across the top of the article—not the one where she was staring out the window. She looked surprisingly like a real artist at work. There was also a photo of one of her in-progress paintings for the field guide. She still needed to document more of the rare birds for that project. Sade had given her a generous amount of time, but she'd expected to have sighted more of them by now and gotten more sketches started to base the paintings on.

As she read the article, Xo began to feel queasy. "Listen to this: 'I dunno how I got into the habit of drawing birds. I like to draw other things too, animals and flowers and such. I'm probably gonna stick around here as long as the jobs last.' It sounds awful. I didn't say that!"

"You mean Alec misquoted you?" Megan took the paper back and skimmed it. "I thought it was good."

"I said that, basically, but not in that way. It sounds uneducated. If *I* had written down what I said, I would never have written it that way."

"It doesn't sound that bad," said Megan. "You do talk that way— not just you, everybody."

"But not in *writing*," protested Xo. "It's supposed to sound professional; it's about my work."

"It's okay, really." Megan pushed Xo's cup forward. "Here, drink your coffee. Ask Alec to print a retraction."

Xo sighed gloomily. A retraction with differently phrased quotes that said essentially the same thing would be pointless, and it would sound ridiculous if she requested it.

At least nobody from her past was likely to read the *Mountain Herald*. Still, it was hardly a good start to her career. What if later articles about her quoted this one, once she became better known? No, never again—she would only respond to interview requests in writing. She re-read the article. Alec had also combined some of her answers in a way that was surely not how she'd said them.

Megan nudged her. "Here he comes now."

Alec entered the coffee house looking quite pleased with himself. "Did you read the article yet?"

"Yes, I did," said Xo, in tones of doom. The newspaper was lying in front of her on the counter, plain to see.

"What did you think?" asked Alec brightly, apparently unable to detect tones of doom.

Xo grabbed the paper, frowning, and beckoned for Alec to follow her towards the back door that led to the alley. She didn't want another scene where she got irritated at him with the whole café watching, but she couldn't let this go by without mentioning it. Instead of going outside, she stopped just inside the door—nobody else would happen by who wasn't on the way to the restrooms.

When Alec joined her, Xo lowered her voice to a loud whisper. "Why did you quote me like that?"

Alec looked surprised. "Like what?"

"Like...like this." She read from the page in a low, goofy voice. "'I'm probably gonna stick around here'—that's not what I said!"

"Well, I'm paraphrasing," said Alec. "We have to. Otherwise you'd always be reading quotes full of 'erm' and 'uh, actually what I meant to say was,' and all that stuff. You had a lot of those," he added pointedly.

"Maybe I had. But why did you have to put stuff like 'gonna' and 'dunno' in writing? I sound like a doofus."

Alec laughed. "You don't sound like a doofus. It makes it sound more genuine, more relatable."

"And here, you described me as *leggy!*" She spoke through gritted teeth, jabbing the offending paragraph with her finger.

"So?" He shrugged. "It's a compliment!"

"The whole thing makes me into an airhead. This is my *work.*" Xo's voice cracked. She folded her arms. She couldn't go on; her eyes were watering and the drops threatened to become actual tears. The pressure of holding them back closed up her throat.

Alec looked uncomfortable. "Heyyy, take it easy." He patted her shoulder.

Xo wrenched away. A wave of loneliness washed over her. When was the last time someone had held her? It felt like forever ago. However, at this moment, she distinctly did not want it to be him.

"I think you're over-reacting." Alec's voice was infuriatingly calm. "I write articles like this all the time, and people enjoy reading them. Nobody's going to think it's unprofessional."

"*I* think so. And it's about *me,*" hissed Xo. "I have to go."

Her first impulse was to exit through the back door, but she switched course and dashed behind the counter and into the kitchen instead: an employees-only zone where Alec couldn't follow. As the door swung behind her, she saw Megan give Alec a look. He shrugged uselessly in response.

Xo leaned against the wall on the other side of the kitchen door and practiced slow breathing techniques until she began to relax, wiping her eyes. Jacqua paused in folding croissant dough to glance at her questioningly, then returned to folding.

After a while she asked, still a little tearful, "Did you read the article about me?"

"Hm. Yes." Jacqua rolled out the dough.

Xo sighed. "I came off sounding so dumb. I never should have agreed to that interview."

Jacqua continued rolling and folding the dough without speaking. After he set the dough aside to chill and washed his hands, he went to the bulletin board that held the employee shift charts and unpinned a newspaper clipping. He passed it to Xo and began organizing lunch foods.

It was a years-old article from when the coffee house had first opened. Jacqua was described as "grim" and "beetle-browed," though the article's tone was positive and it encouraged people to come to the new café. The author—who was not credited, making her wonder if it had also been Alec—looked forward to sampling expanded menu offerings in the future.

Though not an inaccurate description, Jacqua likely found parts of it unflattering. It struck Xo that she would not make a good reporter herself. She would always be concerned about how the subjects of the article would react to it.

"Oh well." Xo tried to sound encouraging. "It seems you've done pretty good anyhow. They say any publicity is useful, right?"

Jacqua made a gesture between a nod and a shrug as he stacked sandwiches.

Xo replaced the clipping on the bulletin board. Jacqua was right: one article couldn't ruin her dream. But for some reason that thought wasn't comforting enough. Alec's involvement made it all so much worse.

❖   ❖   ❖

Elliot worked his way up a switchback trail above Lingen that was easily accessible from the coffee shop. The crisp morning air was gently sunlit through masses of puffy clouds, perfect for Xo to be out sketching birds somewhere that Elliot could randomly encounter her.

His camera strap lay comfortingly across his chest, justifying his presence in any setting with a potential for photos, which was nearly all. If he did not happen to meet Xo, he might still take some pictures for the newspaper. Photos reflecting seasonal changes or wildlife on the mountain were handy for filling extra space and relieving readers from the onslaught of mostly negative real news.

He was glad to photograph only local news when he read about disasters happening elsewhere in the world. These were not things he wanted to document. There was occasional local drama, but it tended to be less gory—except for the Lingen outbreak, of course. He shivered in spite of the sunlight warming his back. Another photographer had been assigned to cover that. He quickly pushed it from his mind, as usual.

Instead, Elliot pictured Xo walking gracefully beside him, occasionally stopping to admire this flower or that finch. Well, perhaps not gracefully. The incident of the shelf-jostling came unbidden to mind. It was not grace, exactly, that endeared her movements to him. There was something else about the way she moved, a sort of litheness and energy, and the way she looked at things as if finding hidden fascination in them.

She reminded him of a mountain lion he had seen early one morning slipping down the rocks, long and sleek, loping unhurriedly. It had stopped and watched him, and he, it. He had masked his rapidly beating heart in the face of its wildness. After a long gaze, it had continued languidly along its path on large, silent paws. Then, a gentle leap into the mist and it was gone.

A crunch on the path pulled Elliot back to the present as another hiker approached from the left fork of the upcoming intersection. He knew even before looking that it was not Xo. The cadence of steps was wrong. But there was something familiar about the figure hulking down the hill.

Elliot cleared his throat. "Francis. Hello."

The man had bulked up some in the intervening years, and his hair was thinner, but it was definitely Francis—out for a casual stroll judging by his thin shoes unsuited to the path. So Francis had come to visit his aunt after all. Elliot admonished himself internally, feeling bad for having concluded that he would never do so.

Francis halted, his arm stilled in the process of wiping sweat from his glistening forehead. "Elliot?" His voice was grounded in absolute astonishment and tinged with something else...it couldn't be fear, but it wasn't good, and it made Elliot study him more closely. Francis's flushed face had gone blotchy and he looked a bit ill.

"Wh—what are you doing here?" Francis spluttered.

Elliot hadn't been expecting an especially warm greeting, despite the length of time since he'd seen Francis, as they'd never exactly been friends. Still, he was a little taken aback. He lifted his camera with one hand. "Just...out. Photographing."

Francis didn't even look at the camera; he continued to stare at Elliot.

Elliot decided to make the best of the encounter. "Er...I don't suppose you passed another hiker on the trail this morning? A young woman?"

Francis shook his head slowly. "You're...alive," he declared.

Elliot eyed Francis cautiously. Francis did not appear to be in a joking mood. "That is the consensus," said Elliot. Francis didn't return his attempt at a smile, and it faded as Elliot's discomfort grew.

Francis had regained his color, and was now watching Elliot as if weighing something in his mind. "So, you didn't die in the epidemic."

Elliot felt a guilty lurch in his stomach, and Francis's eyes narrowed slightly.

"I did not," said Elliot, trying to keep his voice light.

"And...you're not angry? You're over it?" Francis's face was puzzled as he scrutinized Elliot. "I mean, boy. For me, coming here—it just brings it all back." He turned and looked out over the town, a muscle clenching and unclenching in his jaw. "She shouldn't have died. It's so senseless."

There was no point in being mad at death—certainly not ten years on, even if that emotion had come up initially—but Elliot was wholly unprepared to launch into a discussion of a rather personal memory.

"I'm not angry," Elliot finally said. Francis himself seemed a bit agitated. Perhaps, not having been in Lingen at the time, Francis had not had the same chance to process how he felt. As for being over it…Elliot wasn't sure how to answer that. But what he did feel, in the last several weeks in the presence of Xo, was a kind of opening, an untwisting of something he'd held tightly guarded. And he would much rather move on to find Xo than reminisce with Francis, of all people. It would be best to leave Francis alone to work through whatever he was working through.

Elliot made to continue along the trail, but Francis lurched in his direction, grabbing his arm. Elliot nearly lost his balance, eyeing Francis with alarm.

"Were you there? At the end…when she…" Francis trailed off.

Elliot's mouth went dry, his tongue stuck to the roof. "Yes," he managed at last. Hopefully Francis did not want him to relate an account of the final moments.

"Hmm." Francis released his arm, as if in afterthought, and stood looking out over Lingen again.

"I—uh—I have somewhere to be," said Elliot. Francis did not react. There was nothing else helpful that Elliot could think of to say, anyway. He turned and walked quickly away along the right fork of the path, leaving Francis standing there cogitating.

Elliot was left with an uneasy feeling as he stumbled along the trail. He couldn't begin to make sense of why Francis thought he had died, but he also didn't want to think about it long enough to figure it out. He'd relived the days of the epidemic often enough in his mind, and it always made him feel the same, even though it was useless feeling guilty when there was nothing he could have done.

Better to leave these things covered in the layers of time. He could never fully part with them, but he could put them out of his mind, even if anyone who looked at him still had an instant reminder of the virus that had swept through. The memories faded into the background easier around Xo. At least the meeting with Francis had given him guidance on which way to go at the intersection to increase the odds of running into her.

Elliot had lost track of how much farther he'd walked, trying to push the uncomfortable memories out of his mind, when his heart told him almost before his eyes did that he'd finally encountered Xo in the field.

10

THE DEAD BIRD

Xo sat a short distance off the trail, leaning against one of the many large boulders deposited by retreating glaciers in Arin's icier past. The sight flooded Elliot with relief, like a soothing strain of music. As he cautiously approached, Xo was holding her sketchbook on her knees and facing a sprawling tangle of low-growing wild rose bushes. The rose hips had attracted a flock of cedar waxwings. He tried not to startle the birds, but some small movement spooked them and they rose at once and dispersed. Xo raised her head, and since there was no further point in stealth, Elliot relaxed and allowed his feet to crunch the gravel normally as he approached.

"Oh, hey Elliot." Xo's voice was subdued.

"I'm sorry. I was trying not to scare them." Elliot smiled apologetically, picking his way over to where she was seated. A few sketches in her book roughly outlined the birds' poses. Luckily, it did not seem he had interrupted a detailed portrait.

"It's okay," said Xo. "They'll come back. Besides, they're not really what I'm looking for."

"That's good."

Though it might not be, if she was not finding what she was looking for. Elliot felt awkward standing there while she sat on the ground, but she made no move to get up, and from her bemused look he wasn't sure if he was intruding or if he was invited to stay. Xo usually relieved him of much of the burden of conversation, but today she did not jump to fill the silence. Hopefully, it hadn't been horribly distracting to walk up on her while she was sketching.

All at once, he remembered that he had come prepared with topics of conversation! He sighed with relief. He'd almost forgotten them in the course of the unexpected encounter with Francis.

"Are you enjoying that book series?" Elliot began enthusiastically.

"Yes," Xo said. "Actually, I'd been away from it so long that I decided to re-read the series from the beginning, so I haven't finished it yet."

"Good!" Elliot looked around for some other handy words, while Xo stared off into the bushes, leaning her arms on her knees. How had he gotten stranded like this with his advance preparation?

"Have you had a chance to begin that novel, *Precipice and Precipitation*?" he asked.

"Oh! No, not yet. Do you need it back?"

"No!" Elliot protested. "Take your time. The books were only gathering dust. I've read them many times. I merely wondered what you would think of that one."

"Oh, okay." Xo's eyes drifted away again.

Elliot squatted down and grasped his camera. He looked through it experimentally, scrutinizing the bush that Xo was observing as if he were intending to take a picture. As a matter of fact, he had no such notion, but he needed to do something besides stand there. Also, it gave him an excuse to get closer to where Xo sat, instead of addressing the top of her head. He remembered his backup topic.

"I saw that your article came out yesterday." He risked another glance at Xo as he attempted to balance in his supposed photographic squat. As positions went, this was actually more physically cumbersome than standing, but it seemed early to abandon it when he hadn't yet thought of a better one. Just so long as he didn't tip over on her.

Xo heaved a sigh and rested her chin on her arms. "Yes, it did. Did you read it?" She rolled her head to look at Elliot, eyes mournful, as if dreading the answer.

Elliot gulped. Her sadness tore at him. He would do anything to relieve it, but he wasn't sure how, as despite his overwhelming sympathy of feeling he didn't know why she was upset.

"I did read it," he said slowly, then watched in horror as her expression contorted further into a grimace. "Is…the article what is bothering you? You seem…troubled."

He took this opportunity to move to a half-kneeling position. Uncomfortable, as the ground was rocky and damp, but less unstable. He could lean closer to Xo without the risk of tumbling over.

"I hope the photos were not—"

"Oh! No." Xo shook her head. "They were fine. Great, in fact!"

At least he was not the source of her misery. He quietly awaited further explanation, and in due course it came tumbling forth, breaking the dam that her distress had placed upon her mouth. Hearing her talk rapidly again was an incredible relief, though he wasn't completely following every word. It meant he didn't have to keep talking himself, and it might make her less distraught as well, since speaking seemed to be a more natural state for her.

"And so—" Xo came to the end of her explanation. "The whole article was a disaster. I just don't understand why he would do that to me."

Elliot let most of the details go, particularly the reference to Alec, to focus on the key points. The main thing was that Xo was unhappy, and she was talking to him about it.

But he felt powerless. "I…I'm so sorry it didn't turn out as you'd hoped." He longed to put his arms around her and comfort her, but he didn't dare. He'd been feeling a lot more confident when he first set out to find her. Instead, he shook his head. "I feel partly responsible, myself. I encouraged you to do the article."

His feelings were not very strong one way or the other about the article itself. He could see her point of view, but he'd read many other articles like it—especially by Alec—so the tone did not surprise him. However, he did feel strongly about Xo's distress. Summoning all his courage, he reached out to pat her shoulder, but before he could, she abruptly raised her head from where it had been resting on her arms. He quickly withdrew his hand before it touched her.

Xo seemed to pull more tightly into her huddle; maybe she had seen him and was trying to preclude another attempt, in which case he should not have tried in the first place. Though it was possible she hadn't noticed his hand with her head down.

"It's not your fault," said Xo glumly. "The article's probably not that bad. That's what Megan thought. At first, I was shocked, but I get now that it won't kill my career or something. The part that still bothers me, is: what was Alec even thinking? I start wondering again and I get so mad at him. And me getting all emotional about it probably just made him think he was right about how he portrayed me." She turned to Elliot helplessly. "I know there's no point in getting worked up about it, yet I still am, and *that* bothers me even more!"

Elliot looked back just as helplessly. The time for patting her shoulder had passed and there wasn't anything he could think of to do about that either.

"I shouldn't let myself get upset all over again," said Xo at length, more quietly. "It's stupid. It shouldn't matter."

"I believe it is better to have...feelings. Even if they are painfully strong at times." Elliot searched Xo's face, wondering if he could possibly continue down this path.

Xo sighed again. "It doesn't seem to cause anything but trouble, just makes people not take me seriously. Since there's nothing I can do about the article now anyway, I'm trying to focus on other things, I guess." She gestured to her sketchbook. "But I can't concentrate. Not only because of the article, before that too. Who knows how long Sade will even keep me on, if I can't get more done? On top of the weekly newsletter illustrations, there are still some birds I need to get sightings of before she'll let me put their paintings in the field guide. I mean, there are the common ones, those I'm doing okay on, but I actually have to find the rare ones or those won't be included."

Elliot looked at her with real alarm and surprise. He cast about for a possible answer.

"Did the photos earlier help?"

"Oh! Yes, they did. But I need to document some of the other rare birds that are supposed to be in this area. Your photo of the lesser red-backed alpine finch was helpful, but I couldn't tell if it's the subspecies I'm trying to find. I think I need to see them in action. I've been looking for places where they'd be, and nothing. Or the hog-nosed finch, that's another elusive finch. Did you know that Lingen used to be known as the hog-nosed finch capital of the world? Sade says nobody calls it that anymore. They're incredibly rare now, maybe even extinct. But three years ago, two people in unrelated events reported seeing them while hiking higher up. If I could confirm a sighting, it would be a huge breakthrough. Or the turquoise-naped hummingbird. Again, random reports dating back a few years, but no confirmations, and they're easy to mix up with the commoner ones that we know migrate through here. Is it really them? Who knows? What flowers are they coming for? There's so much unknown about the species and it's already threatened."

She cast her hands up in the air in a futile gesture. "I thought I could make a difference here, but...I dunno if I can do any of this."

"Well," said Elliot slowly, "I suppose if they are that rare, then it may take patience and perseverance to find and document them, or it would've already been done. But I feel certain that you are up to the task."

Xo looked at him forlornly. "You must know something about me that I don't."

Elliot gazed back at her. Unfortunately, he had a feeling that sharing what he thought about her would be less welcome at the moment than practical solutions. And he'd just realized he might be able to help in that area. "There is one other thing—though I don't wish to raise false hopes."

"What do you mean?" asked Xo.

"I may...possess a specimen of one of the birds you mentioned, specifically the turquoise-naped hummingbird."

Xo started up in surprise. "Where?"

Elliot rose to his feet as well. "At my house. I was not aware of its rarity, but from the descriptive name I feel it may be what you are looking for. I rather doubt you'll find one on the wing at this time of year. But if you'd like to accompany me…"

Xo was bouncy again, anxious to get back to the trail. "Let's go!"

They set off in the direction of Elliot's house, following the pathway downwards to where it met the road.

"How did you happen to come by a specimen? It's not even confirmed that they're migrating through here."

"I had a hummingbird feeder set up," confessed Elliot. "Although I know nothing about them, I did gather some amusement from watching them outside my window. I was going to take down the feeder last winter after they'd flown south, when one more showed up, so I left it. He hung about for a few days, but there was a cold snap." Elliot paused and cleared his throat. "I found him in the morning on the ground. He must have spent the night perched somewhere nearby, but it was simply too cold."

"Awww," said Xo. "So when you say 'specimen'…"

"It's not professionally preserved," said Elliot hurriedly. "More… naturally freeze-dried. I picked him up and brought him inside. I thought there might be a chance he was in a torpor state, to make it through the cold night, but he was gone. His feathers were still iridescent and so beautiful. I set the body aside, and it remained dried out. Essentially mummified." He sighed. "If I hadn't had the feeder up, perhaps he would not have stayed that night, but would have moved on to somewhere warmer."

"I'm sure it wasn't your fault," said Xo. "If it's a turquoise-naped, it's an amazing find. I could draw from it, if it's in good condition. Even with photos it's hard to capture a hummingbird."

"I hope it is helpful. Then, at least some good would come of it," said Elliot. Despite the sad memory, Xo's enthusiasm cheered him.

Elliot stopped in front of his house, allowing Xo to precede him up the walk. Across the street, Mrs. Dupesh waved at him from her porch. He raised his hand slightly to return her gesture and grinned nervously back at her, without drawing Xo's attention. If Francis was staying at Mrs. Dupesh's house, he must still be out on his walk, and Elliot was glad of it. He didn't relish another bizarre encounter with him, especially right now. Xo was waiting at his door, soon to be actually inside his house, and he was completely unprepared.

He joined Xo on his doorstep, catching his breath. The little square building looked even smaller and older than usual with Xo there. The flower beds on either side of the gravel walkway that led up to the doorstep were scraggly now that the summer had passed. He hadn't noticed until now.

Elliot glanced sideways at Xo. She was rocking back on her heels beside him, waiting with an expression of pleased anticipation for him to open the door.

11

The First Blow

Xo stepped over the threshold and removed her shoes, following Elliot's example. It was kind of him to try to help her, though she knew that her difficulty in completing her work was due to stewing about Alec more than anything else. There was a good chance that the hummingbird Elliot had wasn't the rare one he thought it was; there were several that looked similar. Even if that turned out to be the case, the opportunity to see how Elliot lived was intriguing. He'd spoken more words in a row today about the hummingbird than anything he'd ever revealed of himself. She'd felt, for a moment, that he was going to say something more personal, but she must have imagined it. It must be that her wish for any sort of sign from Alec was making her come up with emotional readings that didn't exist in other people. And she'd gotten all worked up, too—that always made her misread situations. Luckily, talking to Elliot seemed to have a calming effect, so she hadn't made a complete fool of herself in front of him.

Her gaze flicked to the window of the kitchen they had entered. There was no hummingbird feeder outside the window now. Maybe he hadn't had the heart to put one up again after what had happened.

The kitchen merged into a bedroom area on the other side of a breakfast bar that split the room almost in half. Xo could make out a pile of books on the nightstand and dresser beside the bed, and more on a bookcase opposite it. She'd have to investigate that later, after she checked out the hummingbird.

Though small, the house did not seem cluttered because there weren't that many things in it. A bright red wire drain rack held a single cup and plate near the kitchen sink. The room was warm and cozy due to a woodstove in the far corner, near a closet door. Despite the sparseness, there were a few decorative items: colorful curtains on the windows that flanked the front door, a small ornate rug folded neatly on top of the dresser, and some framed prints on the wall. None of them appeared to be photographs. One was a picture of goldfinches.

Xo started to inspect it, but Elliot went directly to a short hallway on the right. She followed him, glimpsing a side door to the house at the end of the hallway and a bathroom on the left, before they entered another door on the right into a laundry room. The other windows she'd seen from the sidewalk must belong to this room. It was bright and sunny and comparatively large, taking up the remaining front of the house. There were more accessories here than in the rest of the house combined: clothes racks, laundry baskets and an ironing board in addition to the washer, dryer, and water heater, and cupboards along the non-windowed parts of the wall. Everything was neatly organized.

Elliot opened a cabinet, revealing boxes of soap and laundry additives, and a folded crocheted blanket. He removed a small cardboard box from the shelf and returned to the kitchen. There he paused, one hand on the teakettle that sat on the electric stove.

"May I offer you some tea, Xiomara?"

"Oh, no thanks. I'm not that thirsty."

Elliot set the kettle back down on the stove.

"So, is this—" Xo pointed at the box. "Did you find the hummingbird?"

Elliot held the box in his palm and gently shook the lid loose with his other hand. "There."

The hummingbird lay on its side, one wing extended upwards unnaturally. Xo took the box and held it by a window, where the sunlight glistened off the bird's feathers. The tops of the wings and most of the body were shiny green, but at the nape of the bird's neck and curving around to either side were a cluster of iridescent turquoise feathers. A patch of magenta feathers shone like scales at its throat. It was undoubtedly the species on her list, though she had never seen one in life. She lifted it by the point of the outstretched wing.

"It's so light!"

"Yes, it's truly amazing." Elliot hovered nearby, squinting in the light reflecting off his glasses. "I suppose that's why I didn't bury it. I hope it will help with your paintings."

"Oh, absolutely." Xo carefully replaced it in the box. It could snap in two easily, it was so frail and dry. "I won't borrow it for long."

Elliot's eyes widened. "No! Please, keep it. I have no use for the poor thing myself, none at all."

"If you're sure…"

"Most definitely."

Xo smiled happily. It was amazing how her future prospects changed so quickly, from the crushing low of the article to now having this unique find to work on instead of moping around with her mind on Alec's baffling behavior. She wasn't going to let a romantic hang-up stop her from following her true interests, which had always been significantly more dependable than people.

"Are you sure you won't have tea?"

It occurred to Xo, rather late, that there was a chance Elliot himself wanted tea and that was why he kept offering. Hopefully she hadn't been rude earlier. She often realized these things after the fact and then wished she'd acted differently, but it was usually too late to do anything about it.

"Sure, I'll have some after all."

"Wonderful," said Elliot brightly. "What variety would you like?" He opened the kitchen cupboard to reveal a dazzling array of colorful boxes and tins of tea.

"Let's see…" Xo scanned the unfamiliar boxes. "I'll have that yellow and green one." She pointed to a tin with an intricate lime-green background pattern and a bright illustration of yellow flowers, which gave no indication as to the flavor of tea as far as she could tell. She grinned. "It's like ordering in another language. I guess I'll be surprised."

Elliot smiled as he began to arrange the tea things, the most relaxed smile Xo had ever seen him give. She settled herself on one of the kitchen stools to wait for the water to heat and watched Elliot busying himself.

At first, Xo had been surprised by his home, expecting something more formal or grand, but now she realized the house matched him, and she felt quite at ease here as well. She didn't have to constantly monitor what she was saying around Elliot, or stop to puzzle out some second layer of meaning in his words like she did when Alec was teasing her. His manner was so different from Alec's, and yet they were apparently best friends. In fact, if anyone were to have insight into Alec's behavior, it would probably be Elliot.

❖   ❖   ❖

Elliot poured mugs of tea and sat on the counter stool next to Xo, angled towards her. It was surreal seeing her here, in his kitchen, dipping her finger in the tea to see if it was too hot. The house seemed smaller by her presence, but more alive. It had been a quiet house for a long time. He could hardly remember what it had been like to live with another person.

Now the thick walls, well insulated against snowy winters, reverberated from the inside with Xo's chatter, her laughter. She spun the counter stool back and forth, making it squeak, and shifted her feet around as if testing different locations on the foot-resting bar. She clunked the cup on the counter when she set it down. The house was full of noise. It was like a car being started after a long time in storage: a bit rough at first, but running again, transformed from a stationary piece of furniture into something that could go places.

Xo rose and walked around the kitchen bar to the bookcase opposite the bed, while Elliot drifted along after her, eager to explain anything she might ask about. She laughed and noted the books they both owned, some of which he had acquired since the photo session. Setting her teacup down on the bookshelf, she pulled out a book, flipped through it, put it back and pulled out another.

Elliot eyed the cup warily, with an odd feeling of excitement. The cup had never sat on the bookcase before in all the time he'd owned it. But then, Xo seemed transplanted into the scene as well, so the cup just added to the dreamlike strangeness of the whole image. It was as if a new color had been discovered in the world and he was seeing it everywhere. With a change like this, anything could happen next.

Xo chose a hefty tome and backed up to his bed, bouncing down on the foot of it as she examined the book. Trying to act as if all was the same as it had ever been, Elliot seated himself gingerly beside her. They were at a similar level sitting down, as most of her additional height was in her legs, and they were now connected by a wave of motion as Xo fidgeted in place while she focused on the book. It was a classic romance novel, and she had shockingly flipped to a random place in the middle to read. Elliot tried to figure out where she was in the text. There was a rather racy passage he remembered, which she might end up encountering out of context.

Elliot realized he was intermittently holding his breath as she read. When he did breathe, it sounded irregular and unnatural. The scent of the outdoors lingered on Xo's clothing. Not wanting to alarm her, he restrained himself from taking a deep breath of the air that surrounded her. He could hear her breathing as well, and the sound of her running her finger back and forth over the edge of the book. Every noise was amplified. The pounding of his heart must be equally loud. Could she hear it? He listened to see if he could hear hers, but his own was too loud.

Xo's eyes stopped moving along the lines of the page, and her expression relaxed, her lips parting a little.

"Elliot, can I ask you something?" she said hesitantly.

Elliot turned the rest of the way to face her, and his eyes locked on to hers. He had to make a second effort to reply.

"Yes—" was all he managed, moistening his lips. He sat frozen in anticipation, his ears still ringing with the sound of her voice saying his name, as he implored her to know what he was thinking.

"Do you…" She dropped her eyes to her lap as if building up courage, then looked back up at him. Elliot felt he might not have breathed for the entire past minute. She continued, "Do you think Alec likes me?"

Elliot reeled. He looked anywhere but at Xo, adjusting his glasses to stall for time. What a fool he had been to build up this moment in his mind—he refused to even admit to himself what he'd been hoping she would say. His wish for her to know his thoughts immediately reversed as he struggled to recover his composure.

Xo had stopped bouncing in place and now sat awaiting his response, sad and distant. Before he had found any words at all, she started talking again.

"I know you guys are friends, and I just can't figure him out. I hope it's okay to ask you. First I thought he was interested in me, but then, I wasn't sure. And now the newspaper article. Has he said anything?"

Elliot managed to choke out an answer. "I'm afraid Alec has not shared with me his…feelings towards you." The notion of saying anything about how he himself felt, the possibility of which had seemed so close moments before, was now miles away.

Xo looked defeated, as if Elliot had been her last hope.

He felt he had no choice but to expand on his answer. "He does not tend to discuss these things." Alec's numerous romances did not seem particularly serious, but rather a matter of entertainment for Alec, an attitude of which Elliot did not approve. However, since his friend did not bring them up or seek consolation, he had not voiced this opinion.

"I know it was a long shot. I hoped he'd said something to you, to help me figure out where he stood." Xo sighed. "It's so frustrating. I wish he'd be clearer: if he's not interested, I just want to know! Then I can forget him and move on and stop waiting for him to do or say something."

Alec sounded non-committal, but this was always the case, as far as Elliot could tell. But surely, if she were truly interested in Alec, she couldn't just forget and move on? It was a marvel that either of them could feel anything so lightly. The notion of "forgetting" Xo and "moving on" made Elliot feel physically ill. He didn't think he was capable of that.

"It's not like we haven't already talked about going out. He's asked me, I've asked him, but nothing materializes," Xo went on. "I can't tell if it's because he doesn't want to, or if he actually has other things going on. People are so confusing."

Elliot's surprise that this had already come up was quickly swamped by a feeling of intense stupidity. He should have invited her out to eat, since she clearly took that as a sign of interest. But if he asked her to go somewhere now, she wasn't going to get that impression—it was too late, as evidenced by the fact that she was at his house sitting on his bed and she was still talking about Alec.

"If you don't mind my asking, what indications has Alec given you on the...uh...subject?" Elliot managed.

"I dunno, really," said Xo. "He touches me a lot, and says things that make me think he's attracted. But then, he hasn't made any moves, if you know what I mean."

Elliot cringed, picturing this, but luckily Xo was not looking at him and didn't appear to notice. "And how...how do you feel?" It might be twisting the knife deeper into himself, but Xo's feelings seemed more attainable than answers about what Alec felt. As well as more important, Elliot thought disloyally.

"I like him," Xo said simply, producing a pang in Elliot. "Sure, I'm attracted to him: tall, dark, and handsome, and all that."

Elliot briefly closed his eyes. Did Xo always assess people so blatantly? More than ever before, he was acutely conscious of being none of those things himself.

"On the other hand, he also annoys me," continued Xo. "I think he would annoy me less if I knew he cared and wasn't just goofing around, but I don't want to fool myself into thinking this is going somewhere if it isn't. I want to *know*." She smiled appreciatively at Elliot. "It's nice that I can talk to you about it. I mean, even though he hasn't told you how he feels, it still helps."

Elliot forced himself to smile back encouragingly.

"I think," Xo said decisively, "That if he's interested he'll have to indicate it further in some way. Otherwise I'll assume he's just a friend and act neutral. I mean, I think I've made it clear that I'm interested by now, while he hasn't. Don't you agree?"

He tried to consider it from Alec's point of view, but it was impossible. Elliot would have acted so differently if at any given time he had stepped into Alec's shoes. She had made it clear—painfully so, and he could say nothing about his own feelings when she was caught up in thinking about Alec.

"Thanks for listening." Xo sighed and leaned against Elliot's arm, dropping her head lightly on his shoulder and causing him to immediately question his decision to say nothing. "I hate waiting, and not knowing, but I think it will make things clearer. Maybe it already has and I'm slow on the uptake. I guess I'll have to see."

Elliot scarcely dared to breathe at the contact. Warmth radiated off her, and he longed to rest his own head against hers, to put his arm around her. Would that be so wrong? Her touch was barely there at all; he wished she would really lean into him. Before he could react, even to offer an appropriate level of friendly comfort, she bounced lightly onto her feet. It had only been a parting gesture. She put his book back on the shelf, and half-turned towards the door, smiling wanly.

Realizing she was about to leave, Elliot leapt up. He pressed the box with the hummingbird into her hand again, lest she forget it. She thanked him with a more enthusiastic smile while he struggled between the crushing weight of her words and the almost cruel hope that had sparked from her touch. At the doorway he halted, caught in its invisible barrier. Xo was moving quickly, already out.

"See you later!" Xo called cheerily, waving, now turning towards him but still walking away backwards. "The hummingbird is great!" She raised the box in her other hand, before spinning away again to direct her feet down the sidewalk.

Closing the door unsteadily, Elliot returned to the bed and sank down where he and Xo had been sitting before. Her teacup was still where she had left it on the bookshelf. In just the right position, he could still smell her, still feel the slight weight of her head pressing against his shoulder. The place where she had touched him felt forever changed.

12

ANOTHER DEAD BIRD

Elliot's remaining energy drained as his mind spun over Xo's visit. Her head against his shoulder. *I like him…attracted to him. Tall, dark, and handsome.* This was poking a wound, testing to see if his heart was still there. He pushed the memory of her words away, but it immediately swung back, like a pendulum, knocking him backwards on the bed so recently animated by Xo. He lay motionless, staring at the ceiling.

So Xo was going to wait for Alec to make a move. This seemed horribly inevitable the longer Elliot thought about it, especially since they'd already been trying to arrange a date. And it was what she wanted. She had no feelings for Elliot, or she wouldn't have chosen to talk to him about Alec. Yet, she had confided in Elliot, another part of his mind insisted. She came to him; he was the one she trusted. She'd said that she wanted to know if someone was just a friend or had feelings for her, for it to be absolutely clear.

No, enough. Elliot sat up, shaking his head. She only wanted to know that because she already liked Alec. But there was a shred of hope in him that would not go away. It seemed even stronger now that she had been here in his house, even if it was to tell him she was interested in someone else. He ignored it, argued with it. If he told Xo how he felt now, he betrayed both Xo and Alec. But if nothing further ever materialized between those two, maybe…

He stayed away from the coffee house, away from Xo's hope-inducing presence. The more days passed, the more likely it seemed that Xo and Alec had united. The thought was horribly painful, but less painful than watching the blow fall. Once he'd heard definitively that they were together, his place would be clear. He would be back where he'd been before getting all these notions stuck in his mind. It was a place containing little life, but he'd survived there for many years. By resuming that place now, he would be ready when he saw them together.

At the office of the *Mountain Herald,* Elliot clicked through a series of photographs on his computer. His eyes were not focused on the screen, instead he was seeing Xo and Alec together in his mind's eye. The vision intended to discourage him had the opposite effect: it made him want to see her in person, just to be sure.

Behind him, reflected in the screen, the real Alec stood and stretched exaggeratedly. "Come on, let's go to the coffee house for lunch."

"I have a…this. To do." Elliot clicked faster.

Alec hesitated. "There's something I've been meaning to talk to you about. I was going to over lunch, but…"

A knot formed in Elliot's stomach, contracting tighter and tighter. "Yes?" He held his breath.

Alec sat down in his chair again, resting his elbows on his knees, and rotated to face Elliot. Elliot turned towards him slowly, bracing himself.

Alec seemed to hesitate again at his expression. "Maybe you've heard…"

"No," said Elliot. He swallowed. "Maybe…go on."

"So, a couple of us—er, the others, but I was there—were pitching around the idea of doing an article, just a small piece, on the outbreak. '*Mountainpox: 10 years later*' type of thing."

Elliot stared at him, rapidly trying to get his bearings again. "What?"

"I know it's probably not something you'd want to read, but I think they'd give me the piece if you agreed to participate, for a perspective."

"I don't—why would you even ask me that?" stammered Elliot. First Francis, now Alec. It was all coming up again. After he'd closed that part of the past and put it away, it still wouldn't rest in peace. Was it going to follow him around all his life?

"Look, Elly, I'm sorry for even bringing it up. But I think they're going to do it either way, so I wanted to let you know. And if I write it, I could sort of control the perspective, and you could…"

Elliot shook his head. Alec didn't get it, somehow. "If you must do this, write about the people who died. They're the ones who deserve mention. Just…leave me out of it."

Alec held up his hands. "If somebody else does it I'm not going to have any control over it. But I can't exactly ask them to give the piece to me on account of an interview with you, and then not mention you."

Elliot rubbed his forehead. He had become conscious that other people in the office, some heading out for lunch, were glancing his way, possibly aware of what was being discussed.

"I'm sorry, but…I can't…be part of this," he said in a low voice.

"Okay." Alec sounded concerned.

Elliot turned back to his computer. "Is the article definitely going to happen?"

"I'll see what I can do," said Alec, rising to his feet. "You sure you don't want to come to the café? Take a break, you haven't come all week." Alec prodded his arm. Elliot shrugged his hand off.

Alec sighed and reached for his jacket. "Suit yourself. Hope Xo's in a better mood today at least, she's been giving me the cold shoulder all week."

Elliot's head snapped up involuntarily as a rush of warmth surged through him. Did this mean she had "moved on?"

Alec had paused with one arm in his jacket. "Coming?"

❖   ❖   ❖

They pushed through the café door. No Xo, only Megan. Elliot's eyes went to the clock: it was ten minutes to noon. While Alec ordered, Elliot found his spot on the hearth, already considering what he should do next if Xo had decided not to pursue things with Alec. She had reacted well to the hummingbird. He could help her find more birds for her field guide assignment, and as they grew closer…

"Hey, Elliot." Xo had come downstairs much more quietly than usual. She sat down in a chair next to the hearth.

"Xiomara!" He laid his book aside, resting both hands on his knees. Xo had clearly come to speak to him, but she appeared unusually uncomfortable. Perhaps she was regretting confiding in him before.

"Elliot, I'm not sure how to ask you this, but—" She lowered her voice. "—Did you bring me another bird?"

"Uh…" Elliot faltered. "I don't have any others."

"No, I mean…" Xo glanced right and left as if expecting someone to be listening in, then thrust out her hand, containing a large grey object. Elliot leaned forward to inspect it, then lurched backwards. It was dead. Recently dead. Oozing. It was fortunate he hadn't eaten any breakfast that morning or it would have made a sudden reappearance.

Elliot swallowed the bile rising in the back of his throat. "You thought I—but why?"

"Well…" Xo put the bird on the table, where its neck lolled at an unnatural angle. Some sort of pigeon, the kind that lived near the train tracks. "It was on the landing this morning, outside my door. I thought of the hummingbird, and then I saw you. I should have known you didn't do it. I just…I dunno what to think!"

"Xo!" Megan's voice rang sharply from behind the counter. "I already told you before with the hummingbird—no dead birds in the food area!"

Alec turned from where he lounged against the counter and flashed a smile at Xo. "Ah, you found my gift!"

Elliot stared at Alec, unwilling to comprehend what he had just heard. Alec walked over jauntily and pulled out a chair from the table where Xo was sitting. He straddled it backwards, leaning his arms on the back.

Alec looked from one shocked face to the other, grinning. "What, did I interrupt a secret meeting?"

"Did you put that thing outside my door?" Xo pointed one finger at the corpse.

"I knocked, but you didn't answer," Alec said cheerily. "Getting your beauty rest, I suppose. I had to get to work."

Xo blinked at him, mouth ajar.

Megan came around the counter with the cups of coffee and stood to one side. "Ew! Get it off the table."

Xo scooped the bird up again, a bit heedlessly, as she flung up her arms, spluttering at Alec. "Why in the world would you think I was in need of a dead pigeon?"

Calmly, Alec took the coffees from Megan and handed one to Elliot. Elliot took it mechanically, still thunderstruck, and transferred it to the hearth beside him.

"Well, Megan here was going on and on about how you were over the moon with that bird Elliot gave you, and how you were in dire need of them to finish your paintings!" said Alec.

So everyone knew about his gift to Xo. Elliot's head very nearly sank into his hands in mortification but he managed to redirect the gesture to appear to be just resting his chin on his clasped hands. Luckily nobody was looking at him anyway.

"Now just a minute!" Megan's hands went to her hips. "You can't pin this on me!"

"Nobody's pinning anything on anybody. I take full credit," Alec said roundly. "Now, Xo, I know you had a bit of a beef with that article, and I'm truly sorry about that. Most people loved it! I've had nothing but good reviews of it—except yours of course—and I can see you're still hung up on it with how you've been acting. I wanted to do you a good turn and show you no hard feelings. And Megan said—"

Megan huffed, but did not leave. She shook her head, denying whatever it was Alec was going to say next.

"Megan said," repeated Alec, as Megan looked away with folded arms, "that you went from being all upset to ecstatic when you came back with that other bird. So, to cheer you up—"

"Alec—" Elliot interrupted desperately. If only Megan had never mentioned the hummingbird to Alec. It was Elliot's moment with Xo, for him to cherish alone.

"Cheer me up?" Xo gesticulated with the pigeon clutched in her hand, causing nausea to roil again in Elliot's stomach. "Would finding a dead bird outside your door first thing in the morning cheer you up?"

"Well now," said Alec. "I'm not one for birds myself. But I was feeling bad about you getting all bent out of shape over that bit of publicity."

"I was not 'bent out of shape,'" snapped Xo. "The article was inaccurate and it trivialized my work. You cannot solve that by leaving a dead bird for me to trip over!"

"What, should I have gotten two, with one stone?" Alec grinned.

Xo glowered at him. "That's a terrible expression."

Alec threw up his hands. "There you go again. What is it then, the wrong sort of bird?"

Megan rolled her eyes. "Yes, it's the wrong sort."

"You didn't tell me any particular sort," Alec complained to her.

"I didn't tell you to do this at all!" Megan stomped back to the counter.

"I don't see what the problem is." Alec sounded like he was starting to get irritated. "I'm pretty sure Mr. Audubon hauled back quite a few dead birds to paint, didn't he now?"

"Well...maybe," conceded Xo. "But look here, I don't want any freshly-killed birds, at all."

"It's a matter of age, is it? Wouldn't you rather have fresh ones than old ones? I can't do anything right in your eyes, can I?" Alec finished in a hurt voice. He sat back and crossed his arms, but since he was sitting in the chair the wrong way, there was nothing to lean back into. He leaned back anyway, into the air.

Xo glared at Alec, breathing heavily. Elliot could sense her sadness and disappointment underneath the anger. Was it only because she'd told him how she felt about Alec that it was so palpable? And now Alec was upset too, he must care about Xo after all, despite the unfathomably disturbing pigeon situation.

"You don't get it, do you?" demanded Xo.

"No, I really don't!" Alec said in a sulky voice.

"I cannot for the life of me understand what is going on in your head!" Xo exploded. "First the article, now this. Why are you doing this to me? What do you want from me?"

"Excuse me for trying to help. No matter what I do, you bite my head off." Alec turned to Elliot. "Can't you talk some sense into her?"

Elliot jumped. "Me?"

Xo said angrily, "I don't need someone to talk sense into me! You need someone to talk sense into you! The hummingbird was rare, not any old bird you can find. And don't go out and start killing a bunch of rare birds, either!"

"I'm not an idiot," said Alec quietly.

Xo took a deep breath, clearly preparing to dispute that with additional evidence.

"Please," Elliot intervened. "Alec, did you actually—kill—that?"

Alec frowned. "Of course not. I just saw it lying on the side of the road."

Elliot heaved a sigh of relief. "I am sorry to have to say this, Alec, but leaving deceased birds at someone's door without prior discussion is, frankly, appalling."

Alec slouched forward on the chair back, defeated. Elliot felt bad for him, but it had to be said.

"All right," said Alec at length. "Look, I'm sorry, Xo. Okay? Megan said—anyway, I just saw it there, and I thought it would help make up for how you felt about the article. I can see I've just made things worse." He stood up despondently.

Xo picked at the hem of her shirt and did not respond. She was undoubtedly crushed, as Elliot knew this was not how she'd been hoping things would go with Alec. If she and Alec parted ways now, she would continue to be crushed. Even if it made it easier for Elliot to step in, it didn't feel like the right way.

And then there was Alec. Elliot couldn't comprehend what might have been going through Alec's mind, but he also couldn't watch his friend go down like this without throwing him a line.

"Wait," said Elliot, as Alec turned to leave. There was only one thing to do: use his earlier idea for alone time with Xo. He turned to her. "You were trying to find more rare birds here on Arin."

"Yes…" said Xo hesitantly.

"I hadn't formed an exact plan yet, but it had occurred to me—we could mount an expedition, so to speak," said Elliot slowly. "You mentioned that most of the ones you're looking for were spotted by hikers, so you might have a better chance of finding them at higher elevations. You could confirm the sightings, take notes, drawings. I could photograph them." He swallowed. "And Alec…"

"I'll be your guide!" Alec jumped in eagerly, as Elliot had guessed he would. "If you tell me where they were seen before, I can get you there. Let me make it up to you. Besides, Elliot needs me to keep him from falling off the wrong side of a cliff, right Elliot?" He jostled Elliot.

Elliot let the comment slide. "Alec *is* an excellent guide. He takes hikers up Arin regularly."

"Don't worry about the camping equipment. I'll manage everything," Alec said. "We'll find you those birds."

Xo inhaled deeply and let it out slowly. "Okay," she said finally. "We'll all go. No killing!" she added to Alec sharply.

Alec laughed. "Agreed. Though I can if you need it."

"No!" said Xo and Elliot together.

Alec winked. "All right, cool down."

"Let's figure out which days work." Xo took out her notebook.

Elliot watched them bend over the notebook together. His plan with Xo was now a plan with Alec and Xo. He didn't exactly regret it, but it might not have been the smartest move. Then, in his mind, he saw Xo's face again as she listened to Alec make excuses. Perhaps Elliot was the idiot, but he couldn't let a blunder like this from Alec be the deciding factor in Xo's affections. He wanted Xo to decide for herself.

13

THE HIKE BEGINS

Alec's behavior was still grating on Xo's mind as she scrambled up the hiking path several days later, already trailing behind the others. The expedition would give her material for the field guide, and she didn't know her way around Mount Arin enough to feel comfortable hiking alone on an overnight excursion. Still, she was glad the expedition had been Elliot's suggestion and not Alec's.

Alec had provided camping gear, as promised, as well as food supplies, and he seemed to know where they were going, but he had eliminated any chance of conversation by immediately outdistancing Xo and Elliot. And there were still issues to resolve. Had Alec been making the next move by leaving her that dead pigeon? Did she even want any further moves at this point? Neither Alec nor Elliot had made any further reference to the incident. At the time, Elliot had appeared to share her revulsion, but as they'd prepared to leave this morning he had resumed acting as if Alec were a normal, sane person.

"I can't believe that it doesn't bother you, what he did with that bird," Xo grumbled, catching up to Elliot as he stopped to take a photo. He had brought two cameras, digital and film, to help with documenting birds. Xo's camera and binoculars both dangled around her neck for easy access, but they were banging against her ribs at every step as she leaned into the hill to counter the weight of her pack.

"It does bother me." Elliot sounded a little surprised.

"Then how can you stand it? How can you just let it go?" It was an ongoing mystery how Elliot managed to live with Alec's behavior. "Does he honestly think that was a reasonable thing to do?"

"I suppose he explained it, in his way," said Elliot.

"And does it make sense to you?" asked Xo.

"No…"

"Then how can you just forget about it?"

"I haven't forgotten," said Elliot. "But…what would you have me do?"

"I just want someone to say I'm not crazy." Xo tightened her grip on the straps of her pack. "What he did is crazy and I'm right for thinking so: acknowledge that for once. I feel like I'm going mad."

Elliot smiled. "I'm mad, you're mad. He's mad. We're all mad here."

"Ha ha, very funny." Xo smiled in spite of herself and started walking again.

"You're not crazy," said Elliot more seriously.

"Then is he? Someone's gotta be," said Xo.

"I don't think he's crazy either," said Elliot. "Any more than the rest of us, I suppose. Why does someone have to be crazy?"

"Because his behavior makes no sense." Xo kicked a loose rock so it bounced ahead of them.

"I guess I don't expect to understand his reasoning."

"But how can you sustain a friendship—or any type of relationship—with someone whose behavior makes no sense to you?"

Her past relationships seemed to have failed over this very reason. Misunderstandings inevitably arose, and before long, it was over and unsalvageable. Not *being* understood didn't feel good either, as when Alec was seemingly unable to grasp why various things he did would bother Xo.

"Understanding would be convenient," Elliot conceded. "But not strictly necessary. Even if his actions don't make sense to me, I still feel the same way towards him. He's still my friend."

"I don't see how you can get along without it," said Xo.

"Can anyone ever truly understand another person, without being that person?" said Elliot.

"Maybe not fully," admitted Xo. "But I would hope for a little bit. Don't you want to find someone who really gets you? Like, the real you?"

Elliot hesitated before answering. "Perhaps that's not the most important factor."

Xo trudged on beside him. If she were right, and Elliot wrong, how had his friendship with Alec endured? She'd always assumed other people got along with each other because they'd achieved a level of understanding that she was never able to. Disconcertingly, Elliot's comment suggested he also didn't understand Xo, yet he seemed to get along with her. Maybe he was just more rational than Alec. She couldn't think of anything particularly strange that Elliot had done so far, but then, was it really rational to be friends with someone like Alec?

She sorted through Alec's past behavior, putting the incomprehensible parts aside to see what was left. There were a few things he had done that made sense: he had written an article to help her, albeit a terrible one, and had brought her a bird to make amends, albeit in a very disturbing way. He was also guiding this hike to make further amends. Surely, he wouldn't do these things if he didn't at least like her, even though he was currently avoiding talking to her. Plus, there was the fact that he thought she was beautiful, unlike anyone else she had ever met.

If the only problems between them were caused by her insistence on grasping Alec's mental process, then possibly she'd been expecting too much of him. Mutual understanding might not be a universal need after all, just an unachievable fantasy. It would be better to work with what she had: a guy who was attracted to her and who seemed to be trying to make some sort of effort. For now, she would try to set the dead bird incident aside, as difficult as that was. If she could manage to tolerate the things that did not make sense in Alec's behavior, perhaps there would be other good things too. He was not very adept at communicating, but there should be plenty of opportunities to try during the expedition.

The plan cheered Xo considerably, and she quite enjoyed the rest of the morning's climb, pointing out birds along the way to Elliot, though they weren't yet at the elevation where she expected to spot anything too rare.

Alec finally stopped and passed out sandwiches for lunch, an hour later than Xo would've liked. She threw down her gear and collapsed against a log to update her notes about the birds she'd seen on the way up. Elliot sat nearby with a notebook similar to Xo's, in which he'd said he would record his own sightings.

Xo felt exhilarated, though exhausted, to look back the way they had come and see the world from so high. Lingen was still visible far below the lunch spot, and at this distance, with little symmetrical subalpine firs scattered over the mountainside, it looked like a miniature living diorama. A tiny red-tailed hawk soared below them, its tail flashing copper in the sun as it banked. Xo twisted around in the other direction to look up at the jagged ridges of Mount Arin. The glaciers clinging to the sides of the mountain seemed lit from within by a greenish-blue light where the sun struck them, calling her to explore them further—though Alec had said they would stay below the snowline on this trip.

Alec got to his feet and approached as Xo began work on her hefty sandwich. It was unclear how he'd managed to gnaw through his already, but she smiled up at him, resolving to be open to possibilities and not demand explanations of Alec's confusing ways.

"I think you broke your camera when you put it down over there." Alec thumbed over his shoulder.

"Oh!" Xo struggled to her feet. Sure enough, the filter had come loose and the plastic ring where it screwed onto the lens was cracked. She pressed the power button, and an error flashed onto the screen. "Argh! I can't believe I did that."

Alec shrugged. "Bad luck."

Xo dug through her pack and found a roll of electrical tape, which she'd brought for such repairs, and a toothbrush. Hopefully the error was just caused by grit in the moving parts preventing the zoom lens from extending properly.

Alec watched with a detached expression. "Looks like it'll be awhile before we get going again, eh?"

Xo clenched her teeth. Alec sounded like he couldn't care less.

"I'll take a stroll while you're busy, then," said Alec. "There's a great viewpoint near here that I didn't think I'd be able to hit on this trip. Elliot, want to come?"

Elliot shook his head, raising his half-eaten sandwich.

Alec paused. "C'mon for a second, anyway." He gestured in the direction he was headed, giving Elliot a significant look that Xo could not read. Elliot hesitated, glancing at Xo.

"Oh, go on." Xo turned back to the broken camera in irritation. Obviously, Alec wanted to say something about her to Elliot out of earshot, and she had a feeling from Alec's expression that it wasn't positive. He ought to say it in front of her so she could at least have a chance at rebuttal.

Elliot set down the remains of his lunch. "I shall return."

Xo watched them walk away. Could Alec be regretting bringing her on the hike already? Megan had said it should be obvious if he was really interested in her. When she'd first met Alec, it *had* been obvious, she was pretty sure. But she hadn't reacted well to his initial compliment, and it had become less obvious since. Maybe her response had set the wrong tone forever, and he just didn't view her that way anymore.

❖   ❖   ❖

When they were out of earshot from Xo, Alec said, "So, you know that article?"

Elliot glanced up. "The one about Xiomara?"

Alec stumbled momentarily, and halted. "No, the '*Mountainpox: 10 years later*' one they were talking about doing." He pushed his hands into his pockets. "It's…well, I did what I could, but it should be coming out around the time we get back from this hike, in case you want to skip reading that issue."

"Ah," said Elliot. He swallowed hard. He should have taken the time to tell Xo—to at least tell her something so she didn't have to find out by reading about it—but every time he thought of bringing it up, he was afraid of how it might change the way she saw him.

He had never detected from Xo the air that so many others had when they talked to him. Even if they didn't know about the outbreak, when he encountered new people there was usually a reaction as they noticed his scars. A guarded question in their eyes, a slight recoil, an overly careful, polite air—or worst of all, pity. Xo had never exhibited any of that, from the first inquiring gaze she had turned on him, as if he were a fascinating species of bird she'd come to watch. It had been a little unnerving at first—his breath caught at the recollection— but in a good way. Nor did she appear to moderate what she said around him as some people did in an attempt to avoid offense. Not that she did so with anyone as far as he could tell, but it was refreshing.

Alec shifted a little and Elliot realized he ought to have made some sort of reply. Alec went on, "I didn't get the assignment myself, but I did persuade them not to mention you. Or Lia."

This, Elliot had not expected. "How—"

"It was nothing, just a little bargaining." Alec shrugged. "I think they ended up interviewing some doctor instead."

"Thank you," said Elliot fervently. Alec had stepped in even though he probably didn't realize how much of a relief it would be not to be pushed to the forefront of everyone's minds yet again, as their memories of the epidemic were refreshed. His recent odd encounter with Francis had only emphasized how badly this might go. That had been uncomfortable enough that he hadn't even mentioned it to Alec.

"If there's something I can do, for you…" began Elliot.

"Nah," said Alec. He rolled his shoulders and surveyed the distant viewpoint he was aiming for. "You guys finish up, then."

Alec waved and headed off, leaving Elliot standing there feeling inadequate. Nobody else at the newspaper had even approached him for an interview about the outbreak, making him wonder how Alec had managed to dissuade the author of the mountainpox article from doing so, and if there would be tension at work when he returned. Trying to smooth things out around the office might be the best way to repay Alec. Perhaps he could take an assignment nobody else wanted.

Rejoining Xo, Elliot finished his lunch while watching her fiddle and tape and finally get her camera working in record time. It was possible she already knew about the history of the epidemic by now—gossip got around easily in Lingen. If so, bringing it up would be drawing attention to himself in the worst possible way. Better to leave it alone. While Xo took some experimental pictures with the repaired camera, he busied himself reloading film in his older camera and tried to think of a suitable conversation topic that was not related to the outbreak.

Xo reached for his digital camera, which he'd taken off temporarily to work on the other one. "Can I see your pictures? Don't worry, I won't break it. Probably," she added in response to his look of alarm.

Elliot swallowed down his rising panic as Xo took the digital camera and turned it on. He had no concern at all about her breaking it, but there were a lot of photos of her on there. Quite a lot. If she saw how many, surely she would wonder, and perhaps misinterpret. Or rightly interpret…

14

BIRDSONG AND LOVELINESS

Xo scrolled through a few of Elliot's more recent bird shots, nodding to herself. She paused at one photo and angled her head sideways, studying it, not angrily, but as if slightly puzzled. Elliot got to his feet, ostensibly to return his film camera to his pack, and leaned over to see what photo she was looking at. He wanted her to know how he felt, and yet, he was terrified of her knowing, of her reaction.

There was a blurry, brownish streak of feathers half out of the shot, difficult to identify perhaps even for her.

Elliot sighed with relief. "Ah, I meant to delete that one."

"No, no. I think what we have here is Meiklejohn's bare-fronted hoodwink," said Xo decisively. "Well done!"

Elliot stared at the blurred image. "Can you tell, then?"

"Oh yes, the hoodwink is easily identified by its customary blurriness and rapid exit from the frame." Xo grinned.

Elliot let out a breath of relief that caught in a laugh. "I think I may be something of an expert in capturing those."

"You and me both!" Xo laughed and passed him back the camera, which he gratefully slung safe across his chest.

He gestured to her own camera, now repaired. "I can't imagine how you fixed yours so quickly. "You're...clever at figuring these things out."

"Ha." Xo laughed shortly, then glanced at Elliot. "Oh, you're serious. I wasn't that clever tossing it on the ground, so I can't really take credit for fixing it." She shrugged. "It's just figuring out what's not working and trying to patch it together, not much of an accomplishment."

"It is to me," said Elliot, who had never managed to fix his own cameras as quickly. He'd noticed Xo's approach before at the coffee shop when the espresso machine ground to a halt for unknown reasons. Even Megan would stand by nervously as Xo dived into the internal workings and somehow came up with it functioning again. It was as if she'd been waiting for it to happen and already had the solution in mind, although he knew that wasn't the case.

"Too bad people aren't as easy to figure out as cameras, then I'd be set," said Xo, more soberly. "I can't even reliably identify the problem, in people. In me."

By her change of tone, she'd been thinking on the situation with Alec, and she wasn't happy about it. But was she ready to see an alternative? Elliot seated himself attentively on the ground near where Xo leaned against her sun-bleached log, repacking her camera and repair tools.

"You know, I read this article a long time ago..." She paused as if flipping through a mental index. "How most girls—they surveyed these girls—said if they had a choice between being beautiful and being smart, they would rather be beautiful. I don't remember how many, a high percentage. When I read it, I thought that was dumb, because it seems like being smart gives you a better advantage in life. But statistics show beauty has a certain usefulness. It's easier for people like that to make connections, get ahead in business, find a mate. Just like birds, they compete against each other."

Elliot watched the movement of her jaw as she talked, throwing out words, taking them back, rearranging, organizing them like she was doing with her supplies as she returned them to her pack. The way her eyelashes raised and fell over her eyes, reflecting while blocking the sunlight, was mesmerizing. The glow of the sun, low in the afternoon sky, gave the appearance of warmth to the chilly scene, illuminating her breath in a cloud.

"Why not both?" asked Elliot, barely aloud.

"Huh?" Xo glanced at him, momentarily distracted, then turned back to her thoughts, zipping her pack and putting it aside. "Well, sure, in a perfect world, you would go for both. But realistically..."

She pulled herself up to sit on the log and picked up a few smooth stones, still sorting now that the actual work was done, and polished them one by one against her thumb until by some process of selection she chose a particular one and let the rest fall, scattered, against the rocky ground. She did not watch them fall, only held the chosen one between her fingers, stroking it against her thumb thoughtfully, elbows on her knees.

"Once, I thought that when the right person comes along, I'll know, because I'll be beautiful to that person even though I'm not to everybody else." She looked down at the stone and shook her head. "But it's transient anyway. One day you're beautiful, and the next...you have nothing to offer." She shrugged, gazing out at the horizon line despondently.

"Uh—that is, you are..." Elliot's throat clenched as soon as the words escaped his mouth. He hadn't meant to let them go, but another part of him cheered their freedom even through his nervousness about what might happen next.

"Hmm? What?" Xo turned and caught him again with her eyes, taking away the remaining words. Whatever look her face had worn before was replaced by gentle incredulity as he trailed off, coughing a bit.

"You have both, smart—" Smartness wasn't a proper word, not to mention being the epitome of not smart...and what had he been going to follow it up with? Beautifulness? Beauty. Now it sounded odd. He gestured with his hand to indicate the obvious conclusion of his sentence while covering his mouth with the other as he cleared his throat.

Xo laughed, cutting him off again, but in the clumsiness of the moment he was grateful not to have to continue.

"I know you're trying to say the right thing, you know, being a good friend," said Xo. "But you don't have to boost my ego or whatever, I know I'm not beautiful. For a while there I just thought maybe it would make things easier."

The reference to *friend* echoed in Elliot's mind, not in a good way. Clearly she was thinking about Alec's comment when he'd first met her, on how beautiful she'd looked, which Elliot had also overheard. Yet Elliot's appreciation of her features didn't seem to signify anything to her. Perhaps Alec's comment was worth more because Xo also considered Alec attractive.

While Elliot's appearance hadn't been anything to brag about initially, the mountainpox hadn't done him any favors. That much was obvious whether or not she knew the source of the scars. Still, he didn't think Xo would evaluate people solely on looks.

"What I am trying to say is…"

He attempted to filter out the words that were not appropriate for the situation: you don't know how amazing you are, and how much I admire you and cherish you and adore you, and long to be closer to you. Beauty doesn't begin to describe it.

Instead, he said, "It's not classical beauty that I am speaking of, necessarily, but when you know someone, they become…"

Xo laughed shortly again. "I know how they say: you're beautiful to someone who loves you. But then, which comes first? The attraction, or the love? If one of them goes away, does the other? How can you tell?"

Elliot's attempts to reach her were like the little waves that always rushed the shore, building in power, a little foam starting at the crests, until they seemed certain to wash over the entire beach—but then, right at the peak, they would subside without crashing at all, spread out, ooze up the beach with all the strength dissipated. The words started off strong in his mind, but seemed to de-energize on the way out his mouth, on the way to her ears, not even reaching the previous damp mark on the sand.

She was looking down now at her knees and at the rock she turned in her hand rapidly. Her head nodded slightly with each turn of the stone, as if she were listening to music conjured from its motion.

"Is it obvious? If you love someone, is it obvious?"

Elliot swallowed hard. "To you, or to the other person?"

Xo looked at him in surprise. "Well, I meant the other person, I guess."

"I..." Elliot's throat went dry. "I—I don't know," he finished lamely. Xo had just told him that morning how important understanding was to her, yet how could he expect her to understand if he kept on like this? Making a great effort, he tried again.

"I'm like the tide..."

Xo gave him a puzzled look. "Like on a fork?"

"No, *tide*." Elliot added a "Whssshh" sound for further explanation.

Xo studied him for a few seconds. "The detergent?"

"Uh...no. The ocean waves coming in...breaking, and dissipating." It was happening again.

"Ohhh, tide. I see. The tide." Xo nodded slowly, looking into the golden distance.

Elliot waited for her to ask him in what way he was like the tide, but she seemed satisfied with his assertion that he was simply like it. He decided the analogy was not worth wrangling at this point.

"Like the time, you wait for no man!" Xo flashed him a smile.

Only for a woman. "You don't accept compliments very easily."

"I know." Xo glanced at him again. "Wait, that wasn't another one was it? No. Okay. Yeah." After a moment she added, "Maybe beauty is just another layer of confusion that keeps you from sorting out if that really is the right person or if you're pursuing a dead end. What you said earlier...maybe my own feelings should be more obvious to *me*. I can figure other stuff out, why not this? It's so hard to tell with people; they're always changing their behavior; they're unpredictable. You know, birds don't suddenly up and do irrational things like people do. You're never gonna be watching a finch one day and find out that it's taken up playing the tuba or something. Unlike with people, there's always a logical explanation, if you gain enough information about the situation."

Elliot smiled. "Not the tuba, but they do sing."

"Well, but there are various reasons for that: to stake out their territory, to attract a mate, and there are warning calls and such," said Xo.

"Are those the only reasons?" said Elliot.

"Why do you think they sing, then?" asked Xo.

Elliot looked to see if she thought he was challenging her authority on birds, but her expression was merely curious. "Perhaps they also sing to express how they feel. Isn't that why people sing?"

"I dunno. Is it?" Xo looked doubtful. "What about people who are doing it for money?"

"They might have feelings to express too," said Elliot, amused.

Xo laughed. "Okay, sure. But still, birdsong is not totally random and inexplicable, like people things."

"It might seem so to someone who never heard it before," said Elliot. "Do you know that bird, the one that sings in the evening, and its song goes up and up and up in a spiral?"

"Swainson's thrush," said Xo immediately.

"Doesn't it make you feel like it's doing something besides staking out territory?"

"I can't tell why a bird is singing by how I feel about it, though. Its actions aren't based on my feeling," pointed out Xo.

"Still, your feeling is based on its actions," said Elliot. "What does it make you feel?"

"Wellll…" said Xo. "I guess I feel peaceful listening to it, but I think that's because the sound is just right for it and I am used to it, so it feels like it's supposed to be there. It's a beautiful song, I love it. But I don't think it's singing to make me feel peaceful, that's just a happy coincidence."

"When someone does something a certain way that you like, and you begin to notice this—it feels the same way, and makes your heart lift up, like the thrush song." Elliot struggled to contain himself and still let the words out. "You see part of how they are, and whenever you see it again, you recognize it, and it feels peaceful and beautiful, like you said. Then you love that bit about them like you love the song."

"This is what you mean by 'beauty?'" said Xo. "That's a pretty unique definition."

Elliot risked a look at Xo. She was staring thoughtfully into space.

"I kinda like it though," said Xo. "I'll have to consider it."

She stretched luxuriously and lay back on the log in the sun's glow. It was Elliot's turn to stare at the horizon line while he took in the entire scene in his peripheral vision, saving this moment. He didn't need a camera to imprint Xo on his memory. It happened without conscious choice.

❖   ❖   ❖

In his mind, Elliot turned back to her again. Words were ineffectual. What he really wanted her to know was how he felt. Now he wished she had discovered it, or that he had managed to say it—maybe there was something to being understood, after all. In the vision she lay watching him, like a cat stretched out after play: relaxed, yet ready to catch hold with its claws, should the game continue. He leaned on one arm on the ground beside her. Her eyes locked on to his, daring him. And then…he lowered his head to hers. Her lips parted.

❖   ❖   ❖

Elliot's focus was drawn magnetically, inescapably, back over to where Xo lay dozing. In reality, her eyes were now closed. After a moment's hesitation, he scooted closer, close enough for her to touch him if she moved her arm, but she did not. He gazed down at her, as in his daydream, but this time he just looked at her face, memorizing it afresh. He could take a thousand photos of her every day and never fail to find a new angle to appreciate.

He ached to kiss her, even just touch her with his fingertips, to involve any other sense: sight alone was overwhelmed. But he couldn't possibly touch her while she lay sleeping. He pictured her recoiling awake, pulling away from him, and his insides twisted painfully.

Waiting on her threshold, he pleaded silently for an invitation to step inside. He must somehow gain the courage to knock upon her door, if no invitation came. He had hoped she would see him standing outside and he would not need to knock, but this was seeming less likely as time went by. She simply did not see him, or if she did, thought he merely wanted to chat through the window. He would have to knock. Politely, gently, and not when she was asleep.

"Ready to get a move on? Come on, you slugs!" Alec's voice broke into Elliot's daydreams, sending the precarious and elaborately balanced tower of fantasy tumbling to the ground. It would always have ended that way, but irritation at the interruption still surged.

Xo yawned, stretched, and stood up. "Ow! Why am I sore already? Is it time to camp yet?"

"Ha! We aren't anywhere near where we're pitching tent for the night," said Alec. "Let's go!"

Elliot collected his things and joined Xo and Alec on the trail again. Alec was full of energy, Xo considerably less so, though she roused eventually and began commenting on birds she sighted. Elliot's mind was still on his reverie and his earlier conversation with Xo. He was both comforted and saddened by her easy, unaware presence, but finally gave in to the comfort, as she clutched his arm and pointed out a new sighting. Allowing himself to be caught up in her enthusiasm and closeness afforded some relief.

After Xo had grabbed Elliot's arm several times, excitedly pointing out various birds and chatting about which ones she had seen so far, he noticed that she was doing the same thing to Alec. Alec put in a few comments of, "I'm not much for birds, myself," before putting more distance between them as the grade steepened.

Xo fell silent and trudged along with eyes on the path, and Elliot's heart began to hurt for her again. What did he want, anyway, for Alec to shower her with attention? That would not make him feel any better, but what was Alec playing at? It was difficult for Elliot to imagine someone not being interested in Xo, but if Alec wasn't, he should make it clear and put this to rest. It was what Xo herself had said she wanted. Elliot had resolved time and again to not interfere, but he wasn't sure how much longer he could refrain.

15

ALEC'S STORY

The evening meal had been eaten, the fire had died down to embers, and all had retired to their individual tents. The chill night descended over the mountainside, but it was too early to sleep, even as tired as Xo was from hiking all day. She zipped her tent open and crawled outside, closing the flap behind her again in case any night insects lingered despite the cold.

Three logs had been pulled around the fire pit earlier as seats, and Xo sat on one with her back to the dwindling sparks, looking down the mountainside. The land below lay dim and featureless, all shadows and crags. A glow behind a ridge to the southwest marked the location of Lingen. Farther still, beyond the jagged edge of the horizon, pale clouds still lingered in fading blue and yellow. The warm colors of the departed sun had left only this cool reflection.

Xo turned to see Mount Arin's outline against the other side of the sky, surrounded by stars, the glaciers faintly visible as ghostly streaks in the dark reaching below the snowline. The mountain did not look like a single peak anymore, as it had from Lingen. From here, the profile was irregular, with many high and low points concealing the true summit.

"You still up?" whispered Alec from his tent opening, where the flap was toggled to one side. Xo could barely see his face outlined against the insect screen. She crept over and squatted down by the entrance and Alec unzipped the screen.

"It's warmer in here." Moonlight reflected off Alec's grin.

Xo hesitated. Was it obvious for her, like it was supposed to be? How did she really feel about Alec? Those weren't butterflies trapped behind her diaphragm, beating against the bars to get out; it was more like a cage of agitated chickens. But here was a chance to find out where she stood with him. The darkness might reveal whatever he wouldn't say in the light.

"I guess I wouldn't mind talking for a bit," she said. "I'm not used to going to sleep this early, but it's so dark without the city lights." Usually she ended up reading until she could no longer keep her eyes open, but she'd realized when packing for the trip that maintaining her nightly reading habit on the hike would run down her flashlight battery, which might be needed for an emergency.

She ducked her head inside the tent. There was nothing to sit on besides his ground mat and his sleeping bag, already occupied. Alec lifted the edge of the bag entrance invitingly, teasing her, and Xo felt her face grow warm, luckily concealed in the dark. She retrieved her sleeping bag from her tent instead and stepped into it, then scooted back into Alec's tent like an inchworm. This resulted in a fair amount of squirming to get into the small space. Alec laughed at her contortions.

"Shush," whispered Xo, suppressing a giggle. "Elliot's probably asleep."

"Heh, yeah," agreed Alec, zipping the screen again.

Xo lay on her stomach in her sleeping bag and propped herself up on her elbows, looking out the mesh entrance at the distant darkening skyline. "How did you and Elliot get to be friends, anyway? You seem so different," she said.

Alec chuckled, then quieted. "It was here on Arin, actually. I guess the mountain has a way of bringing people together." He bumped Xo with his sleeping bag.

Xo waited for more information, and Alec settled himself on his folded arms, looking outside as well.

"Man, it was a long time ago. I was still in college, my final year. I think Elliot had already graduated before he moved here—he's a couple years older than me—but you didn't have to be enrolled to take this class, a mountaineering and survival class. I'd taken several of them by that point; I was already planning to be a guide." Alec smiled. "Back then I had some fancier mountain climbing in mind than what I ended up doing.

"Anyway, each quarter the class finished with a real-life expedition, overnight mountaineering stuff. Everyone had a climbing buddy, and Elliot and I ended up as partners. I didn't know him before that—I mean I'd seen him in class but we hadn't talked much. Us being stuck together…it was rocky at first. This was one of those experiences where you really get to know a person. You either come out of it hating each other or bonded for life." Alec grinned and shook his head, eyes sparkling in the dim light. "He doesn't strike you as much of an outdoorsman at first, you know?"

Xo smiled. "Yeah, I guess he looked kinda out of place when we started today, in his hiking gear. Compared to what he usually wears. Maybe that's why he took the class."

Alec shrugged. "Well, I had the same impression back then, at first. Must've been what, eleven-twelve years ago? I'd seen him around, thought he was too serious for me. He had those funny old-fashioned sideburns even then. And he was quiet, even more so than now. But as we made our way up Arin, I saw that he wasn't as incapable as I'd first believed. He was always thinking, considering. He looked where he put his feet.

"A lot of us were showing off, doing stupid stuff. Seeing how dangerous of a cliff edge we could walk along. In reality, we didn't need to do that because there were already enough real dangers, but we didn't know any better.

"Elliot, he didn't do that stuff. I could tell he liked it up here on Arin, but not for the thrill of danger, for something else. He always had his camera with him too, I remember teasing him about that. This was before people started taking pictures everywhere with their phones. Back then you usually only saw tourists dragging cameras around, so people made fun of him. Of course, he was new to the area, that was probably a factor too. He was already working for the newspaper—I wasn't yet—but I don't think he was taking photos on the hike in any professional capacity, just for himself. He developed them himself too, back then."

"I didn't take many photos before I got a digital camera," said Xo with a laugh. "Too long to get results back. And not very good results at that."

Alec was silent for a moment, but his focus seemed to be elsewhere now—or at least in another time, following the events of his story. "We were pretty high up when the weather started to change. The instructor had us turn around, so we could make camp at a lower elevation. We were way above the snow line, not like here."

Xo's eyes were drawn to the floor of the tent as Alec tapped it for emphasis. He wasn't looking at her, or the tent floor, but off into space. It was as if he had stopped merely telling the story to Xo and was now reliving it. She bit back her questions and stared into the dark like Alec, letting the images play out like a movie in her mind as he spoke.

"We were complaining about turning back, most of us, telling each other we could tough it out. We wanted an experience. There was this dangerous bit, this hairline ridge. We shouldn't have even been on it." Alec shook his head. "But like I said, we were mostly all show-offs, myself included. We were roped in pairs. The footing was bare rock, not much snow or ice in that spot because of the wind and the steepness, so maybe I wasn't being careful enough. I put my foot down and the whole section of rock that I was standing on started sliding. It just broke away. I jumped up, but the part above it was slick with gravel from the piece that broke loose. You've probably done this yourself somewhere on a side-hill. Except this was over thousands of feet of sheer cliff drop.

"We'd read about this type of situation in class, these ridges, and what to do if you slip. Not that we expected ever to have to use that knowledge, shouldn't have even been on it. The deal is, if one person falls to one side, that means your buddy has to go the other way to catch you, to counterbalance the rope, otherwise you both fall together. We were walking on the ridge so we weren't hooked into anything else but each other, but that's what Elliot did. He didn't hesitate when I slipped, just pitched off the other side of the ridge opposite me.

"I didn't even realize he'd done it until I felt the rope go tight. Then I looked up and he wasn't there, and I was hanging with my belly against the slope. I didn't lose a second before I dug my feet in and grabbed a higher rock and I started climbing. I'd only fallen past my body length, close to the top of the ridge, so I quickly regained my bearings as the gravel stopped sliding past me, and hauled myself back up.

"The other teams that had already started descending were coming back to see what happened. I got to my feet and I started talking to this other guy who was in my class. I started laughing with relief. When I fell, my heart was in my throat, and now that I was standing on my feet again, I was cracking up. Only for a second—I hadn't noticed until then that the rope was slack.

"I saw some people looking down the other side of the ridge. It felt like I was standing there for ten minutes before I noticed, but it wasn't. It wasn't. It was a few seconds maybe. I hauled on the line and yelled, 'Elliot!' The wind had come up, blowing snow around the lower slopes, and everything I could see below was white. That's why the instructor wanted us heading down, to avoid being caught in the white-out.

"I kept yelling his name, I went down on my knees looking into that whiteness, until one of the other guys grabbed my shoulder and pulled me back from the edge. The rope—I'd pulled the other end up. It must have caught on a sharp rock somewhere on his side and sliced through. This almost never happens. It must have been after I started climbing again, or I would have felt it go slack. If it had broken before that, I would have fallen myself, and I kept telling the others that, asking how it could have happened without me realizing. Then I wondered if it only sliced all the way through when I tugged on it to pull it up.

"Nobody was taking any notice of what I was saying, though. They were looking over the edge and milling about; they didn't know what to do.

"The instructor came back with the student who was his climbing buddy, and he had told three other pairs to keep going down and find a place to make camp. The rest of us were going to see if we could tell where Elliot had fallen. That's how the instructor put it. Elliot hadn't answered the shouting. There hadn't been a sound. I was still asking about the rope, in my head, but I'd stopped telling people about it. I didn't want to come to the end of that conversation."

Xo had grown quite still, and when Alec stopped talking she felt as if she too were listening anxiously for a sound from where Elliot had fallen. Alec's expression in the moonlight was uncharacteristically serious as he gathered his thoughts and continued.

"We started going down, and it seemed like forever before we reached a switchback that passed underneath where he'd fallen. I looked up the cliff and there was only bare rock. There was snow blowing around our feet where there hadn't been any when we hiked up, but Elliot wasn't there. He'd fallen, or rolled, even farther down, where there was no path and the snow was getting deeply drifted in places by the wind. The instructor sent most of the others down the trail to rejoin the rest of the class, while two groups of us were going to hike off the trail, cutting down and doubling back to try to find where Elliot could have ended up.

"I roped on with the instructor's team. There were three of us tied together, plus the other pair, and the five of us made slow headway. At first, the instructor had wanted me to go down to make camp with the others, maybe because I'd caused all this. But he knew I wasn't incompetent; I'd hiked many times before, with him even. I kept saying I was coming and finally he told me to rope up. The others were hushed and afraid. For some of them it was their first big hike. He didn't want me to make a scene and scare them more, I think.

"We crisscrossed back and forth, stumbling over rocks. The snow was falling thickly now; the blizzard had moved in. I couldn't hear or see much anymore. I followed the tug on the line and moved almost blindly, prodding around in the snow.

"At some point it felt like we were heading back to the trail. I asked the guy ahead of me and he said he was just following the teacher. When we got back on the trail I was sure of it, even though it was hard to see now with the blizzard. I went right up to the teacher—I was taller than him—and I shouted in his face over the wind, 'Where are we going? We can't turn back now!' He said we couldn't see anything now anyway; we had to make camp and wait it out. The way he was so resigned about it riled me up more. I could have pushed him over, but I didn't. I wanted to, though.

"We kept going down the trail, and with each step I thought about unsnapping my rope and going back to keep searching, but I was afraid. It's a cold fact. I knew Elliot was out there, but I was too afraid to leave them and go back alone, and the shame of that kept cutting into me."

Alec paused, his head ducked and shoulders hunched as he leaned on his arms. When Xo looked over at him, he didn't return her glance.

"We rejoined the others and warmed up. They'd made camp not far below and the snow was already piling up against their tents. It was real quiet at the encampment. The wind was howling, but there wasn't much talk once the others learned we hadn't found him. Elliot wasn't a particularly popular member of the class, but still, nobody wished that on him, so spirits were pretty grim.

"I asked if we were going out again as soon as the storm stopped, and somebody said it was almost dusk. The instructor said we'd have to wait until morning. I knew this already because it was in the rules, but I asked anyway. Rescues and safety are covered in class. It's a similar concept to lifesaving in the water—you don't jump in the water and grab somebody; you throw them a line. Or, when your plane is going down, you don't put the oxygen mask on somebody else first; you put it on yourself. These are basic safety rules. You can't save anybody else if you don't keep yourself safe first.

"We all knew these rules. We'd even been tested on the ones for mountaineering. It turns out those rules exist because in such situations, you don't want to follow the rules. It goes against everything in you to follow them. Another thing we'd learned was how long somebody can go before freezing to death.

"I said to the instructor that we had to get out there as soon as it stopped snowing. He shook his head, said it was going to be dark soon. When I looked in his eyes, I saw he didn't have any hope. He already had his answer. I wanted to argue with him, and maybe he was expecting that, but I held myself back. Another team offered for me to share their tent. Our tents were for two, but big enough to fit three in a pinch, as a safety feature, and I didn't have anyone to share with because Elliot was my climbing buddy. I declined, and we all turned in to wait out the night.

"I sat in my tent alone, and I didn't sleep. Fear and shame were fighting inside of me. I'd had several cups of hot tea, but the warmer I got, the colder that icy pit got in my stomach. When I couldn't hear anybody else shifting around in the camp, I opened the flap. The other tents were closed and dark. The wind was still blowing snow around, but it wasn't snowing from above anymore. There was that dusky blue light that comes towards the end of a snowy day, a kind of twilight that tells you it will soon be completely dark, but the snow was reflecting what light was left and making the ground brighter than the sky.

"I zipped my tent closed and walked through the camp. When I looked back at the edge of the encampment, my tracks were already filling in with the blowing snow. This time I had my balaclava and full gear on, and I went back up the trail.

"The area we'd been searching earlier was barely recognizable. I almost walked right past it, but then I saw this big rock at a bend in the path. That was the point where I'd realized before that we were back on the trail, and that the instructor had given up the search.

"I didn't know where else to look, so I turned there and followed the base of the cliff where we'd walked before. There was a little shelter from the wind because of the angle of the rock face. The cliff above me was dark except for specks of snow drifting down after they blew against the ledge. If he was caught up there, I couldn't see it, and the snow on the ground was so deeply drifted in places that I was wading through it. I didn't know what the heck I was doing, or where I should look, but I had to do something, so I crisscrossed back and forth like we did earlier. The wind had dropped some and the moon was out now, so that helped.

"There was a muffled thump from above, and a big chunk of snow bounced off the cliff above me and landed on the ground, scattered. It was a large piece, but there was nothing left when it hit the ground, just a splattered mark. I moved out from the cliff wall to where that chunk had hit. I'd realized suddenly that he probably would've been flung outwards as well, if he rolled all the way down here. I had to be careful not to walk off another ledge in the dark because there was more cliff below me. I was backing up against a big boulder taller than me—safe place to back up because I knew I wouldn't drop off anything—to look up the cliff again, when I hooked my ankle on something.

"I thought it was a branch under the snow and I flipped it off my foot, but then I saw it was a piece of rope. I picked it up to find the other end, and that's when I saw him. He was right against the boulder, out of the wind. In the dark, it was like a wadded-up pile of clothing or something, but I knew instantly that it was him. Whether he landed there, or landed nearby and crawled over, it was the best place he could be, considering.

"Though I knew it was him, I couldn't tell if he was alive, so I dragged him away from the boulder out into the moonlight. I screamed his name and shook him. Incidentally, you're not supposed to do that. Don't do that if you find someone injured.

"I ripped off my glove and pressed my fingers against his neck to find the carotid artery, to feel for a pulse. His face was like ice. The wind was like ice too and the blowing flecks stung the back of my hand. I screamed in his face again, nothing. I pressed my hand into the other side of his neck, and felt something, but I wasn't sure. I put my hand against his chest under his coat. Now that my hand had been out in the cold, I could feel that his chest was warmer and his heart was beating.

"I must have had a huge surge of adrenaline then. I dragged him upright and shook him again, but he didn't come to. There was blood on his face from a big gash on his head, but I couldn't tell how significant it was. It wasn't actively bleeding. I took off my balaclava and pulled it onto his head as a hat, and put his hood back on, and pulled my own hood up again. My face was burning with cold now.

"He was like a dead weight when I tried to pick him up. You wouldn't think he'd be that heavy to look at him, he's so slight. I hadn't built up as much muscle back then, too—I'd be able to do it now. For sure. At any rate, at the time I could only hold him under the arms and sort of drag him along with me through the snow, so that's what I did. After a while I realized the whole rope apparatus that was still tied to him was tripping me up. I picked up the broken end and tied it to myself.

"The moment I did that I knew I should have done it before, because if I tripped and dropped him, I would've lost him down some cliff again in the dark. He wouldn't have been able to catch himself, of course. I opened my coat and tried to wrap it around him to warm him up some more, but I think it just made me colder. I wished I had my tent and stove with me, but then, if I'd packed up someone would have noticed.

"I think I walked around in circles for a while hauling him before I found the path I'd made before through the snow and got back to the trail. The wind had finally died down completely and the moon was illuminating the way.

"Now that I knew he was alive, I was terrified he was going to die on me. With all the jostling about, though, trying to get him into a position where I could carry him, he started struggling, pushing me. I stopped and he pushed away from me and fell down, and lay there on his back. I knelt down in the snow and yelled, 'Elliot! Elliot! Wake up, Elliot!' and finally he opened his eyes and looked at me.

"I don't know if he saw me, really, his glasses were gone and he was kind of out of it, but he struggled to get up, and then I could tell that his leg was broken. Now that he was awake, he was grimacing in pain, but he was able to stand on his other leg, and somehow, he limped along with me. I think that got the blood flowing again, and warmed him up. At least the groaning told me he was still alive, so I was glad to hear it.

"We didn't talk, just kept going down the trail, until I could see the tents. I don't even know how long it took. I started shouting when I was close enough to be heard, and pretty soon a bunch of people unzipped their tents and came out in alarm. I don't think they'd realized I was gone. They simply went off to sleep. Pretty soon we got him in a tent and they were splinting his leg with the first aid kit and somebody was doing something to his head; somebody else got some fluids. I suddenly didn't have anything to do, but he grabbed my hand, fairly tight, so I didn't go anywhere.

"That part is all a blur, though I remember finding him clearly enough. I remember the instructor eyeing me, though. I thought he was angry and he was going to say something to me about how I left the camp, but he didn't; he never did actually. He just started telling people what to do to get Elliot stabilized. The others asked if Elliot was going to be okay, and the instructor finally said that he was. He had to be splinted for the night, which must have hurt, but he couldn't be taken down Arin that night anyway.

"Finally, everybody had to go back to sleep. He was stuffed into his bag and we were back in our tent and I was still terrified he was going to die, but he was breathing loud enough that I knew he hadn't yet. I don't think I slept the rest of that night; I was so wound up on adrenaline. He hadn't said anything except to respond yes or no to the first aid questions earlier—they were trying to see if he had a concussion or what-all was hurt—until we got back in our tent, then we were lying there supposed to rest, and I was trying to lie still and quiet but I was all wound up. And he looked over at me and he said, 'I thought you didn't make it,' and tears just poured from his eyes. All that time he was out there, at least whatever amount of time he was conscious, he thought that when the rope broke and he fell, I fell too, and that's what he thought about. I couldn't get over that. I still remembered how afraid I was to go back, when we were walking away from the search."

Alec fell silent and Xo became aware of how tense her body was, even though she'd known that both of them must have survived in the end. She let out a breath slowly and blinked wetness from her eyes, avoiding looking at Alec. He'd never spoken to her with this much emotion before, or gone on so long about anything without laughing, though he'd begun the story with his customary jollity.

"Did it take a long time for you to go hiking again?" It would be hard, following that sort of event.

"A while," said Alec. "But we got out there. I went back to it first, then Elliot did, when he was able to hike again on that leg. Nothing as extreme, of course," he added. "Normal stuff. Day trips. We encouraged each other. It had to be done. I think we both needed it, to get over it. I went into guiding later, as planned, so I've encountered a few other minor incidents over the years, but nothing like that." Alec paused. "I was never afraid again like that, afterwards. You'd think I'd be more scared, knowing what could happen, but I wasn't." He shrugged.

"I guess that's how you got the guide gig, huh, by reputation?" Xo put a slight tease in her voice to lighten the mood.

"Heh, yeah, I guess so." Alec's voice was gravelly. "I mean, everybody knew what had happened. I never told that story before, though."

"You don't regale your tour groups with it?"

"No." Alec shook his head and his voice was serious. He laid his head on his arms. "Sometimes it feels like finding Elliot was the only really worthwhile thing I've done in my life. And he'd already saved mine—if it hadn't been for my stupidity, he wouldn't have even needed saving. Sometimes, I wonder if I've just been trying to make up for that ever since."

Xo couldn't think of a way to respond without diminishing the moment, so she looked out at the stars without speaking. When she glanced over at Alec again, his eyes were closed, his breathing slow and regular. The telling seemed to have exhausted him. After a minute, she unzipped the screen and crawled out of the tent, pulling her bag after her.

"Goodnight!" she whispered, to which Alec mumbled something unintelligible in his sleep. Then she stepped back over to her own tent and fell quickly to sleep.

16

The Morning After

Elliot folded the pillow around his head, pressing it tightly against his ears, but he couldn't help straining to hear through the barrier. Muffled laughter sounded as the neighboring tent flap unzipped and zipped, and then quiet, intimate voices long into the night. He even imagined he caught the sound of his own name on Xo's momentarily raised voice, but that was just torturing himself. His stomach clenched with unexpected forcefulness, like a black hole had opened at the center of his being. He fought to contain it, to lie still. The low rumble of voices went on and on until he finally fell into a restless sleep.

Morning brought an aching back, a lumpy pillow, and the same queasy feeling as remembrance of the night came back to him. On top of that heaped a burden of shame for feeling this way. Xo and Alec had evidently made their choices. Hadn't he determined that he would be glad for Xo regardless of what she decided? He did want Xo to be happy, he truly did; he just believed he could contribute to that himself. But he could never stand in the way of her looking elsewhere.

Elliot rubbed his face briskly with his hands to restore his reason. He had told himself that if Alec made his intentions known, he would bow out, but that honorable feeling was not making an appearance now, despite searching around for it. Yes, Alec did not have a history of serious relationships, but he could potentially behave differently with Xo. Elliot should be happy that his friends were happy. If they were miserable, he surely would be as well. He imagined Xo's face with the disappointment he had seen on others' faces after Alec's dismissal. No, he definitely did not want that. It was over. Any chance that might have existed for him and Xo had only been in his mind.

He took his water bottle and poured some water into his hand, then splashed his face, wetting the floor of his tent in the process. The mess barely registered. Finally, when he could delay no longer, he joined the others outside.

"Man, I don't think I have slept that well in—I can't remember how long!" Alec said cheerfully to Xo as they puttered around collecting their gear to break camp.

Xo smiled knowingly before noticing Elliot. "Oh! Good morning, Elliot."

Elliot greeted them both in a voice unlike his own and quickly busied himself with packing, after a few bites of his provisions. His aching felt transparent, but fortunately his companions did not seem to notice.

"Oof!" Xo heaved her pack onto her back as they set off along the trail again. "My thighs are killing me!"

Alec laughed loudly.

"How come you aren't sore?" she demanded.

"I do this all the time. You should work out more!" Alec shouted over his shoulder as he sped up the slope.

Elliot felt sicker as the words sank in. He briefly considered vomiting over the nearest ledge, but willed himself not to react, plodding ahead. Still, his mind kept grinding away at the previous night. Hiking on Arin usually made him feel refreshed and unburdened, but today he felt as if he were wading through sand. Keen focus on something else was the only recourse. He averted his eyes from the others, searching for birds he could photograph— preferably common ones that he wouldn't need to bring to Xo's attention in the moment.

Xo stopped for a long break at lunchtime and sat drawing. She complained that she wasn't used to walking all day, to which Alec responded that she shouldn't have stayed up all night.

"You're one to talk," Xo replied.

The morning hike hadn't been rigorous enough for Elliot's hunger to overcome the reaction in his gut at the renewed thought of Xo's and Alec's night together. He put his lunch back in his pack and wandered a short distance away, fiddling with his camera.

Many small birds had come out to explore the cold, sunny day, flitting this way and that, picking at the remainder of the season. Elliot followed a flock up the slope until he was out of earshot. The little cloud of birds rippled in the air like someone shaking out a blanket in the breeze. They settled as a group in a cluster of bushes, then rose again as one unit to move further on as he advanced, seemingly undisturbed, but not allowing him to get too close. They were about the size of juncos, with a red patch between their wings…yes, this was one of the types of birds Xo was specifically looking for! He'd photographed one in the past, but she'd said it wasn't clear enough.

He stopped and adjusted his shutter speed, carefully taking several shots of the birds hopping around on the bushes and ground. Quietly removing the notebook like Xo's that he had procured for the expedition, he checked his list. Lesser red-backed alpine finch. He had written next to it "Different subspecies?" But he couldn't remember what differentiation factor Xo was looking for, something to do with having a white patch. Or was it not having the white? He'd read up in preparation for the trip, to distinguish between birds of special interest to her and the common ones, but now, he couldn't find amongst his memories the detail he was supposed to have known about these particular finches. All he could remember was the moment in time when they had discussed it, and Xo laughing delightedly at him. For a brief moment, then, he had brought her happiness.

Elliot swallowed the growing ache again and quickly jotted down the time, date, and general location, approximating the number of birds of each sex in the flock. He scrolled back through the images on his digital camera. There were enough clear, close-up shots from different angles, so he moved a short distance from the birds before risking hailing the others with a wave of his arm to come and join him.

Xo was sitting against a large rock far below him with her sketchbook on her lap, not drawing, just talking animatedly to Alec, who stood lounging against the same rock. Neither of them looked up at Elliot's wave. The longing he had tried to send away tugged at his heart, but he shoved it aside. Time was of the essence. The flock of birds had settled, but could take off at any moment, and only Xo could determine if they were the ones she sought. He started back down the hill, trying not to make any sudden alarming movements.

❖   ❖   ❖

Xo had awoken that morning with an altered perception of both her companions. As she watched Elliot break camp, a snatch of Alec's tale flashed into her mind. The mental picture was even more vivid than it had been last night, now that Elliot stood before her in real life, and the image of him lying bleeding in the snow made her draw a quick breath. She had an urge to reference the event somehow, to let him know she knew, but for the first time she stopped herself from just blurting out whatever she felt like to Elliot. She had no idea how he would react, and what if he didn't like her knowing?

He seemed different this morning, but maybe it was just her view of him that had changed. How had he decided, in a split second, to risk his life for a virtual stranger by flinging himself over a cliff? Yes, he was following the training, and if he hadn't done anything they'd likely both have been pulled down on Alec's side, but Xo still found it hard to imagine the calculations that preceded plunging off the side of a mountain. In the same predicament, she might have tried to find another alternative...cutting Alec loose to fend for himself, for instance. He might have still managed to gain a foothold and climb back up. Xo shivered. It was just as well she had never been forced to make such a choice. There was a fine line between bravery and rashness, and she preferred options with a higher statistical survival rate.

The story had also given her a more positive impression of Alec, though. His decision to go back and search for Elliot was, finally, something she could make sense of, even though in the daylight Alec was back to his cheerful and more annoying self. Still, it encouraged her to evaluate him further.

They were now stopped for lunch. The morning chill and fogginess had burned off and the day was bright and sunny. Xo considered her next step. Elliot had wandered off, and she'd already filled several pages of her sketchbook with birds that morning. She walked over to the giant boulder Alec had picked out as an eating station and settled against it with her sketchbook and food.

"From what Sade told me, this hike is probably my last chance this year to sight hog-nosed finches," said Xo, trying to get comfortable on the rocky ground. All her padding seemed to have worn flat in one night, and the rocks jabbed her bones right through what should have been an ample layer of protection. "I guess they migrate somewhere else once the snow starts. Dunno where—they haven't been sighted outside the Mount Arin ecosystem for years."

Alec peered at the distant sky on the western horizon, as if reading something in the wispy clouds. "Snow isn't far off, it's nearly November."

"Well, maybe I'll still see them. I got a lot of others already, even an ochraceous pipit!" said Xo.

Alec continued to regard the sky while working through his sandwich, which might be what prevented him from further conversation. The bread he'd made their sandwiches out of was thick and fairly difficult to chew, and seemed to contain an awful lot of extra non-bread material.

Xo examined her sandwich more closely. "What's in this, anyway?"

Alec perked up. "Yours and Elliot's have cheese, I wasn't sure what meat you go for. Elliot's kind of picky."

"Not the filling, the bread."

He grinned. "Like it?"

"It's...chunky." Xo pulled a particularly large unchewable seed out of her mouth and tossed it towards a nearby cluster of dark-eyed juncos. They fled the missile, making her regret the move. "Tastes like birdseed."

"Eat a lot of that, do you?"

"Well, not a lot. I've sampled it of course, to make sure it's fresh, but..." Xo narrowed her eyes. Alec was suppressing laughter. "What, is that really what this is?"

Alec's expression turned to surprised innocence. "Course not! It's just...you're telling me you actually do eat birdseed."

"Not eat: *sample*. For quality control only." Xo glared at him. "Do I need to chuck this away or are you gonna tell me what's wrong with it? It's like chewing a nut-studded sponge."

"This bread," Alec hoisted his sandwich, "is the ideal hiking food. Protein heavy, plenty of carbs, and it doesn't fall apart in packing. And contains no birdseed, because *I* eat people food."

"If you can call it that. The only reason it doesn't fall apart is because it's practically indestructible," grumbled Xo.

Alec shrugged, unconcerned. "I'm not taking food advice from someone who eats birdseed." He snickered again. "Seriously, Xo, birdseed?"

Xo folded her arms and frowned into the bushes, now completely devoid of subjects for her to sketch. She could go on trying to explain herself all day and it wouldn't do any good because he would refuse to get it. Yet if she objected to something he said, he didn't seem to care.

Alec glanced at her with raised eyebrows. "Why are you so ruffled all the time?"

"Why are you so irritating all the time and always laughing at me?"

Alec just chuckled again as Xo fumed at his general infuriatingness, which was heightened by her having to gnaw her way through the rest of her sandwich. So much for picking up signs of peace and beauty. She caught sight of Elliot approaching and sighed with relief, hauling herself to her feet. At last, someone sensible to talk to.

Elliot stopped beside her and angled his camera screen to let her see the photos. "Xiomara, I was wondering if this is one of the birds you were looking for."

"The lesser red-backed alpine finch!" Xo took the camera and paged through the images.

"That is what I was hoping." Elliot leaned over the screen again himself, his head near hers. "But, as I recall, you were looking for a specific variation. I am afraid I cannot remember the particular characteristics."

"Yes, yes! These are the ones. See the patch of white on the male's wing?" Xo pointed it out in the photo. "That's different from the usual coloration. Are they still there?"

"If we hurry, they may be." Elliot quickly led the way up the boulder-strewn slope. There were heaps of rocks everywhere, gigantic chunks of former lava, doubtless shuffled around by glacier movement since the mountain was formed. In the bushes at the top of the rise, there was a faint movement, as if the seasons had turned back and rustling leaves had returned to the bare branches.

Xo felt a spark of excitement as she clambered after Elliot, glad to be unencumbered by her backpack, which she'd left at the lunch rock. It wouldn't be a huge loss if the birds flew away, since Elliot already had several photos, but she still wanted to see for herself. The pain in her legs now seemed like a sign of life rather than an ache trying to persuade her to turn back.

As she climbed the rock pile, Xo reached up for Elliot's hand and felt his muscles tighten as he hoisted her up to the boulder on which he balanced. Being pulled up through space exhilarated her in a way she couldn't remember ever feeling before...though it must have happened before, and she'd just forgotten the sensation. Elliot's arm trembled with the strain, but not for a moment did Xo feel he would let her go. She caught her breath and her balance beside him, her heart racing in the excitement of the moment, then realized she was still holding tight to his hand. She released her grip awkwardly. Luckily, Elliot gave no indication he had noticed her delayed reaction.

Now that they were nearly on level with the flock, Xo advanced more cautiously. "It's them!" she whispered.

Elliot took up his camera again and knelt to steady himself. Xo watched the finches jump about, imprinting their flitting movements and habits on her memory.

Suddenly, the whole flock rose up with a frantic beating of wings and soared right over them, then swerved as one and disappeared into a canyon a short distance away. Xo gasped as they flew overhead, and Elliot dropped both knees to the ground, turning to watch them go.

A sense of wonder swelled within her. "It's like that thrill you get when a train pulls up and blows the whistle," she said softly, to avoid breaking the spell.

Elliot looked over at her. "That's it. Exactly."

17

Xo's Story

Xo was filled with satisfaction at camp-making time that night. She settled on one of the ever-available boulders, organizing the day's notes and sketches quickly to take advantage of the disappearing light.

"Want me to put up your tent?" Alec was arranging the campsite with Elliot.

"Oh, could you? Thanks," said Xo. After the day's successes, not only the lesser red-backed alpine finch but several other choice sightings she'd made, she was even feeling more charitable towards Alec. After all, she had been rather hard on his food preparation skills when she had none to speak of herself. Plus, it looked like they were having some kind of reconstituted stew for dinner instead of more sandwiches, for once.

Alec grinned. "Then again, maybe you don't need your tent. Are you planning on actually using it tonight?"

"I'm not the one who fell asleep early," Xo said airily.

"I didn't realize I had something to stay up for," Alec replied in innocent tones.

Xo pretended to be concentrating on her work, and to her surprise Alec put up her tent without trying to elicit further comment. He didn't even mention birdseed again.

Later that evening, Xo lay restlessly looking out the entrance of her tent. Last night, she had felt closer to Alec, but now they had all retired separately and uncertainty hung heavy in the air. It was desperately lonely lying there in the dark wondering. At last she crept over to Alec's tent door and knocked, or rather batted, at the tent flap. He unzipped it, looking unsurprised to see her.

Xo shifted from one knee to the other. "You accepting visitors?"

"That depends on whether or not you can afford my going rate," said Alec cheerfully.

Xo glowered at him, but it was wasted in the dark. "On second thought, I think I'll go back to bed."

"Aw, come on," said Alec. "Get your bag."

Xo dragged her sleeping bag out of her tent and returned, out of sorts again, to crawl under the flap Alec held up.

"Your turn to talk tonight." Alec poked her in the shoulder. "I spilled my guts last night and you have to give me something in return."

"Okay, okay. I don't have anything as dramatic, though. The most exciting thing in my life has been coming here. It's my first job as an artist," said Xo.

"Really?" Alec sounded surprised.

"I thought I would start illustrating when I got out of college, but it didn't work out. I didn't have the right connections or I bombed the interviews, I dunno. Eventually I had to take a regular job to pay the bills. My parents were relieved I was doing something sensible instead." She hesitated. "I ended up working at an auto parts shop."

She could actually hear Alec grin in the dark. "You don't even own a car."

"I did then, but I sold it. It probably wouldn't have made it over the mountains anyway, it was pretty old," said Xo. "I'll get another eventually once I save up, but it hasn't been as crucial here in Lingen."

"I'm just having a hard time picturing you in an auto shop." He chuckled.

Alec's remark needled her, as a vague judgment about her abilities. "It was mainly customer service stuff like installing batteries and headlights and running the desk, and I was just fine at it," Xo countered. "But it was supposed to be temporary. Next thing I knew years had gone by and my dreams were barely even dreams anymore. That job was no longer something to do until I achieved the life I wanted; it had become my life. But it wasn't *my* life. It was like somebody else's life I'd somehow gotten myself into because it worked. It wasn't going to become the life I wanted without me doing something different. It was like that poem that goes, 'the road is made by the walking.'"

Alec shook his head, unsure of the reference.

"I don't remember it exactly, but the gist is, if I wanted to end up somewhere else, I had to start walking another direction, you know?"

"Very logical," said Alec.

Was he mocking her? "To you, it probably seems like nothing, but to me coming here was a big jump. It was terrifying—what if it didn't work out?"

"Well, what if it doesn't?" asked Alec.

Xo stared at him. "Great. So you think I'm gonna fail!"

"I didn't say that. I just don't get the big risk," said Alec. "You knew you could do the work, so you planned how to get what you want by making sensible choices. Playing it safe."

"Obviously, I wouldn't have come if I didn't think I could get the job. That would be stupid." Xo frowned. "But it wasn't guaranteed."

Alec shrugged. "I'm not saying there's anything wrong with that approach. I do the same thing."

"You make safe, 'sensible choices?'" Xo said sardonically.

"You act like I'm some adventurous daredevil," Alec said with a laugh. "I've lived in Lingen my whole life."

"Well, here are you are telling me about heroic mountain rescues."

Alec grew serious again. "Hardly. Don't forget I'm the one that slipped in the first place." He rested his head on his arms.

"Okay then, when did you ever turn down a chance at adventure?"

Alec propped himself up on his elbows again. "At one point I had this idea I would do investigative journalism, uncover a big crime or something. I even applied for a job I thought would get me there."

"They wouldn't hire you?" Xo softened a little in sympathy.

"Didn't get that far. I was at one of those big offices in the city, waiting on the interview, when I realized it wasn't for me. No mountains, for one. Why would I want to leave a place like this to live somewhere like that? I must've been crazy."

"But what about your idea of doing some good in the world, exposing some big issue through your reporting?"

"Me?" said Alec. "No, I just wanted to get into it for the fame and hot chicks."

Xo groaned as he laughed at his own joke.

"What I'm saying is, just like you I chose a life I thought I'd enjoy more," said Alec. "I guess I like to take it easy more than I like uncovering underground corruption. Plus, there are a few hot chicks here…"

"No, that's not what I was doing at all!" Xo frowned, avoiding responding to the business about *chicks*. "Enjoy more, yes. But I didn't move here because it was easier! The scary part was changing everything. Even if I didn't like how I was living before, I knew it worked. But the job in Lingen was doing something I actually cared about, and somewhere along the line I'd stopped making choices just based on caring about things. I didn't have very many things that I still did care about, so those things were important."

"And is that all you care about now?" Alec grinned.

Xo felt flustered. "Well, I think it's good to add new things." She was glad it was dark so Alec couldn't see her face very well. "But listen, I haven't told you the amazing part of how I found out about the job here—the day I realized I could start walking that new road. It was totally out of the blue."

"I know how you got the job." Alec sounded unaccountably smug.

"Not this part," said Xo. "I was still drawing birds in my spare time when I was working at the auto parts store. That was my remaining shred of sanity, so I wouldn't lose myself completely. I would post the pictures on this website where artists—well, aspiring artists—

share their work to get feedback. Then one day—you're not gonna believe this—I got an online comment posted on my paintings of the Mount Arin birds, the ones I'd painted from photos, saying I should apply at the visitor center in Lingen. That they were looking for an illustrator to do the birders newsletter and stuff.

"That's when I started dreaming again. I'd read about Mount Arin's birds before, but I'd never thought seriously about moving here. That was something only other people did, moving to the middle of nowhere to draw exotic birds."

Alec smothered a laugh, shaking his head. "Not exactly the middle of nowhere."

"Hey, it seemed like that, okay? I haven't moved around that much. I told myself not to get too excited—it'd been years since I'd applied for an illustration position. But Sade liked my pictures, and told me to come in person. I dropped everything and moved. I guess there wasn't that much to drop after all," Xo conceded. "But it seemed huge then."

Alec regarded her evenly with an expression of faint amusement.

"You could be a little impressed," said Xo. It wasn't a rescue in a blizzard, but it had taken courage to save the creative spark in herself that had been on the verge of dying. Even to believe that it was worth saving.

"I told you, I already knew."

"How? Did Sade tell you?"

"No." Alec grinned out into the darkness beyond the tent screen, clearly enjoying his secret.

"Then who?"

"Elliot!" Alec sounded as if it were obvious. "Don't you know he's the one who messaged you about the job?"

Xo gaped at Alec. "What!? Elliot didn't post those comments…I mean, he would've said something if it were him!"

Alec shrugged. "I know for a fact it was him. He told me about finding your drawings on that site even before he wrote to you. I mean, he didn't mention your name, but he was going on about how good they were and how you were already drawing birds from Arin."

Xo stared at the wall of the tent in shock, trying to see through it, back in time, to her first meeting with Elliot. Unfortunately, the exact details of what they had said to each other were gone, leaving only bits and pieces in her memory: different conversations on different days, a scene here or there. He certainly hadn't introduced himself as her online contact, though.

Even if he hadn't known from the start who she was, he surely would've figured it out when she told him her name and went on to the visitor center to interview with Sade.

"How could he not tell me that he was the one who contacted me?" Xo's voice rose to a pitch that made her throat hurt. It was wrong somehow, even deceptive!

"Maybe he thought you knew it was him?" Alec shrugged. "I'd assumed that's how you guys had already met, once you told me you worked for Sade. I'm surprised you didn't try to find out who in Lingen recommended the job to you."

Xo shifted uncomfortably. Yes, that would have been a good thing to do, if she'd only thought of it. She'd never replied again to confirm she'd gotten the job after arriving in Lingen. And there had been no more reason to post pictures on the site now that she had an actual paid illustration position, so she'd just let it drop. Elliot had picked up the connection in person, unbeknownst to her. Some of her distress now might be due to her own guilt about not following up, but still, how could he not tell her in all this time?

"Well, that was fascinating, but I'm about to fall asleep." Alec laid his head on his arms again. "No offense."

Xo was freshly irked. "Are you this hospitable to all your visitors?" Alec was apparently happy to tease her about spending the night, but couldn't care less what she thought about this bombshell he'd just dropped.

Alec propped his head back up on one hand, looking less sleepy now. "Like I said, that depends on the rate and services." He smiled.

"That's not funny," said Xo. "Are you a hiking guide or an escort service?"

"Why do I have to choose?"

"I said, it's not funny." Xo scooted out of her sleeping bag and began rolling it up in preparation to leave. If Alec was just going to keep teasing her, there was no point in sticking around.

"Take it easy. As I recall, you're not paying for the hiking guide services either."

Xo's mouth fell open. "I thought you just offered as a friend. What are you suggesting?"

"I did offer as a friend," said Alec placatingly. "Seems like you're the one looking for more than that."

Anger fueled by disappointment and humiliation burned a path through Xo's insides. Her hands crushed into the fabric of the sleeping bag. There was no point in rolling it up other than to indicate to Alec that she was leaving, since she would have to unroll it again when she returned to her own tent. She kept rolling anyway, making it unnecessarily tight. The whole reason for coming to Lingen was to get her life moving forward again, a life that mattered. But the part of her that she'd finally fed a little bit, given what it wanted, was now ravenous for more—more to care about, more to love. More that was real, and really her. Yet regardless of what she did, she and Alec remained in this undefined state. His denial of his part of the equation was even more infuriating than his inaction. As if she'd forced her way into his tent!

The sleeping bag couldn't hold any more tension. Xo stopped rolling. "What is this, Alec?" There. She'd said it.

Alec shifted slightly where he lay. "It's a sleeping bag," he said slyly.

Xo gritted her teeth. "No. Me and you. What are we doing? What is *this*?"

Alec sighed. Finally, he said, "You don't want to start something with me, Xo."

"What, like a fight?"

"What—?" said Alec. "No! What I'm saying is…you know we're just having fun, right?"

"Me, I don't like fun," snapped Xo.

Alec sighed again.

Xo hesitated. She needed answers from Alec, and now she wasn't even taking the opportunity to get them. She took a deep breath, and biting her tongue, gave him a pointed look to see if he had anything more to say.

"I'm just trying to get you to loosen up, that's all," said Alec. "Everyone likes a bit of flirting."

Xo sat back and stared fixedly at him as if it might reveal answers. "A bit of flirting. That's all."

"Yeah." Alec's smile was relieved, though Xo could not imagine why.

She frowned. "To what end?"

"Er…that's up to you, I guess. Of course, it's up to you." Alec held up his hands in a position of surrender, somewhat hampered by his sleeping bag.

Xo shook her head. "I don't understand what you're saying."

"Look, I like you, Xo," said Alec, slowly.

She coughed, feeling awkward.

"But I'm simply making sure you know: I'm not looking for anything serious, right?"

Xo couldn't stand to look at Alec. She focused on her hands, resting on the sleeping bag roll.

Alec looked around the tent as if help might be available in some corner. "And here I can tell by how you're acting that you're upset. I'm not trying to upset you. That's the last thing on my mind. I just don't want you to get the wrong impression."

"To be absolutely clear, when you say, 'it's up to me,' what do you mean exactly?"

Alec seemed confused. "Just that. You know, whatever you're comfortable with. I'm not looking for a…for something, you know, for a…" He stopped.

"…relationship?" supplied Xo.

"Or that," said Alec. "I mean, I'm not saying you are looking for one, necessarily. I just don't want to give you the wrong idea. Out of respect. Before anything happens."

"Out of respect," repeated Xo.

"Absolutely."

"What I am *not* comfortable with is being in here, now." Xo jerked down the zipper on the tent screen. It got stuck halfway. She forged ahead anyway, shoving her bag out and crawling over the half-open screen with difficulty. Her foot became trapped and she kicked it loose, narrowly missing Alec's head.

"Xo, wait!"

Xo stalked over to her tent and opened the flap there more carefully, threw the bag in, and followed it, zipping up without a backward glance.

"Xo!" Alec's voice came again, more hushed.

Xo heard him struggle to get the zipper unstuck, but she couldn't tell if he was pulling it up or down. After a short time, the noise ceased. He had not left his tent. She crawled into her sleeping bag and pulled the opening closed, and when all was quiet, cried into the attached pillow.

18

The Third Thing

During the night, Elliot awoke to sounds of discord at Alec's tent. Prepared for a second miserable night of overhearing intimacies, he had only just managed to drop off to sleep out of sheer exhaustion. Now, he froze, a sinking feeling in his stomach. There was the sound of Xo emerging noisily and returning to her own tent, unresponsive to Alec's call. Then silence. But not complete silence. A shadow of sobbing drifted over on the night breeze. Elliot held his breath: the sound was unmistakable, each faint cry a cold dagger twisting in his heart.

Should he go to her? Then the sound stopped; possibly she had fallen asleep. He should have gone…but it probably wasn't Elliot from whom she wanted comfort. No, what he really should have done was speak to Alec, much earlier. He had known something like this would happen, yet he had done nothing. He could no longer do nothing. He just had to figure out what he could do.

The camp was unusually silent as they packed up the next morning under a flat white sky, overcast with a whisper of winter in the air.

"We should be back in Lingen tomorrow," said Alec, scanning the campsite for forgotten items and tossing Elliot a pan that had been left out.

Elliot grunted acknowledgement as he stuffed it in his pack, too irritated with Alec for words, yet he needed to find some. He wrestled with the idea of somehow getting him alone and telling him…what? That he'd better not make Xo cry again? That would hardly go down well. Plus, over breakfast neither Alec nor Xo had alluded to the night before, reminding Elliot that he only had guesses about where things currently stood between them.

As Alec struck out ahead as usual, with Elliot's mind still churning over what he ought to say to him, Xo dispiritedly fell in beside Elliot. In other circumstances, he would have enjoyed Xo sticking by him. Part of him still did enjoy it, which only increased the feeling of guilt over not having intervened earlier. Though he wasn't looking forward to hearing details about her and Alec, he resolved to be her support, should she choose to confide in him again. She might even see that Elliot could be more than a confidante—no, he shouldn't imagine that. As far as he knew, she could still be with Alec, though unhappily. Unless she didn't want to be anymore, and that was why she was walking with Elliot. His heartbeat skipped.

Xo said nothing for most of the morning, though she kept looking as if she were about to.

At last, when Elliot stopped to photograph some common birds, Xo stopped as well and pulled out her binoculars. She lowered them almost immediately, her forehead creased.

"Elliot…"

A drop of rain after a long drought. Or possibly his own foolishness.

"Xiomara?" He lowered his camera.

"Oh…nothing." Xo watched the birds, her face dejected. "Never mind."

Elliot nodded. Foolishness.

"Actually," said Xo, "Do you know that poem that goes, 'The road is made by the walking?' It's stuck in my head now, and it's driving me up the wall that I can't remember the rest."

"Antonio Machado?" said Elliot. "*Caminante, no hay camino.*"

"I only read it in English," said Xo, her cheeks darkening in a blush.

Elliot bit his tongue. What must she think of him? He searched his mind, the words of the poem surfacing much more easily than his own words ever did:

> "*Walker, your footprints are*
> *The road, and nothing more;*
> *Walker, there is no road,*
> *The road is made by the walking.*
> *The walking makes the road,*
> *And looking back,*
> *The trail is seen*
> *That will never be trodden again.*
> *Walker, there is no road,*
> *Merely the wake upon the sea.*"

Xo smiled into the distance, the first time he'd seen her do so that day. "I like your translation."

He had done something right, or Machado had, at least. If only all the things Elliot wanted to say to her were as organized in his mind as poetry he had read. Immediately another quote came to mind. "Machado also said, 'Between living and dreaming there is a third thing. Guess it.'"

"I don't know that one. What is it?" asked Xo.

"He didn't say what the third thing is; that's part of the quotation," said Elliot.

"Oh! Hmm…" Xo tilted her head to one side. "What do you think?" She met his eyes for longer than usual, and for a moment, he imagined she could tell what he felt. Then: "Looking?" Xo's amused expression said it wasn't a serious guess.

"I have an idea, but I suppose I'll have to wait and see," said Elliot. "I seem to have the other two things down."

Xo walked down the trail beside him, deep in thought, but seeming in a better mood now that her mind was on the puzzle.

"Okay, so dreaming is inside your head, and living is outside. This guy's a poet, so he shares his inner dreams with the outside world through poetry. But 'poetry' isn't broad enough for everybody. Maybe it's 'communicating.' Expressing your dream turns it into reality."

Elliot turned the idea over in his mind. "Communicating…"

Xo laughed. "I know it doesn't sound very poetic."

"It's a good thought," said Elliot.

"Tell me yours?"

Elliot shook his head. He knew now he'd been wishing she would guess the same as him, but when she didn't, he couldn't bring himself to say it.

At lunchtime, the three of them sat around awkwardly, with Alec not initiating the usual banter and Xo not filling the gaps with random observations.

Finally, Xo broke the silence. "Alec, what do you think 'the third thing' is?" She explained the concept, sounding more standoffish than usual.

Alec chewed his sandwich slowly. "Doing," he said, at length. "Dreaming is thinking about what you want to do, and living just happens. You can lie there and do nothing but eat, drink, and sleep, and still technically live. In between, you've got to actually choose to do something. It's like you said last night."

"What did I say?" There was a warning in Xo's voice as she narrowed her eyes at Alec. Elliot looked from one to the other with trepidation.

Alec continued calmly, as if all were well. "You were talking about changing your job, your life and such. Between living and dreaming you had to do something—that's what made the change."

Xo's expression did not soften as she continued eating silently.

Alec stood up, finishing his last bite. "Let's hit the road. Homeward bound!"

❖   ❖   ❖

"Come on, Elliot, tell me what you think the third thing is," Xo coaxed again later, as they stopped for a rest with Alec nowhere in sight.

While she stretched her soreness out, Elliot found a log to sit on, trying to keep his eyes on a wren hopping over the stones.

She sat down right beside him on the log, almost touching. "Please?"

Elliot looked into Xo's eyes, so very close to his, and knew he had lost. Grinning, Xo hooked her ankles together and swung her feet back and forth. She must have sensed capitulation.

He removed his glasses and cleaned the dust off with his handkerchief. "It's only an idea. But I wondered if it was…'loving.'"

Xo looked surprised. "Go on."

"Well," he hesitated. "That's all, really. Without that, there's not much point to the other two, is there?"

"Hmm…" Xo picked a nearby branch and stripped the leaves methodically, one by one.

Elliot watched them fall. He would give all his love to her if she would only take it, if she would only open her eyes and see. But her eyes were already open and unseeing, looking far away.

"Have you ever been in love?" she asked.

Elliot tried to gauge if he dared make the leap. Much as he longed to, he could not imagine a realistic scenario where he would tell her how he felt and she would jump into his arms, after what must have just happened with Alec.

When he did not reply, she looked at him questioningly.

"Yes," said Elliot.

"Then you know what it's like to wish the other person would see you the same way." Xo picked at her twig.

Elliot glanced at her quickly. Again, there was no indication that she had any sense of his own feelings, unfortunately. Her thoughts were surely elsewhere. In another situation this would be a perfect lead-in, but now it was perfectly the opposite.

So, he turned his mind towards the past, seemingly a lifetime ago. A parallel world, almost. "She did," he said simply.

At this, Xo turned with a look of astonishment. "Oh! I supposed it was one of those unrequited things."

Like this?

"Since you're not with somebody now, I mean," Xo added.

Elliot determined that further explanation was inevitable, much as he would rather not dredge up these memories. "She married me."

Xo looked even more surprised. "But, you're not married now. Are you? I mean...I guess I don't know that much about you."

The sick feeling of last night returned to the pit of Elliot's stomach. How was it possible for one person to feel so close, and the other so far? It was the same distance between them from either side. He must have caused it by avoiding telling her about his past. He couldn't imagine how he would have inserted it into any prior conversation, but he should have found a way.

"No. I'm not married now." He swallowed hard, realizing he couldn't stop there.

"Cheer up! You're better off without her anyway!" Xo patted his back in a bucking-up gesture.

This was going even more poorly than he could have imagined. He removed his glasses and cleaned them again, trying to think of a way to put it, then replaced them without having come to any such decision.

"She died," he said finally. He tried to keep his voice from cracking, but it was only partly successful.

"Oh!" Xo sounded horrified. "I just thought..." She chewed on her lip, looking worried.

"That she left me?" He raised an eyebrow.

"Cheated on you, maybe." Xo shrugged and bared her teeth apologetically in a self-deprecating smile.

"Or I, her?"

"No, I don't think you're that type," Xo said.

Elliot nodded once in affirmation.

"Anyway, I'm sorry, for, you know, your loss," Xo added, wincing. "What killed her? I mean, someone...something must have." She laughed nervously.

"I..." began Elliot, but the words didn't want to come out.

"You killed her?!" Xo gaped at him.

Elliot returned her look of shock. "What kind of a person do you think I am?"

Xo looked confused. "Does that mean you didn't?"

Elliot stared at her. She didn't seem to be joking. "No! I mean... yes, I did not. Of course not. She...took ill." An oversimplification, but he couldn't stomach going into more detail at this point. "And no, I did not poison her, or anything of that nature," he added, an edge of irritation entering his voice despite his efforts against it. Immediately afterwards, he felt bad for getting annoyed with Xo. If she didn't know him any better than that, it was his own fault for not being more open with her.

"Sorry. You didn't actually say no, at first, so I thought...I mean, it could have been an accident or something," Xo said. "What did she get sick from?"

Practically everyone seemed to have it on their minds these last few months, while he would rather have let his memories lie where he had carefully wrapped them deep in layers of the past.

"A virus. Mountainpox." It had been so many years since Elliot had said the word, and just saying it brought up unpleasant associations. He glanced at Xo, dreading her reaction.

Her face remained clear. "I haven't heard of it."

"It's not common." If she'd never heard of mountainpox, no one had told her about him, and she must not have asked about him either. That could be good, or bad.

"Is it only in the mountains or something?"

"The outbreaks have started at high elevations, yes," he said.

Xo looked around. "So it was here? In Lingen?"

Elliot swallowed. "And a few other places." He ought to tell her the rest. "It was...a long time ago," he finished lamely, not feeling very courageous.

"I'm sorry," said Xo again.

"Lia and I were married for less than a year, but it felt like a large part of my life," said Elliot. "Now it almost feels like it happened to a different person. I suppose it did. I'm not the man she loved."

"So there *was* someone else involved!" exclaimed Xo.

"No!" said Elliot. "I mean, I am no longer the same person. That… version of me is gone. I suppose he died along with her. I'm not even sure how to be that person anymore, if I wanted to."

Even Lia's image in his mind was faint, like a beloved character in a book that he had read long ago and far away. The mental picture called up a mostly positive feeling, but laced with guilt. It was a guilt he knew he couldn't explain to Xo, the guilt of an undeserved, inexplicable chance at life while other people died.

"I think I would have trouble moving on from something like that." Xo nodded to herself. "So you never remarried?"

Elliot shook his head.

"Would you?" Xo's voice was curious.

Elliot hardly dared glance at her, but he managed. She wasn't looking at him; she had a habit of looking away when she spoke and then suddenly turning her eyes on him while he was trying to compose an answer, unaware of the inhibitory effect it had. He would never say anything to stop her, though. He lived for those moments.

"Yes. I would," he said quietly.

Xo was so near to him, her hand on the log closing the gap between them. It would take only a slight movement for him to rest his hand on hers, to give more meaning to his words, his useless words.

He hadn't thought he could feel like this, after Lia. Even though it pained him to be forced to think of Lia's final days, which he had become used to numbing out of his mind in order to get by, seeing her in his head just now hadn't been as bad as he'd expected. As long as he shied away from picturing her actual death, he could let her in a bit more without breaking down.

Another memory surfaced, a day near the end. Lia taking his hand, out of nowhere, and telling him that he deserved to be happy. There were times when he had seriously questioned if that were true, but he knew Lia had meant it. All at once, he felt that if Lia could have anticipated Xo coming along years after her death, she would have wished them the best. The notion unexpectedly washed away some of the pain. He hadn't realized how much there still was until he felt it lift, and the afternoon seemed brighter.

❖   ❖   ❖

Towards dusk, Alec finally stopped at his chosen camp location. Xo had given up on him regretting how he'd acted the night before—he'd spent the day either behaving like nothing was wrong or avoiding her, which had left her with Elliot.

It was hard to believe that what Alec had said about Elliot was true. Several times, she'd been on the verge of asking Elliot if he'd really been the person who messaged her about the Lingen job, but she hadn't been able to bring herself to do so. She just couldn't see Elliot deceiving her by never mentioning it, and what if Alec had only said that to rile her up? Furthermore, if she found that it was true, she'd be at odds with both her companions simultaneously. So long as she didn't know, there was still comfort in spending time with Elliot, while happy-go-lucky Alec roved ahead probably wondering why she didn't consider this "fun." But not knowing was also like an irritant against her skin that she could only ignore for so long.

Alec was whistling as he set up his tent for the evening. "So, Xo, was it a successful hike?"

Xo composed her expression. Alec's preferred type of "non-serious" relationship apparently meant not being affected by anything emotional. Admittedly, that would make it easier to deal, if she could achieve it.

"It was fine," said Xo briskly. From a technical standpoint, this was true: the hike had accomplished much of what she'd set out to do. "I have sketches I can base paintings on, and some photos to work from, plus I was able to document the lesser red-backed alpine finch with the white patch. I'm pretty sure it is not a case of isolated leucism now," she finished forcefully.

"You didn't see any of those pig-tailed snipes, did you?" Alec grinned.

"There isn't any such bird," said Xo icily. She shook her tent out vigorously and stomped on the spikes to tack down the edge, hurting her foot through her hiking boot. "If you are referring to hog-nosed finches, then no, I didn't see one. You could at least learn what they're called."

Alec snorted, shaking his head. "Lighten up, I know that's not really their name. You know how many birders I've guided up here?"

"Oh. Did any of your tour groups ever see one?" Xo asked tentatively.

"No idea," said Alec. "I wouldn't recognize one if I tripped over it."

Xo winced. "They're not ground dwellers, hopefully they'd get out of the way."

"Catch." Alec responded by tossing her the mallet he'd been using, causing her to lunge to grab it, to his evident amusement.

Xo had already finished staking her tent with the stomping method, and she had half a mind to fling the mallet right back at Alec and catch him unawares. She controlled the urge and passed it to Elliot, before realizing he was also done setting up his tent. Elliot packed it away instead of perpetuating the game of pass-the-mallet, his concerned face indicating that he had guessed this sport might become dangerous.

"Welp, I'm off to find firewood," announced Alec. He marched away. Elliot leapt to his feet from where he had been stowing supplies and made as if to follow him.

"Wait, Elliot," said Xo. Elliot halted instantly as her hand touched his sleeve. "Can I talk to you?" she asked in a low voice.

Elliot's eyes followed Alec as he disappeared off into the rocks. "Of course." He turned back to her.

Xo sat down on a convenient boulder. If she was going to get the truth out of Elliot, now was the time. She'd managed to handle Alec calmly this evening. She should be capable of handling the conversation with Elliot the same way without causing a rift. And she couldn't go back to ordinary life in Lingen tomorrow without knowing.

"I never thanked you for helping me get the job at the visitor center." She looked at him sideways, trying to gauge his reaction.

"The job was yours on merit." Elliot sounded cautious. "There's nothing to thank me for."

She couldn't tell for sure if Elliot knew what she was referring to. After all, he'd helped her in a few ways. "I mean, helping me…before I got to Lingen."

A look very like panic flashed over Elliot's face. He didn't say anything, but Xo instantly knew Alec had not been lying about that. Which meant Elliot had.

19

CONFRONTATIONS

The wave of disappointment which hit Xo was shockingly heavy. She fought to contain it—okay, Elliot hadn't lied exactly, but he had certainly concealed their past connection.

"Why didn't you tell me it was you who contacted me about the job in the first place?" Xo burst out.

Elliot gulped. "I—I was going to. Originally."

"I don't understand. You obviously knew who I was." Xo tried to keep her voice neutral.

"No, not at first…" said Elliot.

"When? I told you my name, and why I was here!"

"Well yes, then—"

"Then, you still didn't *tell* me you knew!" She was rapidly losing the reins of calm, her frustration galloping out before she could stop it.

"I started to—I meant to. There wasn't a good time," said Elliot, his voice desperate. "Then, the owl…"

"I can't believe you let me go on all this time without knowing it was you!" Xo's voice caught on a sob. To her horror, she was choking up, tears hanging in her eyes. She'd thought she could rely on Elliot, at least, to be straightforward. If not him, then who?

Elliot's eyes widened. "I swear, I had no intention to deceive you. Please, forgive me! When you did not mention how you learned of the job...I...later, I thought perhaps it was not important..."

The strain of holding back all day finally broke her and tears poured down. "Not important? Of course it was important!" Her inability to stop, to try to salvage some shred of dignity, made her cry even harder because of what a fool she was making of herself. She was shaking, unable to catch her breath. Elliot's face was guilty and shocked, but after one glimpse she was too embarrassed to look at him further. Why did she have to become this blubbering mess? She bowed her head to hide her face, but Elliot knelt in front of her, and she felt him clasp her hands in his.

"Please, I am so sorry. I truly am. I did not mean to hurt you."

He touched her shoulder tentatively, and she leaned into him, her entire body aching. As the sobs shuddered out, she felt the strain leaving her. Her face pressed into Elliot's shoulder as he held her, no doubt saturating his shirt disgustingly with tears and snot, but she gave up worrying about impropriety as relief flowed in. Her tears slackened and a beautiful calm settled over her like a heavy blanket, all sense of time departing. Her face, too tired to make any more expression, relaxed, and she sighed deeply.

Elliot's voice in her ear was low, catching on the words. "Is...is this why you were...crying last night?"

Xo shook her head, too tight against Elliot to talk. Last night... no, that could only have been because of Alec acting stupid. At the thought, Xo's eyes popped open, and she raised her head slightly. Alec, acting stupid, and wanting something casual with her. The upset had drained away, and now she was freshly aware of the fact that she was clutching and snotting all over Elliot's shirt and his arms were around her. Elliot: Alec's best friend. If Alec returned and saw this, what would he think?

Xo sat back, her face burning, disengaging herself from the comfort. What was *she* thinking? What in the world was she doing crying on Elliot's shoulder? She should definitely not be feeling like she wanted to crawl right back into his arms. Last night, Alec had literally told her he liked her, he was just not interested in...whatever he considered an advanced relationship. It wasn't like she was going to ask him to marry her or something. But whatever might develop between her and Alec, it certainly wouldn't happen if he found her like this.

"Sorry. I dunno what came over me." Xo tried to erase the blush from her face, or at least mask it, rubbing her face vigorously with her hands. She wiped her wet hands on her jeans.

"No, don't be sorry. I'm sorry! I should have told you," said Elliot insistently. "I hope you can forgive me. Please."

Xo looked at Elliot's stricken face and felt even worse. Okay, so he hadn't told her. That couldn't be why she'd been so upset. That would be ridiculous. It must just be the accumulation of strain after the situation with Alec.

"I do forgive you. It's not you…"

"It's not?" Elliot sat back on his heels.

"I mean, I was upset about that, but…well, I was upset about something else that happened too, and I think it all came together. I shouldn't have lost it like that. I didn't mean to take it out on you."

Elliot relaxed somewhat, though he still looked shaken. After a moment, he shrugged. "You can still take it out on me."

Xo giggled through her residual tears and wiped her eyes again. "Thanks. I think I just need to lie down for a bit before dinner, and then I'll feel better."

She got to her feet unsteadily and headed to the refuge of her tent with Elliot walking beside her. She was calmer now, yes, but worried. If Alec had come back…but he hadn't. He had missed the whole mortifying scene, hopefully. She gave Elliot what she hoped looked like a reassuring smile indicating that she was perfectly fine now, before zipping the flap closed.

Her mind kept going back, with a tinge of guilt, to how wonderfully relaxed she had become as Elliot embraced her. As fast as she banished the thoughts, they returned, threatening to lead to more inappropriate thoughts that definitely would not help her work things out with Alec. She fanned herself with her notebook, trying to cool down and regain control before she had to face them both over dinner. Maybe…maybe she shouldn't have been so insulted by Alec's suggestion, despite how poorly worded it had been. A casual relationship might be exactly what she did need. Such things certainly seemed to keep Alec in good spirits and not bawling over virtually nothing.

Outside the tent, she heard Elliot's footsteps crunch away from the camp.

❖   ❖   ❖

Elliot picked his way over the rocky slope outside the encampment in the direction Alec had gone. He hadn't mentioned that he'd seen Xo's work online to anyone but Alec, so Alec had told her. Of course, Elliot should have told her himself—and when he'd realized who she was, he'd meant to. At first. Before she'd become so important to him. The longer it went on and the more he got to know her in person, the harder it became to go back and rebuild the foundation as he should have done in the first place, without his explanation sounding bizarrely contrived. Everything had changed when she'd stopped being a random talented person he'd encountered online, and had entered his life—and even more, when he'd realized he couldn't bear for her to leave it again.

As relieved as he was that his actions hadn't been the full reason behind her distress, he also felt responsible for the pain Alec had caused. Xo's tears were still wet on his shoulder; his hands still shook from holding her in his arms at last. If he'd said something to Alec sooner, maybe the long-sought embrace would have been a happier one; now it was all wrong. His mission now must only be to keep Xo from getting hurt any further. No more delay was possible, no procrastination or excuse.

He found Alec at a greater-than-necessary distance from camp, having assembled a minimal pile of kindling. Alec appeared to have rejected most of the likely sticks lying around, of which there were plenty at this elevation.

Elliot cleared his throat. "May I ask what your intentions are with Xiomara?" His tone was sharper than he'd intended. Unfortunately, he could not let go of his distress as quickly as Xo apparently had, and his heart was still racing.

Alec straightened up and turned to Elliot with a weary expression. "What did she say now?"

"She did not say anything," replied Elliot tensely. When Alec didn't respond, he continued. "I overheard the two of you the other night. Then last night, she was crying." Best not to mention the more recent tears, for which he shared at least part of the responsibility.

Alec shook his head, looking uncomfortable. "Xo just took what I said the wrong way. You know her—she melts down over practically everything."

"You did not answer my question. What are your intentions with her?" Elliot could not recall ever having pressured Alec to tell him something before, and he did not like doing it, but he no longer had any choice.

Alec snorted. "Who are you, her father?"

"No, I'm her friend." It sounded odd to his own ears, but Xo had said so herself, thereby authorizing him to use the term.

"And here I thought I was your friend." Alec looked at him strangely. "There's a line, man."

"Are you serious about her, or not?" demanded Elliot, swallowing hard.

Alec evaluated him for a moment without answering. Then he said triumphantly, "You're jealous!" He gave a short laugh.

"I am not jealous," scoffed Elliot. It didn't sound convincing, even to himself.

"Then why are you suddenly interested in my relationship status? You've never interfered with my love life before," pointed out Alec.

"The other ladies you've had…liaisons…with weren't my friends. But I've seen what you do, and I don't want that to happen to Xiomara."

"Oh really." Alec looked hurt. "And what is it I do that you find so offensive?"

"You cannot have a…a fling until you tire of her and then drop her. If you're not serious about her, tell her now."

"So you're saying I just use people," snapped Alec.

Elliot didn't respond.

"Not everybody is looking for a permanent relationship, you know. Some people like having a 'fling,' as you call it." Alec folded his arms.

"That's not what she's looking for." The idea of Xo wanting such a thing was appalling.

"Just because you're not interested in something casual doesn't mean the rest of the world feels the same," said Alec. "I've known plenty of people who were quite interested in that, by the way."

"Why would she want that? Why would anyone? At our age?" asked Elliot.

"I'm not so old!" said Alec. "Some people want to enjoy themselves without getting tied down for the rest of their lives. I can't even picture myself that way. A wife…kids." He shook his head. "I'm not ready to give up my life for that."

"What exactly would you be giving up?" Elliot looked around in bewilderment. "Never mind, that's not the point. If you do not want that with Xiomara, how is it going to end? She doesn't seem to me to be enjoying herself, crying herself to sleep. When are you going to stop stringing her along?"

"Who says I'm stringing her along?" protested Alec. "I can't believe that's how you think of me." He looked disgusted.

Elliot hesitated. It had been his initial assessment that Alec wasn't that interested in Xo. But recent events had turned that idea upside-down, and Alec not answering his questions wasn't making it any clearer.

"You told her she was beautiful."

"Does a compliment now mean you're automatically committed? Maybe if women heard that more often, it wouldn't seem like such a huge deal!" said Alec. "Can't I find someone attractive without wanting a relationship with her?"

"*Are* you attracted?" pressed Elliot.

"Aren't you?" countered Alec.

Elliot didn't answer. Attracted was inadequate to describe how he felt about Xo. It was just as well that he'd never fully voiced his disapproval of Alec's conduct with other women; it would not have been worth it. The discussion was already vastly worse than he'd anticipated, with no end in sight. Elliot closed his eyes briefly, feeling ill.

"Why do you care so much, anyway?" demanded Alec. "You've known her how long? And how long have you and I been friends? So she and I had a misunderstanding, that's all. Why are you mad at me?"

When Elliot still didn't say anything, Alec started to look concerned.

"Okay, sure," Alec said finally. "At one point I thought she and I might have a go. But there's nothing. It's nothing." He shrugged and looked away.

"Then don't," said Elliot dully. "If you're not serious, tell her."

Alec watched him for a while. "You *are* jealous," he said finally, in a quieter voice. Then he sighed, studying Elliot's face.

Elliot had said everything he could say, and exhaustion had set in. Between this conversation and upsetting Xo, he might have destroyed everything worthwhile in his world in just one night. He turned away and picked some sticks off the ground for the fire.

Alec followed him silently back to camp with the rest of the firewood. Xo was waiting for them, now with dry eyes and a ready smile, but there was not much talk that night before they retired to their tents.

The next morning, Xo helped a subdued Alec and Elliot pack for the last leg of the hike back to town. After her embarrassing outburst yesterday with Elliot and an unusually silent dinner, Xo had spent an evening of methodical reflection alone, leading to a more sensible frame of mind. If she could manage to discuss matters with Alec before they reached Lingen, the expedition might still end on a good note.

As they filed onto the trail, Xo pulled Elliot aside.

"Hey," she said. "I need to talk to Alec alone. You don't mind if I run ahead for a bit, do you?" Alec was already rapidly gaining distance on them, speeding down the trail.

"Of course not," said Elliot quietly.

Leaving Elliot lingering on the path, Xo hurried after Alec. When she was close enough for her footsteps to be heard, Alec paused and looked back, raising his eyebrows.

"Hang on a sec." Xo reached him and stopped to catch her breath, hands on her knees.

Alec hooked his thumbs under the straps of his backpack and waited, looking especially unenthusiastic. His usual light mood had not returned.

"I've been thinking—I may have overreacted a little the other night," said Xo.

"A little?"

"The bit about being an escort was not funny. It was insulting. Um…you were joking about that, right?"

"Oh, for crying out loud. Yes, it was a joke," said Alec.

Xo expected him to make a follow-up joke about not charging interested parties after all, but he seemed to have finally stopped laughing about everything. This boded well for her planned conversation.

"Anyway…I overreacted." Xo quickly continued, as Alec looked both unaffected and impatient. "I've been thinking about what you said, how you weren't looking for something serious…"

"Yeah?"

"And I thought, maybe that would be okay. You know: see how things go, like you said. I can be…casual. I know you said you don't want a relationship, but I realize it can take time to potentially develop…"

"Whoa! Hang on." Alec held up one hand. "What are you talking about, Xo?"

"Well…" Xo's face grew uncomfortably warm. "You said you were looking for some fun, not something committed."

"Now, just a minute," said Alec. "I'm not…propositioning you for anything."

"No, yeah, I know."

"No, I'm not sure that you do." Alec looked around directionlessly, brushing his bristly hair back with one hand. "Look, Xo. I'm not looking for a relationship. At all."

Xo plowed ahead. "I know 'relationship' is this complicated term…"

"Just stop, Xo. Stop talking," said Alec abruptly. "What I'm saying is, I'm not looking for any…romantic involvement. With you."

"Then why did you say you liked me, and you wanted to flirt and have fun without getting serious if I wanted that too?" demanded Xo. "You said 'before anything happens.' Why isn't it gonna happen?"

Alec sighed. "Come on, you don't really want that."

"I can do that," protested Xo. "You have these casual entanglements with other women, why not me?"

Alec crinkled his face in distaste at the description.

"Don't do that," said Xo. "Megan told me, okay? You may not call it a relationship, but it is."

"Megan, huh. Told you what, that I'm 'easy' or something?" Alec raised his hands to the sky. "Thank you. At last, I find out what my friends truly think of me." He shook his head. "Unbelievable."

"I'm not judging you about it; I'm merely saying I'm aware," said Xo.

"Some people come into your life and they just go out again and that's all they want. And that's all I want with them, too," said Alec.

"Well, are you involved with any of those people right now?" asked Xo pointedly.

"No, but I'm beginning to wish I was, if it would get you off my back. Maybe I should grab the first female I see when I get back to town, huh? Be honest, you aren't looking for a one-night stand or something meaningless like that."

"How do you know what I'm looking for?" Xo frowned, perturbed.

Alec set his jaw sideways, frowning into the distance. "I feel like I was just in this exact same conversation."

This was hardly surprising. "Well, then you should probably stop telling people what they want," said Xo.

"Okay, fine. Is that what you want with me?" Alec turned back to her, his expression a challenge.

What would he do if she said yes? It was excruciating to admit that Alec was right, but deep down, she knew she wanted more.

"Not really, but I'm willing to try. Sometimes these things start off casual and then develop into something long-term." If she was willing to try casual, he should be willing to allow for something else to happen. He couldn't possibly find lasting satisfaction in his approach.

"No, they don't," said Alec. "Yeah, I've had these 'relationships' that Megan so kindly described to you, and none of them has ever magically turned into something else. Not gonna happen. If I wanted something long-term, I wouldn't start it that way. Anyway, I don't. You and me especially, we'd drive each other crazy. We're already driving each other crazy!"

"I'm not that bad!"

"You're not. For somebody *else*," Alec said firmly.

Xo dropped her eyes to the ground, shifting her pack. "Just too annoying for the long-term, apparently."

After several moments, Alec spoke: "I meant it when I said I liked you. As a friend. We're better off that way. I'm pretty sure if you'd think about it, you'd agree."

Xo sighed. That couldn't be all there was. It didn't make sense. "If these relationships you like are so meaningless," she said finally, "Why didn't you have a meaningless one with me at the beginning, and then move on?"

"I'm not gonna just hook up with one of Elliot's friends," said Alec. "He'd never forgive me."

"Oh, so *that's* it. What is this, a 'guy code' thing?" Xo's irritation was building again, fueled by hurt pride.

"Sure, I guess. Something like that." Alec shrugged.

"So you've never done that. Ever. I find that very hard to believe."

"It hasn't exactly come up before. Maybe you haven't noticed, but he doesn't have a lot of female friends. Now that it has come up: no, I wouldn't," said Alec. "I sincerely wish I'd never given you the impression that I would."

"The only problem is that I happened to meet Elliot before I met you, is that it?" demanded Xo, her voice rising. "If I weren't friends with him, you'd have no hesitation getting involved with me? As long as it wasn't for too long?"

Alec folded his arms, frowning back along the trail.

"Well? Am I right?"

Alec's face tightened. He made a slight gesture sideways with his head, in the direction from which they had come.

Now what was his problem? Xo turned to look back.

Elliot stood a short distance away. His eyes flicked from one to the other of them. He looked as if he'd been stabbed, but hadn't fallen yet.

20

End of the Line

Elliot had hung back for a long time, until he heard Xo's voice rise in agitation and wondered if he should step in. Now within earshot, he froze. What had he been thinking? In his delusion, he'd managed to destroy the prospects for both his friends, for the sake of some thin, impossible dream.

Xo had stopped talking. She glanced from Alec to Elliot. Then she turned and walked away from them down the trail, shoulders slumped, arms wrapped around herself.

"She's just mad at me. She'll get over it," said Alec.

Elliot stood motionless. An eternity had passed and he had forgotten how to speak, since there was no longer any point in doing so, but Alec's untrue claim jolted him back.

"I've made a mess of everything," said Elliot.

"No, you haven't."

Elliot swallowed hard. "I heard what she said. I…I shouldn't have, but—"

"That's not what she meant," said Alec.

"No, she's right," said Elliot miserably. "If I were not in the picture, you two might have been happy." He hadn't even been able to stick to his original plan of not interfering.

"You've got it all wrong," said Alec. "There was never going to be anything between me and Xo. We'd be a terrible fit."

"If I hadn't made you talk to her and break things off—" Elliot began.

"There wasn't anything to break off, and you didn't make me tell her that."

Elliot removed his glasses and rubbed his temples. "She must hate me. For being an impediment, and for eavesdropping."

"You were just trying to keep her from getting hurt."

"That is what I told myself," said Elliot slowly. "But perhaps I was just being selfish." He gazed at Xo's distant figure.

"Go ahead and talk to her," said Alec.

"I don't think she wishes to talk to me at the moment." Or possibly ever again. Elliot unstuck his feet and started walking slowly down the trail in the direction Xo had gone.

Alec matched his pace. "You're not going to be able to stop her from getting hurt," Alec said after a while. "Especially if she keeps on this way. You may not think much of my morals, but there are lots of guys who wouldn't hesitate to take advantage, and they certainly won't care how you feel, either. *Not* that I'm holding back because of what you said." His voice was rough. "I'm not the monster you seem to think I am."

Elliot had never felt like a worse person. Anguish ate away at him for everything he had done to ruin the lives of the two people he cared about most. Lately he couldn't think straight through any decision without making a horrible blunder.

He cleared his throat. "I'm sorry for what I said last night."

Alec studied him. "It's okay. Forget it," he said after a moment.

"I thought I might have lost you, too," said Elliot.

"Come on, you can't get rid of me that easily." Alec laughed shortly and jostled Elliot with his pack.

Elliot knew Alec was trying to get him to smile, but he couldn't muster one.

"I don't think you've lost her, either," Alec continued. "She'll cool off."

They kept walking down, through the biting wind that had risen in Xo's wake. Elliot's eyes watered, but not entirely from the cold.

❖   ❖   ❖

There was a sudden alarmed shout from Xo, out of sight ahead. Alec had paused for lunch and was eating a sandwich, while Elliot poked through the remaining tired provisions in his own pack. At the sound of Xo's cry, a shudder of terror washed over Elliot. He dropped his pack and raced down the steep trail as fast as he dared, chiding himself for letting her go ahead alone.

Xo came into view as he surmounted a rise. She was sitting on the ground at the edge of the pathway, examining her knee. Elliot caught his breath in a gasp of relief. She was not lying at the bottom of some gully, at least.

"Xiomara! Are you injured?" He approached and reached out to help her up, but Xo pulled away.

"I can manage," she snapped.

Elliot shrank back, stung. With Xo, it seemed impossible for him to refrain from inserting himself where he was not wanted.

Xo got to her feet with difficulty, tried a few steps, then reseated herself on the higher bank on the other side of the trail.

"I rolled my ankle is all," she said somewhat more gently. She rotated her foot gingerly and poked at her ankle above the hiking boot. "I think it's okay."

"And your knee?" Elliot tried to assess it without getting any closer. The leg of her jeans was torn open and her knee was bloody with bits of gravel in it.

Xo bent over it, flicked out a small rock with her fingernail, and winced. "It's fine, just scratched up."

"I have a first aid kit." Elliot put his hands to his shoulders, but the pack which contained the kit was not on his back anymore. He'd left it behind.

Alec hailed him from the top of the rise; he was carrying Elliot's pack in one hand.

"Well, Alec has it." Elliot turned back to Xo.

Xo was examining the scrape again. "I don't think I need anything."

Elliot braced himself. It was clear that Xo did not want to talk to him, but he had to speak with her before Alec got there.

"Xiomara, I—I shouldn't have intruded on your conversation." He couldn't exactly say he hadn't meant to overhear it. "You wanted to talk privately and…I'm sorry." Again. He uttered a string of futile apologies every time he spoke. Words were worthless after a point.

"It was pretty much over, anyway. But, if you heard what I said at the end…" Xo looked up at him.

He felt as if he were seeing her for the last time. "Yes."

"I didn't mean for you to hear that," said Xo. "I don't blame you, really. I just feel so stupid."

"No," said Elliot. She should blame him, after all.

"I'm glad you're my friend. Even if—well, it's better to have a good friend. Alec said he and I wouldn't have worked out anyway." Xo sighed. "And if I hadn't met you, I mean, I wouldn't even have this job. I wouldn't be at the coffee shop either. I wouldn't be…up here." She gestured at the surrounding mountains.

"You already have those things," said Elliot. "What if I were not here anymore?"

"What?" Xo's head snapped back to him.

"If I just…went away. Out of the way."

"What? No!" said Xo. "Elliot, don't you dare."

"Perhaps it would be better," he said thickly.

❖ ❖ ❖

Alec reached them before Xo could respond further, tossing down Elliot's pack. "Everything okay? Did you trip over one of those ground-dwelling finches?"

She looked up at Alec fiercely. At least her clumsiness had provided a new topic besides their non-relationship, but she refused to respond to his baiting about the hog-nosed finches' habits.

"I landed on the side of my ankle, but I think I can walk on it."

"That's a relief," said Alec. "Wouldn't want me to have to carry you, eh?"

"Absolutely not!" At the beginning of the trip, maybe, but now the idea was horrifying. "It's completely unnecessary."

Alec laughed, and Xo gaped at him. He'd already recovered both his annoying sense of humor and his good mood. Shaking her head in disbelief, Xo reached for the bottle of antiseptic Elliot had dug out of the first aid kit.

Elliot didn't give it up. "Please let me help you. Just this once."

"Oh, all right." Xo was perfectly capable of cleaning out her own scrape, but possibly Elliot knew that and was only trying to make amends. Not that he needed to. She was the one who had hurt his feelings with her angry words to Alec. If allowing him to help made him feel better, she could at least give him that.

"Thank you. This might sting." Elliot gently daubed her knee.

Normally Xo resisted assistance, but he'd already done a lot to help her, and he'd rendered most of it sneakily enough that she hadn't even been aware until recently. Maybe that was why his hidden connection to her job at the visitor center had bothered her so much at first—it had all seemed so coincidental, and realizing it was not had been a jolt. However, he seemed to mean well; maybe he was just one of those people who really enjoyed helping others. Hopefully he understood she was only mad at Alec now, not him. If only Alec hadn't shown up before she'd had more chance to elaborate.

Alec was not watching the wound cleansing operation. He was surveying the surrounding mountains and Lingen, now in sight again below them, as if they provided everything he needed. He acted in far better spirits now than he had before her last humiliating attempt at reconciliation, and that stung a lot more than the scrape on her leg. She really was no more than an object of amusement to him.

As Elliot finished bandaging, Xo had the fleeting impression that he might kiss her knee, like her mother bandaging a scrape when she was small. But he didn't.

"Why are you so nice to me?" she asked, smiling, as Elliot rose to his feet.

He met her eyes wordlessly and offered her a hand up. Even though it was just a little pull this time, she felt a strange thrill like when he'd pulled her up the rocks before.

21

Delivery for Xo

Xo's relief at returning home was mixed with a reluctance for the excursion to end, which she hadn't expected after the fallout with Alec. However, once back at her apartment, a long hot shower temporarily pushed all troubling thoughts from her mind. Under the welcome deluge of heat, it was like she was shedding her skin rather than just a few days of grime. The bed she crawled into afterwards had never been so soft and comforting.

When she opened her eyes again, bright morning light was slanting in through the wall of windows, and tiny specks were falling outside, greyish against the overcast sky. Tempted out of bed, she crossed to the windowsill. A fine, powdery snow drifted down, widely spaced flakes that transitioned to white as they reached the dark pavement. The snowflakes sifted over the ground like powdered sugar and blew up against both sides of the street, which was striped with car tracks.

Another sensation pulled Xo away from the hypnotically peaceful scene and made her rush to throw on some proper clothes: the intoxicating smell of coffee wafting up from the shop below.

"Bring me back to life, Megan!" Xo gasped minutes later.

Smiling, Megan slid a breve over to her.

"Ahhhh…" Xo took a luxurious sip, wrapping both hands around the warm cup. "Coffee from a saucepan over a fire is nothing compared to this."

"Lunch, too?" asked Megan. Breakfast was well over.

"Please! Anything but sandwiches."

Megan grinned knowingly. "Alec made you eat that seed bread, huh?" She put together a lunch plate.

Xo's shift didn't start for another hour, so she sat down to eat. It would've been nice to take another day off to recover from the hike, but vacation hours accumulated slowly at part-time. She'd already had to trade some shifts with Megan to cover the extended weekend. Luckily, Megan had also needed to move things around to babysit her sister's kids.

Megan came around the counter and pulled out a chair to join Xo. The café was mostly empty this morning and the other customers already had their orders. "At least you guys missed the snow!" said Megan. "Once it starts piling up it'll stick around until spring."

"It is pretty, though," said Xo. It was already beautifying the street in front of the shop, and making the inside even warmer and cozier than usual.

"Quit stalling and get to the good stuff!" Megan leaned in conspiratorially. "How was the hike?"

"It was good. I made quite a few sketches to paint from."

"Great, but you know I'm not talking about birds," said Megan. "How did it go with Alec?"

"Ugh. Not good. I basically made a complete fool of myself." Xo gave Megan a rundown of the low points. "I think my pride is hurt more than anything else," she finished. "I was practically throwing myself at him."

"At least you didn't sleep with him," said Megan.

"It feels like I had the fling and the heartbreak without getting anything out of it," said Xo.

"Trust me, you'd regret it a lot more." Megan spoke with finality.

"It's just…I don't think I've ever had a guy act so interested in me before. Even so, I doubted at first that he really was, half the time.

But he kept, you know, flirting or something. Now it turns out he wasn't into me at all. It's so embarrassing."

Megan sighed and shook her head. "Don't beat yourself up, Xo. He acts that way towards everybody."

Xo groaned. "Oh, that's even better."

"I don't know if I should mention this…" Megan glanced around the shop as if to make sure they were not overheard. It was apparent that she was exaggerating for effect, though: the shop was completely devoid of customers now, except for one man lounging near the fire behind a newspaper.

"Well?" Xo frowned.

Megan leaned in again. "Alec left here earlier today with some new chick. They seemed pretty tight."

Xo spluttered into her coffee. "Seriously? I thought he was joking about doing that! What is wrong with him? It seems like everyone I've ever been interested in turns out to be a jerk or a loser."

Megan shrugged and took a sip of her own coffee.

"Does everybody besides me understand how other people think, or are they only pretending to understand? I plain don't get it."

"I don't know about pretending," said Megan. "I mean, it bothers me when guys do stupid things, but what can I say: they're just stupid guys."

Gloomily, Xo leaned her elbows on the table. It was a comforting fallacy, chalking up Alec's behavior to being just a stupid guy, but it wasn't truly that simple. Plus, since the misunderstandings always seemed to happen on her end, that must be where the problem lay.

"When it comes to guys, there's not that much to understand," Megan went on confidently. "They're only ever thinking about one thing anyway."

"What's that?"

Megan laughed loudly. "You know!"

Xo blushed. "Oh."

"Not that I mind. It's mainly what I'm thinking about too," added Megan with a snort. "Right?"

Xo sighed. Wasn't there any more to life than this game, a game she didn't know the rules of, and kept losing? "I dunno why I thought he'd be interested in me anyway."

"That kind of thinking won't help you," said Megan sternly. "You don't want to be that girl he's out with now. We all know how it's gonna end. I know you're all obsessed with being in a relationship, but Alec's not a good candidate."

"Yes, he established that," said Xo dryly. Rehashing it had only added to her emotional exhaustion, rather than bringing her relief in sympathy. Time for a subject change.

"Hey, did you know that Elliot was married before?" asked Xo.

"Really?" Megan's eyes widened.

"I know, right?" Xo shook her head. "I can't wrap my mind around it."

"Actually...now that you mention it, I guess I did hear a rumor about it," mused Megan. "Somebody who died."

"Yeah. He said he loved her." Xo poked listlessly at the foam in her cup with her spoon, then licked it off.

Megan giggled. "I can't see anyone being in love *with* Elliot. It's hard to imagine him doing anything romantic."

Xo frowned. "I dunno about that." Discovering that Elliot's wife had died had explained the wistful expressions and subdued contemplation that she had observed on their hike. In fact, until she'd found out about the death...Xo hated to admit it, but in the absence of any proper attention from Alec, she'd flattered herself that Elliot might have been entertaining thoughts about her.

Once he'd told her about Lia, though, it was clear that he'd just been thinking of his past when he talked of things like love, and she squirmed with embarrassment now to think she'd imagined it could be anything else. After all, Elliot had never pressed the boundaries of friendship with her, never said anything provocative or flirtatious, never touched her in a way that sought to do anything more than give and aid. She frowned harder at her coffee cup. Not once.

"Maybe she cheated on him and he killed her out of jealousy!" Megan smiled deliciously. "Now, he regrets it...the only woman he ever loved..."

Xo revisited her conversation with Elliot in her mind. "No, he didn't kill her."

"How do you *know*?" Megan waggled her eyebrows.

Xo shrugged. "I asked him."

"You what?" Megan shrieked with laughter. "You asked him if he killed his wife?"

"Yup, and he said no." Okay, maybe the question had been slightly inappropriate, but it didn't deserve quite this reaction from Megan.

"Like he's going to admit it? I mean, I don't think he really killed her, but I can't believe you asked him that!" Megan rocked back and forth laughing hysterically.

"I dunno, I believe him." It felt like her talk with Elliot had taken place a long time ago instead of just the other day. "I think he's trustworthy. Solid. I think he would have told me."

"Why would anyone admit that?" asked Megan. "Okay, I guess I could see him confessing out of guilt."

Xo frowned. "Anyway, she died from some kind of pox."

"Oh yeah, the paper had an article the other day about that outbreak, a historical recap or something." Megan looked around for the *Mountain Herald* copy the coffee shop usually had on the counter, but their solitary customer had taken it with him and was on the way out the door. She shrugged. "I don't remember much about it. I mean, I was in high school."

"I didn't realize it was that long ago," said Xo. Maybe it was just the sort of thing Elliot could never get past, even with time. Alec's odd remark about Elliot not having many female friends came to mind. She considered asking Megan about it, but Megan was giggling again.

"I still can't believe you asked him that. You say the strangest things, Xo."

❖   ❖   ❖

Neither Alec nor Elliot came by the shop, and Xo felt ridiculously lonely. There were plenty of other customers to talk to, but they only engaged in chitchat and then returned to their smartphones, or less frequently, to their real friends.

There was no point in mooning about Alec, but his sharp rejection still stung, especially as he'd immediately snagged somebody else he deemed better. How did he do that, and why couldn't she do the same? She'd come here to focus on a part of her that she'd never been able to devote enough time to: her art. Now that she could draw to her heart's content, her heart desired more. Not that the other desire hadn't existed before, it had just seemed less pressing and even less achievable, as—unlike painting—it required skills in which she was severely lacking.

In the evening, Xo put her sketches on the easel, and instead of working on her paintings, spent her free time reading while eating too many snacks. The romances in the books seemed to work out considerably better than hers ever had. Except when the characters died tragically, of course.

The first powder snow melted, but by Friday it was replaced with a thicker coating that made the town even more beautiful. Alec stomped it off his boots at the café door and approached the counter, cheeks red from the cold.

"Afternoon!" He grinned at Xo.

Xo eyed him warily. She had been dreading the next encounter with Alec all week, inevitable though it was. She'd known he would eventually come by the coffee shop, and besides that she was doomed to keep encountering him because they were both friends with Elliot. How Elliot put up with him was unfathomable.

"Hey," Xo said noncommittally. Alec leaned on the counter. When he didn't say anything else, she asked, "Do you wanna order something?"

"Just the usual!"

"To go, or not to go?" Xo looked hopefully at the door through which he had entered.

"That's the question, isn't it?" Alec was in a chipper mood. Evidently the falling out between them continued to have a positive effect on him.

Xo made his coffee in a to-go cup. Maybe he'd take the hint.

"I've got something for you!" Alec was still grinning, as if waiting for her to figure something out.

"A credit card?" replied Xo sardonically.

He handed her the payment for the coffee. "Something else!"

With a deep sigh, Xo rang up the charge. "What."

"Guess!"

"I don't wanna play games, Alec." Seeing him again wasn't as bad as she'd feared, but it was still fatiguing.

Alec sipped his coffee. "I'll give you a clue: it's from Elliot."

"Oh!" Xo looked up in surprise. "Elliot?"

"Aha, that got you." Alec smiled in a self-satisfied way.

"Well, what is it?"

Alec handed her a large manila envelope from inside his coat. It felt thick and substantial, making curiosity overcome her desire to avoid conversation with Alec.

"Do you know what it is?" Xo asked cautiously, reluctant to open it in front of him.

"It's photos from the trip." Alec headed towards his table, raising his to-go cup to her. "Enjoy!"

"But…wait. Why didn't he bring them himself?"

Alec stopped and turned back. "He's out of town. Didn't he tell you?"

So that was why Elliot hadn't been to the coffee shop since the hike. "Doing what?"

"Photo assignment in the lowlands." Alec jerked his head towards the side door as if Elliot were out there. "Nobody else really wanted it."

Xo glanced in the direction Alec had indicated, in spite of herself, and when she turned back Alec was already sitting down.

"Well…when is he going to be back?" And when had he left—had he been gone all week, or had he just not come into the shop while she was working?

Alec was talking to friends and didn't appear to hear. She sighed in irritation, fidgeting behind the counter, then walked over to where Alec was sitting. He didn't look up. She tapped him on the shoulder, annoyed, and he finally turned to her questioningly. Conversation at his table fell silent as his companions stopped chatting to stare at her.

"When's he coming back?"

"Who?" asked Alec innocently.

Xo narrowed her eyes. "Elliot." She held up the envelope.

"Oh, I dunno. Probably sometime next week. He sure seems to be in high demand all of a sudden," said Alec lightly.

"What do you mean by that?" asked Xo.

Alec smirked. "Just that you're not the only one who's been inquiring after him since he's been gone. So I heard."

Xo began to feel like she was being left out of some joke of Alec's, possibly aimed at her, though she wasn't exactly sure what it was. "What day next week, then?"

Alec seemed amused by her expression. "Monday? Maybe Tuesday?"

Tight-lipped, Xo returned to the counter. Alec was already back to laughing with his companions. The rest of the workday was filled with random small frustrations.

After her shift finally ended, Xo opened the envelope in her room and dumped the contents out onto the bed: a stack of large photo prints, a thumb drive, and a handwritten note on a scrap of paper. She picked the note out of the pile.

My Dear Xiomara,

Here are the best photos of the lesser red-backed alpine finches as prints. I fervently hope that they are good enough for you to paint from. Also included please find these and some of the other photos from the expedition in digital form, in case you have need of them.

Yours,

Elliot

Xo read the note twice, miffed. No mention of the newspaper assignment that had taken him away, nor of why he'd sent the pictures with Alec, of all people. Maybe he'd expected Alec to pass along that information, but why, when he knew what had happened with her and Alec?

She went through the prints. Close and detailed, they would indeed be handy as references, but she'd been planning to show Elliot her partly-finished set of hummingbird paintings when he brought her these photos. Oh well. He'd already given her his notebook of bird sightings at the end of the hike, written in the same neat script as the note. She added it to the pile of photos and slid everything but the drive back into the envelope.

Locating her laptop, she plugged in the thumb drive and flipped through the digital photos. Based on the file numbering, he'd already gone through and deleted some, probably those that were too blurry or not relevant, but there were still more photos than she'd taken herself and they included birds she hadn't gotten pictures of. While most of the subjects would have flown to lower elevations by now to avoid the snow, the photos would give her plenty of material to work with through the winter. This did not cheer her much. Maybe it was the thought of them leaving for the season that made her blue.

22

Xo Visits Elliot

The following Wednesday, Xo roused herself earlier than usual to deliver her latest illustrations to Sade. Up to now she'd done this errand after her shift at the coffee house, but with the early winter evenings it made more sense to go beforehand. She left the visitor center again with fresh assignments. There was still plenty of time before she had to be back at the coffee shop, and the sun sparkled brilliantly over the white-coated town, inviting her to extend her walk back and enjoy the picturesque morning. Without deviating much from her course, she came in sight of Elliot's house. He must surely have returned from his trip by now, and she ought to stop and thank him for the photos from the hike.

Xo's footsteps slowed as she approached Elliot's door. It might be a bad idea to stop in unannounced. He could be busy, or sleeping late. And she had not seen him since the last day of the hike—not even for him to tell her he was leaving town—nor since getting back, if he had indeed returned. She stood on the doorstep for a minute, reconsidering.

Her attention was caught by an older woman on a porch up the street. The woman was out in a rocking chair despite the cold, covered with several blankets, and was quite openly watching Xo. Probably wondering what the heck she was doing hanging around on Elliot's doorstep. Did she think Xo was a burglar? If she turned and left now, this neighbor might still make a report to Elliot, which would be even worse than catching him at a bad time. Xo turned back to the door and knocked.

There came the immediate squeak of a wooden stool against the floor, and footsteps. The door opened and Elliot stood there, looking thunderstruck. His jaw actually dropped.

"Xiomara!" He let the door fall open all the way. Despite his evident shock, he did look happy to see her.

"Surprise!" Xo smiled and waved, though they were already standing face to face. "I was on my way back from the visitor center, and thought I'd stop by. I got your envelope." Xo eyed the drifted snow blowing into his house over the threshold.

Elliot seemed to recover. "Please, come in. It's terribly cold out there."

Xo was quite warm, being well bundled up against the weather, but all the heat from the house was going out the door. She stepped inside.

"Oops." Chunks of snow flaked onto the kitchen floor from the treads of her boots. Xo stepped back onto the doorstep and stomped her feet, then stepped out of the boots back into the house.

She had intended to leave them outside, but Elliot picked them up and carried them over to the brick slab where the woodstove stood. He took her coat there as well, after she removed it, and hung it on a coat rack which now stood within warming distance of the fire. His coat was already hanging there.

"I've only just made tea." Elliot returned to the kitchen and turned from one side to another, apparently reorienting himself. "Can I offer you some...?" He picked up the teapot.

"Sure." Xo smiled, now familiar with his routine. "Whatever you're having." She sat on one of his counter stools. There was a partially-eaten piece of toast, with some sort of topping, on a small plate in front of another stool.

"Would you like some toast?" Elliot had seen her glance. "I'm only having a quick bite."

"Okay, thanks."

He got out the bread. "Marmalade?"

That must be what was on his toast. It amused Xo, for reasons she couldn't pinpoint, and she laughed and accepted. While he bustled around the kitchen, she rose and wandered over to the inviting heat of the woodstove to warm her hands. A familiar mug was standing on the bookshelf nearby, right where she had left it.

"Elliot! Is this the same teacup I put here last time?" She retrieved it, smiling curiously at him.

From the kitchen area, Elliot gave her a caught-in-the-headlights look. "Uh…"

She anticipated spoiled milk inside, but there was nothing in it, no leftover tea. Strangely, it appeared quite clean. She carried it over to the kitchen and put it in the sink anyway.

Elliot seemed a little embarrassed, but didn't offer any explanation. He hurriedly placed another mug of tea on the counter, along with a plate of toast and marmalade like his own.

"Here is a fresh cup."

"Thanks." The house seemed neat enough, but maybe he didn't pick up very often. Considering her own lack of housekeeping, she shouldn't be too particular. She took a bite and sipped her tea. "Wait, is this all you're having?" No wonder he was so slim.

"I can get you something else, if you like." Elliot started to get up again.

"Oh, no, I'm fine." Xo had already eaten one breakfast back home. It was highly convenient, living above a café—maybe a little too convenient. Then again, one needed extra winter insulation at these elevations. That probably wouldn't be an appropriate topic of conversation, though. She should explain why she was here. "The photos you sent over, they'll be really helpful, thanks. That's what I came to say."

"I'm glad!" Elliot smiled raptly, angled towards her on his stool.

Xo studied the swirls of milk in her cup. "So…you didn't say you were going out of town." She glanced up.

The smile faded from Elliot's face. "Uh…yes. I had an assignment. For the newspaper." He turned to his half-eaten food. "Did you read—uh, there was an article, recently…"

"I haven't read the paper at all since Alec's article about me." Xo suspected Elliot was trying to change the topic. "You asked me what would happen if you just went away, on the last day of the hike," she said pointedly.

Elliot froze with the last piece of toast en route to his mouth. He put it down on his plate slowly. Guilt was written all over his features.

"It was an assignment…"

"But why didn't you tell me before you went? You were gone for over a week." Furthermore, Alec had acted like Xo would know, though he could have just been trying to irk her.

"I thought it might be better if I were away for a while."

"What for?" said Xo. "I told you I didn't want you to go!"

"To give you time to work things out," said Elliot. "I thought, possibly, without me in the way…"

Xo sighed, exasperated. "Nothing's gonna happen with me and Alec. It wasn't because of you. It's just…not there. I know that now."

"I'm afraid I had to go anyway, for the assignment," said Elliot. "I… I may have lengthened it by finding some other photoshoots to do as well."

"You could have at least told me. I was worried after what you said at the end of the hike," said Xo. "I missed you."

"You did?" Elliot said almost inaudibly.

"Anyway, I wanted to go over the photos with you, and match them up to your notes to make sure I had everything correct. Why in the world did you send them with Alec?"

"I knew he would stop by the coffee house," said Elliot. "And—"

"And what? You don't have to try to push us together. I already said: it's not your fault." Xo sighed and shook her head, returning to her tea.

Elliot pressed the tips of his fingers together, squirming in his seat. "Xiomara—" He stopped, holding his breath.

Xo waited expectantly.

His eyes were filled with trepidation. "There's something I have to tell you."

"What is it?" Xo began to be concerned. He didn't look too well. Was he ill? Was that the real reason he hadn't been around?

Elliot bit his lower lip, wringing his hands together. "I asked Alec to end things with you," he said in a low voice.

"What?!" Xo stared at him.

"You said you wanted to know if he was serious."

"You told him what I said about him? That was confidential!" Xo felt like the room was spinning.

"No! No…" Elliot held up his hands. "I didn't repeat anything you told me. I just didn't want him to…lead you on. I—I don't know if he actually did that." He faltered. "I was afraid you would get hurt. Or already were. So I asked him to tell you, if he wasn't serious—"

"Yes, he made his lack of interest quite clear after that," said Xo grimly.

"I'm afraid I've made a terrible hash of things," said Elliot wretchedly. "I could not stop myself from interfering. So I thought, without me here, perhaps…I'm sorry. I didn't mean to ruin things for you."

Xo shook her head as she looked at the floor, blindsided. "You didn't ruin it," she conceded at last. "I just don't see why you got involved at all."

Elliot was silent for a moment. Then he said tentatively, "From what I knew…I didn't think he was interested in a committed relationship."

"Then why didn't you say so when I talked to you about him in the first place? I didn't mean for you to actually *ask* him!" said Xo, aggravated.

"I didn't know for certain. I only wanted him to tell you one way or the other, before you got hurt any further." Elliot hesitated again. "You deserve to be truly loved."

"Doesn't everybody? But everybody doesn't get that special someone, okay? Why do you, or Alec for that matter, think you can tell me what I want or need? I'm a grown-up; I don't need you to protect me from getting hurt! Anyway, maybe…maybe I don't have to have a serious relationship, I just need something! Although clearly not with Alec."

Xo slumped on her stool. Elliot had no rebuttal, but she wasn't sure if he'd gotten the message—he just seemed braced unhappily against the storm. With a slow breath, she regained her composure, and spoke more quietly.

"Maybe I get lonely sometimes, okay? It's not your problem. You don't have to make sure everyone I'm involved with is right for me, Elliot. That's for me to deal with."

"I understand," said Elliot, in a small voice. "I'm sorry. I've been feeling awful about it ever since, truly."

It was too hard to watch Elliot sitting there sadly; it made Xo feel as if she were in the wrong, instead of him. She averted her eyes, tracing the lines between the counter tiles with one finger to make a square-sided loop of infinity. Maybe she had overreacted, defensive after her own mistakes with Alec. Still, why did Elliot keep getting involved in…everything? It would be different if she'd actually asked him to talk to Alec.

Elliot spoke again quietly. "But…if I had it to do over, I'm not sure I wouldn't do the same thing again."

Xo turned to him in disbelief. "Have I not just said…?"

"Not because you can't make your own decisions," said Elliot quickly. "Because I…I care what happens to you. Alec…he is my friend, but sometimes he—" Elliot stopped. "I know you don't need me to protect you, but I feel I have to. I wouldn't be able to live with myself, otherwise."

"Why aren't you worried about Alec getting hurt?" demanded Xo. "That's kind of sexist." She could feel her anger ebbing against her will. Her outburst had released most of it and the remaining drops slipped through her fingers, leaving her tired and drained.

Elliot sat back, looking flustered. "Well, of course I don't want Alec to be hurt, either."

"But he doesn't need protecting, huh?"

"I suppose it depends on the situation," said Elliot. "If he did need it, I would, of course. Putting that aside—with you, Xiomara, it's different. I feel—"

"Because I'm a woman?" Xo interrupted.

"That is a factor, yes. In how I feel differently." Elliot stuttered to a stop.

Xo looked at him sideways.

Elliot swallowed, looking like he was about to say more. "Xiomara…"

"No, it's okay." Xo stood up, sighing. "I didn't come here to yell at you, Elliot. It's just frustrating. You guys are both treating me like a child. No." She held up her hand as Elliot started to speak again. "It wouldn't have made any difference with Alec anyway. I appreciate you looking out for me, I do. But not like that. Let me make my own stupid mistakes.

"Let's stop talking about it," she continued more quietly. "Just, don't take off on me like that again, okay? At least tell me you're going." She touched Elliot's hand.

Elliot nodded mutely.

She turned towards the door. "I should get going. I have a shift starting soon."

"Of course." Elliot's voice was subdued. "I…your things…" He went to the stove and brought her coat and boots.

Xo felt she had been too hard on him now. "Another day though, do you wanna come by and go over those photos and notes you gave me, from the hike? I need to clarify some of your sightings. And I have these paintings I wanted to show you, of the hummingbird."

Elliot's face cleared a little. "Certainly!"

"Okay, I'll see you, then." She went out into the snow.

"What's going on with you?" asked Megan later that day, during their shared lunch shift. "Not Alec, still?"

"No, not really." Xo shook her head despondently. "I was talking to Elliot this morning, and between him and Alec, sometimes I feel like I'm back with my parents again! Acting like they know what I want or what's best for me when it comes to my personal relationships. I'm tired of being told that I'm incapable of something casual."

"You mean like the watch-movies-and-chill guy?" said Megan.

"Ugh, no." Xo shuddered. "I want to know where it's going, even if it's not long term. I just wish I could be happy as easily as Alec, you know? Go with the flow, meet a random person and hit it off. Not let it bother me when it ends."

"I've known Alec way longer than you have," said Megan firmly. "And he's certainly not 'happy.' He's afraid of commitment. You've just been so hung up on him you haven't noticed anyone else—there must be tons of guys who would kill to be with you."

Xo wrinkled her nose in distaste.

"Not literally!" Megan rolled her eyes. "Stop feeling sorry for yourself and get back in the game. If you're tired of people telling you what you want, stop asking what they think. Go with how you feel. That's what I do."

"What I feel usually turns out to be an overreaction." Xo sighed. "I end up misreading people. I know I should be doing something to move forward, but I dunno what."

"Tell you what," said Megan. "A group of us are going out tonight to that Italian place. There's live music. You should come along."

"Oh!" Xo knew Megan hung out with some of the other baristas and customers, because they mentioned plans from time to time, but Megan had never before asked Xo to join her clique.

"I already know Alec can't make it," added Megan reassuringly.

"Maybe…" Xo said hesitantly.

"No maybes. Definitely. You've got to get out of your apartment and see what's out there. Live a little!" Megan looked her up and down. "And wear something else for a change."

Xo surveyed her outfit. "I'm not gonna wear the apron, of course."

Megan rolled her eyes again. "I mean sex it up. Wear something dressy. Put on some makeup, for goodness' sakes."

Whatever Megan's idea of 'sexy' was, Xo had a feeling she wouldn't be comfortable wearing it.

"Isn't it cold out for a dress?"

"If you want to attract a guy's attention, you've got to *look* like you want to attract a guy's attention. Put out some bait, and you'll have plenty of opportunities to figure out what you want."

Xo tried not to look too disgusted, since Megan was trying to help.

Megan checked the clock. "My shift's almost over. We'll come by at nine and get you, okay? We can walk over together."

"That's pretty late." Xo was usually in her pajamas by then, snuggled up with a book. "And you start work so early, how can you go out during the week?"

Megan just laughed. "See you then! And be ready—I'm not letting you get out of this!"

"Okay." Xo's anticipation was growing, in spite of Megan's garish depiction of the evening. There should be time after her shift to pop out and buy something a little different to wear before the shops closed for the evening. A whole new outfit wasn't in the budget, but maybe she could try something outside of the regular Xo, since the regular Xo evidently wasn't working.

23

THE ACCIDENT

After Xo left, Elliot slowly washed up the plates and put them in the dish rack. He stared at the place on the bookshelf where Xo's teacup had been. Her first visit could have been a dream, except for that cup: her mark, her out-of-place footprint. It had been the only visual indicator of the change he'd felt inside. At night, its white luminosity had been still visible, barely, through the dark as he fell asleep. Each morning, it had still been there. Proof.

Unfortunately, due to the leftover tea originally in it, Elliot hadn't been able to leave it exactly as Xo had done. He had washed it out and returned it carefully to the same position, which was almost as good, minus the spoilage issue. It was fortunate Xo hadn't pressed him any further about what the cup was still doing there today. It would have been impossible to explain without her questioning his sanity. Except for her surprise visit, it might have stood there forever, but now that she had returned it to the sink herself, he couldn't reasonably put it back on the bookshelf. What if she came by again and saw it, and this time demanded an explanation?

Elliot shook his head resolutely to pull himself together. He put the cup back in the cupboard, then nudged it slightly apart from the other cups, mentally deriding himself for doing so. Enough. He closed the cupboard firmly, but his mind continued to whirl. Despite Xo's natural dismay to learn how he had interfered, it had been a relief to tell her, even if he hadn't managed to explain the whole truth about why he'd felt compelled to meddle.

He tried to recall what Xo had said she wanted, but her other phrases kept coming to mind instead and overriding how contrite he ought to be feeling: *I missed you...I was worried...I didn't want you to go...I get lonely.*

He pressed his hands to his face. What else had she said? She didn't appear to be grieving about not being with Alec, and combined with Alec's own insistence that there was nothing between them, that weight had finally floated free from Elliot's shoulders. Could he dare to believe that Xo might be open to something else, with him? She had come to see him; she cared that he had gone away and returned. That might not justify this surge of hope, but there it was.

Except what if he was wrong? It was easy enough to see why she'd been interested in Alec. The words she had first used to describe him now sprang to Elliot's mind. In contrast, Elliot could not recall ever having attracted anyone's interest himself, except for Lia, those many years ago. It had never been clear what Lia saw in him, though, and he would not have realized she was interested at all if she had not spelled it out, so that was not helpful in the present situation.

Could Xo have meant something more in telling him how she felt lonely and missed him? He would never say such things casually. He ought to tell her how he felt, in the kind of sweet words Lia had always wanted him to use. Lia had been forced to endure his inability to explain his feelings to her, and that still pained him. Of course he had told Lia he loved her, and other clumsy things, but she had wanted more. He had known it at the time yet had been unable to deliver.

The words he did manage were oddly-sized boxes that did not properly contain what he meant to put in them. If he were to present them to Xo, would she not reject such an ill-packaged gift? In doing so he could lose the friendship she gave him now.

Elliot's mind shifted back and forth throughout the day. As the time approached for Xo to finish work, his feet, more sure of a path, found their way down the slippery, snowy sidewalk in the direction of the coffee house.

A sledder careening off the curb of the sidewalk at high speed abruptly tore Elliot's thoughts away from Xo. The snow had deepened over the past days, and on this particularly steep section of the road, young people were taking advantage of it on sleds. There was no traffic here: the slope of the hill already encouraged drivers to find another route in this weather.

His heart rate still elevated after the close encounter, Elliot started downhill again. Before the next intersection, he encountered a barricade blocking cars from turning up the hill, but it was only a sawhorse with red and white stripes and reflectors along the top—nothing to prevent sledders from overshooting the intersection, and the sledders were not using much care. The teenage girl who had narrowly missed Elliot had continued past the barrier for another block, although the sledders' usual aim seemed to be either to crash into the barricade or to turn just before it and collide with pedestrians or parked cars. Luckily, most of the sleds upset earlier.

Elliot glanced back over his shoulder in case of further surprise encounters, as his mind sought to return to Xo. Now a low, plastic, boat-shaped sled occupied by a small child lying on its stomach came zipping down the hill. Elliot registered this at the same time as a large beige vehicle lumbered into the intersection just ahead, barely pausing at the stop sign. It was moving slowly, but the driver, doubtless not expecting traffic from the barricaded road, was not looking up the hill.

Elliot started into the street. "Look out!" he shouted, to no effect on either party.

The sled shot directly between the legs of the barricade. Elliot was not going to be in time to block it. With a running jump, he launched himself in its general direction, and his shoulder hit the back of the sled with a resounding crack as it went past, causing Elliot, the sled, and its rider to spin around. The sled flipped, dumping its occupant. Elliot's trajectory over the polished snow continued several feet farther until his back slammed into the side of the vehicle's wheel and rebounded a few inches.

It was a few moments before Elliot regained his bearings. He had come to a halt. Miraculously, his glasses were still on, though specked with snow. He withdrew his arms from the protective position they had assumed around his head and peered upwards at the vehicle in whose shadow he lay. The driver had paused and was looking out the window at him. Apparently satisfied that he was alive, the head withdrew and the car slowly pulled away.

This was how a hockey puck must feel. Dazed, Elliot crawled over to the upside-down sled. The little boy who had been riding it pushed himself upright. He looked about four years old. There was silence as he caught his breath and looked around, then he let out an earsplitting wail.

"There, there!" Horrified, Elliot reached out to pat the child's shoulder, but the boy twisted away out of his reach and got to his feet, still wailing. Fortunately, he did not appear to be injured, despite the unnaturally loud noise emanating from him.

The boy grabbed the string of the sled in his mitten and walked towards a nearby house, tugging the sled behind him, the pitiful cry continuing unabated. The plastic sled had a large crack in it, no doubt courtesy of Elliot's shoulder. Just as well that it was not of more solid construction, he already felt like he'd been hit by a train.

When the boy was halfway across the yard, a woman opened the door, presumably the boy's mother. The child buried his face in her knees, continuing to sob as she bent over him. His mother took the sled and leaned it against the wall beside the front door, giving Elliot a dirty look. Perhaps the child had pointed him out as the breaker of the sled. Which was true. The door closed, and the sounds of sobbing faded away.

Before Elliot had time to ponder further, another sled, this time again operated by a teenager, whizzed towards him. The driver expertly flipped it at the barricade, spilling himself onto the snow.

"Woo hoo!" he shouted, grinning at Elliot, who was still on his hands and knees in the middle of the road.

Elliot stared at him. "You should really block off this whole road if you're going to sled here," said Elliot, sounding like he had ice in his throat. Maybe he did. "So no one slides into the intersection."

The sledder's eyes widened. "That's a good idea! HEY!" He shouted at somebody else in a yard up the street.

By the time Elliot managed to stagger back to the sidewalk, several enthusiastic sledders were rolling car tires down the hill from a nearby yard. One of the tires escaped, to excited shouts, but it did not go far before stranding itself against a parked car. The owners of the tires assembled a dam across the road, before the barricade. It was not impenetrable, but it might help.

A quiet voice caught Elliot's attention and he turned around. An onlooker who had halted on the sidewalk behind him was whispering to her companion, "Did you see...?"

Elliot's skin prickled uncomfortably, and he quickly continued down the sidewalk, brushing the snow out of his hair. His mind was still spinning around in circles on the road. How thin, this line between life and death that these children toyed with. Yet Elliot should know better than they how easy it would be, in a mere moment, to lose the chance to ever let Xo know how he felt. He'd had people he loved snatched away from him before, but at least they'd gone knowing they were loved, without words left unsaid.

Images swam in disarray in his mind: the crying child, the door closing as his mother took him inside. An acute ache arose within him, unrelated to his physical bruises, but at the same time his head cleared. The question of whether or not Xo would reject him was unimportant. He had to tell her how he felt, with whatever words he could find. It was as clear-cut as the moment when he'd turned to run into the street—there was no further thought required in either case, no real decision, it was just that any other course of action was instantly ruled out, impossible even to consider.

Elliot scanned the counter as he pushed open the door of the coffee house. Xo wasn't on duty anymore, and a quick check of the clock told him he'd missed the end of her shift by a few minutes. Without pausing he walked to the stairs and ran up them two at a time. On the landing he caught his breath and knocked at the door. He had no idea what he was going to say, but the recent rush of adrenaline had heightened all his senses and prepared him for any action. At this moment, he could speak without thinking.

The rapid heartbeat in his ears gradually slowed, but there was still no sound from within the apartment. Elliot bit his lip and knocked again. Silence. Glancing down, he saw there was no light shining from under her door. She must have gone out directly after her shift. Slowly, he lowered his arm.

No, this was good. This was fine. He could sort out what he would say, now.

He turned back to descend the staircase, a bit dazed and dizzy-feeling, but with a smile on his face and a firm resolution within. Tomorrow, then. Now that he was certain of his course, one day couldn't make that much difference.

24

XO'S NIGHT OUT

Xo was back at her apartment and ready by nine that evening. She'd gone shopping after work and purchased a new top that was both velvety and sparkly, a rare combination. She touched up her mascara and adjusted the shirt, stroking the fabric. It might not be what Megan had in mind, but it was comfortably cozy.

A knock came at the door.

"Are you decent?" It was Megan.

"I think so?" said Xo.

Megan let herself in, looking glamorous. Her dark hair was extra curly and shiny, and she was wearing more jewelry and makeup than usual, along with a stretchy navy-blue dress with a miniature design all over it.

"Aren't you gonna get cold in that? There's snow on the ground," said Xo. The dress was quite short and seemed to barely contain Megan, which was probably the desired effect.

"You sound like my grandmother. It'll be warm in the restaurant, and I've got a coat." Megan studied Xo critically. She sighed and tugged at Xo's clothes.

Xo petted her sleeve back into place. "Doesn't it feel soft?"

Megan pursed her lips doubtfully. "Here, this should work on you." She handed Xo a tube of lipstick from her bag.

Xo took it reluctantly and removed the cap. It had already been opened, though it wasn't the color Megan was currently wearing. "Is it really hygienic to share these?"

Megan made an exasperated sound.

Xo went into the bathroom and leaned into the mirror. She gingerly touched the side of the orangey-red stick with the tip of her finger and dabbed it in the middle of her lips, rubbed them together to spread it around, and then capped the tube and returned it to Megan.

"Come on, the others are waiting outside," said Megan.

They left through the side door at the bottom of the stairs that Xo used when the coffee shop was not open, joining Megan's clique on the sidewalk. Xo was sure Megan's legs must be freezing as they walked over to the restaurant.

Other friends of Megan had already arrived, claimed a table, and gotten garlic bread which no one was eating. Xo helped herself to it and ordered a cup of tea to warm her hands. She was easily the oldest woman in the group. Megan couldn't be more than five or six years younger than Xo, but some of Megan's friends were younger still, pretty and petite enough to fit anywhere they wanted to. Those at the table rotated constantly as they got up to greet others elsewhere in the restaurant, while new people that everyone else was acquainted with sat down. All talked at once, their speech peppered with current catchphrases that Xo mostly understood but couldn't imagine herself using. There was no continuing thread of conversation beyond two or three related verbal exchanges, so the words must simply be contact calls to keep in touch and identify each other as members of the group.

"Quite the crowd tonight, huh?" said Megan. "We should get this band to play at the coffee house, drum up some more business."

"Sure, maybe," said Xo. The music was drowned out by the sea of conversation that swirled around her. It had been a long time since she'd willingly put herself in such an uncomfortable situation. It wasn't the number of people—it was that they all seemed to be one flock and she was not of a feather. Still, she must be a closely-related species, since interbreeding was theoretically possible if the mating rituals were mastered.

During a lull, Megan elbowed her. "See any cute guys you like?"

There were plenty of folks sitting around listening to music, but no one stood out. So many people, looking generic until one got to know them. Should she pick at random? Was that what Alec did? How did one choose someone for a casual relationship, without worrying about the outcome?

"Just don't hit on any of our regular customers," Megan added. "Awkward."

"Which ones are our regular customers?" Xo scanned the room again. She hadn't realized she knew anyone else here, besides a few other baristas from Megan's group.

Megan discreetly pointed out some individuals. "You know Jacqua's son over there, for instance."

"Jacqua has a son?"

"He has a whole family," said Megan. "You've got to start asking about people's connections."

"That seems invasive," said Xo. "Anyway, people look different when they're ordering coffee," she added in a low voice. She would probably recognize them in the café.

Jacqua's son waved at them.

"Now I gotta go talk to him," said Megan. "Just pick somebody, and start talking, Xo! And not about birds. You better not still be sitting here when I get back." She melted away into the crowd.

There was no reason to say anything bird-related at the moment, nor did Xo need to be told. She stood reluctantly and surveyed the room. There were several guys sitting at the counter, apparently alone; one of them was glancing over a newspaper. Reading was a good sign. Xo made her way over. Though she couldn't judge with full accuracy while he was seated, he seemed tall, about Alec's height but bulkier, with pale cropped hair and a ruddy complexion. She wasn't sure if he would be considered "cute" according to Megan, but he looked approximately in the right age range. No wedding ring. Maybe a list of what to look for wasn't so hard after all.

He appeared to notice Xo standing there, and smiled pleasantly. Xo made her way over and sat on the stool next to his.

"Well, here we are. Listening to the music," said Xo. Great, now she was channeling Alec's annoying habit of stating the obvious. On the other hand, it must work for him. She rocked back and forth slightly to the beat. It was easier to hear now that she wasn't trapped in the conversational whirlpool at Megan's table.

He looked amused. "Can I get you a drink?"

"Oh, I have one." She clutched her teacup in her lap.

He indicated the band. "Not bad."

"They're okay." The band's name was Featherduster, and there was a picture of a crow on their poster with feathers drifting around it. It should be an ostrich, or a turkey. Feather dusters were not made from crow feathers. Xo concentrated on not mentioning this, per Megan's instructions. If he brought up the name first, it would be all right, though. She hoped he would. Aside from that, the music was pretty good.

"Have you heard them before?" Xo asked.

"No, they're local, right? I'm just in town for a little while, visiting some old friends," he said. "How about you?"

"Oh! I live here. I mean, not here, in the restaurant. Nearby. I work at a coffee shop. Nearby." Xo laughed nervously. If he was only in town briefly, this was a perfect opportunity. No lasting damage if she screwed up, which was already looking likely.

"A barista! That's very impressive."

"Not really," said Xo. "It's just a day job."

"Oh?" He leaned one elbow on the counter as he faced Xo. "So, what do you do on these cold nights?"

"Draw?" Technically, she didn't do this at night most of the time, but sleeping or reading didn't sound very interesting. The inaccuracy made her uncomfortable, though.

"Ah, an artist. Even more impressive!" He smiled.

Xo smiled back, wondering if his smile was as mechanical as hers felt right now. All these layers of polite interaction seemed ultimately self-defeating, because didn't people go through these routines with the goal of finding someone with whom they could drop the routines and just be themselves? Or was that just her? But it wasn't as if she made connections without them. That was called Not Making An Effort.

The man continued, "Do you ever tackle the male form? I could model for you."

Xo stared at him. "I mostly do birds." There had been no alternative this time. Luckily, Megan was lost in the crowd somewhere, presumably out of hearing distance.

"That's too bad. Let me know if you change your mind." He sipped his drink.

Wait, it was possible he had just been joking about being a model. This was the "flirting for fun" thing! She could handle that sort of talk, as long as she didn't actually have to draw him.

"Maybe I will. Let you know," Xo said in what she hoped was a casual tone.

His attention returned to her, and he smiled again. "Do you want to get out of here?" he asked abruptly. "I could do with some fresh air."

It was pretty stuffy in the restaurant. "Okay, I guess."

He stood and offered her his arm. There was nothing else to do but take it, but it was a relief to have to let go again as they filed through the crowded room. She still didn't see Megan, and she'd had to leave her partially-consumed tea at the bar.

"Ah, this is better," he said, once they were outside. "Look at all the stars!"

It was starry, but it was hard to appreciate them with him standing there. Xo unfolded the coat she'd been carrying and put it on, and they walked along the snowy sidewalk, where quite a few other people also loitered. Cigarette smoke hung low in the chilly air. They crossed the street to escape the cloud, and she put her hands into the opposite sleeves of her coat to warm them up.

"Cold?"

"Just a little," said Xo. He draped an arm across her back.

They passed in front of a lighted lobby, and he paused, pulling open the glass door with his other hand. "It's warm in here."

Xo hesitated for a split second, then allowed him to guide her inside. He was being considerate; the temperature had definitely dropped. The snow on the street they had just crossed had frozen into a slick, polished surface.

The lobby turned out to belong to a hotel, and the concierge gave Xo a little wave and a smile. "Hi, Xo!"

"Oh, hey." The woman must be a customer of the coffee shop, as Xo had no idea who she was, and had never been inside this building before. It looked better from the outside, in the daylight. Not that there was anything specifically bad about the lobby: it was clean and smelled of cloves.

The warm air was making her overheated in her coat. She moved back towards the door. The arm released her shoulders obligingly to push the door open for her, and a blast of cold air blew in.

"You're pretty cold still," he said. "Want to come upstairs and warm up?"

"Upstairs?"

"I have a room here." He smiled, releasing the door to gesture upwards. As the door swung shut, the hand came to rest on her back again.

Xo glanced up at the ceiling of the lobby, then quickly away. She shouldn't be surprised. He was visiting Lingen, and would need a place to stay. It made sense. Somewhere behind the million alarms that were going off in her mind, it made sense. The scented air was suffocating, and it confused her thoughts as it wafted around, fading and then unexpectedly making her notice it again. How had she ended up in this situation? It seemed considerably less fun than it was supposed to be. Was she doing what she wanted to, or being incredibly stupid, or both?

Xo stalled for time. "Maybe later?"

He bobbed his head agreeably. "Your friend called you Xo—is that short for Zoey?"

"No, it's really Xiomara." As the concierge was possibly listening in the background, it was best not to point out that they were not actually friends. She was moving behind the desk in a bustling sort of way, as if she might soon leave the room, and Xo felt a sudden desire to keep her around. Maybe she could get her to stay if she inquired about the spice smell in the lobby. But the guy was still talking.

"That's a pretty name," he said. "What does it mean?"

Xo launched into her usual explanation, momentarily relieved by the familiar topic. "She was a historical figure. A Roman soldier raped her, so she had his head cut off and gave it to her husband. She said she preferred that only one man who'd had sex with her should remain alive."

There was a prolonged silence. "That's an…interesting story."

"Oh?" said Xo. "There's more to it, if you're interested. You see—"

"Actually, that's okay," he interrupted, coughing a bit. "You mentioned you work at a coffee shop near here, right?"

"I think it's the only coffee shop."

He chuckled. "I forget how small Lingen is. I bet everyone in town comes through your shop."

"It's not mine. I just work there."

"A lot of my old friends probably buy coffee from you. Say, you ever see a guy named Elliot in your shop? Short, blond. He was a photographer."

Xo shrugged out from under his arm abruptly, turning to face him. "What!? *You* know Elliot, too?"

"So he's still around? Thought maybe he'd moved."

"This is unbelievable! Unbelievable!" Xo crossed her arms and stared at him accusingly. "Yes, he's…around. Just…not recently. But yeah, he comes into the coffee shop quite often. Or he used to." She turned away, frowning.

When she looked back, the man was smiling down at her appreciatively, which was not what she had been expecting after her outburst. "I do love a passionate response."

Xo eyed him stonily, her insides curling as if she'd swallowed something bitter. Of all the random people she could have picked, it had to be another friend of Elliot, just like Alec. All at once, she felt disgusted with the evening, and with herself.

"Look, I have to get back. The people I came with will wonder where I am," she said coldly.

"Sorry to hear that. I was hoping we could get to know each other better."

Xo pushed out through the lobby door and walked briskly across the slippery street towards the restaurant, almost falling in the process.

"It was nice meeting you!" he called after her.

She forced her way back into the claustrophobic restaurant. What a ridiculous evening. Had she really considered going up to his room? Why was she even here? It was now completely clear what she wanted: the comfort of her own empty, quiet apartment. She searched for Megan in the crowded room, which stank of too many people out too late. The new top she was wearing was no longer comfortable; the tag she had neglected to remove was poking her in the side below her bra. Between that, and the noise, and the smell, and that guy, she was so jumpy she wanted to crawl out of her own skin.

Finally, she found Megan deep in a cluster of friends. Xo touched her shoulder and Megan turned to her brightly.

"I'm gonna head home."

"So soon?" Megan looked surprised, searching Xo's face for the reason.

"I'm tired. It's late for me."

"Do you want some of us to walk back with you?" asked Megan.

"Nah, it's okay." No point spoiling their evenings. Plus, she didn't feel like keeping up a chirpy countenance, which would be necessary around Megan's friends. "See you later."

Leaving hurriedly, Xo glanced up and down the street between the restaurant and the coffee shop. Luckily, nobody was hanging around the sidewalk on this side of the restaurant. The night was a mix of bright lights, icy snow, and shadows. She skidded across to the coffee shop and let herself in the side door, which locked automatically behind her.

Inside was velvety dark and quiet and warm, smelling comfortingly of espresso, but she couldn't stop to enjoy it or even stand still for a moment, she was too tense. She ran quickly up the stairs to her studio and locked the second door behind her, squirmed out of her clothes and rolled up tight in the heavy quilt on her bed. The twitchy feeling left her skin gradually as she wedged her back against the crack where the bed met the wall, counting breaths to slow her racing heart. A momentary delusion of normalcy had made her agree to this outing with Megan, that was all. It was a huge mistake, but it was all over now, and nobody had to know about it but her. No lasting harm.

She fell asleep as the rain began.

25

ELLIOT'S CONFESSION

Elliot's stomach clenched in nervous anticipation of what he was going to say. This time he had arrived at the coffee house well before Xo's shift ended, and it was a good thing: though there were minutes to go, Xo was already tidying the area for the next barista, who was tying on an apron.

"Oh! Elliot!" Xo smiled at him. "Can I make you something?"

Her expression reaffirmed his purpose and filled him with warmth. He gladly reflected her smile. "I was merely hoping to talk to you, when you're finished with your work."

"What's one more cup?" Xo was already heating the milk on the espresso machine. "I don't mind."

"I would be delighted, then, thank you." He did not need any, but he couldn't say no, and it gave him more time to prepare himself.

Xo handed him the cup and hung her apron in the kitchen. "Did you come by to go over the photos and notes, and see those paintings I'm working on?"

"I would indeed love to, but…" Elliot cleared his throat. "Would you like to accompany me for a walk first, while it's still light?"

"Sure, it would be nice to get outside. Let me get my coat." Xo paused on the way upstairs. "You said you wanted to talk. Does it have anything to do with an old friend who was looking for you the other day?"

"No…" said Elliot.

"Whew. Okay. Never mind then. I'll go get changed." She ran the rest of the way up the stairs.

Now was not the time to puzzle out the reference, so he let it blow right back out of his mind to make way for the much more important words he was soon to lay at her feet, in some order as yet undetermined. It had seemed more straightforward yesterday in his moment of clarity, when she was not in front of him, but while her presence flustered him, it also strengthened his resolve.

As Xo did not immediately return, Elliot sat on the hearth, sipping at the coffee. It was difficult to sit still, but his hands were starting to shake and he was afraid he would spill it if he remained standing. When Xo reappeared he sprang up, abandoning the cup, and they went outside together.

The snow had mostly melted in rain that had come in the night, but the ground was semi-frozen on the path overlooking the town. As they ascended the trail, they left Lingen below wreathed in wispy fog. Xo chatted happily while Elliot arranged his thoughts.

Presently, he said, "There's a part in *Precipice and Precipitation* that's been on my mind." This was when the protagonist realized his true feelings, a moving scene and pivotal turning point in the novel.

"Oh, don't tell me!" said Xo quickly. "I still haven't finished it. I was going to last night, but then I went—well, I got sidetracked. No spoilers!" She laughed and covered her ears. Elliot lapsed into silence again, figuring out a new tack to try.

At a high point in the trail, Xo sat to rest on a broad boulder next to the path, gazing over the valley. The town was now completely hidden by a layer of clouds that stretched out below them, encircling Arin and filling the passes up to the mountainous horizon beyond.

Xo sighed rapturously. "It's like we're on an island surrounded by a sea of clouds."

The top of the sea of clouds was rumpled by slowly billowing cloud waves, moving almost imperceptibly. They appeared still unless Elliot glanced away and then back again to detect their movement.

Elliot sat down beside Xo on the boulder. This was it. It had to be here and now. If this really were an island separated from all the rest of the world, and Xo were stranded on it with just one other person, would she want it to be him? He couldn't bring himself to ask it aloud. Instead, he joined her in gazing out over the cloud bank, lit in constantly changing colors by the sinking sun, and tried to think of something more to the point. Fortunately, Xo didn't seem to be in any hurry.

"Xiomara—" Elliot turned towards her. By starting, he had ensured that he had to continue. He tentatively reached out and took one of her hands, then the other. She did not resist, looking at him with wide eyes.

"Do you remember when you said, it isn't my problem if you get hurt, it's not my business?" He swallowed hard. "I want it to be my business. I want to have the right to protect you, to worry about you. To take care of you. To love you. I want to marry you. I don't know when I started loving you, but it is never going to end. I don't want to go through another day without you, another night…" He stopped at the look in her eyes, afraid he'd gone too far. One word had tangled with the next, drawing them out in a jumble that one should not dump on another person all at once—he knew that, but his mouth only seemed to know all or nothing. He hadn't planned it that way, but it was the truth, and now it was out.

Xo stared at him. She seemed stunned.

"Oh, Elliot…" It wasn't a particularly happy sounding exclamation.

Elliot waited desperately.

"You don't know what I'm really like," Xo said finally, shaking her head. "I just—I can't…You love me?" Her face was incredulous.

"I do. I do!" said Elliot fervently.

"Oh, Elliot," she said again, taking her hands away. She folded her arms on her knees and laid her head on them, breaking away from his gaze.

He slid off the boulder and knelt before her on the rocky ground. If only she would look at him again.

"Xiomara, please give me a chance. You don't know how much I love you. I adore you."

"Why did you have to say this *now*?" Xo looked up bleakly.

"I've tried to show you I care, but…I suppose I didn't do it very well, so…I had to tell you. I meant to do it better. I would do anything for you."

Xo looked away again. "I—I'm not ready for this. I can't. I'm sorry, I know I'm being awful to you." She closed her eyes and rubbed her palms against her knees.

"No, you are not." Elliot's eyes stung with tears that he willed not to fall.

"How can you—" Xo sat up suddenly, grabbing his arm. "Don't go away and leave again, promise. You're very dear to me, Elliot. Understand? I don't want to lose you. As a friend."

"I will be whatever you want." Elliot choked on the words.

"Promise you won't leave?" she insisted.

He nodded mutely.

Xo got to her feet, twisting her hands together. "I'm so sorry, I can't think right now. I have to go. We'll see each other again, okay?"

Elliot watched her numbly. He didn't ask why she'd said no. There were too many potential reasons.

"Let's go back." Xo turned and walked a few steps.

He couldn't move. The rocks he was kneeling on were poking into his shins and knees painfully. If he could allow that feeling to spread to the rest of his body, perhaps it would override the other pain.

Xo returned and tugged on his arm until he stood up and followed her.

They cut back down the hill. The sun was behind the cloud bank now, and Elliot welcomed the concealing dusk. With each step he felt his knees might buckle, but somehow, he reached the street along with Xo.

She stopped outside the coffee house. "Just…give me some time, okay?"

He nodded once. She turned and went into the building.

Elliot turned in the other direction, blindly, and started walking.

"Hey, Elly!" A voice called out behind him. Not now. A few more blocks and he would have been home.

Alec caught up and walked cheerfully beside Elliot. "I've been looking for you!"

Elliot kept his eyes on the sidewalk and didn't answer. His voice might betray him.

"Did you hear about the sledding incident yesterday on this very street?" Alec was grinning.

Elliot moved his eyes to Alec for a few seconds, then back to the direction he was walking. "No."

Alec laughed. "Come on, I know it was you. I've already interviewed the witnesses. Let's do a short article about it for the paper."

"No." He just had to keep going. He would be home soon.

"We desperately need some 'feel-good' pieces," said Alec. "There's been a whole rash of car crashes from that bit of snow we had, with all the tourists up here for the winter, and it's nothing but bad news."

Elliot tried to keep his voice level. "I do not want to do a feel-good piece."

"Come on," pleaded Alec. "It would cheer things up."

Cheer was the furthest thing from Elliot's mind. Why wouldn't Alec go away? With every step, it was getting harder and harder to keep the pain inside.

"Give me a few quotes, that's all."

"No!" Anger edged into Elliot's voice, and he choked it back again. The anger gave slight relief to the pain, but it was like opening a floodgate. The rest would push out if he didn't rein it back in, and he wasn't sure he could turn all of it into anger instead of grief. Regrettably, he had broken down in front of Alec before, but that didn't change the fact that sobbing in front of him was not acceptable. Alec himself would never be so affected—he was sure to be horrified and repulsed by such a reaction, no matter what the reason.

Unfortunately, dealing with angry people who didn't want to speak to a reporter was familiar territory to Alec. He seemed momentarily surprised to see it coming from Elliot, but quickly rebounded.

"Is it too personal? Look, I get it, but listen: in a town like this, everything's personal, and nothing's personal. It adds a bit of human interest, you know that!"

Elliot swallowed down the lump in his throat with difficulty. "No comment."

"What's going on with you? Why can't I write it?" asked Alec.

"No," said Elliot.

"Can't you say anything but 'No?'"

"No."

Alec continued to match Elliot's pace, glancing over at him. "Bad day?" he said after a while.

Elliot couldn't very well say "No" to that. He focused on the sidewalk ahead. It seemed inconceivable that he was still moving, that his feet kept working on their own.

"Okay," said Alec at last. "I guess I'll see you around, man."

Despite his extreme desire not to talk to anyone right now, Elliot couldn't completely blow him off. "Yes," he said. It came out strangely.

Alec gave him a half-smile and wave, and turned off in another direction. Elliot sagged in relief. Somehow, he had made it home. Out of the corner of his eye, he saw that for once Mrs. Dupesh was not out on her porch to intercept him, and he breathed a prayer of gratitude.

Elliot pushed open the door, peeling off his coat. Leaving the lights off, he found his way to the shower and stood under the torrent until the hot water ran cold and he felt he had washed out every tear he was capable of producing. His entire body ached, whether from slamming into the car wheel the day before or the emotional blow he had received today, he could not be sure. Crawling into bed, he found that he had not yet exhausted the supply of tears after all, but they brought no relief.

26

Xo's Reaction

Xo entered the coffee house in a daze and stumbled up to her studio, continuously replaying fragments of what had just happened and then retreating from the emotions that welled up as a result. To find order in the chaos, she reviewed past interactions with Elliot. She couldn't have been this oblivious. She could tell when a guy was interested. Right? There were signs, like random touching, or suggestive comments, such as Alec did. Of course, she'd been wrong about Alec…so were those the right signs, or were they the signs of someone who didn't truly care about her? Elliot didn't act that way at all.

After standing in the middle of her apartment for some time, she realized it was well past dinner. She took off her boots and opened the refrigerator. Deep down, a tiny part of her acknowledged that she had known for some time that Elliot cared about her. A lot. He'd even said so, she'd just sort of brushed it off. Maybe he cared in a different way from all the guys she had known before, and that was why he acted differently. Though he did touch her…sometimes. His hands were different from other people's then, too; he didn't seem to be taking something away from her. It was more like an electric current recharging her, one that was hard to break away from.

The refrigerator door beeped, startlingly: a warning that she had been standing there too long letting out the cold air. Xo opened the freezer compartment. It contained a few frozen burritos and the dead pigeon. She closed the freezer again and considered the choices in the refrigerator.

What would Elliot have done if she'd ended up with Alec—never said anything at all? She felt sick remembering how hurt Elliot had looked. He'd be even more hurt if he knew that while he was lovingly thinking of her, she was considering flings with random people—no, even worse, a *friend* of his—at that restaurant instead of thinking about him. She prayed he never, ever found out about that. Clearly she wasn't the kind of person Elliot was, or the kind he thought she was. He hadn't just started by saying he liked her, but that he wanted to *marry* her. Though maybe he was trying to show her that he was serious, different from these other relationships he had apparently been trying to protect her from. And she'd panicked…just like she panicked last night with that guy from the restaurant, at a decidedly different suggestion.

She had no idea what she wanted anymore, there was too much whirling around in her mind to tell. Every memory of Elliot had now taken on a new meaning, a layer she'd been unaware of before.

The refrigerator beeped again. She was still holding it open, staring into it blankly. Food at least should be a decision she could manage, and it would help her think. She scanned the shelves, mostly leftovers from downstairs: day-old pastries and lunch foods, which Jacqua doled out generously enough. The workers on the closing shifts tended to get the savory items, but that was okay. A piece of pumpkin pie was a balanced dinner: vegetable, egg, crust.

Xo sat on the edge of her bed and warmed each spoonful of pie slowly in her mouth. Married to Elliot…what would that even look like? It was easy to imagine Elliot here in her studio, as he'd been here before in real life. She pictured him kneeling beside the bed, as he had done while she sat on the boulder earlier, telling her how much he loved her. A piece of crust that was still jagged went down her throat in a giant lump. It was too much. He was so earnest. She couldn't help but believe every word he had said, but why? Why did he feel that way about her? It seemed like she must be deceiving him in some way for him to want to be with her that much. She had given him nothing at all.

It was much later, and still without answers, that Xo finally put the dish on her nightstand and managed to find sleep.

❖   ❖   ❖

The next day, Xo was considerably quieter and more distracted than usual during the shared part of her shift with Megan.

"What's the matter, Xo?" asked Megan, as the lunch rush began to taper off. She lowered her voice. "Did something go wrong at the restaurant the other day?"

"What? Oh…no. Well, not exactly."

"You left in a hurry," Megan pointed out.

All Xo could see in her head was Elliot. She forced her mind back to remember the night with Megan, even though that made her want to disappear. "There was a guy there…I know this won't make any sense, but I felt gross. Not that he did anything in particular."

Megan shrugged. "Sometimes you have to go with your gut."

Xo looked at her in surprise. "Really? I mean, I didn't have a good reason to ditch him." Unless knowing the wrong person was a good reason, but more likely it was just an excuse she'd come up with.

"There doesn't have to be a reason," said Megan.

"If there's no reason, how do you know it's a good decision?"

"Well, do you regret not going with him?"

Xo shivered. "Not at all."

"There you go, then," said Megan. "So, what's eating you?"

"Not that guy." Xo picked at a speck on the counter. "It's Elliot," she said finally.

"What about him?"

Xo darted a glance at Megan. "He told me he wanted to marry me."

"What!?" Megan laughed loudly. "You've got to be kidding me. Elliot? Wow."

"What's so funny?" said Xo. "I'm serious."

Megan chuckled. "I noticed he had a thing for you, but I didn't expect that."

"A thing?" said Xo blankly.

"I've seen the way he looks at you." Megan poked her in the ribs.

"I didn't realize he felt that way," said Xo. "Why didn't you say anything?"

"I figured you knew! Don't think I haven't seen you looking at him, too."

"Well, I mean…of course, I like him. But, we're friends," said Xo. "I thought you said it should be obvious, or it isn't worth wasting time on."

Megan stared at her for a moment, grinning. "Maybe some things are more obvious to the people who aren't involved."

So Megan could tell. And Xo could tell, maybe, a little, she had to admit. But this was more than just knowing he liked her.

"I don't think I would have been…as shocked, if he hadn't also said he wanted to marry me." She bit her lip. And if she hadn't just had a near miss with some random guy, which thankfully Elliot didn't know about.

If only she'd never agreed to go out with Megan. It had been all she could think of while Elliot was declaring his love: how he would be thinking of her quite differently if he knew what she'd been up to. Why couldn't he have told her *before* that he loved her, like when she went to visit him? She still would have been shocked, but the evening might have ended much better, and that thought made her intensely sad. How could she make things okay between them again, when she still didn't even know how to answer him? It was so far out of the realm of anything she had dealt with before.

Megan was watching her closely, no longer laughing. "You didn't say yes when he proposed, did you?"

"I didn't," said Xo slowly. "I didn't know what to say. I mean, he didn't exactly propose, he just told me how he felt. Does that qualify? I think…I know I hurt his feelings." Her insides twisted uncomfortably.

She couldn't remember her response or if it had made any sense, but she could clearly remember Elliot's reaction and what he had said. She'd replayed it in her mind constantly.

"Well, no doubt, but you couldn't exactly say yes! My goodness." Megan shook her head, back to laughing.

"He's a perfectly nice person," countered Xo. "He's done so much for me. I think he really cares about me, maybe that's why he has. Well, I know he does, he said as much." It didn't feel right to tell Megan exactly what he had said, though.

"He's kind of...I dunno, odd." Megan shrugged. "But then..." She gave Xo an evaluative look.

"What? I'm odd too?" It wouldn't be the unkindest description Xo had been given.

"Well, anyway, you don't marry someone just for helping you out."

"He's not odd. I think he's sweet," said Xo. "And I do...care for him. I dunno if I'm ready for something like that, though. I mean, how do you know?"

"Are you ready to give up wearing heels?" Megan grinned.

"I don't wear heels." Xo frowned as Megan's words sunk in. "And what's that got to do with anything, anyway? I could wear them if I wanted to."

"Can you picture being married to him, though? You'd have to sleep with him, can you imagine?" Megan giggled.

Ever since last night, Xo had been having trouble getting herself to stop imagining it. Her face grew hot.

Megan eyed her. "Listen, I know you're having some kind of mid-life crisis about not being in a relationship, but that doesn't mean you have to accept the first guy who asks. Being a good friend doesn't mean he's marriage material. I like my friends, but I wouldn't marry them! Though I can think of several who would go for it in a heartbeat."

The number of Megan's friends who were willing to marry her was highly debatable, but Xo didn't want to delve into that, they were getting sidetracked. "I just didn't think of him like that before. I'm not used to things developing that way."

Megan wrinkled her nose. "Are you even attracted to him?"

Xo pictured Elliot looking at her adoringly, taking her hand. There were many times he had looked at her that way, but she hadn't known what it meant. She felt an unusual twinge inside. And there had been that time he held her, on the hike. She had felt it then, too, along with worry and guilt about Alec. How stupid when Alec didn't care anyway. If she'd done something then…she wasn't exactly sure what, but being in Elliot's arms had felt so good.

"He has something about him," said Xo.

"I guess he's not my type," said Megan. "I suppose he could improve some if he shaved the mutton chops. Might make the scars on his face more obvious, though, so maybe not." Megan glanced at Xo. "Do you know what they're from? Did he have really bad acne or something?"

"Umm, I haven't asked." It had not occurred to Xo until that moment that he might keep his sideburns long in order to cover up some of the scars. The hair there was almost as long as on the rest of his head, wavy and fair. It would be soft to the touch…

"Anyway," continued Megan. "You could do better, Xo, you're way out of his league. Especially if you cleaned yourself up a bit." Megan peered at her face. "You could try waxing—I would totally have a mustache if I didn't do it. You're almost working on sideburns yourself with that peach fuzz."

Xo turned away in irritation to line up cups on the counter, jabbing them into their row more vigorously than necessary. The conversation certainly didn't need to include her body hair. Bringing up Elliot had been a bad idea, and she still had no clue what to say to him. At least Megan's shift would be over soon and Xo could spend the weekend alone to get her head in order and figure out what to do. If the weather was clear, she would go out and sketch somewhere that she wouldn't run into anybody, especially Elliot. She needed time to herself to think.

Megan shrugged. "Or give him a try. Whatever floats your boat, I guess. You don't need to settle down for life at this point. Keep it casual, that's what you were looking for the other day."

That didn't feel right either, when Elliot had basically told her he was all in, and she'd decided she might not be cut out for one-night stands.

"I don't think that's what I want anymore," said Xo. "And I don't think it's what he wants either. Plus, what if it didn't work out?" The idea of losing Elliot's friendship was like a punch to her stomach, on top of how bad she already felt about how she'd left him when they parted.

"If it doesn't work out and you're just together casually, trying things out, it won't be as big a deal," said Megan lightly. "It'd be a lot harder if you got married and then things went south, then you'd both really care about the outcome."

Xo stared dispiritedly at the line of coffee cups she had made, which gave her no answers. What if she and Elliot already really cared about the outcome?

27

ELLIOT'S REACTION

Elliot searched Xo's face for the unspoken answer, holding his breath. She gave him a half-smile, as if daring him to read her mind, but he did not dare. Supposing he had been wrong…

"Yes!" she squealed gleefully, clasping his hands in hers and shining her radiant smile upon him. It was almost blinding, like the sun that was filling all the space behind her.

Elliot's stomach somersaulted against his heart. "Xiomara, you have made me so happy. You will not regret it. You may rely on me. I shall treasure this moment, and you, forever." He had hoped, but hardly dared believe that she would accept him. His elation now threatened to overwhelm him entirely.

"Shush!" Xo placed her finger against his lips. Elliot nearly fainted at the contact. His glasses were slipping down, but he didn't want to adjust them with her in such close proximity.

Suddenly, Xo threw herself, along with the incredibly voluminous dress that she was wearing for some bizarre reason, into his arms, an impetuous movement for which he was wholly unprepared. As her fingers entwined in his hair, she pressed her lips against his half-open mouth. He careened off balance, scarcely able to remember how to breathe, and now completely blinded by the sun as he tipped backwards.

Elliot closed his eyes against the light and sought to return her embrace, hitting the ground hard as he fell. His hands clutched nothing but yards and yards of fabric. What on earth was she wearing? Opening his eyes again cautiously, squinting in the light, he tried and failed to focus on the ceiling, then gradually took stock of his surroundings. His arms fell back against the tangle of sheets and blankets and he stopped moving, letting his head sink listlessly to the floor where he had landed, one foot still hung up on the bed.

After a moment, he reached up and found his glasses in their customary place on the nightstand and put them on, resolving the blurriness. It was a meager comfort. Emptiness hollowed him out as he recalled the actual events of the previous day. How foolish to have still dreamt a different reaction. He had little energy even to kick himself mentally as his mind flooded with cold reality.

Of course she'd said no. The feverish, dropping, plunging feeling came back to him. It was as if he had been poised on a cliff, waiting to find out if he would fly or fall, and he had fallen. Of course anticipating anything besides falling would be delusional, yet he had seen other people who must have taken flight, loving one another and enjoying the small pleasures of life together. The feeling was worse than when he'd actually fallen off a cliff, though admittedly pain had a peculiar nature of fading in memory and sharpening in the present moment. The pang inside was physical: a stabbing, burning sensation, like an ember that had failed to extinguish and now threatened to consume the whole. He had read about people who supposedly wasted away from "melancholia." However, it was plain from past experience that this was unlikely to happen to him. Life would go dully on, as he plodded along trying to smother his pain.

Slowly, Elliot got to his feet and mechanically went about the maddening mundanity of brushing his teeth and getting dressed. It all seemed ultimately pointless, like there was no use to his life besides the part Xo inhabited and made fascinating. She had only to turn her head, or gaze at something, or smile slightly, to engage his entire focus. If he didn't know enough about what she was like, as she'd claimed, he wanted to know everything, and that would surely take a lifetime. He wanted to spend a lifetime.

If only he'd been able to express himself better. Or earlier. Or later. But perhaps he would never be engaging or exciting enough to spark the same love and admiration in her that she did in him. She'd said she would see him again, that he was dear to her. Could it ever be more than as a friend? The pain welled up, filling his rib cage with pressure. It would be better if he did not imagine her feelings changing.

His hope, sprung up again during the night in that ridiculous dream, seemed stubbornly impossible to squelch even in the face of bleak reality, and it was that hope which prolonged the ache. He wished he could sob as he'd done as a child, to the point of exhaustion and relaxation. After a certain age, tears no longer helped; it seemed he had forgotten the valve that would let his pain overflow along with them.

Only one bright spot remained, and that was the prospect of seeing Xo again. Yet this brightness also burned, blindingly. Somehow, he must manage to speak to her again and carry on as before, and do his utmost to continue and enhance the friendship. The alternative was the only truly unbearable possibility. Never to see, never to speak to her again would be a complete end to the light, a perpetual night of gloom. Any pain caused by seeing her again was surely worth it. He had managed before, until he had manufactured this unreasonable hope of salvation. He could retreat to that mode once again. The only difference would be the humiliation of having offered his inferior self and having been rejected, but this was nothing his love for her couldn't bear. He must move forward, his aching heart concealed, and glean what wintery warmth he could that shone from her sun in passing.

Resigned, Elliot went to the kitchen to make the morning tea, but when he opened the cupboard, there was the cup. Xo's cup. He reached for it, fingers shaking, then halted. He would probably fumble it and break it. It was better to leave it there, untouched.

Instead, he moved to the laundry room, methodically sorted a load, and started the machine. The soothing thrum and scent of detergent filled the air. In the cabinet beside the laundry treatments was a suet feeder. After the hummingbird, he'd been afraid of luring more birds to their deaths, but Xo would say that the winter regulars would be more equipped to deal with the cold. He could get some more sightings for her; she might accept that form of contact. With the aid of a stepladder, he hung the feeder outside the kitchen window.

After putting away the ladder, Elliot found himself on the way to the visitor center, for the first time since the owl incident. Sade sold booklets designed to log bird sightings with date, time, and location. This would be a better format to give to Xo rather than the scrawled notes he'd kept on the expedition, which she'd said needed explanation. Not that she probably still wanted him to go over them with her.

He pulled open the door of the visitor center, setting off a tinkling of bells attached to the handle, a new addition. Xo would not be here, unless she had come by chance to deliver her illustrations.

She had not. Only Sade was there.

Elliot found the birder's booklet. "I would also like to sign up for your birding newsletter, if I may." His voice sounded rusty with disuse.

Sade pushed a sign-up sheet towards him, and he put himself down for both the online and paper editions, feeling negligent for not subscribing earlier. The current print edition of the newsletter, like a small magazine, was available on the counter. He added one to his booklet for purchase.

"Becoming a birder, are you?" Sade sounded suspicious, or maybe sarcastic, he wasn't sure.

"Only an amateur." He touched his camera, hanging as ever at his side.

Sade rang up the purchase, looking as if she agreed with his assessment.

Suddenly, Elliot remembered the old list Xo had given him of birds for which she was particularly looking, ones he didn't recognize. He hesitated, as Sade was already handing back his change, then took the plunge. "Do you happen to have a...a field guide that includes the rarer birds...?"

Sade evaluated him for a moment, then said, "I will have, once I get the illustrations in and finish writing it."

Elliot felt especially thickheaded. He had known Xo was still working on the paintings, that was why she needed the sightings.

"Is there a particular bird you're trying to identify?" asked Sade, sounding less antagonistic than before. "The regional guide I have here is still a good general handbook, it's just not specific to Arin."

Elliot shook his head. The thought of Xo had robbed him of further speech.

"I did have some older editions that contained more of our special birds," Sade continued, glancing up at the shelf behind her which held assorted books. "But they tend to get snapped up quickly by dedicated birders."

Unlike him. The idea that he'd hoped to accomplish anything by bringing Xo more pictures from her list seemed cringingly pathetic at this point. It wouldn't change how she felt about him.

Elliot collected his purchases from the counter and slid them into his coat pocket. He would try to photograph the birds anyway. After all, if he saw a bird that he could not identify from the book he already had, it would probably be one she was interested in.

"Xo told me about this 'expedition' you all went on," said Sade, causing Elliot to pause on his way out the door. "I was pleasantly surprised to hear everyone made it back in one piece."

Elliot glanced inadvertently at the shelf where the owl used to be, and when he looked back, he saw Sade had been looking there as well, doubtless thinking of the last time he was here.

"I do apologize for the damage I caused before," said Elliot in a low voice. "But I assure you, I would not have let any harm come to Xiomara on the hike." He swallowed hard. "Any that I had the power to prevent," he amended, feeling only too well his powerlessness.

Sade was studying him with an appraising look. "The girl has talent. I'll forgive her if she's a bit lacking in sense about some other things."

"I can agree with you on the first part of that statement," said Elliot stiffly. As unlikely as it seemed, he got the impression that Sade was commenting about him in some way. Probably she thought Xo ought not to have gone hiking with him. Or worse, Xo had told her of the more recent event.

Sade chuckled, which did nothing to put Elliot at ease as he departed.

Xo's shift at the coffee house would be over by now. She might not want to see him yet, but he could not think of a single other thing to do. He would not seek her out, but if she happened to come downstairs, she might say something to him. Or she might not. Then he would know. Perhaps, a ray of light. Perhaps, his last hope would be crushed, and that, too, would put him out of his misery.

Elliot collected his coffee from the barista and sat on the hearth. He removed his current book from his coat pocket and spread it on his knees, but the words were incomprehensible symbols on the page, refusing to provide their usual help. He was conscious only of Xo's absence. Was she in her apartment upstairs, or had she gone out, meaning she would at some point return? The waiting was almost unbearable, but not as much as the staying away.

The waiting was abruptly interrupted by a hand which grabbed his shoulder, wrenching him to his feet and flinging him backwards. The book went flying as Elliot staggered against the fireplace, barely managing to keep upright.

"F—Francis?"

Francis's face was red, and even though he was grinning, he did not look at all happy. "Elliot! At last. You're a pretty hard guy to track down, you know that?"

28

THE ACCUSATION

Elliot stumbled to one side, out of arm's reach, watching Francis warily. "I did not know anyone wanted to find me."

"I didn't so much want to find you," spat Francis, the veins in his neck standing out, "as for you to admit the truth! You see, I've come to realize something. Lia didn't die of the mountainpox."

Elliot stared at him. Francis seemed to have a lot of difficulty grasping whether people were dead or not, between this and their last encounter when he'd been astonished to find Elliot alive. He'd never struck Elliot as particularly bright, but this was going a bit far. "She definitely died."

"But not of the mountainpox." Francis banged his fist on the table, the one Alec usually sat at.

"Yes." Elliot moderated his voice as well as he could, as he knew Francis had been a big part of Lia's life once. Before she met Elliot. "It was an epidemic. The mountainpox is extremely contagious, and deadly. Even her doctor died from it."

Francis turned abruptly and paced away, shoulders hunched, glowering at empty air. A hush had fallen over the room as other people turned to watch, and although Francis spoke more quietly now, his words seemed louder as a result. "Yes, I've been reading up on this mountainpox." He tossed a newspaper cutting that he had been clutching down on the table, and Elliot, sparing it only a glance in order to keep his eyes on Francis, grasped that it was the recent article from the *Mountain Herald*.

"So contagious, so deadly, that once exposed, no one can survive it." Francis stopped and braced both hands on the table behind which Elliot now stood warily. "Except you, apparently. You admitted you were present when she died. In fact, no one saw her after she got sick except you and her doctor, who conveniently also died. Bodies all buried immediately, of course. So how is it that this incurable disease didn't affect you? Because she didn't have it! You used the epidemic to cover up the fact that you murdered her!" Francis finished triumphantly.

Elliot choked. "Wha—Why would I kill her? I...she was my wife."

"Don't act surprised. I'm not the only one who guessed. I heard the same rumor right here in this café, while you were avoiding me—not at home, not at work, nobody able to tell me where you were. You must have heard I was back and realized I'd figured it out, now that I knew you were alive." Francis spoke slowly as he worked his way around the table counter-clockwise, one deliberate step at a time.

"What? Who..." Elliot stumbled backwards, trying to keep the table between them. He glanced nervously behind him, where he had heard a few people gasp and murmur at Francis's words, but he couldn't afford to take his eyes off Francis long enough to look inquiringly at other customers. What rumors? Who had told Francis he was dead in the first place?

Francis looked increasingly menacing. Elliot poised himself to do something...flee? Pick up a blunt instrument to protect himself? Nothing was handy—a coffee cup wouldn't do, and a chair seemed excessive, though possibly he could use one to block an attack if necessary.

"I thought it was odd how coolly you received me when we ran into each other up on Arin, claiming you weren't angry at me. You must've had to think fast to pretend you didn't care about the affair, but you had guilt written all over your face. I just didn't know why yet. Finding

out you were alive, after I'd been told you died with her, threw me off
at first. But you slipped up by admitting you were with her at the end.
I've done my research now: if she had died of the mountainpox, you
wouldn't be standing here."

"Affair? Lia...she was not having an affair." Elliot spoke icily,
fighting to suppress the anger rising within him. "And I certainly
didn't kill her. Lia and I were perfectly happy together. Ask anyone."

Nobody in the café spoke to back up Elliot's account, though a
fair percentage must have known Lia, and they were clearly all
listening. Of course, the way Francis was carrying on, no one would
want to be his next target.

"You couldn't be bothered to attend her memorial service," went
on Francis. "You weren't even touched by her death. Don't try to save
face, everyone knows now. I just want you to admit it. Go on, confess,
in front of everyone. You killed her when you found she was planning
to leave you, for me."

All murmuring in the coffee shop had come to a halt, apparently
awaiting his answer. Those customers who had been in the process
of leaving had settled back down to hold their empty cups.

Elliot stared at Francis. This concept was so ludicrous that for a
moment he could not even muster a response. "That...that's
ridiculous. She wasn't..." Elliot's thoughts tripped and stumbled over
the accusations. Yes, Lia and Francis had been a couple once, but the
man had moved away from Lingen around the time Elliot and Lia
married. That was the last Elliot had seen of him until the run-in a
couple of months ago. His obsession with Lia had obviously gone
further than Elliot had ever imagined, to the point where it interfered
with his common sense.

"Neither of you caught the mountainpox; that epidemic was just a
handy way for you to kill her and cover it up. Everybody's dying,
what's one more? And no one the wiser. Admit it!" Francis swept his
hand around the room. "We're all waiting. Confess."

Elliot didn't dare take his eyes off his unstable accuser, but in his
peripheral vision, everyone did seem to be waiting along with Francis.

"You can look up Lia's death record. My wife," Elliot emphasized
the words, "died of the mountainpox. I had to watch her die from

it." By now, he couldn't suppress the memories flashing into his mind anymore, the way he normally did. An old familiar sickening feeling of fear and grief twisted his insides as he recalled the final moments of her life draining away, and him unable to do anything. He tried to hold on to his anger at Francis's accusations, to cover the other feeling.

"Then how are you still alive?" Francis nodded his head as if he had discovered an astonishing fact. "Can you explain how you were with her at the end and didn't catch it, when it's so contagious and deadly?"

Elliot hesitated, and a look of satisfaction spread over Francis's face.

"I...have an immunity," said Elliot.

"Is that so?" Francis's voice dripped with disbelief.

"I had it before, when I was younger." As if it weren't obvious. "I thought you knew."

"That's not possible. A weakling like you couldn't have lived through it." Francis sneered. "And I've done my research. There have only been five outbreaks of mountainpox worldwide. You expect me to believe that you were not only in Lingen for this outbreak, you also went through a completely different outbreak which you miraculously survived?"

"You can tell that I've had it." Elliot's skin prickled under the eyes of the people watching. He should not have to explain this, but he was not going to be held accountable for Lia's death.

Francis looked him up, down, and sideways. "Am I supposed to be seeing something?" He laughed harshly, glancing encouragingly at the other people in the shop.

When Elliot raised his head enough to see the onlookers, they seemed to have busied themselves with activities demanding immediate, but not completely thorough, attention. He felt himself, at this minute, the town fool. Not because he was in the wrong, in fact, the only reason to continue to subject himself to this degradation was to prove he was in the right: not just to Francis, but to his neighbors, and he had thought, friends. People who respected him. Knew him, at least. However, at the same time he was allowing himself to be put on display, a setting with which he was not the least bit comfortable.

Elliot clenched his teeth. "The scars. On my face," he growled in a low voice. He angled his head to the light.

Francis squinted at him, acknowledging nothing.

Suddenly, Francis leapt the rest of the way around the table and grabbed Elliot's shirt by the collar before Elliot could react. "I *know* you killed her! You can cover it up all you want with this supposed immunity, but I know you wanted her dead!"

Francis was shouting now, and shaking Elliot back and forth. Elliot's camera strap cut into his neck as the camera swung wildly. He grabbed Francis's wrists with both hands and dug his fingers into the larger man's tendons, trying to force him to release his grasp, but Francis didn't even seem to notice. Then Elliot lost his footing as he struggled to brace himself, and there was a loud rip as the fabric of his shirt tore at the collar. He kicked his feet trying get them beneath him again, or alternatively to force Francis to release him, but accidentally hooked a chair instead, which fell clattering to the floor.

In the cacophony, Elliot found himself uncomfortably slammed backwards: first against the table, triggering an ominous crunch from his camera as it caught between him and the wood. Then his back was rammed repeatedly against the bannister of the staircase. Francis's grip was impossible to twist out of, even at the expense of his shirt. A noise arose of many voices, then one deep, loud voice. The other people in the coffee shop had finally mobilized and surrounded the scene, now that it had become violent, and were crowding close.

Jacqua, the owner of the loud voice, placed one large hand on Francis's shoulder and pressed him down vertically into a nearby chair that was still standing. Francis was seething but he released Elliot in the process. Jacqua's other hand supported Elliot's shoulder, and Elliot slowly unfolded himself from the bannister. His collar was partially torn loose, the shirt now untucked and missing numerous buttons, gaping open, one shoulder and sleeve ripped at the seam as well.

"He has the scars," said Jacqua.

It was unnecessary. Everyone present now had a full view in the light of the hanging lamp which had originally been over the askew table. Elliot focused on remaining upright rather than on the words that had just been uttered. It was unexpectedly difficult to hear them spoken aloud. The scars on his face, now ducked against the light, were mostly confined to his cheeks, and the sun-roughened skin made the contrast with the pockmarks less obvious. On his paler skin which was usually covered, they stood out like craters. The light glared over the pockmarks now visible covering his chest and stomach and the exposed parts of his arms. It was not a secret, yet he felt naked. At least it would be clear who was in the right now. That was the one consolation.

Taking in the scene and Jacqua's words, Francis noticeably relaxed, though he was clearly still on edge. The close attention of everyone in the coffee shop didn't seem to unnerve Francis; if anything, it was encouraging him. He sat in his chair as if he owned it.

Elliot remained standing unsteadily against the stair railing. He would rather have left the building on that note, but he wasn't sure of his ability to stay upright at the moment. His glasses had fallen off. Someone, he couldn't see who, placed them back in his hand. When he put them on, his helper had faded into the restless crowd surrounding the scene.

"Listen," said Francis, stabbing the air in front of him with one finger. Jacqua set a fallen chair upright and stood eyeing him, but Francis made no move to jump up.

Francis's voice was moderate again, almost reasonable sounding. "The last thing I heard from Lia was that she was going to tell you about us and end it with you. Next thing I knew, she was dead. In my grief, and good-heartedness, I was foolish: I thought both of you had been the victims of the epidemic, and it was just horribly unfortunate timing. But I realize now, there are no coincidences here.

"So what if you are 'immune' to mountainpox. I may have been wrong about that. I admit it." He looked around the room. "I can admit my mistake. But I'm not wrong about the rest of it. When she told you about me, or when you found out, you killed her. You killed her in some way you could be sure that no one would suspect, and you used the epidemic to cover it up." His voice rose. "You just couldn't bear to be made a laughingstock when she left you, with your stinking pride!"

This last word was shouted with a snarl of added spittle, but Francis still made no move to get up. His legs jutted out at odd angles from his seat, as if they had used all their energy, and his face was shiny from sweat, spit, or both.

Pride, right. Standing here being yelled at, accused, practically stripped, in front of everyone. Xo was probably here somewhere too, seeing him like this. If she'd been in her apartment, she would have come out with all this noise. Elliot's stomach turned.

"It is a documented fact that Lia died from the mountainpox." Elliot's voice came out in a monotone, his own energy depleted. Why was he even replying? What was his role in this conversation, if it could be called that? He found himself watching Francis with a creeping sense of detachment, as if he were merely observing him from afar. It was not worthwhile trying to reason with this man. At some point, Francis would stop talking. At some point, Elliot would go home. There it would be dark and quiet.

He unwillingly tuned in to Francis's words again as the man's voice became more animated.

"That's it! I know what you did." Francis's eyes narrowed. "You infected her! You knew you were immune and would be safe, and no one would suspect because of the outbreak! All because you couldn't stand for her to be happy with me!" As Francis's voice rose, the crowd started to murmur restlessly again.

Elliot had never liked Francis, but until today he had not realized how unhinged he was. No wonder Lia had often remarked on how calm and reliable Elliot was in comparison.

"I always thought you were just ugly, but you're disease-ridden. You're a carrier! Are those pockmarks still contagious?" Francis drew back in his seat, as if to put more distance between himself and Elliot. "Or is the disease alive in your blood? Or maybe you found another source of the virus, one of these research laboratories." His hand found the newspaper clipping that he'd previously discarded on the table and crumpled it. "Knowing that she would die and you would be safe. You thought no one would realize the connection, that you were protected with your…immunity!" He spat the word like it left a bad taste. "But I figured it out. You covered it up for ten years, pretending to be dead, before I put the pieces together."

Francis turned to address the rest of the room. "Do you see now what kind of person is in your midst? He's killed before and he could do it again. Any of you could be next!" He swept his arm across the table and most of the crowd jumped back.

Francis leaned towards Elliot again, but spoke to the room rather than to him: "This man brought a contagious disease into your midst, *knowingly*, and he uses it as a *weapon*! For all we know, he started the whole outbreak. Sure, it caused some collateral damage along the way, but that just made it easier for him to conceal his crime." Francis half rose from his chair. "The game is up, Elliot. Even if you won't admit it, everyone knows now what you are."

Jacqua, still standing nearby, did not budge. The other people in the room, however, milled around in agitation, speaking in low voices. Francis settled back in his seat almost comfortably.

"That is the most ridiculous—you cannot possibly believe what he's—" spluttered Elliot to nobody in particular, as more and more people glanced at him suspiciously. His head ached. The world was going mad. Surely, no one was listening to this raving lunatic?

The raving lunatic in question was not raving anymore, he was sitting and watching, grinning triumphantly as if he had made the final point in a joust. Was Elliot seriously expected to mount an argument against this outlandish line of reasoning? His conversation with Xo about Lia's death sprang to his mind. She'd been so quick to ask if he'd killed Lia. At the time, Elliot had thought Xo was just saying whatever came into her head, as he had to admit she often did, but…she couldn't really have believed that, could she? Would she believe this? Was she here, now? He still couldn't see her. Other people were moving around, grabbing their things to leave, looking askance at him. The show was over, and they were anxious to get outside where they could talk it over amongst themselves, or perhaps just anxious to get away from him.

Jacqua started straightening chairs and tables and clearing cups. Elliot shifted his weight off the bannister of the staircase and back onto his unsteady feet. He kept Francis in his sight, but Francis only met his eyes challengingly and did not get up. The dizziness increased as Elliot moved. He tried to remember if he'd hit his head while being rammed against the various hard objects, but couldn't recall. He stumbled to the side door near the bottom of the stairs and made his way outside.

It was still light, which momentarily caught Elliot off guard, as it seemed more time had passed. The sun was as low as it could be in the pale winter sky, grazing the horizon and glaring on everything so he couldn't see well. The pain in his head spiked again. Gradually, he became aware of renewed aching in his back and shoulders, and of how cold it was outside. He tried to pull his shirt together, but it was a hopeless mess, and his coat was left behind on the hearth in the café.

As he stood on the sidewalk, several people along the street looked in his direction and then turned to their companions in huddled conversation. A few simply stood and gawked at him openly, as if they might actually believe Francis's claim.

Francis had not followed him outside. After a moment of disorientation, Elliot turned and started in the direction of his own home.

After what seemed like hours, but was not according to the sun still melting on the distant peaks, he let himself into his house, locked the door and closed the curtains. The semi-dark thus created felt better than the bright, flat afternoon light. At the little porcelain bathroom basin, he washed his face and hands with cold water, slowly removed his tattered clothes and placed them in the laundry basket, and methodically dressed in another set of clothing. Then he lay down on his bed and stared up at the dark ceiling. He hadn't thought the week could get much worse, but it had.

The notion that Lia had been planning to leave him to reunite with Francis was the absurd fantasy of an obsessed ex-lover. That, he was sure of. But digging its way upward through the layers of embarrassment and the dread of his next encounters with all the people who had witnessed the confrontation, a tiny thread of doubt crept in. It was impossible what Francis had said, wasn't it? That the illness that had stricken him as a young man had somehow transferred from him to Lia?

Of course, Elliot had never intentionally harmed her in any way, let alone tried to kill her. As for the mountainpox lying dormant in someone who had recovered from it and then arising again, he had never heard of such a thing, but there were few who recovered. In fact, he didn't know of anyone who had, besides himself.

His uneasiness might only be a resurgence of the guilt he felt from living through a disease that had taken so many others. It surely could not be possible that he had brought this on Lia, and thence the rest of the town. If it were possible…a spark of fear flickered and went out, dulled by exhaustion.

It must just be that the evening had played out so irrationally that he could no longer judge what was real. None of it really mattered now anyway; he was alone, and alone he would remain. There was a harsh comfort of cold familiarity in that.

29

THE VISITOR

Elliot jerked awake to the noise of loud banging on his door, his first thought that Francis was attempting to get in. He twisted over in bed to look at the door, wrenching his neck in the process. His body still ached from yesterday's altercation and he was in no hurry to repeat it.

A figure silhouetted against the frosted window of the front door raised its arms to its head and pressed against the glass as if trying to see in. Elliot hesitated. If it was Francis and he was in the same mood as yesterday, he would probably kick the door down or break the window, and lying in bed would not be the most healthful way to receive him. On the other hand, if it was someone who would give up and go away, Elliot preferred to wait that out.

"Elly! It's me! Come on, open up."

Elliot sagged with relief at the sound of Alec's voice, though he didn't particularly want to talk to Alec right now either. Even though Alec was unlikely to kick down the door, Elliot found his glasses and staggered over. After the display yesterday, and that cataclysmic conversation with Xo, Alec might be his only remaining friend. He opened the door and peered out, squinting into the midday light.

"You look terrible!" said Alec cheerfully.

Elliot acknowledged this with a noise that started as a laugh and died as a snort, without opening the door any further.

"No, no, I'm coming in." Alec pushed the door open enough to slip by, with Elliot only feigning resistance. As Alec closed the door, Elliot collapsed onto the bed again—a little too vigorously for his back, which throbbed in protest.

Alec was carrying Elliot's coat, which he must have found at the café. He hung it on the rack and straightened it, brushing it off, as if it were Elliot he were setting on his feet again. There was a sound of crinkling paper from the pocket: the birding newsletter and pamphlet which he had shamefully abandoned as he essentially fled the scene yesterday.

Alec sat down on the bed. "I heard what happened."

"I am only surprised you didn't see it for yourself." Elliot gazed dejectedly at the nightstand. "Everyone else was there."

They'd all looked at him so suspiciously, no one speaking up to defend him. People he had lived amongst for years. Well, Jacqua had stepped up, but he might have just wanted to make sure his furniture didn't get destroyed.

"Pretty much." Alec grinned. "You're the talk of the town!"

Elliot groaned.

"I guess Francis was pretty compelling. I mean, I know you didn't kill Lia." Alec patted Elliot's shoulder. "Perish the thought even. Still, people are listening to him."

"He was not compelling at all. He was nonsensical." Elliot sat up, since Alec showed no signs of leaving. "If you had been there, you would have heard how ridiculous he sounded. Why anyone would believe him…"

Alec shrugged and stood up. "They don't know you like I do, that's all. They'll come around. Just impressionable people buying into the excitement." He peered at Elliot closely. "I never knew you to pay that much heed to public opinion anyway."

What Elliot wanted to ask was if Xo had been there. There was a good chance that Alec and Xo would have discussed the incident. What did *she* think?

"And, if I'd been there," continued Alec, as he moved to the sink to fill the kettle and put it on the electric range, "Francis wouldn't have been able to keep running his mouth like that, by golly." He shook his head. "You can bet I would have taken him out! He can take a seat or he can take a sock to the mouth, that's all." Alec jabbed the air, a satisfied smirk on his face.

"This is not making me feel better." Elliot rubbed his face vigorously to wake up and ran his hands through his hair, resting his elbows on his knees. He had slept a long time, but he felt bleary. "It is not necessary for you to fight on my behalf." He didn't particularly appreciate the implication of his inability to defend himself, though he had to admit Francis must outweigh him by well over a hundred pounds.

"Look, I'm not saying you should have engaged him," said Alec. "You did the smart thing not to. I bet that's what he wanted, even: an excuse to swing at you. Then where would you be, brawling? Nah, I can't see it." He chuckled. "Trust me, it wouldn't have gotten your point across any better."

Presumably, then, Alec hadn't heard a play-by-play. Kicking Francis while being smashed into the staircase doubtless counted as engaging him, though Elliot wasn't sure if Francis had actually sustained any damage.

"I'm just saying I would have defended you, not stood back and listened to him talk to you like that." Alec shook his head in disgust.

Elliot tried to look appreciative of the sentiment. At least if Alec still thought he was innocent, perhaps others did too.

"What I can't make out is how everybody seems to believe this guy," added Alec, briskly mixing up two cups of tea and bringing Elliot crashing down again from his tentative hope. Alec handed him a cup of tea and pulled out a stool.

Elliot reluctantly moved from the bed onto another stool, so he could rest the scalding cup on the counter. It was hard to figure out where to begin countering Francis's story—he hadn't done a very good job of rebutting it at the time, he'd been so taken aback. How could anyone take it seriously?

"Maybe I should have mentioned this before," said Alec, "But I heard after the fact that somebody came by the newspaper office a week or so ago looking for you, while you were out of town. I guess it must have been Francis."

Elliot looked at him in alarm. "What did he say? The same...?" It would be horrifying if Francis had gone on about this at work, though by this time everyone he worked with had probably heard what had happened at the café.

Alec shrugged. "He didn't identify himself or leave a message besides that he was looking for you, and I doubt anybody in the office besides us would have recognized him. But he hasn't been in town for years, so why now?"

Elliot sipped his tea, frowning. "I did have an odd encounter with him a couple of months ago."

Alec's head jerked up. "He was here another time?"

Elliot nodded. "I think Mrs. Dupesh asked him to visit. I got the impression that, until he ran into me, he thought I had died when...Lia did, in the outbreak ten years ago. I cannot imagine why though."

"Heh...actually..." Alec shifted on his stool. "I might have something to do with him thinking that."

"You?"

"Funny story. Well, not really." Alec's thumb fidgeted uncharacteristically with his teacup. "Francis showed up at Lia's memorial service."

A guilty, murky memory stirred. "I should have gone to that." There had been an event after the burial, but Elliot had not been able to make himself go: to stand there, stoic and grave like he should have, and accept condolences out of protocol for the sake of whoever else was there. Now, his absence at the memorial felt like evidence for Francis's lies.

Alec interrupted his gloomy thoughts. "Nobody faulted you for not going. You were...in no state. I understood that. I'm sorry to bring it up. Anyway, Francis came back to town for it, and he asked me—well, he noticed you weren't there. He was sort of wound up, and afterwards he asked me something like, did Elliot catch it too. I said yes. Technically you did, at one point. I guess he didn't know you'd had it before, and I didn't correct him. I mean, I let him think that you caught it, and…didn't make it."

Elliot stared at Alec. "But…why?"

Abruptly, Alec turned to face Elliot. "Look, you have to understand, he was acting unbalanced. Going on about all sorts of crazy stuff. I didn't want you to have to deal with him, if he took it into his mind to come talk to you about Lia or something."

It was true that Elliot hadn't been in any frame of mind to talk to Francis after Lia died. However, if he had done so, Francis probably wouldn't be coming around now thinking Elliot had caused her death. But it wasn't fair to blame Alec for that. If Francis had been acting as irrationally at the memorial service as he was at the coffee house the other day, Alec's decision to send him astray began to make sense.

Elliot sighed. "So that's why he was acting so oddly when we ran into each other on Arin."

"Yep. I mean, honestly, I never expected him to show up here again."

Elliot hadn't either, but then he hadn't given Francis much thought. He was a person from Lia's past whom Elliot had never cared for, and the feeling had clearly been mutual.

"Did you hear what they're saying about Lia and Francis?" said Alec, glancing at Elliot.

"Naturally, I heard," said Elliot dryly. "I was there."

"Of course, Lia would never have done that," said Alec a little too heartily.

Elliot eyed him sharply, and Alec hurriedly took a sip of tea. There had been doubt in his voice. And Alec had said *they*, so other people were repeating that part of Francis's ridiculous claim, too.

It didn't seem that anyone was capable of comprehending Lia and Elliot's dedication to one another, despite the briefness of the marriage before her death. However, in the end, it did not matter what the others thought…unless he was going to have to deal with Francis again.

"Is Francis still in town?" asked Elliot.

"So I've heard, but I haven't been able to find him," said Alec. "I don't know what else he's after. If he wanted revenge, he could have just knocked on your door and shot you or something."

"Yes, how much simpler that would have been," said Elliot morosely.

Alec waved away the comment. "What do you think he wants?"

Elliot sighed. "Apparently a public confession that I…did away with her, to prevent her from going back to him. Which obviously I can't give him." Elliot's mind kept returning to the tiny speck of doubt about the virus. It was impossible that he had caused her death, but he still felt responsible somehow. "Of course, it's not true," Elliot added, studying Alec.

Alec's eyes widened. "I believe you! The point is: how do we make him go away again? He needs something to satisfy him." He tapped his teacup with one finger, thinking.

"If it's a question of Lia's and my devotion to each other, many people who knew us both could surely attest to that." Elliot frowned.

"We-elll…" Alec squinted up at the ceiling. "After the scene he made, I don't know how many people are going to be coming forward to tell Francis that. I just have not heard many affirmations of that myself, in the retelling. There is a lot of retelling going on."

Elliot groaned.

"I mean, I'm happy to tell him myself, but I doubt he'd be convinced if it came from me." Alec paused, thinking. "Doesn't his aunt—Mrs. Dupesh—still live right up the street from you?"

"Yes," said Elliot. "Lia used to stop by and visit with her often. They were friends."

"Come to think of it," said Alec, "Aren't you surprised Mrs. Dupesh never set Francis straight about you being dead?"

"Why would she have reason to?" said Elliot. "I certainly don't go around randomly informing people that *you* are still alive. She probably didn't realize you'd been spreading rumors of my demise."

"I feel kind of responsible in a way," Alec began. "I mean, if I hadn't…"

Elliot shook his head. "No, you didn't give him this crazy idea about Lia. And he was bound to find out eventually that I'm alive."

"Yeah, now that he's seen you, I think the ship has sailed on that one." Alec chuckled.

Elliot had no vested interest in pretending to be dead, so it was well that it was all in the open now. It wasn't like he had anything else to lose. Xo's face surfaced in his mind unexpectedly at this, and the tea felt more than usually bitter on his tongue. Was it even possible to recover from this, explain it to her in some way, whatever she'd heard? Would she even want to hear his explanation?

"Perhaps Francis would listen to Mrs. Dupesh though, about Lia and me," said Elliot. "This idea that Lia wanted to get back together with him, it's ridiculous. But it seems to be why he thinks I—"

"...killed her, yeah," finished Alec.

Elliot winced.

"Of course," Alec went on, "There is the fact that Mrs. Dupesh hasn't actually spoken in years."

Elliot considered this. It might present a problem from Francis's viewpoint. But Mrs. Dupesh had been a near constant witness to his and Lia's relationship, at least as much as she could see from her porch.

"Still worth a try," said Alec. "Francis may not believe you about Lia's last days, but he has no reason not to believe his aunt, and she was right here. If it doesn't work, I still leave open the offer to punch him out." Alec smiled encouragingly.

What was the point in catering to Francis's crazy ideas at all? Elliot felt drained. Then again, the next knock on the door might be Francis, wanting to exact his personal revenge on Elliot. He couldn't spend the rest of his life inside, cowering. What else could he do...go to the police? Francis had ranted and raged but not actually threatened him, despite the rough treatment. Plus, considering the lack of public support, Elliot now was doubtful of the law stepping in should another such event arise. They might simply look the other way, or watch to see what would happen like everyone else. He could even envision Francis responding by formally accusing him of murder, followed by a trial. He shuddered, his stomach knotting at the thought of reliving the details of Lia's death.

If only he could go back several days, before Francis, before he'd poured his heart out to Xo. What if he'd simply left town before Francis arrived? But he couldn't have gone, even if the time warp were possible. Xo was here. And for some reason, she'd made him promise not to leave.

As Elliot floated these thoughts in his teacup, Alec poked around in the refrigerator and cut some thick slabs of cheese and bread which he assembled into unappetizing-looking sandwiches.

"Here, eat up, and we'll go talk to Mrs. Dupesh," Alec said enthusiastically. "You can't sit here all day moping, anyway. We'll get it taken care of." He bit into his sandwich.

"Thank you." Elliot picked up the other sandwich, unable to share Alec's confidence. He did not mention the other reason he was reluctant to leave the house and face all the prying eyes again: the burning shame of everyone having evaluated his scarred body, and having rejected his defense anyway. He shouldn't have even mentioned his prior immunity to Francis, since the man seemed incapable of listening to reason. Elliot had only humiliated himself and given Francis more irrational ideas, to boot.

That entire part of the confrontation hung unmentioned in the air now. He half-wanted to bring it up, to hear Alec's possibly reassuring point of view, but at the same time it was too embarrassing to discuss.

Alec spoke again, but he, too, avoided that topic. "Say, how did he get this idea that you somehow infected Lia, anyway?" He frowned, chewing his sandwich. "I mean, you fight off the disease, and it's gone, right? Your body kills it. Didn't you have it when you were pretty young, anyway?"

"Goodness knows how he gets any of these ideas," said Elliot. "He's obviously not in his right mind."

❖   ❖   ❖

Mrs. Dupesh was sitting, as always, in the rocking chair on her front porch. Today she was swathed in a voluminous pink fuzzy shawl against drafts. Elliot could almost see Lia sitting there next to her on the padded wicker stool, talking to her animatedly as she always used to do. He felt at times a need to fill in for Lia in this capacity, though he was a poor substitute. Luckily other neighbors often stopped by as well, recounting the latest happenings in Mrs. Dupesh's ear. Despite not having spoken in a good many years, or maybe because of this, Mrs. Dupesh was a popular sounding board for local chitchat, ideas, shocking news, and even requested advice, which she doled out with a smile here, a nod there—much of it likely interpreted according the whim of the listener.

"Howdy." Alec stopped at the bottom of the porch stairs, grinning.

Mrs. Dupesh smiled back and set aside her crochet as they climbed the steps. Though she did sell quite a lot of her crochet, Elliot guessed that it mainly gave her something to do as she waited for people to come by and visit, while keeping an eye on those who walked past and did not stop to talk. Elliot had one of her blankets himself.

Alec had plunked down beside her, inquired after her latest crochet project, and already worked his way through the usual pleasantries to the purpose of the current visit. "So you see, we were hoping you could help straighten out this misunderstanding with Francis, seeing as you were living here during the outbreak—settle him down a bit? He has this notion, as you've doubtless heard…tell her, Elliot."

It was awkward to begin the conversation, or monologue, in this way; however, Mrs. Dupesh beckoned to him. Elliot knelt near her to be at a similar and more sympathetic level.

"Mrs. Dupesh, you must know that I had only the deepest admiration for Lia, and never would have hurt her."

Mrs. Dupesh smiled and nodded.

"I'm afraid Francis only thinks this because he has this idea that Lia was going to…" Elliot grimaced, trying to find an appropriate way to put it, "…leave me so she could be with him, and that I wished to prevent that. Even though it is not true that I used the outbreak as a cover to…" He waved his hand along, advancing the unspoken thought.

"To kill her," supplied Alec. "Using it as a cover does make more sense than you somehow infecting her."

Elliot gave him an irritated look.

"Not, of course, that this is what happened," added Alec hurriedly.

Elliot sighed deeply. "The point we need to convince Francis of is that I did not wish for—let alone cause—her death. There is no question *how* she died."

The mountainpox rash was indisputably clear before death. Neither Alec nor Francis had seen anyone in the last stages of infection from the miserable virus, as Elliot had more than once, but even though he had warned Alec to stay away to avoid infection at the time of the Lingen outbreak, he at least should remember the newspaper pictures. Of course, Elliot shouldn't have to bring up any of this, since he had not killed anyone.

Elliot composed himself. "Mrs. Dupesh, you saw us together each day. You knew we were happy. Please, somehow, help Francis understand that." He tried to convey every speck of truthfulness in his soul. She had to believe him. "Perhaps you might write Francis a letter telling him how things were, how I had no role in Lia's death. The mountainpox swept through…"

Elliot trailed off, staring at the porch woodwork as his mind replayed fragmented visions of the outbreak. He realized he had stopped talking, and turned back to Mrs. Dupesh. Her eyes were kind, and she patted his shoulder in a comforting way. It was a great relief that she did not appear suspicious of him, as everyone else seemed to be now.

"It would help Francis, as well." Elliot felt uncomfortable asking for a personal favor—better to phrase it as something benefiting a greater good. "He is highly agitated about it."

In response, Mrs. Dupesh looked down the street expectantly. Elliot turned in the same direction, then rose to his feet, tensing. Francis was approaching, carrying a bakery sack. He must have gone to fetch something for Mrs. Dupesh, since she was obviously anticipating him, but from the way he was striding towards them purposefully, he had now spotted Elliot and Alec on the porch. Alec stood up as well. He looked not alarmed, but interested to see what would transpire and prepared to meet it.

Francis tucked the sack under his arm, his eyes narrowing as he reached the porch. "So!"

An appropriate response refused to come to Elliot's mind, so he straightened even further, met Francis's eyes steadfastly and said nothing. What had happened yesterday in the café must not occur again on Mrs. Dupesh's porch.

Alec spoke pleasantly but in a no-nonsense tone. "I understand there have been some issues raised, and Mrs. Dupesh has most kindly agreed to shed some light on the subject." He smiled graciously at Mrs. Dupesh. "She was Lia's good friend and can easily speak to the state of affairs around the time of Lia's death."

Francis frowned at Alec. "How exactly is she going to do that?" He added in a loud whisper, "She doesn't *speak* at all."

Mrs. Dupesh touched Francis's hand to get his attention and then raised her elbow as if she expected to be helped up, seeming unoffended by his poorly concealed comment. Francis gave her an arm as she rose from her chair. Mrs. Dupesh enforced politeness upon everyone, and it made Elliot relax a little. Mrs. Dupesh took the bakery sack from Francis and walked slowly into the house, leaving them all standing there.

Francis, Alec, and Elliot automatically adjusted themselves to form a rough triangle as rustlings came from inside Mrs. Dupesh's house. Francis folded his arms, eyeing the two of them, his expression guarded. The silence wore on uncomfortably, broken only by the porch creaking as Francis shifted his weight.

Finally, Alec said evenly, "You staying here with your aunt?"

"You kidding?" muttered Francis. "I'd go crazy. I got a hotel."

Alec pursed his lips. "Just in town temporarily, then?"

Francis did not answer.

Alec's thumbs were hooked in his belt loops in the appearance of relaxation, but the twitch of his shoulder revealed he was tightly coiled within. Hopefully Alec was not planning to take any of the previous actions he'd described wanting to do to Francis. Elliot was sure he had made it clear that it wasn't Alec's fight. As mortifying as the previous encounter with Francis had been, it would only be made worse if Alec got into it with Elliot's neighbor's nephew on her own front porch.

Mrs. Dupesh interrupted the standoff by re-emerging, at a maddeningly slow pace. In her hand, she carried a paper folded in thirds. Finally! Elliot waited, wishing to leap forward and take the paper and hurry the process along, as Mrs. Dupesh regained her seat, tucked her shawl around her, and pulled up her blankets. When she was fully settled, she held out the paper to Francis. Looking puzzled, he took it from her hand, then stepped back and began to read it silently.

30

THE LETTER

"Hah!" shouted Francis after a moment, clutching the letter with both hands. He bit his lip and kept reading, breathing hard.

As he watched Francis's face, Elliot had the sinking feeling that Mrs. Dupesh might not support his innocence after all. Francis choked, his eyes watering. With a gasp, he finished the page, then turned to Elliot.

"What did I tell you! What did I say?" Francis sounded both triumphant and unhappy.

Mrs. Dupesh beckoned to Francis and shook her head, her finger on her lips. She gestured for him to give the paper to Elliot, and Francis slowly held it out. Uncertainly, Elliot took it.

Mrs. Dupesh pulled Francis to her side and nodded her head towards Elliot. Francis watched him, looking almost as distraught as he had been at the coffee shop, restrained only by his aunt's presence and her slight grip on his wrist.

Elliot unfolded the letter. It began oddly, with more than the usual sentiment, but perhaps Mrs. Dupesh was much closer to Francis than he had thought. The cursive he was reading was hauntingly familiar. An icy knot formed in his middle as he sped through the page, hardly daring to accept what he was reading. He turned the paper over with shaking hands. There was no more. He flipped it back and started to re-read it.

Elliot had thought himself well-insulated from the long-ago feelings that he'd buried with Lia, but now it was as if he'd been dragged back to the very moment of her death, and worse. He staggered against the post holding up the porch roof, tearing his eyes from the letter to stare at Francis, aghast.

"You *didn't* know," said Francis dully. "I can see it in your face." He sagged in disappointment. "He didn't know," he repeated to Mrs. Dupesh. "But she said…"

"You didn't know what?" asked Alec.

Elliot shook his head slowly, staring through the paper.

"Here, let me see." Alec reached for the letter. "Seems like I'm the only one who doesn't know what's in this thing."

Elliot's hand gripped the paper tighter, then he realized what he was doing and gave it over to Alec.

Alec scanned the page with little emotion. "Who wrote this? It's not signed."

"Lia," croaked Elliot. "It's her handwriting." He had lost the ability to inflect his voice.

He could scarcely believe what he had read. It was like another version of reality, a nightmare. His mind flashed back and forth between present and past, trying to make sense of this new information. Lia, asking Francis to come and take her away with him.

Alec said, "Maybe she changed her mind? Looks like she never mailed it."

"The date on the letter…she wrote it after she got sick…" said Elliot hollowly. The memory was vivid. Her voice, shaking with fever, asking him to bring her the paper pad, the pen. She didn't want the laptop. *It's for Mrs. Dupesh, you know she doesn't use email.* Lia had placed the envelope in his hand herself. He had put it aside, to deliver later when it was safe to leave the quarantine of the house. Telling himself, forcing himself to believe that Lia might recover, as he had done. And Lia had perhaps believed that too, at least when she wrote it, before she got worse. She'd said in the letter that if she lived, she wanted it to be with Francis, who must come as soon as it was safe. The concept that she'd been thinking of Francis on her deathbed…it was almost impossible to believe.

Elliot reclaimed the letter from Alec; he had to read it again. It was exactly as it had been before, if not worse. Francis was the one she had loved first, she'd written, everything since was simply a mistake. Elliot's name was not even mentioned. He was only referred to obliquely, presumably included in the mistake. She wrote as if she'd inexplicably ended up in the wrong house, an accident she regretted when she realized the precious last minutes of life might soon run out. The incongruence of the contents of the letter with his memory of that time, of one he loved, was nearly incomprehensible.

"I gave this letter to Mrs. Dupesh. After." Elliot's words to Alec came slowly, through the layers of time that suffocated him. His own voice sounded far away. Mrs. Dupesh hadn't mailed it, but she must have known without any additional instruction that she was meant to pass it on to Francis, though she obviously hadn't done so. Because it was too late? Was Mrs. Dupesh aiding Elliot, or was she an accomplice in this affair?

His glance flicked over to her, the rest of his body paralyzed. She only gave him a sad, sympathetic look. Elliot couldn't bear it and averted his eyes. He did not know whether to be angry or grateful towards her—it was difficult to sort out any other feelings besides the betrayal from the one he'd thought loved him, even so long ago. Already crushed by Xo's rejection, this new discovery pushed him still lower, and the painful ache inside him surged beyond what he thought was possible.

Francis interrupted his thoughts. "She did mean to tell you," he said, as if trying to defend Lia. "She swore she would, dozens of times, but in the end I guess she was just too damn kind-hearted."

Elliot stared at him. "Dozens…"

Francis was wiping his eyes, clearly touched by having been in Lia's final thoughts. "I can't believe you never found out anyway, after all these years. But I saw it when you read her letter. You didn't know. You wouldn't have had reason to kill her." Elliot sensed that Francis would have been happier if his theory had proven true and he could have worked out his feelings through another attack. He seemed at loose ends now that his battle had been stolen from him.

"Reason to kill *you* now, though!" growled Alec to Francis.

Elliot found his voice again. "Stop."

Alec looked at him questioningly.

"Let him go," said Elliot. Nausea churned his stomach. His thoughts crashed down one after another in disarray. He couldn't form a cohesive idea, any conclusion, about anything. Everything was shattered. It would be better to think nothing, and to feel nothing, nothing at all, if he could only accomplish that, but he couldn't clear his mind.

"Don't you have anything to say?" Francis raised his voice, his expression incredulous. "Aren't you capable of showing any feeling? I never knew anyone so cold. No wonder she wanted to come back to me."

Alec glared at him. "Take a hike. You got what you wanted, it's over."

Francis did not leave. His eyes moved to the letter in Elliot's hands. Elliot looked down at it as well, an otherworldly thing, something that did not belong in this reality. He could hardly bear to hold it, let alone read it again, but part of him urged exactly that: to read it, torturously, over and over, until something changed inside him. That change would undoubtedly be for the worse.

Francis cleared his throat. "Can I have my letter?"

"Why, you…" began Alec indignantly, stepping towards Francis.

Elliot intercepted Alec with an outstretched hand, holding out the letter to Francis.

Francis took it slowly. He retreated off the porch with a nod to Mrs. Dupesh and walked away.

Elliot's arm, freed of the letter, dropped to his side, and he turned away, shuddering. He did not want to be there anymore, or anywhere. The emptiness and pain kept compounding. He stumbled down the steps. The ground tipped up towards him, but he caught his balance at the last moment.

Alec dashed off a few words of thanks to Mrs. Dupesh in the background, but caught up to Elliot as he reached his front door.

Elliot turned to him stiffly. "Thank you," he managed. "For believing me. And—" He stopped, searching Alec's face. It couldn't be, but something made him ask anyway.

"Alec…did you know?"

Alec waited a moment too long before answering. "Come on, I don't listen to gossip. Certainly not about you."

Elliot turned away, facing the closed door in front of him.

"Elly…" Alec trailed off.

"Let me be alone," said Elliot.

"Are you sure that's a good idea?"

Elliot closed his eyes, gritting his teeth. "Please."

"All right," replied Alec hesitantly. "But I'm right here if you need a friend."

Elliot nodded once, then stepped inside and closed the door. He leaned against the inside, waiting until Alec's footsteps crunched away down the path, then slid down slowly to sit on the floor, accidentally banging his head against the door in the process. The physical pain gave expression to the pain in his mind. He did it again. Now his head rang in protest, and he stopped and slumped forward against his knees. The coldness outside soaked through the door into his bones.

His mind flickered over the letter. He had scoffed at the very idea of an affair just the day before, at how ridiculous it had seemed. It still did seem ridiculous, in a way. In his memories, he tried to find some clue. When had Lia become detached from him? The negative parts of their relationship were hard to locate in his mind; they were not what he had replayed in the aftermath of her death.

But something Francis had said had sparked a memory. Lia had gotten upset with Elliot once—no, more than once—saying Elliot acted like he did not care. Couldn't Elliot tell her or show her how he felt, or did he feel anything? She had yelled something like that, eerily similar to what Francis had just said to him. And Elliot had said…he must have said something to her in response, but he couldn't recall what. He'd wanted to convey how he felt to her, but his way of doing so would never have been like Francis's. Was that what she'd missed? He sometimes felt he might burst apart from the force of his emotions, but it never actually happened, they only soaked out slowly, whether they were good or bad. Was that what she'd wanted, for him to rave and shout like Francis?

Had she ever actually broken things off with Francis, even when she got engaged to Elliot, and later, when they got married? Perhaps she had never really loved Elliot. Or perhaps she'd once loved him and then somehow changed her mind…no, he could not even conceive of that, not in the case of real love. Lia's long-ago love for him had been, unbeknownst to him until now, a large part of the foundation upon which his subsequent life rested. It had crumbled, it had been an illusion, and now everything that had happened after was unstable too. Who was she? More to the point, who was he?

Maybe this was why Xo had been surprised to find that he'd once been married, why she was shocked when he told her he wanted to spend his life with her. He had tried to show her, to tell her. But he hadn't done that the right way either. And clearly he'd failed just as much at his earlier attempts to communicate his feelings to Xo, considering how she'd reacted when he did tell her.

Heretofore, he had seen himself as someone who was at least capable of inspiring love in another, but that was no longer proven. He might always have been completely unlovable, his belief that Xo might ever return his feelings founded on a lifetime of delusion. Everything in his experience had to be re-evaluated, as if the bleak discovery had shattered the previous laws of physics and required a completely different understanding of the universe, one he had yet to form.

His mind drifted back to Francis. Once, raving lunatic—now, the person who had an affair with his wife. In spite of that, he could not summon anger against Francis anymore. For that matter, he could not even find any anger towards Lia. There was nothing left to feel but shock, betrayal, sadness.

Francis had suggested Elliot would have a motive to kill Lia if he had known of the affair, and that was the only thing he could feel even a little angry about. If he had known, of course he would have let her go. He would have been heartbroken, yes, but if that was what she wanted…Elliot sat back in sudden realization. If he'd found out about the affair before Lia got sick, and she'd left Lingen to be with

Francis as a result, she would have escaped the mountainpox outbreak altogether. She would have lived. More than anything, this thought cut through him like a knife. Could he still be responsible for her death after all, through his own obliviousness? It was all too terrible to think about, and yet he could not stop turning over the details.

There came a point, it might have been the next day, when he was again disturbed by knocking, but this time he did not respond.

❖   ❖   ❖

As Xo emerged from her apartment to deliver illustrations to Sade before her noon shift, Megan hailed her from downstairs, erasing her hopes of slipping out unnoticed.

Time spent alone over the weekend, reading and drawing on the mountainside until the last light, should have helped her figure out what she wanted and how to deal with Elliot, but now it was Monday and her head was still muddled. She was not ready to discuss Elliot with Megan again. Whenever she talked to Megan, Xo's opinion seemed to shift to the exact opposite of whatever Megan was saying, but she wasn't sure if it was truly how she felt or just a need for contrariness.

By now, Megan was jumping up and down to get her attention, so Xo reluctantly crossed the busy coffee shop to the counter. In the background noise of customers, she imagined hearing Elliot's name—doubtless the result of too much time spent thinking about him. She checked the hearth in spite of herself, but he was not in his habitual place.

"Where have you been? I knocked on your door like five times this weekend!" exclaimed Megan.

Xo blinked in surprise. "Oh, I've been mostly out. Why?"

"Have you heard about Elliot?"

Xo lost her breath for a moment as her lungs seemed to constrict. "Heard what?" Please don't let anything have happened to him, she prayed silently. It couldn't. Not after how they'd left each other.

"You dodged a bullet, that's what!" Megan seemed to be savoring the reveal. "You're going to be thanking your lucky stars you turned Elliot down."

This did not sound quite as fatal as Xo had first imagined, an image she quickly suppressed since it was too horrifying. "Well? What happened?"

Megan leaned across the counter. "Remember Elliot's wife, Lia, who died? Turns out she was having an affair with this guy Francis, who used to live here. Get this: Francis showed up here the other day and accused Elliot of murdering Lia to keep them apart!"

Xo stared at Megan. "That's ridiculous."

Megan's eyes were wide. "I'm telling you: they were right here in the coffee house fighting about it!"

Setting aside the unlikeliness of Elliot being in a fight of any kind, Xo focused on the larger inconsistency. "You can't possibly think Elliot would kill somebody!"

"I dunno, Xo. People do extreme things when they find out they've been cheated on."

"No…" said Xo slowly. "She didn't cheat on him, I asked. She got sick."

"Except Francis was saying that Elliot infected her with mountainpox on purpose to kill her," said Megan. "He was already immune to it."

A voice behind Xo broke in, causing her to jump. "I thought it was that he killed her and just used the outbreak to cover it up." It was a customer waiting to order.

Xo moved aside, feeling edgy. "You know about this too?"

"Saw it go down," said the man, after ordering. "Pretty much like she said."

A hint of smugness crossed Megan's face as her story was validated.

"But, that's impossible! What did Elliot say during all this?" protested Xo.

"He didn't say a whole lot to defend himself." The customer scratched his head. "Doesn't look good. I mean, I don't really know

Elliot, but he definitely had something *wrong* with him." He gestured vaguely, grimacing.

"What do you mean, something wrong?" asked Xo, freshly alarmed.

Megan wrinkled her nose. "Those scars he has…they're like, marks from this mountainpox virus. Elliot said so himself. They were all over his body."

Megan's words reverberated dizzily through Xo's head. Elliot hadn't mentioned having the mountainpox himself, when he told Xo about Lia's death. Why had he not? She frowned. "That doesn't prove anything." Then she turned angrily to the customer. "As you said, you don't know Elliot. He wouldn't do that."

The customer shrugged, leaving with his coffee, completely unconcerned.

Nothing added up. There had to be more to the story of what had happened between Elliot and this Francis person. If only Xo had been there. Or if only Elliot had told her when it happened…but she could hardly expect that after how she'd left him, broken-hearted. She was the last person he'd want to talk to now.

Megan touched Xo's arm. "It could all be a misunderstanding." She sounded doubtful.

"It is a misunderstanding!" said Xo. "I know Elliot!" The accusations, and the fact that anyone was taking them seriously, were hard to comprehend. How could anyone believe that about Elliot, the nicest person she knew?

Megan shook her head. "You may think you know somebody, but how can you really know for sure?"

❖   ❖   ❖

Her mind cloudy with worry, Xo handed Sade her stack of illustrations. Sade flipped through them, paused, and spun one around on the counter to face Xo.

"I think you mislabeled this, unless we have a bird native to Cameroon," Sade said dryly.

Xo snapped back to attention. "What? That's a Lewis's woodpecker…" Her voice died away as she saw with a jolt that she'd clearly written *Elliot's Woodpecker* below the drawing. Burning with embarrassment, she scrambled back through her memories of creating the picture, trying to figure out how she could have made such an error. And how could she not even notice it afterwards?

"I'll correct it in the printing," said Sade, her voice tinged with amusement. "Since that's the longest I've ever heard you stop talking."

"I don't know how I did that. It won't happen again," said Xo.

Sade's mouth twitched. "Maybe it should."

"I mean…oh."

Right, stop talking. Xo took the list of next week's assignments and stumbled out the door, back to the café to start her shift. But if getting Elliot out of her head had been difficult before, it was impossible now at the coffee shop. As she woodenly ran shots of espresso, murmurs of the claims against Elliot swirled in the background. They were unrealistic and unfair, but she couldn't even begin to explain this to people without growing hot and angry and entirely unconvincing as a result, so she simmered silently at the counter. There was no new information to go on, nothing to ease her concern for Elliot's well-being.

Towards the end of Xo's shift, Megan popped back in and made herself a coffee. "I'm covering the shift after yours today," she said in response to Xo's surprised look. "Here, check this out." She slid a newspaper over to Xo.

Xo scanned the page, glad to have something to talk about besides the troubling rumors. "This isn't the *Mountain Herald*."

"No, it's the college paper," said Megan.

"Our team is the Hoary Marmots?" Xo asked dubiously. "Why don't they use this opportunity to promote the local birds, like the flammulated grosbeak?"

"You really think that's better? Nobody's going to be intimidated by some weird bird."

Xo studied the mascot image, a sort of cartoon groundhog. "This thing doesn't look very fierce."

"Those guys are big!" said Megan.

"Then how come I've never seen one?"

"They're in their burrows for the winter," said Megan. "Anyway, I didn't give it to you for the sports. Read below."

Xo flipped the folded paper over. *Is Mountainpox a Current Threat?* screamed the headline. "Did they write this piece over the weekend or what?"

"It's a hot topic," said Megan. "Plus, there was that mountainpox article a while back in the *Herald*. The two newspapers can get a little competitive."

"That outbreak was ages ago, though. Why would it be a 'current threat?'" Xo frowned. "Is this because of what that guy said about Elliot infecting his wife?"

Megan shrugged. "Seems relevant. It's not just opinion; they got a quote from some medical research guy who's apparently an expert."

Before Xo could launch into all the reasons why it wasn't relevant, Alec entered the shop. His arrival brought unexpected relief. Surely, he would be an ally in this, taking Elliot's side.

"Alec!" Megan popped up enthusiastically. "What's your take? You don't think Elliot actually killed her?" she added in a confidential voice.

"That's a load of..." Alec's glance fell on the paper in front of Xo and he snatched it off the counter. "What's this rag doing here?"

Without waiting for an answer, he chucked it into the trash can by the door.

"Hey!" said Megan. "Customers might want to read that!"

"Then they're idiots," said Alec flatly. "Xo, are you off yet?"

"No." It was plain that she was still working, since she was on the other side of the counter and wearing her apron.

Alec remained standing at the counter expectantly, without ordering.

Xo decided to be charitable, in light of Alec's support of Elliot. "But I'm off soon, why?"

"Elliot needs you," said Alec.

Xo's heart skipped a beat. "Did he say that?" she asked cautiously.

"Of course he didn't, it's Elliot. He's not going to say that he needs you. I just know that he does," said Alec.

So, Elliot must not have told Alec about his proposal, or her rejection. Xo started to untie her apron, turning to Megan. "My shift's almost over. Do you mind if I...?"

Megan held up her hands powerlessly. "Go ahead. I'll cover for you."

Alec lingered by the coffeehouse door until Xo followed him out. She managed to keep up with some difficulty as he walked briskly up the sidewalk.

"Is Elliot okay?" asked Xo anxiously. "Everybody's saying these awful things."

"As it turns out, there was something going on between Francis and Lia before she died." Alec shook his head. "Elliot's taking it pretty hard. He didn't know."

"What did this guy Francis do to him?" she asked, unable to keep the worry out of her voice.

Alec hesitated. "Made a big scene, but we got rid of him."

"What do you mean, you got rid of him?" Xo trusted in Elliot's innocence, but she wasn't so sure what Alec would do if pressed.

"The fight kind of went out of Francis when he realized Elliot didn't know about the affair. But Elliot is pretty broken up, he won't even talk to me now. I thought maybe he'd talk to you."

Not likely. He'd completely shut down after she refused him. The memory of it stabbed at her. She was glad, somehow, that Alec was coming with her.

When they reached Elliot's house, Alec knocked on the front door. "Elliot! Open up. I've brought Xo."

There was no sign of life from the house, and the front curtains were drawn. Alec knocked again. Xo stood next to him on the doorstep, looking around uncomfortably. The watcher on the porch up the street was there again.

"Elliot!" Alec yelled, banging the door loudly, apparently completely unconcerned about what the neighbors might think.

There was no response. He paused, leaning on his forearm against the door, then walked around the left side of the house. Xo followed. There was now a bird feeder outside the kitchen window, with black-capped chickadees at it. The birds flew away as Alec and Xo approached, leaving Xo with a desolate feeling. The kitchen window curtains were also closed, so Alec gave up and returned to the front step.

"He wouldn't just leave," said Xo, partly to reassure herself. "He promised!"

Alec sighed heavily. He tried the door, but it was locked.

"Maybe he went to the store or something," said Xo uneasily.

"I don't think so." Alec reached down to the planting area beside the door and flipped over a particular stone with his hand.

There was a key underneath. He picked it up and brushed off the dirt on his jeans, then inserted it in the lock.

Xo watched him, aghast. "Are you sure we should be doing this?" she hissed in a loud whisper.

Alec glanced at her, his hand on the doorknob. "It'll be fine," he said briefly. He opened the door quietly and leaned in. "Elliot?"

Xo peered around him, afraid of what they might find, afraid of whatever Alec anticipated that led him to break in. The house was warm, but dark. The only sound was her own heartbeat.

After a moment, Alec entered, turning on the light. Xo followed and closed the door behind them. The house appeared unoccupied. Alec walked through the kitchen and around the bed, scanning the room and tracking snow on the floor.

"You should take your boots off," said Xo. "Elliot's not gonna like that." Alec did not appear to hear her.

Xo was stranded on the inside doormat, so she took off her own boots and left them there, joining Alec as he turned into the hallway that accessed the right half of the house. He ducked his head briefly into the open bathroom doorway and then went into the laundry room.

Xo followed tentatively. It didn't feel right to poke about like this. She halted as she entered the laundry room. The room was filled with pile after pile of clean laundry on every surface, ironed and neatly folded in stacks, as if Elliot had decided to wash all the clothes he owned. Her mind tripped over trying to figure out what could have precipitated this, but no plausible explanation surfaced. It was the only clue they had to his disappearance, though.

"Do you think he spilled something in his dresser, or…?" Xo trailed off.

"Nah, this is just what he does," said Alec absently, leaving the room again. Xo trailed behind in puzzlement.

Back in the main room, her eyes were drawn to the framed print of the goldfinches that she had noticed on an earlier visit. As she examined it more closely, it became clear why it had first attracted her attention. It was one of her own paintings, though a low-quality print of one, reduced in size.

"Hey, Alec," Xo began, then stopped, reconsidering calling his attention to it. Alec, at the far corner of the room, opened the closet door by the woodstove and flicked on a light inside.

"Why are you looking in the closet?" Xo came up behind him.

"It's not a closet." Alec entered the room.

Xo lingered in the doorway. It was still technically a closet, as it didn't have any windows or other exits, but it was larger than she had expected and did not contain any clothes or vacuums or the other sorts of things people usually kept in closets.

Instead, there was a small desk with the kind of shelves above it that were used to sort letters at the post office. Various papers and photographs were on the shelves, and a few books, while a closed laptop sat on the desk. There were several strings tied from wall to wall above Xo's head level, with tiny clips on them, like miniature clotheslines. More photo prints were stacked on a filing cabinet.

"He used to use it as a darkroom. Maybe still does." Alec glanced around, then picked up a photo of a woman that had been leaning against the side of one of the cubbyholes above the desk. After regarding it silently for a few seconds, he put it back and turned to leave the room.

"Is that Lia?" Xo leaned around him, curious to see what she had looked like.

Alec gave her a funny look as he went out of the room. "No, it's you."

Xo stepped inside the room slowly and, almost against her will, picked up the photo by the edges. She felt like a thief. It was indeed a print of her, close up, in black and white, but it was a version of herself that she did not know. The woman in the photo wore an expression she had never seen in the mirror, sort of confused or astonished. Feeling strangely intrusive, she replaced the photo in the shelf and left the room, closing the door again behind her.

"Well, he's not here," said Alec, standing by the bed with folded arms.

"Ya think?" At times like these, Alec's statements of the obvious irked her no end.

Alec surveyed the room, chewing on the inside of his cheek. "When Lia died…" he said slowly, "Elliot didn't do too well, Xo."

"Why would you expect him to do well?" asked Xo, with growing exasperation. "Some people are capable of having feelings for others, you know."

Alec looked annoyed. "You don't understand."

"Understand what?"

"Elliot." Alec shook his head.

"I understand better than you!" said Xo. "Naturally, he'd be upset… about Lia. You wouldn't even know what it's like to be devoted to someone."

Alec turned to face her. "And you do?" He looked truly irritated, to Xo's surprise.

She started to say yes, and then stopped herself. There was no evidence to give for her claim. "I can imagine it, anyway. Shouldn't we go look for him?"

"Well, hold up. He could be anywhere," said Alec. "We should wait here and see if he comes back."

"I don't think we should be here," said Xo uncomfortably. She didn't like the sound of the "if," either. "I'm going to find him."

Xo marched over to the front door, opened it, and then froze.

Elliot stood on the doorstep, staring at her in surprise.

31

ELLIOT'S STORY

Elliot was too startled to speak.

"Alec let me in! We were worried about you," exclaimed Xo. She seemed to realize she was still blocking the doorway, and backed out of the way.

Elliot stepped inside. "You don't have to worry about me," he said quietly.

"Maybe I want to worry about you." Xo's voice sounded unsteady. She spun away from him and opened the kitchen cupboard. "I'm going to make some tea."

Elliot put his boots and coat by the woodstove and sat on a counter stool. A long-absent feeling of amusement twitched his mouth at the concept of Xo offering him tea in his own house. He hadn't smiled in days. Hadn't known it was still possible.

He'd thought that seeing Xo again would be almost unbearably painful, but her presence was unexpectedly comforting despite how they had parted. There was pain, but it brought life back with it, like warm water on icy hands after coming in from the cold, burning as the blood surged back in.

Alec appeared out of nowhere and waved a hand in front of Elliot's face. "Are you okay? You had us worried sick."

"I was only walking," said Elliot.

His subconscious had gone to work in the night, quietly sorting through his mind's spilled contents and putting it back into the little boxes and compartments that made it possible to go on living. On waking, he had begun to walk, knowing time and exposure to the icy wind would numb the ache inside. After an unknown number of hours, he'd found himself beside the tracks. The train used to seem like a wild card, an emergency option if he couldn't take it anymore, just as he'd once fled his old life to come here. Now, it only reminded him of the day he met Xo.

As for Xo's miraculous appearance in his doorway, he would have counted it a delusion if his outing in the biting cold had not already forced him to separate physical reality from his inner experience.

"Alec told me what happened." Xo settled on the stool next to him as the tea brewed.

"You weren't...there?" Elliot asked haltingly.

"No. I wish I had been." Xo's eyes went to his camera, zeroing in on the crack in the lens cover.

"I am glad you were not." Elliot shuddered.

"Megan said there was a fight," said Xo. "Were you hurt?"

Elliot shook his head silently. If she didn't know about that part, he didn't want to tell her. There were more important things to say that he should have told her long ago.

Alec patted Elliot's shoulder. "I'm going to leave you two to talk. Take care, okay? Don't give us another turn like that."

Elliot looked up in surprise. "Thank you."

Alec smiled and went out the door.

Xo shifted in her seat. "Do you want me to stay?"

"Yes. That is...if it's what you want," he added quickly.

"I want to. I just want you to be okay," said Xo.

Elliot took the cup of tea she had made him and stirred it. "I felt no one believed me. At the café. That they actually thought I could have killed her. Perhaps...they all knew about Lia and Francis." Not a pleasant thought, but likely. "You asked me about Lia, once."

Xo cringed. "I shouldn't have said what I said back then. I believe you."

"No, I should've told you the whole story," said Elliot. "It's…not easy to talk about, but I want to tell you. Lia…she was with Francis, before I met her. I thought it was over between them. It's still hard to believe it was not. She…helped me manage, after I broke my leg."

"From the mountain-climbing accident?"

Elliot stopped, momentarily derailed. Xo had made some inquiries about him after all.

"Alec told me." Xo's cheeks tinged with pink.

"Uh…yes," said Elliot. "It took some time to recover. We became better acquainted…and we married. I wonder now if she simply felt sorry for me." That was a new, unpleasant theory.

He set the idea aside and continued. "Francis moved away. I thought nothing more of him. I suppose they must have been in contact. Alec told you about the letter?"

"Briefly," said Xo.

"It read as if…there had been other letters." Elliot tried not to dwell on the contents. "At any rate, we weren't married very long before she became ill. I recognized the symptoms immediately. There was a similar outbreak of mountainpox in my hometown, when I was fifteen." He stopped. "Everyone else who caught it died. My parents…" He adjusted his glasses. "There's not much one can do, once the rash appears. Most people do not recover. My parents did not. I did, for some reason."

Elliot rested his teacup in his hands between his knees, studying it. "I finished high school. Finished college. I suppose I didn't know what to do but continue my studies. One just keeps going. But when I finished with that, I had nothing else. I couldn't stay there. Anyone who saw me knew I had lived through it." He touched the marks on his face. "Scars everywhere. It's…more extensive than it looks." He risked a glance at Xo. She was staring at the floor, so he continued. "Everyone there knew: about me, about my parents. Somehow, I couldn't stand their pity. So I left."

"What made you pick Lingen?" Xo's lack of polite sympathy was a relief. It was hard enough recalling the way people used to look at him with an evaluation of his suffering on their faces, hard enough admitting to her how it had made him feel.

"I saw a picture of Lingen on a postcard, and I just picked it. When I came here, it was like another world: it was beautiful, and people here didn't know about the mountainpox. To them, it was only a small, faraway news item when it happened.

"When Lia got sick, it all came back," he continued. "It was hard to believe that it was all happening again. They isolated everyone right away, so not as many people caught it here. Lia was one of the first. I stayed with her, figuring I was probably immune. I knew it wasn't likely, but there was a small chance she'd live, as I had. I'd lived through so many things that I felt it was possible—irrationally, perhaps. She only lasted a few days. At least she didn't suffer very long.

"After that, I suppose life went on. I thought that was it: the best part of my life over, and the rest…just filler. For a long time, Xiomara. Sometimes you simply keep living and you're not sure why. I moved on, eventually. I thought I did. And then, I met you." Elliot sought Xo's eyes. "And everything changed, again."

"Aren't you angry at her, to find out now that she was having an affair?" Xo frowned. "I don't see how she could do that to you."

Elliot sighed. "I tried to be, at first. I was shocked, yes. Sad. But I'm not angry. The thing is, Xiomara, she didn't leave me. It's possible that she would have—she considered it, judging from the letter. But she didn't. She was good to me, as far as I knew at the time, and now, she's gone. Since a long time. So what does it change, in the end? What's the point in being angry about it? I simply can't.

"When I found out, it was as if I discovered I'd never had what I thought I'd lost. I could wish that she'd left me and not been here for the outbreak. Or that she'd loved me. If she did, it was in some way I cannot comprehend, not in the way I loved her. But it's too far away in time. Perhaps what didn't happen, never could have happened…I don't know. What might have been is a story that never got written, and never will."

"Do you…still love her?" asked Xo.

Elliot considered. "I don't suppose it ends, exactly, does it? When you love someone. It is just…far away now. Not still growing, not alive and beating, filling up every fissure."

He allowed himself a look at Xo, then turned back to his teacup. "More like a memory of love. Though I cannot say it is still a memory of *being* loved. Knowledge does alter the way you feel about memories, sometimes. Isn't that strange? You'd think they would stay the same as when they were formed, before you knew.

"I don't feel any differently towards her than before I found out, if that's what you mean. Mainly, I feel differently about myself. Doubting my own perceptions, wondering how delusional I really am." He laughed slightly. "I guess I'll keep on being a fool, until I learn whatever it is I'm supposed to learn."

Elliot fell silent. He had been talking for too long, and he was exhausted. Probably he shouldn't be speaking of love to Xo, making her uncomfortable—but with her in the room, the alive, still-beating love had grown to obscure almost every other feeling, even his residual sadness. It was hard not to talk about love now that he had started, and now that she knew how he felt about her, but the memory of his last conversation with Xo kept him in check, thankfully. He wasn't sure how many more blows he could take in such a short time.

"You'll be okay, won't you?" asked Xo.

Elliot nodded. "It just took a while to register, I suppose. It was so sudden. I didn't mean to alarm you and Alec. Thank you, for coming. I didn't know if you would want to…to see me."

"I still want to see you," said Xo. "I want to see you again."

Unbelievably, Elliot's heart began doing its tricks again, flipping about. How much would it take to crush this feeling? It seemed impervious to reality or common sense, or else how could he still feel excitement and hope? Was it insanity?

"You still owe me a visit to go over those photos and notes." Xo smiled and rose, collecting her coat.

"And your hummingbird paintings."

"Tomorrow?" asked Xo.

"Yes." In his mind, she kissed him, and it wasn't goodbye.

❖   ❖   ❖

Elliot's walk to the coffee shop the next day seemed longer than usual. People he passed on the sidewalks paused and commented quietly to each other. The surreptitious glances took him back to the days when he was coping with the aftermath of the first outbreak. People had stared and whispered then, too. In time, he had adjusted to the way things were. The move to Lingen had helped, and eventually those long-ago issues had faded from his awareness. Until now. Was it just his frame of mind from talking to Xo the night before about events long past? Or perhaps the confrontation with Francis, reminiscent of other mortifying incidents of his youth, had awakened a self-consciousness that he'd thought was long gone.

The general populace had seemed quite ready to accept that Elliot had killed his wife in retaliation for the affair, despite Francis's particularly poor argumentation skills. This topic was surely the fuel for most of the gossip going on just out of his earshot, and it was a blow to his confidence in the general humanity of his adopted town.

Elliot pressed on, giving no outward indication that he noticed the added attention. Xo's belief in him was his armor against the world. He pushed open the door of the coffee shop, the scene of his humiliation—even more so now, since at the time he hadn't believed there was anything between Lia and Francis. Several people actually turned around in their chairs to see him enter, but Elliot focused on Xo, smiling behind the counter. She'd said she wanted to see him again. That was the only thing that truly mattered.

It was still a quarter of an hour until her shift ended, so he prepared to wait for her. He was grateful to see Alec at his usual table. Elliot sat nearby on the hearth.

"You're looking better," said Alec approvingly. "Good to see you in here."

"Thank you," said Elliot. "It is nice to see a kind face in the crowd." He shifted uncomfortably, aware that eyes were still on him.

"Don't let them get to you," said Alec. "Those rubberneckers aren't fit to shine your boots."

"All the same, I'm not sure I would have come if Xiomara had not made me," said Elliot. "I'm afraid I have given her a mess of photographs and notes, and not organized them with her as promised."

"I hope I did the right thing, bringing her by the other day," said Alec.

"Yes," said Elliot. "Thank you. Again. Not just for that." As usual, Elliot failed to adequately reciprocate Alec's role in his life.

Alec waved the thanks away, leaning back in his chair and tipping it on two legs as he surveyed the rest of the room. The murmur of voices that filled the shop was louder than usual. Alec sat forward again suddenly, thumping the chair down onto the floor, and several heads swiveled in their direction.

"All right, you lot," said Alec loudly. He twisted in his seat to fold his elbow over the back of the chair, addressing the entirety of the café floor. The noise level in the room dropped abruptly. "Anybody has a comment to say, they can come right up here and say it out loud instead of whispering in corners. I'd be happy to discuss." He clipped his words crisply. "No takers? I thought not. I'll leave it open." He swung back around to face Elliot, shaking his head. "Idiots," he said in a quieter voice.

"Much as I appreciate the gesture," said Elliot placatingly, "I don't think Jacqua would enjoy a second fight starting in his café within such a short time. We'll both get banned at this rate."

Alec chuckled and stretched, scanning the crowd again. A few people left hastily, possibly to continue their conversations outside.

A book on the mantelpiece above caught Elliot's eye. It turned out to be his, the one he had been reading when Francis interrupted—someone must have found it and put it there. And another person had handed him his glasses after the altercation. Perhaps he still did have supporters out there, they were just the quieter sort. Comforted, he found his place in the book and settled in to read.

Inadvertently triggered by some phrase in the text, his attention drifted back over to the counter where Xo was working. Her movements even at this distance were unlike anyone else's as she attended to some espresso-related crisis. If only it were enough to sit and watch her.

Alec broke into his reverie, giving Elliot a sideways look. "You really like her, don't you?"

Elliot continued to gaze at Xo. "I love her." The words he had once found so difficult were so simple to say after all.

Alec nodded. He didn't seem surprised by the revelation.

When she finished her shift, Xo made a fresh breve for herself and a latte for Elliot and walked with a mug in each hand over to where he sat. Elliot gathered his coat and stood as she approached. She handed him his cup and received thanks and a smile in return, but it wasn't exactly the same smile as he always used to have when she would give him his coffee. Likely the adoration had been there before, but caution had now replaced nervousness, and she feared that pain had replaced a certain endearing eagerness that had once broken Elliot's composure on a regular basis.

She wished she had not caused any of that pain. The news about Lia might not have hit him so hard if Xo hadn't already broken him first.

"What, none for me?" Alec grinned.

"Very funny," said Xo. "I'm sure you can get a coffee yourself if you mosey on over there and pay for it. Now, if you'll excuse us, we have business to attend to." She could tease him right back if he continued to insist on that.

Alec took it well enough in stride. He clapped Elliot on the shoulder as Elliot followed Xo past the table.

"Good luck!" Alec said in a loud whisper.

Elliot looked embarrassed. Knowing Alec, Xo decided it was best not to ask what he was referring to.

When she unlocked her apartment door, Elliot hung back, and she finally had to tell him to go in. She followed, kicking the door closed behind them with her toe. It bounced against the doorjamb without shutting properly. She'd noticed that morning that the strike plate was getting out of alignment with the latch, but at the moment her hands were full of keys and coffee, and there were more interesting things to attend to.

"Okay, first things first!" Xo put her coffee cup on one of the shelves at the back of the room and picked up the finished turquoise-naped hummingbird painting from where it leaned against the wall. "What do you think?" She held it up for Elliot.

"It looks so…alive. Especially considering your unfortunate subject." Elliot smiled, looking it over. "You've really done it justice, Xiomara."

Xo watched him examine it. She'd painted it in a style to be used in the field guide, showing the male bird based on the specimen, plus a female. A second male was pictured with wings folded and back to the viewer, to better show the turquoise patch on the nape of the bird's neck.

"I had to use a photo reference I found online for the female, but they are similarly plumed, just with a smaller gorget. I do prefer to sketch from life and then paint based on that, but since we have proof it lives here—or at least died here—I think Sade will still accept it for the field guide without a current sighting."

She held up another painting she'd been waiting on, feeling slightly nervous. "This one was just for fun."

The iridescent feathers of the bird had deserved more than the limited colors reproducible by the book printer, so she'd made a second painting with metallic pigments to imitate the effect of the feathers. This one showed the hummingbird at a flower. It was a bit silly; it certainly couldn't be made into a print that way, but in person the painting showed some of the shimmer that the hummingbird possessed in life, and even in death.

As she held it, Elliot touched the frame hesitantly, angling it to the light from the window so the iridescence showed.

"You amaze me, Xiomara." Elliot's voice was low and soft, but the words came out in an irregular rhythm, like silk catching on roughened hands. She felt a warm quivering in the core of her body, especially when it was her name that caught unevenly. He always did sound this way, she reminded herself. It was nothing new that she should take notice of it.

He looked at her now as if he might say something further. Then he sighed and returned his eyes to the painting, letting his hand fall away from the frame. She set the picture back down, feeling overheated. How could he still look at her that way, after she'd refused him, after everything? Or was she mistaken about the look? Did she want to be mistaken?

She took a deep, cooling breath. "Here are the lesser red-backed alpine finches." Xo placed the painting on the easel. "I'm not happy with this composition. I think I'm gonna redo it. This one's also for the field guide."

Elliot tilted his head. "Which part will you change?"

"I dunno exactly, but it didn't come out like I imagined. I want to highlight the difference in plumage, in case it turns out to be another subspecies, so it has to be right."

"Were the photographs enough?"

"It's not that. I just need to try a different arrangement or something." Xo frowned at the painting. "That's one of the things I like about painting, I guess—I can make it exactly like I want, and change it if it's not right."

Elliot smiled. "Or even bring it back to life?"

"Only in the picture." Xo found the acrylic box where she'd stored the specimen of the hummingbird, along with a packet of silica gel to help keep it free of moisture, and showed it to Elliot. "I was thinking now that it's modeled for me, I should let Sade display it at the visitor center. She did finally let me patch that owl back together, but it looks a bit wonky, and I kinda feel like I owe her a replacement bird. If it's okay with you, that is."

"It makes sense," said Elliot.

"Plus, if I knock this one on top of you, it won't be as heavy."

Elliot shook his head. "It was entirely my fault for startling you."

"Nah," said Xo. "I was totally being clumsy. You were very heroic."

Elliot ducked his head, examining the hummingbird painting again. It was hard to resist teasing him, but unfortunately it had caused him to stop talking.

"What are you thinking?" prompted Xo.

Elliot took a moment to answer. "I was thinking that I would not be able to make a hummingbird seem alive again, no matter how I framed the photo. The beauty in the world that I'm able to record— to save a small part of—is so intricate and astonishing that I could never imagine it, were it my task to invent in a drawing. I can only marvel at it."

"It still makes a difference what you include in a photo," said Xo. "I saw this photo of the Taj Mahal which showed all this garbage near it that people usually crop out. It did give a different perspective."

Elliot nodded. "If I go to an event with another photographer from the newspaper, we'll capture different images. And depending on which photos run, it gives a different impression of what happened—or at least, how the photographer feels about it."

Xo thought of the photo of herself in Elliot's closet darkroom, not how she saw herself at all. "Which photo tells the true story?"

"Well...both." Elliot rubbed his coffee cup pensively with his thumb. "As much as any one person's view is the truth of the matter."

"Why did you ask me to marry you?" said Xo.

Elliot had been in the process of taking a sip from his mug, but now he started abruptly and sloshed most of the hot liquid down the front of his shirt.

"Ahh!" He winced and bent over, pulling the scalding shirt away from his chest, but quickly looked back up at her. "I...I love you, Xiomara. I still do."

"But...marriage?" persisted Xo. "It's a lot to take in."

Elliot held the mug away from himself, cupping his other hand under it, though the coffee had also poured down the arm that held the cup. "When I told you how I feel...it just followed. I could not ask for your love without offering you everything I'm capable of giving in return. I know it's not much..."

Xo smothered an inappropriate laugh at Elliot's appearance. He looked incredibly serious, standing there covered with coffee.

"I'm afraid that's going to stain." She eyed the white shirt ruefully, thinking of his mysterious piles of laundry.

Elliot seemed to sense that he'd been released from answering further questions for the moment, and he relaxed, surveying the damage.

"Cold water. If you'll excuse me—" Elliot gestured towards the doorway that led to the kitchenette area and adjoining bathroom.

"Go ahead." Xo shooed him along.

Elliot walked hurriedly out of the room, and she heard the water in the bathroom turn on.

Xo could not stop smiling, despite the interruption in their conversation. She set the painting back on the floor and began hunting for the envelope with Elliot's notes, to discuss when he returned from rinsing his shirt.

A door creaked. At first Xo thought it was Elliot returning from the bathroom, but then the apartment door swinging open caught her eye. At the sight of the figure standing there, she froze.

32

REPERCUSSIONS

The guy Xo had met at the restaurant lounged in the doorway of her studio. He smiled widely. "Door ajar? That's what I call an open invitation."

Xo stood immobile, holding the envelope of Elliot's photos and notes. "What are you doing here?" she blurted out.

"You weren't that hard to find, and you did say you might like me to model for you sometime." He stepped into the room, giving her a sample pose. "Or do you prefer the nude form?"

"Umm...No! Actually, I am no longer considering that—that subject," said Xo robotically. "Strictly birds."

At any moment Elliot was bound to reappear. The sound of water running in the bathroom basin had ceased.

"Another form of recreation, then? I won't be in town much longer. You left so abruptly last time."

"No, no—I think we had a miscommunication before." This wasn't strictly true, nor did Xo want to get into the specifics of who had said what that night, as it wouldn't support her case. "I am not available for any type of...recreation." Her voice came out unnaturally high.

A movement from the kitchenette doorway caught the attention of both the man and Xo.

"Get. Out." Elliot's voice was a growl. He stood in the doorway glaring at the other man, his shirt still dripping wet from rinsing out the coffee. Xo's heart felt like it had tripped over her lungs. Elliot's reaction shocked her even more than the sudden appearance of the restaurant guy.

"Well, well," the man said—rather nastily, considering he'd said he was friends with Elliot. Then again, the situation was unlikely to bring out the best in either one of them. She had never seen Elliot look like this before. How much of the conversation had he overheard?

"I said, get out," Elliot repeated in threatening tones, stepping forward slowly. Only half the buttons on his shirt were buttoned, presumably because he'd thrown it back on in a rush, but the buttons were not lined up correctly. He buttoned another without looking as he advanced, compounding the issue.

The other man folded his arms and regarded Elliot with a sneer. "How long did it take you to sew those buttons back on? The other look suited you better: shabby, like you. Or is it too disturbing for the lady to see the taint of disease on your body?"

Elliot did not answer, but stepped between Xo and the other man, facing him.

"Please, just go," said Xo, with growing unease.

"Which of us are you addressing?" asked the taller man in an oddly cheerful voice, over Elliot's head.

"She is addressing you," said Elliot.

"I wouldn't be so sure," said the man. "You've never been very good at figuring out what women want, after all."

"Our business is finished, Francis," said Elliot. "And you have none with Xiomara."

Xo groaned in dismay. It was even worse than she'd originally thought. If Restaurant Guy was Francis, how could Lia have chosen him over Elliot? Although...Xo had nearly done that, herself. She didn't even know why she'd pulled out of the evening with Francis—she'd acted on an undefined feeling without having a logical argument to back it up. It was scary to realize that even though she'd avoided a truly horrible mistake, she still didn't know what had stopped her.

But she was not like Lia, Xo told herself, and she hadn't known then how Elliot felt. Even so, she'd made enough of a mistake that it would hurt him, yet again. Perhaps damage their connection irreparably.

"You should go, Francis," Xo said firmly. "What Elliot said is true. I didn't know who you were before, and I don't want anything to do with you." It would not do to have any misunderstandings at this point.

Francis looked displeased and taken aback. However, he didn't bother to reply to Xo, and instead addressed Elliot again.

"I can pick you up and break you just as easily as I did before." Francis narrowed his eyes. "I guess you didn't get enough last time."

"Just try," said Elliot, not moving.

"Oh, now you've got something to fight for, eh?" Francis's eyes flicked over to Xo and back to Elliot, who appeared indeed ready to do just that. "Lia wasn't worth that to you."

"Lia is…dead," said Elliot.

"She never loved you," spat Francis. "Lia just couldn't resist somebody who needed taking care of. She settled because she thought you were safe and dependable, but it was me she wanted."

"What's wrong with safe and dependable?" countered Xo.

Francis ignored her. "But she wasn't safe, was she?" he said to Elliot. "I can't believe I thought you had the ability to mastermind a murder, when you were too stupid even to see what was happening right in front of you." Francis's face twisted in disgust. "I'm still not sure you didn't somehow infect her without even realizing—it'd be like you to be so oblivious. You're just lucky stupidity isn't a prosecutable crime. You should've died of that disease long ago and spared everyone from looking at your sorry face."

"Shut up!" snapped Xo.

Francis continued speaking to Elliot. "And if you believe that whore behind you cares any more for you than Lia did, you're wrong. I happen to know!"

Xo scowled at Francis. His eyes finally flicked over to her for just a moment, but far from being cowed by her reaction, he was smiling nastily and triumphantly as he focused on Elliot again.

"She didn't tell you, then, about our little…dalliance?"

Even though Francis implied far worse than the truth, the truth was bad enough. Xo's face burned as she anticipated Elliot's reaction, but Elliot remained silent and tense in response to the taunts.

She watched Francis's eyes move between her and Elliot, and she glared back defiantly. It was two against one this time, and no audience to impress. Maybe that had been what spurred him on before, because after an almost interminable pause, he straightened up and took a step back.

"Well. Lucky for you, she's not worth my time," he said to Elliot. "And neither are you anymore. I wouldn't want to *catch* something." He reached for the door and stepped backwards through it, treating Elliot to a parting sneer as he closed it. Xo listened to his footfalls descending the stairs.

Elliot quietly stepped forward and opened the door enough to see out.

Xo peeked through the crack as well, over his head. "What are we doing?" she whispered.

"Making sure that he leaves," said Elliot in a low voice.

They watched the café door swing closed behind Francis. Then Elliot stepped back and let out a ragged breath while Xo closed and locked her apartment door. She stared at Elliot. He met her eyes with an expression of concern.

Once again, the enormity of what she had done hit her. This awful feeling combined incongruently with the relief of having avoided another fight between Elliot and Francis. She could now imagine the details of what had transpired before.

Xo stumbled over to the bed and sat down, grabbed the pillow, and hugged it to her chest, burying her face in it. She was terrified of the moment when Elliot would ask how she knew Francis, why Francis had come to her room. Seeing his disappointment in her would be unbearable. She hadn't wanted Elliot to know about that evening when it had been some unknown guy, but now it was a thousand times worse.

"Are you all right?" Elliot's voice was tentative, from near at hand.

Xo groaned. The fearful anticipation was even more unbearable. Why didn't he ask how she and Francis knew each other, and get it over with?

She felt Elliot sit down on the bed next to her, not touching.

"I won't let him…do anything to you," he said, after a minute.

He probably thought she was afraid of Francis coming back. While that was not a pleasant notion, Francis wouldn't have any reason to return. She'd made herself pretty clear this time.

"That's not the problem." Xo moaned into the pillow, against her knees. Elliot didn't say anything, so she wasn't sure he had understood. She lifted her head. "That's not the problem," she said more quietly.

"What is it?" asked Elliot softly, bending to catch a glimpse of her expression.

Xo hid her face in her hands, leaning her elbows on the pillow across her lap. She wished, irrationally, that Elliot would angrily demand to know what association she had with Francis, and stop being so nice. That was the response she deserved, and then she could get mad back at him, instead of feeling so ashamed.

It was becoming apparent that he wasn't going to make those demands, though. She would have to force the confession out of herself, and make an end of it that way.

"Elliot…I'm a terrible person. I did something incredibly stupid. I told you, you don't know what I'm really like." Xo's voice cracked.

"I know you're not a terrible person," said Elliot.

"But I am." She groaned. "I met him at this restaurant I went to with Megan. I swear I did not know it was Francis. I didn't even know there was a Francis, then." She forced herself to look at Elliot beside her to see what his reaction was, but he only appeared confused.

"I was just…The thing with Alec was pathetic. And then, I was so lonely. You went away…" As soon as the words were out of her mouth, Xo regretted them. It wasn't Elliot's fault, it was hers. She plowed recklessly on. "I dunno what I wanted, to be like Megan or

Alec and not care as much. I don't even know, now, what I was thinking. I started talking to Francis…and sort of encouraging him. I guess I wanted to see what it would be like, to be…wanted, maybe." She stopped, her face burning. "It didn't feel like I thought it would. Then I found out he knew you…Oh, Elliot, I think I even told him where he could find you!"

Xo covered her face with her hands again as the sense of horror grew. "I was disgusted with myself. I feel even more stupid now. I never guessed he would find where I live."

It had always been possible that he would come into the coffee shop and order something, but she'd expected to be able to handle that, plus he'd said he was only in town for a few days. She'd forgotten to worry about it, with everything that had happened since.

"And now, I'm sure, you're disgusted with me too." Xo reluctantly turned to Elliot to assess the damage.

"I could never be…I can't even say it." Elliot looked pained. "There is no shame in being lonely. I wish that I had been there for you. If you wanted…someone to talk to." He swallowed. "It was I who failed you. I should never have left."

Technically, Elliot had already come back from his work trip at the time, and she'd ended up yelling at him over his interference between her and Alec. And then she'd gone out and wound up with Francis the very same day. She couldn't judge anyone accurately. She'd felt dirty enough after considering a rendezvous with Francis before she knew what a scumbag he was, but now she felt worse. No matter where she turned, she was a clueless idiot: with Alec, with Francis. With Elliot. Why was Elliot not more upset with her? She ached to lean into him, to feel his arms around her, but surely that would not be fair to him.

"It's not because you left," said Xo. "It's just me. How can you stand me?"

Elliot's eyes gave her the answer before he spoke. "You know," he said after a moment.

She did know. But she didn't understand. "I keep making these terrible mistakes. I dunno what to do, to get where I want to be." Xo sighed.

"The road is made by the walking. Remember?" said Elliot.

"Well, I keep finding out that I took a wrong turn somewhere and made a dumb path," said Xo. "Then I want to back up and take a different direction."

"You are not alone in that. I've made so many wrong turns, Xiomara." Elliot's voice caught in his throat. "I think everyone does."

"Then how do you get back on track? I keep getting more lost." Xo sighed again.

"When it gets very dark, I look up and orient myself by the brightest star in the sky: Xiomara." The corner of Elliot's mouth twitched up.

Xo laughed a little despite her mood. "There isn't a star called Xiomara."

"You can't be Sirius?"

"Did you just make an actual joke?" asked Xo in mock astonishment.

"I can make jokes." Elliot smiled sideways at her.

Xo laughed again, following it with a deep breath, trying to relax. "If you don't hate me now, and for some reason it seems like you don't…let's look at your bird notes. No point in letting Francis ruin another day. He doesn't deserve it." She stood up.

"I am at your service," said Elliot.

"I'll get the laptop," said Xo. First, she went into the bathroom, splashed cold water on her face, and took more deep breaths until she was calmer. She collected the laptop from where it was charging in the kitchenette and returned to sit on the bed, picking up Elliot's notes again along the way.

It was a relief to do something practical and known. Much less confusing than wondering if she could hug Elliot instead of the pillow. She couldn't hurt him even more just because she needed some comfort. What if she did go down that road, and it ended? Considering her relationship history, this was quite likely—something always went wrong. She would probably lose him as a friend then, as well. She'd realized when she started telling him about her association with Francis that there was a lot at stake. Too much.

Xo took refuge in the task in front of them, to distract herself from such incomprehensible issues. Placing the notes beside her, she pulled up the photos on the computer. Elliot had correctly identified many of the birds, as far as she could tell, but others he had not been sure about or had written a description that she needed to confirm.

"Let's start by matching up the photos you sent with the descriptions, because there are more descriptions than photos," said Xo.

"I removed the hoodwinks," said Elliot.

"Aw, I was looking forward to those."

Elliot smiled. "A few might still qualify."

Sitting next to her on the bed, Elliot took the laptop and balanced it on his knees, scrolling through the photos he'd brought her.

"This is the same." He made a notation next to one of his written descriptions with the name of the matching image. "And this."

Xo watched his fingers move delicately over the keyboard. His hair curled over his forehead, falling forward as he bent to write something on the paper. Uncomfortably, she noticed a purple bruise on his neck when he leaned over, extending down his back under his shirt. Once, she would simply have asked what had caused it, but now she held back. It was probably a horrible vestige from his previous fight with Francis. And yet, moments ago he had been ready to endure more of the same.

Abruptly, Xo realized she had been using this notes-sorting session for a while to try to get Elliot to visit. Now that they were finishing it, what would be next? Would they drift apart again? Everything seemed so uncertain since the proposal, and her refusal.

Elliot turned to her, interrupting her thoughts. "This one, I was not quite sure about. I did not manage a photo."

She took the notebook. "It sounds a bit like a sandy-sided sapsucker, but it would be unusual at this time of year. Here, let me show you a picture." She reached over and tapped a few keys on his lap, pulling up photos. Soon they fell into a comfortable rhythm.

"I saw you had a bird feeder up last time I was at your house," prompted Xo after a while, as Elliot worked mostly quietly.

Elliot ducked his head a little. "One never knows, one of your rare birds might come. Nothing yet."

Xo smiled. "I doubt they visit feeders much, or there would've been more sightings over the years."

"Yes. But one never knows," said Elliot.

"I like that you have it up," Xo hastened to add. "No, it's nice. I mean, I guess even the elusive ones have to land and do ordinary stuff sometimes, right?"

"Yes." Elliot was looking at her again, and she felt herself growing warm all over. She quickly flipped through the notebook to check another entry.

In the end, all that could be noted or verified had been.

"I suppose that's everything." Elliot passed Xo the laptop.

She set it aside with the stack of notes, without getting up.

"Not quite." Xo bit her lip.

Elliot looked at her questioningly.

Xo reached out and took hold of his shirt collar with one hand, pulling him towards her. He caught his breath audibly.

For interminable seconds they faced one another without speaking. Elliot had completely frozen.

She had felt so sure of herself a moment ago, but now, doubt began to swim in the space between them and nibble away at her judgement.

"Your shirt buttons are all cattywampus," she said.

Xo unbuttoned the top button and carefully matched it to the correct buttonhole. Elliot's shirt was still damp from being rinsed, but she could feel the warmth of his skin radiating through it. She slowly progressed down the shirt, unbuttoning and rebuttoning. Her fingers were fumbling by the time all the buttons were lined up properly.

"There." Xo took her hands away.

Elliot hadn't moved during the entire proceedings. His eyes searched hers, and there was too much hope and anguish in them for her to sustain the gaze. It reminded her that she was not making rational decisions, could not make them while looking into that swirl of emotion.

She pulled herself away and stood up unsteadily. Crossing the room, she put the laptop and notes on the shelf. "Oh…" Xo picked up her coffee cup, and took a deep breath. "I forgot to drink my coffee, now it's all cold. Shall we go down and get some more, and have something to eat?"

Elliot unfroze himself. "Uh...yes."

They went down together.

Much later, when Xo returned alone to her apartment, she noticed a piece of scrap paper on her easel. The handwriting on it was Elliot's, and he could only have written it while she was off washing her face and finding the laptop.

On the paper was a cartoonish line-drawing of a mountain peak poking out of a sea of clouds. It was labeled, "Mt. Xiomara." Another label with an arrow pointing to the clouds said, "My love for you." At the bottom he had written "E."

Xo smiled, sighing, and wiped her eyes.

33

THE DANCE

When Elliot entered the coffee house with Alec for lunch, Megan and Xo were at the counter, deep in conversation.

"Hey, Alec, the music is go!" said Megan. "Xo said she doesn't mind if we stay open late and keep her up all night."

"Well, not all night," Xo interjected.

"Don't go changing your mind now," said Megan. "Jacqua said you had to agree. It'll be a blast, and good for business."

"All night sounds good." Alec grinned. "I have a friend in the band," he added to Xo.

"Maybe you could get them to fix their poster," said Xo.

Elliot anxiously searched Xo's face as she talked to the others. By now she would have discovered the note he'd left, which perhaps he should not have left. It might have been wrong to bring up his feelings again, but she'd seemed so upset, so sure he would not be able to see past whatever had occurred between her and Francis. Merely telling her that it had no impact on his love for her did not seem to be enough.

Then there had been that moment between them. Elliot had replayed it in his mind a thousand times without coming to a definitive answer: had it meant something to her? Should he have done something, or was it just buttons, and he was imagining everything else? When it came to interpreting her intentions, it was difficult to distinguish what was real from what he only desperately wanted to be real. In his recollection of the moment, there was also music playing in the background of his mind, and that was certainly added on afterwards.

"Are you listening to the music?" Xo asked Elliot.

Elliot stared at her in alarm. Surely, he wasn't already over the brink. "Pardon?"

"The band that they're lining up to come here." Xo indicated Megan and Alec, who were leaning on the counter debating what should go on a flyer advertising the event. "Featherduster. They're pretty good. Sounds like it might be a fun evening, dancing and such." She gazed dreamily at the ceiling.

"Yes." Elliot decided on the spot. "I am. I will." Xo smiled happily at him and his heart pounded.

"Oh!" said Xo. "I have something for you. Wait here." She walked around the counter and ran up the stairs to her apartment, leaving the door open and Elliot in a whirlwind.

Megan handed Elliot his coffee, and as Xo didn't immediately re-emerge, he sat in his usual place. The only thing he had left behind in Xo's apartment was that note.

Xo reappeared carrying what was obviously a framed painting wrapped in a large black plastic trash bag. She sat down next to him.

"The bag is to keep the snowflakes off on your way home." Xo pulled open the drawstring, lifted out the painting and put it on his lap.

It was the painting of the goldfinches. Elliot held it in shock.

"I saw the print in your house." Xo smiled mischievously. "How long have you been stalking me, anyway?"

"I—I only put that up after we met," Elliot stammered. "You had mentioned online that it was printed in a magazine. I—uh—found the issue."

"My one published work, before I got the job at the visitor center," said Xo. "I'm moving up in the world! Was that just the page of the magazine then? It was a terrible reproduction."

"I'm afraid so."

"Well, you deserve a better version of it," said Xo. "I want you to have the original."

Elliot ran his hands down the frame, swallowing hard. "Thank you. I don't know what to say. Someday, this will be worth millions, and I shall refuse to sell."

"What do you mean, 'someday?'" Xo laughed.

Elliot examined the painting again, then carefully pulled the protective bag up around it. Xo's gift had completely caught him off guard. He had put up the print because it did not seem within his rights to display an actual photograph of Xo. Not that he'd meant for her to see it—she just had a way of arriving in his house without time for advance preparations. The painting, the fact that she'd given it to him, meant much more. He was never prepared for what she would do next, but he would willingly be thrown for a loop as many times as she wanted to throw him.

"I love it." Words were so insufficient.

"Good," said Xo. "Because you have to promise to do something for me, in return."

Elliot's mind whirled with possibilities, both positive and negative. However, ultimately it didn't matter what she was going to ask: he already knew he would agree. "Anything."

Xo hesitated. "I want to draw you."

This was not one of the possibilities that had come to mind. "Me?"

"Yes, a portrait. You have to sit for me." Xo tilted her head, considering him. "Possibly more than once, until I get it right."

Elliot shifted self-consciously on the hearth. "But...why do you want to draw me?" There were countless better human subjects, and he'd never seen any portraits of people amongst her collection anyway.

"I just do. Deal?" Xo reached out towards the painting in slow motion, as if to take it back.

"All right." He couldn't refuse her request, as discomfiting as it was.

"Great!" said Xo, as if she'd known he would agree, which she probably had. She stood up. "I'd better get back to work now, but I'll figure out a time when I can draw you. We'll do it at your house—you might look more comfortable there."

Xo headed back to the counter, turning to smile and wave at him. Elliot lifted one hand in response, then returned it to the painting on his lap, still feeling stunned.

❖   ❖   ❖

"Tonight could be your big chance, Elly," said Alec, as he crunched alongside Elliot in the freshly fallen snow later that week. They followed the sidewalk downhill towards the coffee house, breath fogging in the chill evening air.

"In what way?" said Elliot.

"You know: music, dancing." Alec waved his hand around briefly before jamming it back in his coat pocket. "Women love these things. Puts them in a romantic mood."

It was true that Xo had made frequent references during the week to this evening's event. She had also not forgotten the drawing session, which she had scheduled for an upcoming weekend. Elliot felt more prepared for tonight, but it would still be best not to let his imagination get carried away.

"Did you bring a book?" asked Alec suddenly.

"I always bring a book."

Alec groaned to the sky.

"If it's too loud to read, then I could take photos," said Elliot, a bit defensively.

"Well, it could be good press," admitted Alec. "We could do a story. They might have other musical evenings if it goes well."

Elliot nodded.

"Okay, but listen," said Alec. "You got me off track there. This evening isn't about avoiding boredom."

"Problems could arise," Elliot agreed. "I intend to look out for Xiomara."

Alec frowned. "I heard Francis finally went home, at least. But that wasn't what I meant."

"What, then?"

"She didn't ask you to come so you could 'look out' for her," said Alec. "Maybe you should demonstrate that you're capable of having a good time. I get the impression Xo thinks she should have more fun and excitement in her life. Though you already seem to get into enough trouble around here for all concerned—not exactly sure how."

"Isn't the musical entertainment supposed to provide the fun and excitement?"

"It's supposed to provide an opportunity for people to loosen up and enjoy themselves," said Alec. "You might want to give that a try. You didn't used to be quite this serious all the time."

Elliot sighed. "Yes, well, I've had a series of traumatic events of late. You may be familiar with some of them."

"There are more?" Alec raised his eyebrows. "Well, can't say I'm surprised, but appearing traumatized isn't usually the way to the maiden's heart. Don't get stuck in the past. Tonight is about the here and now!"

Alec pushed open the café door, preventing any rebuttal that Elliot might have come up with, given more time. He grinned back in acknowledgement of this as Elliot followed him in.

The coffee house had been re-arranged to accommodate the event by moving the tables to the sides and front of the room, creating an open space in the center. The band was setting up their equipment in front of the fireplace, where Elliot usually sat. Some customers were watching expectantly, but several heads turned as Alec and Elliot entered, giving Elliot a familiar uncomfortable feeling.

"Hang your coats over on the wall tonight." Megan shooed Alec and Elliot in the direction of the coat rack. "And Elliot, you can manage a chair, they're plenty comfortable. You always look like you're about to jump up and leave suddenly when you're sitting on that hearth."

Elliot regretfully parted from his coat, with his book in the pocket. "Sometimes one has to leave suddenly."

"None of that, we're here to party." Megan disapprovingly eyed the camera in Elliot's hand, which he'd removed to take off his coat. He quickly looped the strap back around his neck.

"We might do an article," supplied Alec helpfully.

"Yeah? Awesome!" Megan ran off to accost more incoming customers.

Since the hearth was blocked, Elliot made his way over to the stairs and sat down a few steps from the bottom, watching the room fill and the band test their equipment. Alec had broken away to help them find electrical outlets for their gear, chatting with his friend who was part of it.

Under the dull roar in the room and the band starting their first number, Elliot felt footsteps on the staircase above him. He turned to look up and gulped. Xo was descending, as luminous as ever plus a bit more so, in a garment that was unusually sparkly. She walked down the stairs directly towards him and sat beside him with a radiant smile.

"You look…nice," said Elliot. Stunning. Breathtaking. Lovely. Gorgeous. These concepts always became so mired on the way to his mouth and ended up lackluster.

"Thanks, you too," said Xo. "I like this top, but things didn't go so well last time I wore it. I'm gonna try to make a better memory association with it tonight, so I can keep on liking it."

Elliot wondered if he should have dressed up more. He was wearing his good vest, as it was an evening event, but that wasn't saying much. Hopefully his usual habit of dressing neatly would suffice. Come to think of it, what else could he have worn? A tie would likely have been too much.

Xo smoothed the soft nap of her shirt with her palm, and Elliot's mind flooded with the imagined sensation of doing the same with his own hand. He averted his eyes before she could notice, swallowing hard. He should say something. Any unrelated topic would do at this point, if only he could think of one. His eyes fell on the poster the band had put up on the wall behind them.

"Of course, one doesn't make dusters with crow feathers," he said.

"Ha!" Xo turned to him with shining eyes. "I know, right?" She laughed delightedly.

Elliot could only watch her in mute amazement. If she was happy, he was happy, it didn't matter how or why.

"I gotta go make sure they have everything taken care of in the kitchen." Xo jumped to her feet. "Back in a bit. Do you need anything from there?"

Elliot assured her he was fine, and she wove away through the room, which was more crowded now that the music had started. It might be a good time to take photographs. He climbed the stairs to get a better view and snapped a few pictures from the landing outside Xo's apartment, then waited, scanning the room. What he really wanted was a picture of Xo when she came back out of the kitchen. She wasn't working tonight, so she was bound to reappear shortly.

Sure enough, Xo emerged from the back room and paused with her hand on the door frame. Elliot raised his camera and captured the pose. She stepped sideways and started around the counter. He panned the camera and adjusted the zoom, taking a step forward. His knee banged against the balusters of the railing and he stumbled, reaching out one hand to steady himself on the rail.

Except it didn't steady him. Where there should have been resistance as he braced himself against the rail, there was none. The whole four-foot section of the balustrade he had leaned on had come loose from the wall and was tipping forward into the room. And Elliot was falling with it. He let the camera drop to the end of its strap and grabbed the rail with both hands, but of course this did not help.

Quickly, Elliot snatched at the neighboring section of railing, no longer connected, standing aloofly back where it belonged, but it was already out of reach. There was an ominous creak as the nails attaching his section to the floor of the landing pried out under his weight. Nobody else appeared to notice it over the music, until with a loud crack and splintering of wood the section flipped completely upside down.

Elliot, still holding on, somersaulted over it with a terrific jolt and ended up hanging from the edge of the railing in midair. Several people screamed. The closest table evacuated in complete disarray.

Elliot's camera had deserted him in the middle of the flip, bouncing off his face to land somewhere below. Clearly, he should have been wearing the strap more securely across his body this evening, instead of around his neck. This thought was interrupted by another loud creak from the section of railing, now dangling by a few bent nails, as it announced that it was not going to remain connected to the landing much longer with his weight pulling it down.

Taking what seemed the better of two bad options, those of falling either with or without the railing, he chose the latter and let go before the railing did. There had been a small chance of landing on his feet, but it was not to be. He did roll with the fall, though, away from the hearth, fetching up against one of the hastily abandoned chairs.

His letting go had triggered a few more screams from customers, but now there was silence. At some point during his descent, the band had clued in to what was happening and stopped playing. The silence was broken by the drummer playing a sting. Several people laughed nervously in response, including Elliot himself now that he had caught his breath. He adjusted his glasses back where they belonged and propped himself up on one elbow. The railing still dangled from the landing above, relieved of his weight.

Then Xo was there, pushing through the crowd. The gathered onlookers had started talking animatedly, describing to each other what had happened, with those who hadn't seen trying to get closer. The general mood appeared upbeat, except for Xo.

"Elliot! Are you okay?" Xo knelt beside him, her hand on his shoulder, her face creased with concern.

"Uh…" Elliot coughed in embarrassment. "Yes." He glanced up at the rail. "I'm afraid I can't say the same for your bannister."

"What was he even doing up there?" said somebody in the background to somebody else. Elliot didn't hear the answer and hoped Xo didn't either.

Xo ineffectually tried to help him to his feet, but he managed to get up in spite of her efforts.

She touched his cheek softly. "Your face…" Her touch burned more acutely than the bruise which had preceded it.

"Bludgeoned by my own camera." He retrieved it from the table where it had landed and turned it on and off. This digital camera was more finicky than his film camera, but it had survived. Perhaps it was time to consider an even more durable model.

"I can't take my eyes off you for two seconds!" Alec elbowed his way through the other customers to where Elliot and Xo were standing. He stared up at the railing, then back at Elliot, and began dusting Elliot off. "This is not what I meant by enjoying yourself."

"Enough of that." Elliot arrested Alec's hand.

"Did you get a picture on the way down? This is going in the article!"

"This is *not* going in the article," said Elliot firmly. He added in a lower voice, "Could you tell your friend in the band to start playing again?"

Alec obliged, and as the music started back up, people drifted away from the scene to return to their own tables, except for the table into whose midst Elliot had fallen.

"Try offering them complementary pastries or something," suggested Alec to Xo, indicating the people who were still standing around looking doubtfully at the section of rail overhead.

"Oh! Good idea." Xo started for the counter, then paused, turning back to Elliot. "Are you sure you're okay?"

"I am, thank you. Please, go ahead," said Elliot quickly. Jacqua had arrived at the scene and stood surveying the dangling section. Elliot stepped over to him as Xo hurried away.

"I'm terribly sorry," said Elliot. "I will, of course, pay for the damage—"

"No," interrupted Jacqua firmly, holding up one hand. He steered Elliot over to the counter, where Xo was collecting two plates of free pastries to appease the displaced customers. They had been re-seated at a safer table.

Jacqua handed Elliot a pastry as well and made him a cup of coffee, then picked up a toolbox he'd brought from somewhere and climbed the stairs. He began removing the loose section from its precarious position. Elliot stared dazedly at the pastry and coffee cup in his hands.

Xo approached again, looking worried. "We could go sit down while you recover. I wouldn't mind, really."

Elliot looked up in surprise. Much as he'd like to feel her touch on his cheek again, he wished she wouldn't look so concerned. He was not giving her the fun evening she'd been talking about all week, he realized, with 'dancing and such.' But it was not too late.

He smiled. This seemed to alarm her further.

"I'd rather dance," said Elliot. "Will you join me?"

A few people stood on the periphery of the cleared dance area, bending their knees and bobbing their heads, but not really dancing. Elliot put the pastry and coffee on the counter and took Xo's hand, leading her towards the middle of the room. She went along with him, wide-eyed.

A peculiar sense of freedom filled him. He had already made a complete spectacle of himself that evening, on top of the malicious gossip he'd attracted thanks to Francis. If people were going to stare at him now, well, they'd already been staring anyway.

Despite his resolve, his heart was pounding as he stepped into the open area and turned to face Xo, her hand still in his own. Xo glanced back towards Alec and Megan with an expression of bewilderment, then laughed and covered her face with her free hand. She stepped forward to join him, trying to mirror what he was doing. And their rhythms aligned, and they were actually dancing.

Elliot concentrated on Xo, and the noise of the other people blended into the music. Xo was not laughing anymore, but still smiling, her eyes fixed on his shoulder. The hand he wasn't holding landed there of its own accord as she stepped closer. Everything else merged with the background except Xo, so close to him, and the places where their hands touched each other, her scent, the sound of her breathing. The heartbeat in his ears grew louder and merged with the drum until there was only one beat left to follow, but it served.

34

Xo Draws Elliot

Xo awoke filled with a fluttery impatience: today was the day she would try to capture Elliot's likeness, as he'd promised she could. Ever since the dance, the anticipation of this time alone with him had grown.

Every time they saw each other, which was at least once a day when he came into the café, one half of her urged a headlong rush. The other decidedly stronger half, trained for years to control the impulsive side, had so far successfully kept her contained. Each day in Elliot's presence she hoped for another sign from him that would push her over the edge, but he had already put all his cards on the table. It was her turn, if she could only figure out a decision.

To say she was in love sounded so juvenile, impractical: not a suitable reason. Inside, she still felt like she had when she was little, unsure of how people decided what to do in the adult world. Being a person had never come naturally, and she'd spent a lot of time trying to figure out how a person was supposed to be, before eventually realizing that she was stuck with herself and had to work with that.

There was also the reality that her relationships rarely worked out. Even friendships were a challenge. She would be sure she was on the same page with someone, and it would turn out not to be even the same book. And there always came a time where she pushed too hard for an explanation, or broke down emotionally and scared the other person away.

Xo wiped her face briskly and sat up straight. Letting the past bring her down wasn't going to help her future. She had to think in terms of Elliot only. And Elliot had never run away from her demands or tears.

She reached for her notebook and opened it on her knees. Elliot: pros and cons. Her pencil hovered above the page. This type of evaluation hadn't pointed her in the right direction with Alec...or Francis. Her lists must be leaving out something important that she couldn't figure out how to describe or quantify: those vague discomforts, soaring warmths, twinges in the center of her body, leaps of joy, and whatever it was that moved her to tears. Things like the burning feeling of wanting to see Elliot right now, and more than see: to touch, to hear his voice like nothing else, to feel him clasp her hand again. It was so easy to be in his accepting presence. It was easy to be *her* around him—that was what made it easy. And he loved her anyway. In spite of her.

She tried to picture Elliot with a list of pros and cons about her, but she couldn't manage it. The failed attempt made her smile, improving her mood a little. Elliot figured things out some other way, and he didn't seem to look at marrying her as a practicality, either. Her gaze drifted over to her easel, where he had stood, dripping coffee, telling her he could not offer her anything else except everything. He was trusting her with...well, the rest of his life, all of him. Could she do the same, throw caution to the wind? The idea thrilled and scared her, but she couldn't tell if it would be wise or stupid.

Noticing the clock on the shelf behind the easel made her jump. Quickly, she closed the notebook without entering anything and grabbed her bag and a drawing board, shoving her feet into her boots.

Bright morning sunshine was slanting through the high window above the landing as Xo left her apartment. Jacqua had strung yellow plastic "CAUTION" tape across the gaping hole where the railing was missing. He must keep a supply of this tape handy for such situations, though she'd never seen it lying around. It could be a useful thing to get Elliot, though he'd probably need to be wrapped in it himself for it to do any good.

The entertaining mental image of wrapping Elliot in caution tape was banished as Xo peered over the edge, and her insides clenched at the sudden recollection of his fall. For a moment she allowed herself to remember the clash in her mind that night: the horror of seeing him fall, the fear of what she might find when she reached him. Did the danger create the tangle of emotions in her, or did it merely illuminate a pre-existing truth of how much he meant to her? The memory held too much terror for his well-being to comfortably examine it further, so she pushed it from her mind again as she descended the stairs.

The tables and chairs were back in their customary locations now, but Xo paused in the middle of the room to imagine it cleared again. She couldn't remember another time that she had danced in public, at least not since she was a little girl. She didn't even know how to dance. Almost certainly it was not something Elliot did regularly either, but no one else could have successfully persuaded her to join in. Maybe this kind of protection, the sense of safety to do such things, she could accept.

Xo headed up the snowy, sunlit sidewalk, adjusting her drawing board under her arm. She had drawn Elliot many times before in her mind, unbeknownst to him. She would watch him sitting on the edge of the hearth with a book balanced on his knees as he waited for her to finish work, or looking up in response to Alec's latest remark. Then she would trace the lines: his tousled hair, eyelids, glasses, the way his sideburns curled over the sharp angles of his face. Her fingers would move ever so slightly throughout the mental exercise, as she imagined how the pencil would record each mark. It was a very satisfying exercise, but it didn't stay in her mind after he was no longer in front of her, like it would if she really drew him—not as a whole picture. Once she made the real drawing, though, it would become a perma-nent mental image that she could always call up, even if the sketch itself were not present.

This time Elliot was expecting her at his door. He ushered her in with an apprehensive smile, and Xo noted approvingly that the painting of the goldfinches was in its proper place. While Elliot made tea, Xo sat on a counter stool and folded up one knee as a place to rest her drawing board, taking a sheet of heavy paper from her large sketchpad.

Elliot put the teacups on the counter and settled gingerly on another stool. For someone who photographed others on a regular basis, he looked awfully nervous about being drawn. "Shall I sit here, or...?"

Xo smothered a smile of amusement. "Sure, but once you get situated you can't move around a whole lot, okay? Oh, and the rule is: you can't look at the drawing until I'm done. No peeking."

Elliot nodded. He sat up straight with his knees together, hands resting on them, and faced her directly with a fixed expression.

Xo adjusted her drawing board and taped the paper down at the corners, and then regarded Elliot further, hesitant to begin. His posture was incredibly unnatural.

"Are you sure that's the position you want to stay in?" she asked. "You don't look very relaxed. Or even your usual non-relaxed."

Elliot rolled his shoulders and tipped his head around in what was presumably an attempt to loosen up. When he became still again, the effect was exactly the same as before.

"Okay." Better to just get started. Xo managed well enough with birds that weren't posing for her, but then, people were harder. And when she had drawn Elliot mentally, he wasn't looking directly at her like this, but was occupied with something else. She sketched for a while. Every time she looked up, Elliot was frozen in the same position.

It was hard to focus on anything besides Elliot's eyes with him staring so intensely at her. The different flecks in his irises had always made her uncertain about their actual color, green or hazel. Sometimes, depending on what was around him, they seemed to take on a more golden hue, but there wasn't anything else green nearby now to enhance the color, and they were still extremely green. Green then. She wasn't sketching in color anyway. His gaze was completely unwavering, like he was watching her eyes for a glimpse of something deeply hidden, or waiting for it to reappear at the point he had last seen it.

Xo blinked and shook her head, taking a deep breath. She felt like she had stepped back from the edge of something that went too far down to be leaning over like that. The drawing was not progressing very well.

"I can't really concentrate with you looking at me," she said finally. "Maybe it would be better if you focused on something else."

Elliot's gaze finally broke, flicking from one of her eyes to the other, and he sat back. "Where should I look?" He sounded confused.

Xo scanned the room for inspiration. "Could you try reading a book or something? You might get in a better position then, too."

"All right." Elliot retrieved one from the bookcase and returned to the stool, spreading the book open on his lap. Sandy lashes shaded his eyes.

"Just don't look totally down, or I can't see your face at all."

Elliot turned partially and propped the book between one knee and the counter so his head was not bent as much.

"That's good." Xo sighed in relief and flipped the paper over to start fresh. "Are you actually reading?" she asked after a moment, as he was still completely immobile.

"No," admitted Elliot. "I'm sorry, I'm afraid I'm being a poor subject."

"No, I just have to find the right angle." Xo sketched away, trying to sound reassuring. "I'll admit it's slower than photography, but at least it doesn't hit you in the face, right?" she added cheerily. The welt from his camera had developed a few new shades of color.

Elliot's lips twitched in amusement. "I didn't prepare very well for the portrait, did I?"

"Don't worry, I'm not putting the bruise in. Artistic license."

"Perhaps you can make other improvements as well," said Elliot.

"Did you always grow out your sideburns?" asked Xo after a few moments, as she worked on that area of the sketch.

Elliot laughed. "Is that one of the improvements?"

"Oh! No, that's not what I meant. I like them. I was just curious, as they're not very common around here." Xo could feel herself blushing. Luckily, Elliot looked back at the book to hold his pose.

"I've kept them since they started growing, for the most part. I suppose I'm accustomed." He paused for a moment. "It was... challenging to shave there without cutting myself, initially."

Because of the scars. Elliot had survived mountainpox, but Xo suffered from foot-in-mouth. She felt horrible. "I didn't mean to make you uncomfortable."

Elliot glanced over at her without altering his pose. "I don't mind you asking, Xiomara. You can ask me anything you want."

Xo's heart beat faster. She hesitated: he was a captive subject here...did he really mean *anything*?

"Please," said Elliot.

"What do you think makes one person fall in love with...another particular person?" she asked.

Elliot's face softened and he thought for a minute without answering.

"I would tell you if I knew," he said eventually. "Isn't it one of the mysteries the ancient philosophers pondered? And then the poets tackled it for centuries, trying to find the answer. And when people stopped believing in poets, science took up the question. I don't know that they're any closer to the answer, even now."

"I wish they were. I've...thought I was in love before," said Xo slowly. "But then it would end. When it would happen again, it felt like the last time must not have been real love at all."

"It could merely be that it's different each time."

"Then how do you know it's not going to end? I don't know many people who've lasted a lifetime—I can barely even remember what it was like before my parents split up."

"I guess it's what they call a leap of faith," said Elliot. "One can't even prove, for certain, that the sun will rise again. But we trust that it will, because it always has, and because we have to believe that, even though we know there's a chance it may not."

"Relatively speaking, the failure of love seems a lot more likely than the end of the world."

Elliot smiled without moving his head. "It may be that this is another juncture where poets and scientists disagree."

"You're one of the poets, right?" said Xo. "I mean, for real, are you?" He probably had a collection of his own poems tucked away somewhere.

"Only so far as a carpenter who is unable to use any tools could call himself that," said Elliot. "If I am, it is only at heart. Words…are difficult to work with sometimes."

"When you were married before, it seems like Lia had a change of heart or something…" Xo wasn't sure if she should bring up the subject. "How can you pick someone, knowing you might fall out of love again or get interested in a new person?"

Elliot paused before answering, but he did not look offended. "I cannot pretend to understand her decisions, so I only speak for myself on this: falling in love may not be a choice, but you choose what you do next. You can choose to dedicate yourself to…the one person. To cultivate that love, nurture it. Sometimes, people choose not to. They withhold care, or walk away and let it die. Even try to crush it."

Xo switched to drawing Elliot's hair to avoid recording the expression which was now a little melancholy. "So, you're also a gardener! But you know, sometimes a plant dies no matter how well you take care of it."

"It's possible that I would do better at gardening than poetry," said Elliot, with a look of amusement. Xo was quick to capture it with her pencil. "But, yes, you do what you can, and hope for the best. And believe in the sun rising again."

"I dunno how you can have so many things go wrong in life, and still have faith that it will all turn out."

"That's when you need it the most," said Elliot. "Don't think that I don't fall into my chasms of despair, Xiomara. But even when I think it must be gone, there is that hope again. Here—"

Elliot flipped through the book he was holding, looking at it attentively for the first time. One angular hand traced lightly down the page. The skin on the backs of his hands was slightly translucent, with ridges of bluish veins standing out in relief. She should have put his hands in the sketch to record them as well. There was no way to do so now in the amount of space left on the paper, unless she gave him an uncharacteristic pose.

"You might like this," Elliot said, reading aloud:

> " 'Hope' is the thing with feathers—
> That perches in the soul—
> And sings the tune without the words—
> And never stops—at all—..."

"That is Emily Dickinson," he said. "And very apropos, for my ornithologist."

Xo felt one of those peculiar twinges inside; she could almost believe it was that thing fluttering in her own soul. When she looked down at her sketch, the drawing was all wrong. The individual parts of it were like Elliot, but they did not look right when they were all put together. She took out a new sheet of paper and began again, while Elliot read to her.

35

Xo's Confession

Xo finished her shift at the coffee house and went upstairs to get her coat before Elliot arrived. She paused on the way out of her apartment to flip through the stack of illustrations she'd made for Sade this week. Despite how difficult it had been to capture Elliot's likeness, when she'd returned to her birds they'd practically flown out of her hand onto the paper. The portrait had been the exercise she'd needed, and drawing him had been enjoyable in a way she'd almost forgotten it could be.

The final drawing of Elliot, the product of not one, but several sessions she'd spent with him, lay on her dresser next to the novel he'd lent her some time ago. The sketch wasn't quite as accurate as she would have liked, but it still served to evoke Elliot in her mind, not only his image but the sound of his voice, his way of moving. A lump rose in her throat as she surveyed the drawing. It still wasn't enough. She wanted him to be there in reality. To always be there.

She took a deep breath and went out onto the landing, looking down into the café over the repaired railing. As if in answer to her wish, a familiar figure was perched in his customary spot on the edge of the fireplace, tawny head bent over a book, waiting for her.

As she stood there, Elliot looked up, and it was as if the sun came out in his face. "Xiomara!"

"Want to go for a walk?" asked Xo.

"Of course." Elliot marked the place in his book and stood up.

Xo stuffed her mittens in her coat pocket and hastened down the stairs. The toe of her hiking boot knocked something off the last step of the staircase and it skipped across the floor. Elliot bent and picked it up. It was a button.

"You could use it," said Xo. "Almost looks like one of yours."

He examined it pensively, and then slowly put it in his pocket. "It is."

Elliot's gaze went to the bannister. His face had a faraway, grave look.

"Oh." From his demeanor, the button must have ended up here during the altercation with Francis. Xo's first impulse was to ask what he was thinking about it, but then he'd have to keep thinking about it, and she would see the pain increase in his eyes remembering the betrayal. Talking about things didn't seem to help him as much as it did her; it would only make him feel worse if she pressed him. And this day, in particular, needed to go very differently.

"Never mind Francis, whatever he said, he was wrong," said Xo.

She slipped her hand into Elliot's to draw him towards the door. The effect was instantaneous. It was like a magic power she was only recently discovering how to use. Elliot raised his head. His eyes had cleared, and it was plain that every thought of anything except her had just left his head. She smiled at his reaction and tugged him along, and Elliot followed her wordlessly out the door into the lightly falling snow.

Xo turned her face up so the flakes melted on her cheeks, and sighed delightedly. "So beautiful."

Elliot looked at her. "Yes."

The snow made a soft noise of its own as it fell, muffling all other sounds as they walked along.

"Where are we going?" asked Elliot.

"Oh, it doesn't matter," said Xo. "I just want to walk with you."

Her fingers, however, were beginning to stiffen in the cold, so she dug her mittens out of her pocket and put one on her free hand. She tried unsuccessfully to stuff her and Elliot's conjoined hands into the other mitten, but they would not both fit and she gave up, laughing.

"You put it on," said Elliot with a grin. "I don't want your hand to get cold."

"Very chivalrous!" Xo turned him loose and put the other mitten on, rubbing her hands together to warm them up. "You are, you know. You are the most chivalrous person I know in real life. And the kindest. The sweetest."

Elliot lowered his eyes. "But?"

"That's nice too," said Xo slyly. Elliot laughed self-consciously, making her grin. "But I like your smile best," she went on. "You make me feel strange. And you make me feel like it's okay to be strange." She paused. "Those are two different kinds of strange I'm talking about. The second one, I guess I always was, but the way you make me feel is…different than I've felt before."

Xo could feel Elliot looking at her, and she knew exactly what his expression would be like, but she couldn't fall into his eyes now or she would lose her train of thought. Instead, she gazed at the ground beneath her feet as they walked together, at her hiking boots making neat, fresh prints in the pristine snow.

"I finally finished *Precipice and Precipitation*," said Xo.

"What did you think?" said Elliot.

"I don't think she should have rejected him."

Elliot stopped walking, and Xo did as well.

"She didn't reject him…" said Elliot.

"I shouldn't have," said Xo. She bit her lip and met his eyes now, through the falling snow.

"What—what are you saying?" said Elliot shakily.

"Can I go back and change my answer?" asked Xo. The walk through the snow had warmed her, and now that they were standing still, she was overly hot as she waited for Elliot to reply.

"You can go…forward."

Xo took a step closer and placed her mittened hand against Elliot's chest. "Yes," said Xo. She could feel him shivering. Snow was collecting in his hair. "You should have worn a hat."

"Yes," said Elliot almost inaudibly.

Snowflakes were also accumulating on his glasses. Xo moved them, pushing them up in his hair.

"Now I can't see you," whispered Elliot.

She put both hands over his shoulders, and taking a deep breath, stepped forward again. "What if I'm really close?"

Elliot blinked the snow off his lashes. He didn't appear to be breathing.

"I love you, Elliot," said Xo.

"Xiomara…I love you."

Tentatively at first, Elliot's hands slid around her waist, returning her embrace. Then at last she learned what his mouth felt like against her own. Her heart fluttered in her chest, then soared. He was holding her, kissing her tenderly, making everything she'd bungled on the way to this moment not matter. All the rest of the outside world seemed to swirl around the two of them along with the snowflakes, but at the quiet center, time slowed almost to a standstill. She could have happily stayed there forever, wrapped in his warm arms.

Except that Elliot abruptly released her.

It felt like his lips had touched hers for only moments, or at any rate not nearly long enough, when he jerked backwards, catching his breath with a gasp.

"What's wrong?" Xo searched his face. Elliot looked terrified.

He gulped, still holding on to her arms, but now with considerable distance between them. "I…I love you," he stammered.

"Yes, I love you, too." Maybe Xo hadn't been clear enough in her acceptance. "And I do want to marry you, Elliot."

"What have I done?" Elliot stumbled back further with a groan, letting go of her to run his hands through his hair. His fingers encountered his glasses, and he put them on, his gaze returning to Xo with an agonized expression.

"What's going on?" A little off balance after the kiss, Xo caught hold of Elliot's sleeve. He seemed on the verge of taking off. She could still feel the softness of his lips on hers, and transitioning out of that sensation to try to figure out what was the matter was disorienting.

"What if—Francis was right?" Elliot choked out the words.

"Francis? Why would Francis be right about anything? The guy's an idiot," said Xo, nonplussed.

"He was right about Lia. Partly. Perhaps entirely." Elliot clutched Xo's hand. "Xiomara, what if I did kill her?"

"You didn't kill her," said Xo adamantly.

"Not intentionally...but...what if she did catch the mountainpox from me? If it transferred from me to her..." He looked down at Xo's mitten and dropped her hand as if it were on fire. "Oh, God! I could already have infected you!"

Xo stared at him open-mouthed. "Elliot! You're not contagious. If you were contagious people would be dropping like flies around here."

"Not as contagious as when I first had it, but...I still could be. Lia was one of the first—possibly the very first—to get sick in the outbreak here. She might have caught it from me, somehow." Elliot gasped. "Xiomara, if I infect you with this, I could never forgive myself."

Xo folded her arms. "How long have you thought you were contagious?"

"Until now, never. I simply did not think." Elliot hit his forehead with his hand, roughly. "I should have. It was irresponsible not to consider it. It never occurred to me until Francis brought it up, and it seemed he was just spewing nonsense. Then, when I found out about Lia...there was so much on my mind. It felt like nothing mattered anyway, except—" Elliot looked desperately at her.

Xo shook her head. "Elliot, slow down."

He caught his breath raggedly and continued, somewhat more slowly. "I tried not to think about it anymore...the past...the outbreak. I...I should have but...I shut it out. I always force myself to stop replaying those memories. To look forward. Thinking about you, even though..." The way Elliot looked at her made Xo's chest ache. He went on, "And now. Impossible happiness. Then I remembered what Francis said last time: maybe I infected her, would infect you, without knowing. He could be right, again. It could be…" Elliot glanced around himself as if searching desperately, and then stared at Xo in increased horror.

"It could be transmitted in saliva!"

"I don't think there was much saliva transmitted by that kiss," said Xo dryly. Probably because he had apparently been thinking about Francis and Lia during it, while Xo had only been thinking about him.

"You should rinse your mouth. You'll have to use snow." Elliot gathered fresh powder from the ground.

"I am not washing my mouth out with snow," said Xo firmly.

Elliot looked at her pleadingly, offering her the handful.

"No, I refuse!" said Xo. "This is getting ridiculous, Elliot. You are not thinking about this logically. Let's go inside and talk about it." They were already some distance from the coffee house. "We'll go to your house." She started walking in that direction.

Elliot remained frozen in place. "My house…it could be contaminated."

Xo resisted rolling her eyes, with difficulty. "Elliot, I've been in your house before, as have numerous other people who haven't died yet. Come on." She trudged onwards through the snow, and while he seemed reluctant, he followed.

Inside, Xo made them both cups of tea, keeping an eye on Elliot. He was still shivering. She handed him his teacup and went to stoke up the woodstove. Elliot remained in the kitchen, eyes fixed on her with a haunted expression.

"Come over here and warm up," said Xo impatiently. "If you could infect me by standing somewhere in my vicinity, I would've caught it ages ago."

He approached, holding his cup and looking chagrined.

"Now, what makes you think you could still be contagious?" asked Xo. "Why couldn't Lia have caught it another way? How does the mountainpox usually get started?"

"I don't think anyone knows," said Elliot darkly. "There have only been a few outbreaks."

"Okay, but from what you told me it's very contagious when it gets going, and you obviously aren't very contagious," pointed out Xo. "You had it, what, twenty years ago? You recovered."

"Perhaps it reactivated and infected her," said Elliot. "The virus might not have gone away entirely. It could have had a…a resurgence. Flared up."

Xo considered. "The chicken pox virus does that," she said, reluctantly. "I know it can resurface as shingles, and then other people can sometimes catch chicken pox from the shingles infection."

"Exactly," said Elliot gloomily. "And shingles is not as contagious as the original chicken pox."

"Yes, but don't you think you would know if it came back?" asked Xo. "With shingles, there's a new rash. Did you get anything like that around the time Lia got sick?"

"Not that I recall," Elliot admitted. "But it might not have been as obvious as the original infection. I might not have noticed, or I might not remember, because I did not connect it with anything significant. Or I was too focused on what was happening to her. It never occurred to me to consider myself as the source."

"Even if that's the case, it doesn't mean you're contagious now, or that it would reactivate again," insisted Xo. "I think it's a stretch anyway."

"But I *could* be contagious now. I could have been all along, just less so than before. It's too great a risk." Elliot shook his head frantically. "You don't know…So many people have died. Lia. My parents. Countless others. You *cannot* catch it, too."

He put his teacup down and sat on the edge of the bed, raking his hands through his hair. The dampness of the melted snow had made it curl more.

"Those people didn't die because of you," said Xo gently, sitting beside him. She laid a hand on his back. Elliot flinched.

"Stop recoiling from me," said Xo sternly, unclenching one of his hands with difficulty and holding it in her own. "Regardless of what we know about this disease reactivating—if it even does that—it clearly doesn't spread through casual contact."

He groaned, attempting to extricate himself. "How do you know?"

"Think of all the people you've had contact with since you recovered from the initial infection. Every handshake. Every doctor visit. Anyone who has ever touched you, or you've ever touched. For that matter, any interaction with Lia before she got ill. Has a single one of those people other than Lia ever caught this?"

"I have to talk to Alec!" said Elliot, biting his knuckles. Xo captured that hand to hold along with the other one.

"Maybe he would talk some sense into you, if you won't listen to me," she said. "But don't do it in this state. Think about it. It's clearly not *that* contagious! Even if it 'reactivated' as you say, it would've been that one time, not constant contagion for the last twenty years."

Elliot looked at her wildly, both hands trapped.

"Breathe," said Xo.

Elliot swallowed and took a deep breath, then another. Xo watched him carefully.

"Let's just figure this out." She tried to sound more soothing. "Surely there are medical records of how mountainpox can be transmitted, and there will be documentation if anyone else ever had it reactivate or infect somebody years later. We can research it. Then we can get this idea out of your head."

"You don't believe me," said Elliot in a low voice. "You have not seen this virus in action." He shuddered.

"It's not that I don't believe you," said Xo. "It just sounds very unlikely. But we'll investigate it, together. Okay? You have to calm down about it. Maybe I can get vaccinated or something."

"There is no vaccine," said Elliot dully. "No cure, either."

Xo frowned and reached out to cup his face in her hands. "I still love you. I still want to marry you. Do you still want that?"

Elliot touched her wrists with shaking fingers. "I love you, Xiomara. I want to be with you forever. I feel as if no one has ever loved anyone as much as I love you."

"That is statistically improbable, but I'll accept it," said Xo. "Will you marry me, or not?"

"Yes," said Elliot, "...if I can be sure I'm not going to infect you."

"I guess that's the best I'm gonna get for now," said Xo. "Now, will you please kiss me?"

"I'd better not." Elliot looked pained. "Perhaps the reason I didn't infect anyone besides Lia…" He cleared his throat. "Well…I haven't been…intimate with anyone else."

"It sounds like you're talking about more than saliva," said Xo, smiling.

"We cannot be too careful. There could be more than one means of transmission." Elliot stood up.

Xo gestured to the cup she'd brought him. "I drank out of your teacup."

"What!?" said Elliot, in abject horror.

"I'm kidding," said Xo. "Seriously, Elliot, if you don't settle down about this, I'm going to pin you down and lick all your scars until you accept reality."

Elliot reeled slightly on his feet. "I am trying…" He wrung his hands together. "I'll call the clinic. They might be able to tell me something."

"They'll be closed now. You can make an appointment tomorrow," said Xo.

"There's an emergency line, I think."

Xo watched Elliot roam around the room. "They're not gonna tell you anything about this disease on the emergency line. It's not an emergency. It's just information." She caught his hand again as he paced by and took the phone out of it. "I know you're worried about it, but worrying isn't going to help tonight."

"You're right. You're right. Xiomara…" Elliot knelt at her feet, then jumped up again and went into the laundry room. Xo stared after him. He'd always had such a calming effect on her when she was upset, that she'd never have guessed he could get so agitated. Even when he'd spoken to her with passion before, literally shaking, he'd never been so worked up as he was this evening.

There was the sound of a drawer opening and closing, then Elliot returned, looking slightly more relaxed, to Xo's relief. He knelt before her again. "Xiomara, will you have this ring? It belonged to my mother." He paused, then added, "It's been cleaned. I…I do not think it could be a source of infection…"

"It's beautiful." Xo intervened before Elliot could second-guess the thoroughness of the ring-cleansing. "Was it her wedding ring?"

"Yes," said Elliot. "She gave it to me when she was dying. My parents...I didn't think of any future then, but they did. For me."

Xo wondered if Lia had also worn the ring, until she died, too. Luckily, Elliot continued without prompting.

"I never gave it to Lia." He sounded a little ashamed. "I suppose I wasn't ready to part with it, then. I am now. Xiomara, I want you to have it. Even if...I find out that I'm still contagious and cannot marry you."

"That's not gonna happen," said Xo. "But I would be honored to wear it, and marry you with it. Doesn't the ring part come later, though?"

"Does it?" said Elliot. "I thought it was on becoming engaged."

Xo smiled. "I guess now is good."

Elliot slipped the ring on her finger carefully. It seemed he was still trying to avoid touching her skin.

"I have never felt like this before, Xiomara." Elliot gazed up at her. "I will do anything, for you. I would die for you."

"Please don't die for me." Xo pulled Elliot up beside her. "Are you sure you won't kiss me?"

Elliot moaned. "I can't," he whispered.

"Okay." Xo leaned her head against his shoulder. Elliot swallowed hard, put his arms around her, and closed his eyes.

36

LOOKING FOR CLUES

Elliot called the clinic the minute it opened the next morning to make a same-day appointment. He had barely slept the night before, after Xo had gone home promising to return first thing in the morning. She had arrived with coffee for both of them and was now using his laptop, looking up details about the mountainpox. She'd assured him that she was going to find out as much information as possible while he was at the appointment, to put his fears to rest.

He was not sure this would put his fears to rest. Every nerve he possessed had been activated, and he did not know whether to jump for joy, or scream, or cry, or run. The delirium at Xo's acceptance and love fought with the paralyzing terror that he might bring her to her doom. It was difficult to remember to do anything else in the midst of this, such as breathing, let alone optional things like eating and sleeping.

Now he paced around the waiting room at the doctor's office—a room poorly designed for waiting, as there were a number of chairs to trip over. He tried to keep calm in the way Xo had instructed him, through the use of regulated breaths. The effectiveness of the method was doubtful, but as he had to breathe anyway, it was worth a try.

"Dr. Rotariu will see you now," said a nurse, at last.

Elliot sprang forward and followed to his assigned room, where he waited again until Dr. Rotariu appeared. She greeted him pleasantly, after looking up his name on the paper she carried, and sat in front of her computer to pull up a new record.

Elliot perched gingerly on the edge of the paper-covered bed. The bed was for patients, not him—he had come for information only—but there was nowhere else. Unfortunately, it had been impossible to simply discuss his questions with the doctor over the phone, according to the receptionist with whom he had made the appointment.

Dr. Rotariu swiveled on her rolling stool to face him.

"So, Elliot." Dr. Rotariu referred to her notes again. "I see that you are concerned about the contagiousness of the virus commonly known as mountainpox?"

"That is correct."

"Forgive me for saying so, but you look like you've already had it," said Dr. Rotariu.

"Yes. I have."

"As far as we know, survivors acquire immunity," Dr. Rotariu continued.

"Yes, I know," said Elliot. "I'm not concerned for myself; I'm worried about someone else contracting it. You see, I'm hoping to be married."

"Ahh." Dr. Rotariu nodded.

"Yes, and I'm concerned that she might catch it."

"As dreadful as it is, there's a fairly slim chance of that happening," said Dr. Rotariu. "There have only been..." She glanced at the computer, where information about mountainpox was pulled up on the screen. "...Five documented outbreaks of mountainpox."

The receptionist must not have conveyed Elliot's entire message about the purpose of the visit. "But you see, my wife—my first wife, that is—she did catch it. And died."

"I'm very sorry to hear that," said Dr. Rotariu.

"Yes, thank you, it was a long time ago," said Elliot, a touch impatiently. "The point is: I think she might have caught it from me, and I want to know if that's at all possible."

"Well, it's quite possible."

"It is?" Elliot gulped. His back became drenched with sweat, followed by a clammy feeling everywhere else.

"Well, it's an incredibly contagious disease." Dr. Rotariu eyed him critically over the top of her glasses, as if he ought to know this.

"I...realize that," said Elliot. "But I initially caught it when I was fifteen. What I mean to say is: I wonder if I...transmitted it to her later. Ten years later."

"You think she caught it from you, even though you recovered from it years before?"

"Precisely." Elliot held his breath.

"No, that's very unlikely," Dr. Rotariu said. "Why would you think she caught it from you?"

Elliot let the breath out again. "I wondered if the mountainpox could have remained in my system. Inactive, but still contagious. Possibly less contagious than before. Or if it could have reactivated, rather like shingles."

"Have you had shingles?" asked Dr. Rotariu.

"Me? No..." said Elliot. "I've only read about how it happens."

"Online, I take it?" said Dr. Rotariu disapprovingly.

"Uh...yes, some."

"With so much information out there, it's easy to get an idea like this which seems plausible, or is even supported by certain websites, when in fact there is little basis for it," said Dr. Rotariu. "We don't have any evidence of that kind of transmission for mountainpox. If it worked that way, presumably we would have seen more cases, considering how contagious it is in the active stage."

"But few people even survive the active stage to potentially transmit it later," said Elliot. "Perhaps there are cases, but they're undocumented. Don't you think it is suspicious that out of only five known outbreaks, I was present in two of them? And that my wife may have been one of the first people to contract mountainpox in Lingen?"

Dr. Rotariu turned back to the computer. "Your wife was in the outbreak here in Lingen?" she repeated, looking something up. "Ah...hmm. Did you share your concerns with her doctor at the time?"

"No. It did not occur to me, then," admitted Elliot.

"It looks like Dr. Barker treated most of the patients in the Lingen outbreak," mused Dr. Rotariu. "I wonder if he could lay your fears to rest. He would be more familiar with the disease than I am."

"He died from it, too," said Elliot. The fact that Dr. Rotariu did not already know this gave him a sinking feeling.

"Ah. I see."

While Dr. Rotariu was checking her computer again, Elliot chanced a quick glance at her framed credentials on the wall, and deduced that she would have been studying on the other side of the country at the time of the Lingen outbreak. She would only have heard about it, then. Seeing it was different: the speed, the devastation of the disease as it spread, and the complete lack of any method to combat it, except to isolate the sick and wait for them to die painful deaths, in fevered delirium by the end if they were fortunate.

With a small jolt, Elliot realized Dr. Rotariu was looking at him expectantly. She had caught him examining her degrees and was waiting for him to say something. There were no words to explain. He shifted uncomfortably, causing the paper on which he was sitting to rustle loudly and bunch up. Trying to flatten it again only worsened the issue—the crackly paper clung to his sweaty palms, and once damaged, refused to return to its former smooth state. Dr. Rotariu waited silently until Elliot finally abandoned the effort to fix the paper, now completely mangled, and faced her again.

Dr. Rotariu pressed her fingertips together. "Elliot, I can see that this is concerning for you, but we simply don't have any evidence for the reactivation of mountainpox. As far as we know, if subjects recover from it, they are no longer capable of spreading the disease."

"As far as you know?"

"It's difficult to establish these things with absolute certainty. However, I feel safe saying that I don't think your fiancée is going to catch mountainpox from you."

"Then, how did the other outbreaks start?" asked Elliot.

"That hasn't been firmly established, but theoretically there's a non-human host where the disease typically resides. It's probably not as lethal to the host as it is to people. There may also be a vector, such as an invertebrate, which transmits the disease from the host to the human population," said Dr. Rotariu.

"Once an outbreak is contained, the mountainpox goes away until another transmission from its original host occurs." She glanced at the computer again. "While the host hasn't been determined for mountainpox, most likely it seldom comes in contact with humans, potentially only in mountainous areas. Or perhaps the virus also exists at lower elevations, but the cold temperatures at high elevations increase the likelihood of the virus crossing over from the host. There is still much we don't know, since mountainpox occurs rarely and the survival rate is low. You can consider yourself one of the lucky ones!"

Elliot would have laughed at this assessment of his luckiness, if the situation were not so serious. "How do you know that the subsequent outbreaks weren't triggered by those who recovered from the first outbreak, like myself?"

"We don't have any documentation of that."

"But has it been investigated? What about in Lingen. Did anyone live through the outbreak here?"

"I don't think we keep records of the local disease mortality rate here at the clinic, unless someone reports to us that a patient of ours died. But I wouldn't be able to give you information on survivors, regardless. Patient confidentiality laws would prohibit that," said Dr. Rotariu firmly.

Elliot closed his eyes in frustration. He pictured Xo and took a deep breath. If she were here, she would know exactly which questions to ask to cut to the chase and get the right information. He kept ending up back where he started with every query, while the doctor remained infuriatingly calm in the face of this life-and-death situation.

"There's a colleague of mine you might find it helpful to consult with," said Dr. Rotariu, when Elliot looked up again. She wrote a name and phone number on a piece of paper and passed it over to him.

He sighed with relief. Finally, they were getting somewhere. Scanning the paper, he tucked it into his coat pocket. "Is this person familiar with the disease?"

"He specializes in psychiatry. Have you ever received treatment for anxiety in the past?"

Elliot stared at her. "No," he said flatly.

"Anxiety disorder is a condition that can be very treatable," said Dr. Rotariu. "You have a wedding coming up, and this is a time of great stress for many people. It's easy to become overwhelmed by fear or panic…"

Elliot tried desperately to scrape together words that would get through to the doctor. "I am not panicking. I am worried legitimately for my fiancée's safety. For that matter, it could well impact the safety of many other people—" He realized his voice was shaking and broke off.

Dr. Rotariu watched him with a look of detached sympathy. "I hope you'll give my colleague a call."

Elliot stood up. He removed his glasses and rubbed his temples, then eyes, with his finger and thumb, finishing at the bridge of his nose. One more try. Replacing his glasses, he turned back to the doctor.

"Is there anyone else to whom you can refer me, who has more knowledge of the mountainpox?" he asked as politely as possible.

The doctor raised her eyebrows and stiffly turned back to the computer, scrolling through a few screens. Clearly he hadn't been polite enough.

"It looks like a Dr. Adams was involved in investigating the Lingen outbreak. He's now a research physician in the microbiology department over at the college. He doesn't take patients, but it says here he worked with the virology team who assembled what limited information we have on mountainpox." She jotted his name down on another scrap of paper.

"I'm only giving this to you because, as a survivor, becoming involved with efforts to understand and eradicate mountainpox might help you move forward," said Dr. Rotariu. "Talk to Dr. Adams and put your mind at rest. And at least for the sake of your fiancée, talk to someone about your anxiety as well."

"Thank you," said Elliot, and left. Xo would be waiting at his house for him to report, and he had failed to get any useful information.

Still, when she greeted him on his return, the comfort of seeing her again gave him strength. How wonderful it would be if she could be here every day.

"How'd it go?" asked Xo.

Elliot leaned against the kitchen counter, mentally pushing aside a great deal of useless talk from the appointment to isolate the relevant information.

"The doctor didn't have any documentation of contagion after the initial recovery, but neither could she tell me for certain that it *couldn't* happen." He sighed and rubbed his face. "I—I don't think I was able to convey how catastrophic this would be, the gravity of the situation."

"I read up on the mountainpox," said Xo, her voice gentle. "I doubt I found out anything you don't already know, but at least I think I understand it better now."

She reached out and ran her hand lightly over Elliot's hair, tracing the place where it came to a point on the back of his neck and making him think of things he could not do without potentially infecting her. He closed his eyes and drew a shuddering breath.

"It does sound like a pretty awful disease to go through," Xo said after a moment. "Painful. Does it…still hurt?"

"No. It…I cannot remember exactly how it felt." Elliot tried to give her a reassuring smile. There was much that he did remember about it, but there was no point in going into detail about that aspect, or making Xo feel as discouraged as he did after the morning's experience. His fingers closed on the slips of paper in his pocket. "I did get one good thing from the appointment," said Elliot. "She referred me to another doctor."

"Oh!" Xo sounded surprised. "Who is it?"

"There's a Dr. Adams at the college who's more familiar with the virus. I hope he can provide some answers. If I can…ask the right questions." But if this doctor, too, proved unhelpful—Elliot swallowed hard. He didn't have any steps beyond that.

"Are you going to see him now?" asked Xo.

"I was—unless—I don't suppose…" He stopped.

"What?"

When Elliot still hesitated, Xo leaned her head to one side. "You have to tell me what you're thinking, Elliot. I can't read your mind."

"I…could wait until after your shift at the café, if you wanted to come and talk to him as well. You don't have to, of course," Elliot added quickly. "I could simply tell you what he says when you get done with work." He glanced at the clock on the stove. "I'm afraid you're going to be late. I've kept you too long already."

"No, I'll come with you," said Xo decisively.

Elliot nodded. He'd made it through the night; he could make it through the next few hours until Xo finished work.

"And we'll go now," Xo continued. "I'll call Megan and see if she can find someone to cover for me. I told you, we'll figure this out together."

❖   ❖   ❖

To Elliot's relief, finding Dr. Adams was easy once they located the campus directory. He was even in his office, which had a less clinical air than Dr. Rotariu's office, another thing Elliot found relieving. There was a definite feel of ongoing study, with papers on his desk, different types of microscopes set up on the counter behind, and notes in progress on a whiteboard to one side.

Dr. Adams stood up from his desk to shake Elliot's hand, as Elliot explained how he'd been referred by Dr. Rotariu. "Elliot, you say?" He scanned Elliot's face more closely and smiled broadly. "If I'm not mistaken, you've had mountainpox yourself. It's a rare honor to meet with a survivor. You have a personal interest then, as well as a scholarly one?"

"Uh…yes," said Elliot, uncomfortable under the scrutiny. It felt worse in front of Xo, but he was glad she was there after how his last appointment had gone.

"And you?" Grinning widely, Dr. Adams offered Xo his hand.

Xo's smile sparkled. "I'm Xo. Elliot and I just got engaged! You're the first person I've told."

"Well, well, this is a fine day!" replied the doctor cheerfully.

Xo gave Elliot a look he had been longing to see for what felt like a lifetime. He knew how fortunate he was to be with her, but a part of him was amazed that she seemed to be as ecstatic as he. At least, as he had been before he'd realized he might become an agent in her death. His heart ached with the hope that he would not disappoint her, now that she'd finally come to see him the same way. Not by infecting her—he would never let that happen—but by being unable to fulfill his promise to marry her after all, if it turned out he had the potential to infect her.

Elliot cleared his throat. "Our betrothal is somewhat related to why we are here. I need to find out if it's possible for me to still be contagious."

"Could he still infect someone from bodily fluids or something?" put in Xo, as Dr. Adams reseated himself, stroking his chin thoughtfully. "Could it reactivate like shingles?"

Elliot was grateful to Xo for getting to the point, though slightly embarrassed. She'd already covered as much as he had in his entire conversation with Dr. Rotariu, and without sounding panicky at all. Though that could be because she didn't believe he was contagious.

Dr. Adams leaned back in his chair, gesturing for them to sit. "It's an interesting theory," he said, cocking his head to one side. "One I have considered before. Certainly, there are conditions that re-emerge this way, not only shingles. Herpes simplex remains latent in the system and reactivates contagiously on a regular basis, for instance. Of course, it's not nearly as lethal as mountainpox. Typhoid fever can remain dormant and asymptomatic for years and still infect others. You've doubtless heard of it. Do you have reason to believe that your mountainpox infection has returned?"

"Possibly," said Elliot. "I had the mountainpox when I was young, before I moved here. When it broke out in Lingen…I was married to someone else at the time, Lia. She caught it. Could she have contracted it from me? Even started the outbreak that way?"

"Wait a minute." Dr. Adams sat forward, looking excited. "I know who you are!"

"He already told you who he is," Xo pointed out, settling in one of the guest chairs.

"Yes, but I know now in the context of the Lingen outbreak," Dr. Adams said. "I'm very pleased to meet you!" He reached over the desk and shook Elliot's hand again. "Sit, sit!"

"Thank you," said Elliot uncertainly. There was no other option, so he hesitantly sat on the edge of the other guest chair.

"You're mentioned in here!" The doctor dragged a folder out of a cabinet and tapped it with his finger. "I've always believed it was because of you that we got this outbreak under control so quickly. Dr. Barker had no idea what it was, until you said it looked like what you'd had yourself," he finished frankly.

Elliot felt considerably less elated about this revelation than the doctor appeared to be. "I thought he knew what it was when he was treating Lia."

"Well, he did after you brought it up, and the tests confirmed it. That's when I became involved. I'd actually known Dr. Barker before, briefly, when he was interning. At one time I thought he was brilliant, really going somewhere. But, his decisions in practice were—shall we say—shortsighted at times.

"I'd devoted much of my career to researching the prior mountainpox epidemics, so naturally I jumped at the chance to come to Lingen amid a real outbreak. Unfortunately, the outbreaks have been so infrequent and small that there are few opportunities for study, and not enough research money has been allocated to it," said Dr. Adams in a disappointed voice. "At the time, I even thought of being the one to develop a cure through my studies." He sighed, with a look of fond remembrance.

"So yes, I remember you, Elliot. We didn't talk in person, of course, but I knew you existed." Dr. Adams leaned forward again, regarding him with acute interest.

Elliot shifted uncomfortably. "Then...is it possible that I caused the outbreak here?"

"Well," said Dr. Adams. "I'll tell you this. We don't have any concrete records of the mountainpox virus re-emerging from latency to become infectious again, but it's an intriguing idea. I can't rule it out, either, because we haven't discovered exactly how the outbreaks do start."

Even though Elliot had feared as much, it was far worse to hear Dr. Adams acknowledge it. The light in the room seemed to dim. An expert who'd made mountainpox his life's work thought it could be possible for the virus to reactivate, and yet still didn't know for sure. Elliot felt immobilized, trapped by the unknowns, a trap of which he couldn't even see the boundaries to figure out a way to escape. At that moment he couldn't even feel his body, though he could look down and see himself sitting there motionless, caught by the steel arms of the guest chair.

"Can't you tell if Elliot is the one who infected Lia?" Xo sounded upset. "Who got sick in Lingen first?"

Dr. Adams shuffled amongst his records and spread a map of the town out on the desk.

"We tried to determine where the outbreak started, but Lia visited several public locations on the day she developed the rash." Dr. Adams gestured to sites marked in color on the map. "She could have been the primary case, or she might have caught it from someone else that same day. It's hard to pinpoint exactly with mountainpox since this virus moves so quickly—it's not contagious before the rash appears, but once it does, it spreads rapidly through coughing or other transfer of bodily fluids.

"Luckily, it doesn't survive long on surfaces outside the body, and victims develop such a high fever that they're soon confined to bed and no longer exposing as many people. Elliot here," Dr. Adams gestured to him, "identified the rash that evening and asked Dr. Barker to come to the house. If Lia had gone to the clinic, we might've had an even larger outbreak, though of course we soon learned of other victims as it had already begun to spread."

The doctor shook his head, frowning. "I'm afraid Dr. Barker himself contributed to the spread of mountainpox here in Lingen. After he caught it, he inadvertently infected his patients who wouldn't have otherwise been exposed. Still, we did contain it better in Lingen than anywhere else."

"If it's so contagious, how did you avoid catching it when you were collecting all this research from the patients and working with Dr. Barker?" asked Xo.

Dr. Adams smiled. "Naturally, I took special care to avoid catching it myself, knowing it is generally deadly. Also, despite how contagious it is, there are always some people who just don't catch it, or are asymptomatic, even if they come in contact with infected individuals. We don't know why that is; some people are simply less susceptible. I wasn't banking on being one of those people myself, though." He chuckled. "I do know something about working with diseases safely in the lab."

"You don't seem too concerned about catching it from Elliot right now." Xo gave Elliot a significant glance.

"I'm not too concerned about that," said Dr. Adams to Xo. "It's safe to say that if latent reinfection is possible, then it's either much less communicable than the original infection or it's asymptomatic, otherwise we'd have more examples of contagion. But there could be other cases out there besides Elliot's suspicions of transferring it to Lia. I'm going to look into it."

Dr. Adams turned to Elliot. "We don't know exactly what causes re-activation in other diseases, but it's often associated with weakened immunity. For example, another illness taxing your system or prolonged stress. It's likely, though not certain, that you would have some symptoms if you were shedding live virus; you might feel sick or get a milder version of the rash.

"What I can do, if you like, is take some samples from you, and then I can tell you if you have an active infection now and if you're shedding any live virus—that is, if you're contagious. I think it's unlikely at the moment, but it might give you peace of mind."

Elliot sat forward, the spell of immobilization broken. "Please, do. I need to know."

"I also might be able to tell from studying your antibodies if you even have the same strain that caused the outbreak in Lingen."

"You mean it might not even be the same disease?" asked Xo eagerly.

"He had a version of it, since it conferred immunity and has the same presentation, but it's not necessarily the same strain of mountainpox. If I can determine that it isn't, then yes, we could rule out reactivation in the case of the Lingen outbreak."

Xo hugged Elliot delightedly. Though he wasn't quite ready to let down his guard, he felt a glimmer of hope.

"Thank you," said Elliot to Dr. Adams. "I didn't know if you would take this seriously."

"Oh, it's quite interesting to me," said Dr. Adams. "You don't know how excited I am to work on this again! As it happens, I'm still interested in developing a vaccine or even a treatment to increase the likelihood of survival. Your samples could be helpful for that research as well. We don't have many to work from, since few people survive."

He retrieved some vials from a cupboard and prepared a syringe. "If you don't mind, I'll collect blood, saliva, and a skin sample. Very non-invasive, don't worry."

"Take whatever you need." The idea of a vaccine was considerably more heartening to Elliot than anything else.

As the doctor did this, Xo leaned on the desk, examining the outbreak map. "So, could you track down other people who survived and see if they had any connection to other outbreaks or infecting anybody later on?"

"I did collect info on every person we knew of who caught it in Lingen," said Dr. Adams as he swabbed Elliot's mouth. "Unfortunately, that wasn't the case in the initial outbreak that sickened you, Elliot, because nobody was on top of it. I don't think the mountain-pox even got a name until most of its early victims were dead. Back then, it was still so unusual that when it didn't occur again for a while it was let drop—except by those with a particular interest in it, like myself. There were two survivors documented here in Lingen. It may be that a few other people survived the other outbreaks as well, but I don't have their info. I only had access to the pools of shared data made available when we were actively researching the Lingen outbreak.

"One of the Lingen survivors died shortly afterwards of something unrelated. Car accident, I think. The other one...I think he moved away..." Dr. Adams flipped through a file and then closed the folder again, turning back to Elliot. "Roll up your sleeve, please."

Elliot did so, exposing numerous pockmark scars on his arm. He glanced at Xo, but she was studying the map.

Dr. Adams followed his glance. "You're worried about Xo catching mountainpox from you."

"Yes." Elliot winced as Dr. Adams stuck him with the needle painfully.

"Let me try your other arm, it might be easier to find the vein." Dr. Adams stepped to Elliot's other side and inserted another needle as he talked. Elliot tried to focus elsewhere, feeling sick.

"You probably know that I can't give you contact information for the remaining Lingen survivor," said Dr. Adams. "However, in the interest of research, I'd be happy to try to locate him myself and find out if there's been any indication of the virus resurfacing. He might be willing to participate in further research, like you."

"I can't thank you enough for this," said Elliot, as Dr. Adams scraped the surface of a small area of scarred skin with a blade.

"It's really my pleasure. This was always a pet project of mine," said Dr. Adams. "Now, Elliot, I don't think you should worry too much. The chances of you being contagious right now are quite low. I'll give you a call soon about your test results and let you know definitively, and I'll see if I can get anything helpful from the other survivor. In the meantime, you two try to enjoy yourselves!"

Xo slipped her hand into Elliot's as they left the office. "It's gonna be okay," she said. "He'll be able to prove you're not infectious, and you probably didn't even have the same version that was in the Lingen outbreak."

Elliot returned her smile as enthusiastically as he could, but inside he still felt tense and worried. He knew that feeling would not go away until he could be sure he wasn't putting Xo in danger, but at least there was the possibility of a good outcome. Still, the follow-up call from Dr. Adams couldn't come soon enough.

37

TELLING PEOPLE

Xo couldn't help grinning excitedly as she came downstairs to start her shift on the following day, even though Elliot's sudden concern over contagion had slightly marred the happy occasion of their engagement. The pictures and descriptions of the mountainpox that she'd found online had been disturbing, but the likelihood of her catching it seemed low except in Elliot's mind. His concern for her did seem a little excessive at times. Hopefully, he would soon be able to relax about it, and then they could focus on their happy future together.

This was primarily where Xo's thoughts strayed. Looking over her sunny apartment that morning, she'd felt only a little nostalgia at the idea of moving out. Her apartment was nice, but she liked Elliot's house, and more importantly, it had Elliot. Waking up next to him would be better than waking up to the smell of already-made coffee, as delightful as that was.

Xo sashayed behind the counter and tied on her apron, unable to stop smiling. "I do appreciate you covering yesterday," she said to Megan.

"Yeah, that was really last-minute, Xo," said Megan. "I had homework to do, and I'd already put in my eight hours."

"I know. I'm sorry," said Xo. "I'll make it up to you."

"How about you take my shift next Wednesday?" said Megan. "I have a final exam and I really need to study beforehand. I'm sure I can get somebody to take your afternoon so you're not here all day, but nobody ever wants mine."

"Sure, of course!"

"Really? My whole shift. From before the crack of dawn."

"Yep, got it!" said Xo cheerfully. "Put my name down."

Megan folded her arms and gave her a suspicious smile. "Okay, Xo, what's up with you? You can't possibly be grinning over that. Spill it!"

Xo held up her hand with Elliot's ring on it. "Elliot and I are engaged!"

Megan squealed and grabbed both of her hands, jumping up and down with her as Xo laughed giddily.

When they stopped to catch their breaths, Megan poked her in the ribs. "Now I know what you were doing yesterday!"

"What? No, we were…something else came up."

"Then when did this happen? Tell me everything!" demanded Megan.

"Well, you know he asked me a while ago." Xo hesitated, remembering Megan's reaction to Elliot's proposal, but she was too happy not to want to share the news. "I guess I just had to think it over."

"Have you guys picked a date? Where are you getting married?" To Xo's relief, Megan did not bring up her previous evaluation of Elliot.

"We're still working out the details." At this point, there was no need to mention the concern over the virus, and Elliot's somewhat conditional acceptance. She wasn't sure how rational the contagion issue actually was, but she was pretty sure it would sound silly if she tried to explain it to Megan. Plus, it would soon be resolved, once they heard back from Dr. Adams. He seemed like a sensible person, and he'd certainly had no hesitation in interacting with Elliot. He'd shaken his hand twice, even though he was reputedly more careful about contagion than Lia's ill-fated Dr. Barker.

"Let me see!" Megan took Xo's hand and rotated the ring on her finger. "Wow, it's really old-fashioned."

"Well, it is old, it was his mother's," Xo said a little defensively.

"Ooh, can I be in the wedding party?" asked Megan excitedly.

Xo laughed. "I dunno that there's gonna be a party, per se. I mean, I'm not really into that stuff."

"Come on, you have to have a party, this is the biggest day of your life! You get to dress up, and have a big cake and everything!"

"Is that really required?" Xo wrinkled her nose. This sudden notion generated more stress than the off-chance of catching some rare disease. "Not saying I'm anti-cake—cake is always worthwhile. But who would I even invite?"

Megan shrugged. "Old friends? People from your hometown?"

"Mm…" said Xo noncommittally. There were acquaintances, perhaps quasi-friends, in her past, but nobody who could be expected to travel this far to attend her wedding. For that matter, she had not gone to the weddings of anyone from college or even from her previous job, though she had noticed them getting married, one by one. Some had been married and divorced and remarried by now. Most she had not talked to in years.

"What about your parents?" prompted Megan.

Xo sighed. "They'd probably come, but they don't really get along. They'd argue with each other the whole time."

Plus, her mother wouldn't be any happier with the decision to get married than she had been about Xo's move to Lingen in the first place. Xo wasn't sure she even had a current phone number for her father. It had been years since they'd talked regularly. Elliot would meet them eventually—hopefully on separate occasions. And Elliot would handle it well, he was always polite. But it would be easier to see her parents again when she was feeling more established in her work.

"I get it," said Megan. "No drama like family drama."

"I guess," said Xo. The people she knew in Lingen didn't call up the same feeling of discomfort when she imagined them at a party, but hosting an event was completely different from handing out coffee across a counter in her official capacity. Was it possible to be an

outsider at one's own wedding? "I don't think we'll have a big event—
it just seems like a lot."

"What about Elliot, doesn't he want some sort of proper traditional
ceremony?" asked Megan.

"We'll probably just go to the courthouse. I have to talk it over with
him still." Elliot did know more people here than Xo, but hopefully
he wouldn't want something fancy. If anything, he'd probably be less
at home hosting a party than Xo.

"I bet Jacqua would make you a cake!" said Megan enticingly. "We
could bring in a band again! Of course, you'd have to keep Elliot off
the stairs…"

Xo laughed, but it caught in her throat with a pang as she remembered his fall. Was that when she had known how much she loved
him, or before? It all came rushing back.

"I don't need a party. I think I really just want to be with Elliot, you
know? I don't ever want to lose him."

Megan looked puzzled. "Well, you guys think about it, okay?"

"Alec, I have to talk to you." Elliot sat on the café hearth, wrapping
his icy hands around the cup of coffee that Xo had just given him.
Her loving smile had only underscored the enormous responsibility
he now held.

"Congratulations," said Alec genially.

Elliot looked at him in surprise. "You heard?"

"I'm always the last to know," said Alec, feigning sorrow. "But
seriously, I'm really happy for you and Xo."

"Thank you." It wasn't what Elliot had been planning to talk about,
and he felt like a poor friend for not telling Alec the news himself.
Though Alec exaggerated, he really did sound a little hurt. Xo must
have told him, or she'd told someone else who'd told him—as Elliot
should have realized would happen.

"What I don't know is why you look so miserable," said Alec.
"Shouldn't you be all happy now?"

"I may have made a terrible mistake in asking Xiomara to marry me," said Elliot hollowly.

"What are you talking about?" said Alec. "You're not that bad." He grinned and fake-punched Elliot's arm.

"No, stop. You need to know this. Francis may have been right," said Elliot in a low voice. "When I asked Xiomara, I didn't think I could still infect anyone with the mountainpox."

"Has that ever happened before with this virus?" asked Alec skeptically.

"No one knows. We talked to a professor who researched the Lingen outbreak the other day, and he admitted it *could* have started with me infecting Lia. Even worse, it could happen again."

Alec did not look appropriately worried, only mildly concerned. Elliot glanced around the room, but luckily no other customers seemed to have overheard him. It was now apparent that the wary treatment he'd gotten before from the general populace had been justified.

"This all sounds pretty hypothetical," said Alec. "If nobody knows if it can even happen…I think you're putting way too much blame on yourself at this point."

"You sound like Xiomara," said Elliot gloomily. "The thought that I could cause her to catch this—"

"Hey, nothing's happened yet. She's perfectly fine, see?" Alec gestured to the counter where Xo was working, quite happily, it appeared. "She doesn't look too worried. You said you talked to an expert on this disease. Can't he find out?"

"He just got back to me." Elliot ran his hands through his hair in frustration. The phone call had made everything worse. "He was testing to see if I had a different strain of the mountainpox from the Lingen outbreak, but the results were inconclusive. It still could have been me who started it by infecting Lia. Also, when the doctor contacted the only other person who is still alive after catching it in the Lingen outbreak, he didn't want to talk."

Dr. Adams had told him that the first time he called, he'd left a message, but the second time, the man hung up after Dr. Adams identified himself.

"Well, that's too bad, but why do we need to talk to this guy?" asked Alec.

"To find out if he's infected anyone else. Alec, I cannot marry Xiomara if there is a chance of giving her this disease."

Elliot felt like a walking time bomb. After all this, he was going to be the one to hurt her. His coffee was sloshing from his hands shaking, so he put it on the hearth beside him and clasped his hands together.

"We can get to the bottom of this." Alec grabbed Elliot's shoulder. "Are you going to give up now? Isn't she worth it?"

"She is. But what else can I do? No one will give me more information; everything is confidential. There are too many unknowns. I keep hearing that the risk is low, but…if it happens, it's nearly a death sentence. I cannot do that to her, Alec—" Elliot broke off.

"Pull yourself together. I have an idea," said Alec. "There was newspaper coverage of the outbreak. We'll go through the records down at the office. It's likely one of our reporters interviewed this other survivor or called him to fact-check, or at least mentioned him in an article. We're going to find out who he is."

Elliot looked up despondently. "But the doctor said that this man didn't want to talk."

"Finding him is still going to tell you something. If he's been contagious in the past ten years it may have turned up. Not everyone is as fastidious as you are about sharing bodily fluids," Alec added with unnecessary amusement. "We might find out if he was connected to any of the other outbreaks since then, or individual deaths. If, on the other hand, he has a big happy family and six kids and nobody has caught it from him, what does that tell you?"

"It is still only one person." But the spark of hope had returned. It was harder to find when Elliot was just thinking things over to himself.

"It's one more person than you have now, considering it doesn't sound like there's much evidence to lean either way. This may be the only survivor besides you that we have a chance of finding. And we do have a pretty good chance, in my opinion." Alec stood up.

"Let's go," said Elliot.

❖   ❖   ❖

After hours of poring through old articles and journalists' reference notes for the names of people involved in the Lingen outbreak, then cross-referencing them against obituary listings and death notices, a likely candidate emerged.

"This 'Hector' keeps coming up," said Elliot, for the third time.

"It's got to be him," said Alec. "There's no death record. It looks like he got married, too. You going in person?"

"Yes. He may be more willing to talk face-to-face." Unfortunately, Hector had indeed moved in the intervening years. Elliot copied down the address they'd found online, hoping it was current.

"Tell him we're doing an article about mountainpox survivors. That'd be a lead-in," said Alec.

Elliot shook his head. If Hector wouldn't even talk to the doctor, he wasn't going to want to talk to the newspaper, and it would be deceptive anyway since Elliot had no intention of letting Alec do such an article.

"Or not. Just an idea."

"I know. Sorry," said Elliot. "I never—I never felt like a 'survivor.' That word makes it sound like I fought something and won, while those who didn't survive failed. It was not an achievement. I didn't *do* anything."

"Your immune system kinda did."

Or it betrayed him by not actually killing the virus, so it could spread to others later. Elliot sighed and folded up the paper with Hector's address and put it in his pocket.

"It's too bad the guy doesn't live in Lingen anymore," said Alec. "They're predicting heavy snow in the passes tonight. Do you want to borrow the truck? You know your car isn't up to it."

"There's no need." Alec had already done too much for him. They'd been at the office so long that it was pitch black outside, and well past the time Alec usually had dinner. "I'll take the morning train."

Elliot turned from putting on his coat and saw that Alec had been holding out his keys.

Alec tossed them in the air and caught them again, returning them to his pocket. "Have it your way."

Elliot felt wretchedly ungracious. "Alec…thank you for helping me find Hector. I don't know what I would do without you. Thank God I haven't infected you."

"Yet," said Alec jovially.

"Please don't even joke about that."

38

ELLIOT AND XO

When Elliot got home, Xo was sitting on the doorstep.

"Xiomara! How long have you been out here?" said Elliot, aghast. It was well below freezing and the snow was piling up rapidly.

"Oh, not too long." Xo blew on her mittened hands and held up a plastic bag containing takeout boxes. "I got teriyaki for dinner. It might be cold."

"But—why didn't you go inside?" She must have known where the key was, since she and Alec had used it before.

"I wasn't sure if you'd mind," said Xo. "It's not a normal thing to do, is it? I only went in before because I was so worried. This time wasn't an emergency: I knew you were off with Alec and bound to come back eventually."

"I mind you freezing to death." Elliot was awash with guilt. He hurried her inside, shedding his coat, and climbed onto his knees on one of the counter stools to reach the top shelf in the kitchen, where he kept another spare key.

Suddenly, he felt icy hands on his back, underneath his shirt, which had come untucked as he reached up. Elliot gasped and nearly fell off the stool.

"Just trying to warm up," said Xo impishly, as he turned around.

"Please, use this whenever you need to." Elliot pressed the key into her hand.

Xo frowned at the key. "This isn't as warm." But to Elliot's relief, she took her key ring out of her bag and attached the key to it.

Elliot dished up the food on plates, thanking her for bringing it, and carried it over to eat by the wood stove in hopes of warming her up more safely.

"Did you find out anything more?" Xo took her plate and leaned against the warm bricks on one side of the stove, while Elliot did the same on the other side of the corner.

Elliot gave her the bad news first. "Dr. Adams could not determine if I had the same strain as the Lingen outbreak. But I now have the name and address of that man who recovered from it and moved away: Hector." He paused. "I'm going there tomorrow on the train."

"To do what?" asked Xo.

"I'll talk to him and try to determine if he was present at the locations of other outbreaks at significant times, or infected anyone else. Or if he lives in close contact with people who haven't been infected," said Elliot. "He's apparently married."

Xo ate silently for a few moments. Then she said, "Did the doctor confirm that you aren't shedding live virus right now?"

Elliot nodded. If not, he wouldn't be standing here with her.

"Are you gonna be satisfied if this surviving guy has never infected anybody, even though he's had the opportunity?" Xo asked. "If there's no evidence of the virus ever reactivating?"

"Except for what happened here in Lingen," pointed out Elliot.

"That's not evidence," said Xo. "If the tests were inconclusive, it might've had nothing to do with you."

Elliot thought for a long time before answering. "I don't know…if I will be satisfied," he said at last.

Xo regarded him sadly. "And what are you going to do, if you find out this guy did have it reactivate and infect someone?"

Elliot looked down at his plate. He set it aside, feeling nauseated.

"You promised me that you weren't going to leave without telling me," said Xo. "Are you planning to get back on that train and never return if it turns out the mountainpox does reactivate? Is that it?"

This specific idea had not occurred to Elliot, but would that be for the best, after all? If he found out he would always present a risk of infection, he couldn't remain near her. Or Alec. Or anyone. The future in such a scenario was an endless void with nothing to fill it— he could barely bring himself to look into it. He had to hope it would not come to that.

"Perhaps in that case...you can 'forget me and move on,'" Elliot said hoarsely.

"I can't forget you, and I don't want to move on!" Tears sprang to Xo's eyes. "I love you, Elliot."

Elliot felt his heart was being wrung out. "And I love you, Xiomara. Can't you see this is why I could never put you in that much danger?"

He could be putting her in danger even now. The fact that he hadn't been actively shedding live virus when Dr. Adams tested him was a cold comfort. Until he ruled out the possibility of the virus reactivating, there was a chance he could become contagious again without knowing it and begin infecting people at any time. He might not even realize it had reactivated until Xo got sick. He was a fool for never considering he could be the source, back when it happened to Lia.

"Why are you the only one who gets to evaluate how much risk is too much around here?" demanded Xo. "Doesn't my opinion count? It seems to me that you have a very skewed view of how likely it is that the mountainpox will re-emerge and wipe me out, let alone the rest of the town."

She took another bite of food, stabbing at her plate with the fork. "Anyway, even if I caught it, who's to say I wouldn't survive? Then at least we could stop having this conversation, which is beginning to sound like an excuse not to be with me. You won't even touch me."

Elliot let his arms fall limp. "Xiomara, you cannot be serious. If you did catch the mountainpox...it is extremely unlikely that you would live. And even if—"

"If what? You wouldn't still want to be with me if I'm horrifically disfigured from the ordeal?" snapped Xo.

❖   ❖   ❖

As Elliot flinched, Xo realized she'd said the wrong thing. Horribly wrong. He had turned, if possible, paler than he already was.

"I'm sorry," said Xo quickly. "That's not what I meant at all...I didn't mean you were..."

Elliot just looked at her. It was as if she had hit him with a sledgehammer. And then herself.

He turned away silently, picking up his plate to return to the kitchen. At last, he spoke from the other side of the counter in a low voice. "I was going to say, even if you lived, I couldn't bear that I should cause you to suffer that way."

Xo followed him. "That was an idiotic thing for me to say. It came out wrong."

Elliot put the dish in the sink and began to wash it as Xo shifted from one foot to the other, feeling awful.

"And I would want to be with you regardless of...your appearance," said Elliot after a long wait, adding another shovelful of dirt to the pit Xo had dug for herself.

"I know," she whispered, tears welling up. "I feel the same way. I don't think of you that way—that's why I didn't think." Whatever she said only magnified her earlier words and made them a thousand times worse. "I just can't stop talking sometimes. It's stupid. I'm stupid. Say something, Elliot."

Elliot finished washing the dish and put it in the drain rack, turning around at last. "I love you," he said quietly. "I have to prepare for sleep now. The train leaves at six tomorrow."

He went to the dresser and took out some folded pajamas, then walked out of the room. Xo sank in despair onto a kitchen stool, rocking back and forth.

Elliot emerged from the hallway a while later with damp, curlier hair, wearing the pajamas. He halted abruptly, looking surprised to see her still sitting in the kitchen.

"Uh…I hope you'll excuse me," he said.

"I'm not going anywhere," said Xo. "And you're not getting on that train without me."

"But what about your work tomorrow?" protested Elliot.

"Elliot, tomorrow's Saturday."

Elliot blinked. "Right."

Xo eyed him with concern. It wasn't like Elliot to forget what day it was. She did still have illustrations to work on over the weekend, but there was no way she could let him get on that train alone, not knowing if he was coming back. Especially after her thoughtless words. He hadn't even denied that he might never return.

It might also be best if Xo could hear for herself what the other survivor had to say. Considering how Elliot had been acting lately about her getting infected, he might not interpret whatever information he got tomorrow in a rational way.

Elliot went back to the bathroom, returning a few minutes later. "I've sanitized the shower, in case you want to use it." He lay down on the far side of the bed, facing away.

A shower might help her relax, as well as prevent her from saying anything else hurtful to Elliot. If she gave in to the urge to keep talking and apologizing right now, she was sure to inadvertently cause more damage. She walked around the bed to where Elliot was lying and took another pair of his pajamas from the dresser to change into afterwards. Elliot watched her uneasily.

"What? I didn't know I needed to bring extra clothes," said Xo.

"It's just that…" began Elliot, then trailed off.

"You think this thing is transmissible via pajama?" said Xo incredulously.

"I used bleach, at least." Elliot still sounded doubtful.

Shaking her head, Xo took the pajamas. Later, when she put them on after her shower, they were of course too tight. Oh well. She could still wear them, looking ridiculous. Luckily, the pants were the drawstring style so there was more room in the hips than Elliot needed, though they'd turned into capris on her.

She sniffed her freshly washed skin. Elliot had stashed his in-progress bar of soap somewhere she couldn't find it, so she'd had to open a new one for her shower. Between Elliot's pajamas and the faint perfume of sandalwood from the soap, his scent was all over her. It was comforting, in a way, but she would rather have it on her skin directly from him. He was pulling away from her more and more.

Xo returned to the main room and turned off the rest of the lights, letting her eyes adjust to the flickering orange glow from the wood stove door. The fire burned gently, with a faint rumble. Elliot was on his side in the same position as she had left him, seemingly asleep. She lay down on the other half of the bed.

"Elliot?" Xo whispered, touching his arm. "Do you forgive me?"

Elliot rolled onto his back, his profile visible in the dim light. "There's nothing to forgive."

"Forgive me anyway?"

He turned his face to her. "I do."

Xo moved her hand to rest on Elliot's stomach, which rose and fell shallowly. This time he didn't flinch. The buttons of his shirt slipped open easily at her touch, and she felt his heartbeat accelerate. Small hairs curled around her fingers as she ran them over the rough surface of scarred skin. She raised herself on one elbow and studied the constellation of scars scattered over his stomach and chest.

"What do you think?" Elliot's voice was low.

Xo traced her finger from one mark to the next. His chest was still now as he held his breath.

"I think I can see Orion's belt."

Elliot laughed quietly, and that smile he often used to have flashed back on his face. Maybe he truly had forgiven her. She bent to kiss him, but he tensed and pulled away, triggering a sinking ache deep inside her that seemed to force the air out of her lungs.

"Elliot, you're not contagious right now, Dr. Adams said."

"I could become so," said Elliot thickly. "I might not ever be able to…be with you."

Xo lay back down beside him, but the space between them had never felt so wide. She could have cried from frustration. "I want to touch you. I want you to touch me. I need to know."

"To know what?"

"That you love me," whispered Xo.

"Xiomara…" Elliot's voice caught. "I do love you. I don't have to touch you to love you."

"Touch me anyway."

After a long moment, Elliot rolled to face her where she lay on her side. He reached across the chasm between them and tentatively traced her cheek, across her shoulder, and down her side, his hand coming to rest at the curve of her waist. His fingers left a trail of heightened sensation. Xo almost expected to see a line of phosphorescence in their wake, where his touch had awakened her nerve endings and triggered the warm wave spreading throughout her body. She scooted down to put his hand in a better location and heard his sharp intake of breath.

When her fingers touched his skin again, he was trembling. She met his gaze, soft and beautiful and full of love, and this time let herself fall in, sinking into a pool of unknown and unfathomable depth. The intensity was overwhelming, but she wanted to see where it led.

She held the power to make him look that way. To make him react that way when they touched. And to hurt him cruelly—as she wished she had never done, all the times that she had. Was that why he was so afraid?

"No saliva, I promise," she murmured, pulling him closer.

39

THE TRAIN

It was much later when an unidentified noise woke Xo. She opened her eyes a crack and scanned the room sleepily. It was still dark, but there was a light on somewhere. Elliot was nowhere to be seen. The distant sound of an engine made her bolt upright. The train!

"Elliot!" she yelled frantically.

Elliot appeared almost immediately from the hallway into the other part of the house, looking alarmed. "Xiomara? What is it?"

"I thought you left or something." Xo rubbed her eyes.

"No!" Elliot hastened to her side. "I was…uh…doing laundry. I couldn't sleep."

"Oh." Xo squinted at him in confusion. Gradually it sank in that the sound she'd heard was the washing machine. Or possibly the dryer. There was a fresh pile of smooth, folded clothes on the dresser: the ones she had been wearing pre-pajama. The last time she had seen them was in a tangled heap on the bathroom floor, she remembered guiltily.

"Is it time to get up?"

"No," said Elliot. "Please sleep. I won't leave without you, I promise."

Xo fell back into a troubled sleep, and he didn't.

❖   ❖   ❖

By the time morning had supposedly come, if not actual sunrise, they were on the train heading down the pass. Xo scrunched down into her seat, hoping for a little more sleep even as the sky brightened, but Elliot seemed remarkably alert for having been up half the night washing clothes. Although Xo appreciated having something clean to wear, it did not suggest that he had reached a sensible place in his mind about the disease.

"Does this guy know we're coming?" she asked.

"No," said Elliot. "I'm not even certain this is his current address."

Since she'd inserted herself into the trip at the last minute, Xo decided she had no right to complain that these details should have been nailed down in advance. It was too late anyway; they were descending elevation at a brisk pace. The fir trees rushing past the windows didn't even have much snow on them anymore, and it was becoming proper daylight.

If she weren't in the picture, Elliot surely wouldn't go to these lengths to determine if he could become contagious. Maybe he would simply isolate himself from all further human contact. She wanted to be more appreciative of his efforts, but what if he couldn't find the evidence he was looking for? Her previous attempt to tackle this topic had gone so poorly that it would be better not to try again until after they talked to Hector. Best case, she wouldn't have to, because the meeting with Hector would be enough.

❖   ❖   ❖

It was drizzling as they walked along the road from the train station, and though it was December, Xo felt overdressed in her winter coat. If there had been any snow down here, it had melted. The lowlands, regularly drenched in rain from the distant ocean, were green and relatively warm compared to the mountains they had just left. The strip of grass beside the street was mucky and soupy, and the road itself had numerous puddles.

Elliot stopped to check a mailbox number. "This is the place."

Xo surveyed the house. Several random objects sat in the yard, including a faded plastic slide that couldn't be too useful, since it was only about a foot high.

Elliot lifted his camera off over his head. "I don't want Hector to think I…Would you mind putting this in your bag?"

"Oh! Sure." Xo tucked the camera away, while Elliot seemed to be trying to figure out what to do with his hands now that he couldn't rest at least one of them on his camera. He opened and closed them a few times, then approached the house. Xo followed him onto the step where he rang the doorbell.

"I don't think it works," said Xo after a moment. "I didn't hear any sound when you pressed the button."

As soon as she spoke, a frantic barking erupted inside. The cacophony approached, accompanied by running feet which sounded both human and canine. Sounds of pushing and shoving and barking came from the other side of the door, then a set of feet went pounding off again accompanied by a child's voice shouting, "There's somebody at the door! They're just standing there and not knocking!"

Xo and Elliot exchanged a glance, then Elliot knocked hesitantly.

More footsteps. The door opened a crack and a woman looked out inquiringly, blocking the opening with her knee to prevent one of the eager dogs from squeezing past. Xo scanned her face quickly. No scars like Elliot's pockmarks.

"Hello," said Elliot. "I'm very sorry to intrude, but I was hoping I could speak with Hector."

The woman stared at him so blankly that Xo was sure they had the wrong house. Then she said, "Just a sec," and the door shut.

After a muffled conversation within, a man emerged, closed the door behind him and stood in front of it with arms crossed. Hector was heavily built, with an abundance of dark hair and pockmarks on his face, arms, and as much of his chest as was visible at the opening of his shirt.

Elliot produced a nervous smile. "I live in Lingen. My wife was in the mountainpox outbreak there."

Hector's guarded stare went to Xo.

"Uh, not her," clarified Elliot. "This one died."

Xo groaned inwardly, hoping she wouldn't always be introduced this way.

"As you can probably tell, I've also had the disease..." Elliot continued.

Hector glanced back at the house. "Let's walk," he said to Elliot, setting off across the spongy lawn.

Xo trailed behind them, trying to avoid puddles. She and Elliot had a long walk back to the train station for soaked feet. Hector stopped beside a woodshed a short distance from the house, turning to face Elliot in the same attitude as before, feet apart and arms folded, oblivious to the drizzling rain.

"What is it you want?" Hector sounded suspicious. "I got a call from up there the other day. Already told that doctor I want nothing to do with him."

"You see..." said Elliot. "It's come to my attention that it may be possible for the mountainpox to reactivate, becoming infectious again."

Hector ran his tongue over his teeth. "Is that so?"

"Have you visited these cities...?" began Elliot, removing from his pocket the list of the locations and dates of subsequent outbreaks.

Hector took the list out of his hands, glanced over it, and thrust it back. "No. Are you accusing me of causing the other outbreaks?"

"No! Uh...not exactly."

"Then what's this about?" Hector's voice was a monotone that Xo couldn't read, but it made her uncomfortably wary. She stopped walking towards them, lurking under a nearby cedar for shelter from the rain. Hopefully Elliot knew what he was doing.

"Have you ever been aware of any...resurgence of the rash? Or other symptoms?" persisted Elliot.

"No," said Hector.

"Has anyone else—that you know of—ever caught the disease after you did? People that you have associated with?"

"No," Hector said again, in exactly the same tone.

Elliot hesitated. "Y-your wife has never caught it?"

"She has not. Pretty sure we covered that." Hector took a step towards Elliot, who took a step back.

Xo was growing increasingly uneasy. She should have tried again to talk Elliot out of coming down here.

"And you have been…uh…intimate with her?" asked Elliot.

Hector shoved one forearm against Elliot's chest, bringing it up under his chin and pressing him against the wall of the woodshed.

Fear surged through Xo, closing her throat as if the hairy arm were on her own neck instead of Elliot's. She tried to shout but it came out as a squeak.

"What are you implying?" Hector peered closely at Elliot.

Elliot made a choking sound. "Nothing!"

Xo caught her breath. "Leave him alone!" she yelled, springing forward. "He only wants to know so I don't get infected!"

"Xiomara, get back!" Elliot said in a strangled voice.

Hector turned his head slightly to see Xo, who was not getting back. Slowly, he released Elliot and looked him over. Elliot lowered his chin to a more natural position.

Hector spoke slowly and deliberately, with a menacing edge to his voice. "We've been married for eight years and have three kids. Any more questions?"

"No," said Elliot.

Hector eyed Xo challengingly, and when she said nothing, he turned back to Elliot. "Then I suggest we don't see each other again."

"Thank you for your time," said Elliot quickly. He crossed back over to the road, and Xo hastened to join him, looking over her shoulder at Hector. She wished they would get out of sight faster. When she checked again, Hector was walking to the house. He went inside.

Xo turned to Elliot. "I know I'm tops at saying the wrong thing, but what were you thinking? Do you have a death wish?"

"I had to know," said Elliot unrepentantly. He looked unshaken, somehow.

She shuddered. "Well, now you know, right?"

That was the one good thing. She sighed in relief. The tenseness of the moment started to slide off her shoulders as it struck her that Elliot could now give up the idea of reinfection.

As they walked back to the train station, the rain stopped and the sun parted the grey sky for a moment to warm her back. Red-winged blackbirds started singing, *co-o-ooeeeeoo,* in the cattails beside the road. Other unseen birds twittered deeper in the marsh, celebrating the winter sunbreak, and Xo tried to spot them amongst the brown dead grasses.

Could this be where the hog-nosed finches hid out over the winter? It would certainly be effective camouflage. Xo smiled at the idea and glanced over at Elliot, but he was lost in thought, eyes on the road before his feet, and he didn't seem to have noticed the bloom of birdsong.

Aboard the train again, Elliot followed Xo to the sparsely populated café car and looked for a place to sit while she went to the counter to order. His stomach had been cramping uncomfortably all morning and food was not going to help. Finding an empty booth, he sat and gazed out through the condensation building up on the windows. Xo clearly did not approve of how he had dealt with Hector, but he could not think what he should have done or said instead. There was no tactful way to approach the question of infection, and to Hector, Elliot probably represented a bitter phase of his life that he'd rather not be reminded of, let alone its possible recurrence.

Xo reappeared, releasing a double handful of bagels and cream cheese packets onto the table. She hung her soaking wet coat on the edge of the booth, where it dripped steadily onto the floor, and plunked down into the seat facing Elliot, putting her feet up on his side underneath the table.

"So," said Xo. "I'd say that was a successful trip!" She spread cream cheese on the halves of each bagel and bit into one, looking quite a bit more cheerful than Elliot felt.

"You would?" said Elliot.

"Unless you were looking for a different answer," said Xo, between bites. "From Hector."

Had he been? Unfortunately, it seemed the only definitive answer would have been bad news. No, he hadn't wanted that, but he was no nearer to a resolution, to a feeling of relief that Xo would be out of danger.

Xo pushed the remaining bagel towards Elliot.

He shook his head. "You have it."

She chewed slowly, watching him and looking less cheerful now.

"Hector does not seem to have infected his wife, at least. Or children," conceded Elliot. "That is more likely than infecting other people. Though I suppose we can't be certain about his children..."

"Why can't we?"

"We didn't actually see them. We only heard them," said Elliot.

"Do you really think that's likely?"

"They probably didn't catch it," he admitted. "The very young would be even less likely to survive."

Xo sighed and crumpled her napkin. "Great. Elliot, you can't go on like this. Why can't you accept that it's good news?"

She ticked items off on her fingers: "The one survivor we can find doesn't have signs of reinfecting anybody. He's married with kids and everybody's alive and well. The doctor says you have no live virus at the moment, and he didn't seem to think there was any immediate likelihood of you infecting me, him, or anybody else. The test didn't prove you even had the same strain of the virus that sickened everybody in Lingen. Nobody's gotten sick since then, despite contact with you. For ten years. Not to mention another ten years between you catching it and the outbreak in Lingen, during which time you didn't infect anyone."

"That I know of," said Elliot. "I might not have had enough contact to infect anyone besides Lia."

In fact, he'd had more contact with Xo last night than was wise. Just the memory of her touch was overwhelming, but he'd been an idiot to give in to his senses. How had he ever justified...

Xo gave him a severe look that effectively interrupted his thoughts, and continued. "There's no record of anybody else with this disease having any resurgence. You even said yourself that you didn't remember having any symptoms when the Lingen outbreak started, and the doctor said that if it reactivated there should be signs." She spoke matter-of-factly, but her underlying agitation showed.

"I'm out of fingers." Xo held up both hands. "What else will prove to you that you're not going to infect me?"

"Everything you said makes sense. But…when I think of the chance, however small, of you catching this…" Elliot shifted in his seat, unable to find a comfortable position.

"We can't keep fighting this battle indefinitely; there's no opposing side." Xo got up from her seat and scooted in beside him. She interlocked her fingers with his, her touch only adding to the feeling of needing to protect her at any cost.

"Can you think of anything else we can do that would put your mind at ease?" asked Xo.

Dr. Adams might succeed in developing a vaccine; he'd asked on the phone if he could draw more blood for research, and Elliot had agreed. But developing a vaccine could take a long time, longer than he could ask Xo to wait—if it was even possible. Even the idea of the vaccine didn't give Elliot much comfort now. The paralyzing feeling inside him was not directly related to any of the things Xo had mentioned. He looked out the window, not wanting to meet her eyes. The trees outside were a dim, dark-green blur through the wetness.

He couldn't dispute her reasoning; she must be right. The only thing left, then, was fear. Worse, it wasn't only fear for her safety, it was also fear of his own loss. Fear of losing everything he loved, yet again. He was a coward. Xo probably wouldn't be surprised by that— she had doubtless already realized it—but he still felt ashamed.

"No, I can't think of anything else," said Elliot quietly. "I am just— terrified—that you will die from this, and I will lose the most important thing in the world." His words crowded around him, clogging the air.

"It's a risk I'm willing to take," said Xo, briskly dispersing them. "Elliot, that stupid disease could strike here tomorrow, through no fault of yours, and I could catch it and die no matter what you do. Or any number of other disasters could happen. Are you willing to go through those unknowns with me, including my potential horrible freak-accident death, or are you not going to because you're afraid of what might happen? Didn't you tell me love involves taking chances?"

"Taking a chance on love is not exactly the same thing as taking a chance about inadvertently killing the other person," said Elliot.

"It's the same thing," said Xo. "I'm taking a chance that I'm gonna marry you and dedicate my heart and life to you, and that you're not gonna fall off the next staircase you come to and break your neck. Or whatever other outrageous hazard you end up in. Realistically, I think that's more likely than me catching this disease. Now, if you want to be with me, you're gonna have to risk it. It's a small risk, in my opinion, but it's there. I can think of bigger risks that you didn't seem to be worried about when you were talking about taking chances."

"It's not because of how small the risk is that you take the chance," said Elliot.

"It's a factor. What about when Alec fell on that hike and you jumped off the cliff?" asked Xo. "On some level you must have calculated the risk and concluded—unfortunately incorrectly in that case—that the rope was unlikely to break."

"In that kind of situation, it is not really a choice," said Elliot. "Or, it's the only choice."

"But it wasn't the *only* thing you could have done," insisted Xo.

"It was the only thing *I* could have done." He wished he could explain better.

"Okay. Maybe it would be easier to follow my heart if I could just *feel* what's the right thing to do," said Xo. "But I start second-guessing myself—especially if it's, well, an emotional situation—and then I don't know if my decision is the right one or a stupid one. Then it's worthwhile to look at the available evidence and see what level of risk makes sense."

Elliot had the feeling that he'd already been proven wrong somewhere in the conversation. It was true that his emotions swayed every decision when it came to Xo. Were they really that untrustworthy?

"And the evidence is in: the risk of me ever catching mountainpox is small," went on Xo. "Is your love for me stronger than the fear of this very small risk?"

Elliot looked at her. "I love you more than anything I know."

"And I love you," said Xo. "Now do you still want to be with me forever, or at least until one of us dies in a horrible freak accident?"

"I want to be with you forever," said Elliot.

"Then do you still want to marry me?" said Xo. Her wide dark eyes were fixed on his, waiting, hopeful.

It was one of those times when no other course of action was possible anymore.

"If you'll have me." Elliot pushed the icy fears down, down. They were, as she'd established, foolish. He could pretend, perhaps, that they did not exist....

Xo cupped his face in her hands, tangling her fingers through his sideburns and into his hair. Then she kissed him, and the idea that he'd ever thought there could be any other path seemed like the most ridiculous notion in the world. How he'd not seen this before, he couldn't imagine. How many other people were in the train car possibly watching, as Xo's knee went over his and she pressed him back against the seat, he did briefly consider, but only for a moment until he realized he didn't care. His head spun dizzily as he pulled her into his arms, so that he would have lost his balance if he hadn't already been sitting.

"Then let's go get married," said Xo, when they came up for air.

40

HAPPY DAZE

"I can't believe there's a waiting period after applying for the marriage license. I was ready when we got off the train yesterday," said Xo. She was arranging her paints in a cardboard box that had once held food supplies for the coffee house, one of several contributed by Jacqua to pack up her apartment.

"Only three days," said Elliot with a smile. He had already waited with such longing that the legal requirement felt like next to nothing.

"I know, but that puts the earliest day we can get married on Tuesday, and I already agreed to cover Megan's shift the very next day. I wish I could take some time off like you did, but I haven't got any left."

"We could delay it, if you like," said Elliot. It was on his account that she'd missed work before in the first place. He had taken the whole next week off to help arrange Xo's belongings in the house and to spend as much time as possible with her. Though his schedule was already quite flexible, he wanted to make up for how their engagement had started.

"Nope, no delays! I don't want you developing any more doubts between now and then." Xo's eyes were teasing, but Elliot wasn't sure she was entirely joking.

"I never had any doubts about you," said Elliot. Only about infecting her, but bringing that up again would not reassure her. Perhaps he should not mention that he had another appointment with Dr. Adams tomorrow.

"Can I set up my easel in the laundry room? I like the light in there," said Xo.

"Of course," said Elliot. "There's not much space in that house, is there?"

"I like your house," said Xo. "We can put our kids in the darkroom."

Elliot laughed. The darkroom wouldn't do, of course, but there was enough space on the lot to add a room at the back of the house. Imagining Xo living in his little house flooded him with warmth. He pictured holding a wispy-haired baby who closely resembled Xo in his arms, as the real Xo snuggled against him on the bed. The peacefulness of the scene brought a lump to his throat.

The real-real Xo interrupted his vision by chucking several items off the shelf into another box. "I dunno how I managed to accumulate so much stuff. Of course, half of these books are yours."

She flipped through one of them and handed it to Elliot, cocking her head to one side. It was *Precipice and Precipitation*. "Were you trying to seduce me back when you lent me this?"

Elliot took the book with a sheepish smile. "Possibly."

Xo laughed, shrugging. "I guess it worked. If only I'd been a faster reader!"

He put the book in the box. His heart was so full that it hurt. "I wish you could hear what I feel inside, how much I love you. When I try to tell you, it's not enough."

"You could show your love by helping me pack," said Xo lightly, handing him another book.

"But I need to tell you. My words are so inadequate. You don't know how much you mean to me, Xiomara. You make me see the world as a different place, a beautiful place, just by being there and seeing it with me. You are extraordinary."

Xo shook her head, smiling. "I love you too, Elliot. You don't have to flatter me; you've already got me."

"It's not flattery. I mean it."

"I know you do, it's just…hard to hear about myself. I don't feel that amazing. Most of the time I have no idea what I'm doing. It's like being a real, fully-fledged adult is a hobby I'm not very good at." Xo surveyed the stacks of paintings she had assembled for transportation. "I'm better at being an artist, but I still feel like an amateur there, too."

"Do you feel you are back to 'being yourself?'" asked Elliot.

"Yeah, I think I'm going the right way. I just have more work to do. You believe in me; that helps." She smiled and stroked Elliot's cheek. "Please don't think your words are inadequate."

Elliot's mind was no longer on packing, if it ever had been. He caught her hand and turned his head to brush his lips against it. "Xiomara—"

Xo reached for one of her notebooks with her other hand and flipped it open. "I got your note." She indicated his drawing of "Mt. Xiomara" paper-clipped to the inside cover. "I never said anything about it, but I should have. That day Francis was here…you made me feel like you would love me no matter what. And I know you didn't do anything stupid like I did, but I would love you no matter what, too."

Elliot swallowed hard, holding her hand in his. "I have my own stupidity."

On Monday, while Xo was at work, Elliot stopped by Dr. Adams's office to provide another blood sample. He still had not told Xo he was going. This omission made him vaguely uncomfortable, but not as much as telling her the day before their wedding and making her think he was giving in to foolish fears and worrying about contagion again. Which he was not going to do. If anything, the visit should help him keep those fears at bay, where they belonged.

"Thank you for doing this," said Elliot, as the doctor took his blood samples. Elliot had told himself repeatedly that Dr. Adams would not find anything new, but it was still best to do it now, before the wedding day.

"No trouble at all," said Dr. Adams. "Give me a call any time."

"I spoke with Hector," Elliot added.

Dr. Adams looked pleased. "You found him after all! Diligent work."

"He did not appear to have infected anyone in his family," said Elliot. "That seemed encouraging."

Dr. Adams looked up from scrutinizing the blood work. "Yes, I quite agree. You may be interested to know that I've been working with your samples to develop an experimental treatment, in case we ever have another outbreak. It could help people in the early stages of infection. Now, it's nothing you would need if your mountainpox re-awoke: in that case your immune system should recognize it and suppress it. But, if it ever appears that it has reactivated and infected someone else, or Xo ever shows any symptoms…"

Elliot tensed as the doctor hesitated. Xo had convinced him beyond reasonable doubt that this would not happen, but away from her influence…He tried to remember all her reasons that he should not worry about this.

Dr. Adams continued, "Well, in such a case, this treatment might help. But as you saw, this other fellow has been married for years with absolutely no sign of infecting anybody." The doctor smiled re-assuringly. "And your blood shows no signs of infection at the moment either. I really don't think you need to worry about being contagious. Enjoy your wedding. And congratulations, again."

Elliot forced himself to relax and concentrate on the joy of marrying Xo. It had been worth coming again to talk to Dr. Adams, who had only validated what Xo had said. She would be happy to hear that. No—she was already convinced—it would only concern her that he was still worrying about this. Which he was not, because there was no basis for it.

❖   ❖   ❖

Elliot and Xo stood before the judge. A peculiar vibration that Elliot could not quell had hummed in the middle of his body since he woke up, increasing in anticipation of this moment. His palms were sweating and he had to keep reminding himself to breathe. Xo also kept reminding him to breathe. She did not seem as nervous, but her cheeks glowed darkly and her eyes were shining, lovely as always. Alec and Megan had accompanied them as witnesses, and they stood to one side, dressy and excited.

Elliot listened to the words in a daze and spoke at the appropriate time. His heart raced until he felt like he might collapse. When the judge said they were married, Elliot slowly kissed Xo and wrapped his arms around her, shaking. He did not want to let go of her ever again. Somewhere in the vague background he could hear Alec and Megan cheering.

"I love you," whispered Xo in his ear. She was crying.

Elliot pulled back and examined her face cautiously, but they were happy tears. He wiped them away and got mascara on his hands. Finding the handkerchief that he generally used to clean his glasses, he cleaned the mascara off his fingers so it would not transfer onto her outfit. As he put the cloth in his pocket, Xo took his other hand, smiling.

They turned to Alec and Megan, who were congratulating them and hugging them. Elliot held tight to Xo's hand, as if she might slip away. He had to keep reminding himself that this was real. They walked out of the courthouse into a world coated in golden light as the earth rolled away from the setting sun.

"Come on back to the coffee house." Megan dragged on Xo's other hand. "There's a surprise for you two." Megan kept bouncing, and her hair kept bouncing when she bounced. It was unusually jarring. Elliot returned his focus to Xo instead.

"Oh, I said I didn't want anything." Xo's voice was doubtful, but she was still smiling.

When Xo and Elliot entered the coffee house, the people inside started clapping. At a table near the door, Elliot recognized Jacqua's wife sitting with Sade and her husband, and beyond them, Alec's parents.

"There's no party," said Megan. "These are random customers who happen to be here at the moment."

Xo laughed, then stopped and looked up. There were white paper birds and flowers up all around the room. "Did you do all this between me getting off work and you joining us at the courthouse?"

"Yes, I was in charge of decorations," said Megan gleefully, pointing out additional enhancements.

"Why don't I get any credit?" complained Alec, who had suddenly reappeared at Elliot's other side. "I hung them up."

"That's only because you're tall," said Megan.

Xo scrutinized a large red-and-white banner above the mantel congratulating them. "Did that used to say 'Go Hoary Marmots'? I know I saw something similar near the campus."

"Maybe it did, maybe it didn't!" said Megan airily. They all laughed, and Elliot heard himself do so as well, somewhere nearby.

"Well, it all looks lovely." Xo smiled and leaned against Elliot and he felt her smile flow into him as he held her.

Jacqua produced a large cake from the kitchen and set it on one of the tables. It was decorated with two goldfinches made from a frosting-like material, quite beautiful, and clearly inspired by Xo's painting. Jacqua dished it out, looking pleased with himself, as Xo exclaimed over it.

"How did you know about the goldfinch painting?" Xo asked the others in confusion.

Alec tipped his head back and laughed. "Sometimes it seems like you two think you live in a world of your own. It's not like the rest of us couldn't see what was going on around here."

Someone raised the volume of the music that was playing in the background. Megan was trying to get Alec to dance and meeting with resistance, but eventually he gave in, as did a few other people in the coffee shop.

Xo turned to Elliot. "Do you wanna dance?"

"I always want to dance with you," said Elliot.

The song was slower than the music they had danced to before, thankfully, as Elliot wanted to keep holding on to Xo. He could only think how amazing it was that she was here in his arms. Could it really be true that she always would be?

Many dances later, they walked back to Elliot's house, to their home, the streetlights on the snow making everything bright and cozy despite the cold. Every few steps, something caught Xo's eye and she stopped to look at it, and Elliot looked at it with her, then she ended up looking at him, and he ended up looking at her, until the cold made them remember to keep moving again. A few times they were nearly forced to let go of each other's hands to keep their balance on the icy sidewalks, but they made it home together at last.

When they entered the warm house, Xo paused just inside the threshold and turned to face him. "Remember how I'm working Megan's shift tomorrow instead of mine? I'm gonna have to leave for the coffee shop pretty early in the morning."

"Ah," said Elliot.

Xo's voice dropped. "So, that means we should get to bed early." She flicked off the light he had just turned on. "Elliot..."

He felt her mouth against his neck and closed his eyes. "Ah...Xiomara..."

"I want to use lots of saliva this time," said Xo softly in his ear.

Elliot leaned back against the closed door and accidentally clunked his head, hard.

"Unh," he gasped in pain, involuntarily.

"Oops, sorry." Xo pulled away.

"No, come back," Elliot whispered. He found her again in the dark and clutched her to him, kissing her and kissing her again, and they melted into each other's arms.

Elliot awoke into a state of lightheaded bliss. He licked his lips, remembering Xo's kiss when she left for work hours before in the dark, and groaned, pushing his face back into the pillow. It was firm and uncuddly, no substitute for Xo's soft warmth. Did she have to take the early shift *this* morning?

He debated staying in bed longer, but he was too thirsty. As he sat up, the edge of the covers dragging across his chest enacted a searing pain. He looked down, and the bottom abruptly dropped out of the world. His stomach and chest were dotted with a red, blistery rash.

41

Rash Decisions

Elliot stumbled to his feet, wide awake in an instant. His breath caught in his parched throat. He was sure the rash had not been there earlier that morning, before Xo left. And he was sure that she hadn't had these marks on her own skin when she dressed—but was he sure enough? Hours had passed since then. But how many, and how long until she returned home?

He reached for his phone on the nightstand, froze, withdrew his hand. If Xo knew, she would return home immediately. Since she hadn't come home already…she might be well. Lia had been ill even before she went out that day, not realizing what the rash meant, but Xo would know. Wouldn't she? If she had been sick that morning, or was now, she wouldn't stay at the coffee shop. She had missed work for lesser reasons. If she saw a rash, she would know what it meant.

He wasn't sure he believed himself. The idea of observing her unnoticed at the coffee shop, to determine if she was ill, came to mind. No, it was too dangerous for anyone to come in contact with him. Yet Xo would be returning here soon—even sooner than usual, since she was working Megan's shift.

As Elliot threw on a shirt it became clear that the rash had spread to his back as well. When the cloth touched the scattered blisters that were forming, it was like being stabbed with shards of glass. The memory of that feeling abruptly returned, as did the remembrance that soon he would be tossing with fever and his ability to act or think clearly would be severely impeded.

Xo had once accused him of planning to get on the train and not come back, if he discovered he was infectious. Faced with actually doing this, however, the implications were horrifying—he would start a new outbreak amongst any number of innocent people. Even if he drove his own vehicle, no matter where he went, he would bring destruction: anywhere he stopped, or stayed, or bought supplies. The roads were so snowy it was unlikely he could reach a location remote enough to avoid the possibility of someone approaching the vehicle, and it was too cold to stay overnight in his car anyway. He should have come up with a better plan before—not now, with his head spinning, and the ghastly result of any potential action paralyzing his mind.

He tugged the sheets and blankets off the rumpled bed in one armful and dumped them into the washing machine, then walked through the house quickly, collecting his coat and boots. Feverishness was setting in, whether generated by the mountainpox or his frantic thoughts, he wasn't sure. At the sink, he started to reach for a glass to fill with water, then cupped his hand to drink instead, turning off the faucet with his sleeve, suppressing the urge to cough. The house was a crime scene, and he was the criminal. Nothing must be contaminated.

Retrieving his most-loved photo of Xo from its place in the darkroom, he looked over the image of her face before tucking it into his shirt pocket. The cozy future with her that he'd imagined was now shattered, even further from reality than when he'd taken that photograph. If he stayed here, he sentenced her to death. If he left, he might still be abandoning her to the same fate, but at least there was a chance she had avoided infection. He was her worst enemy, having pulled her into his field of destruction where everything he touched suffered. He might temporarily cease to be contagious if he fought off this infection, as before, but then what? Xo would never be safe now that it was clear the virus could reactivate. Nor would anyone ever be safe from him.

If only he could be sure that she had not already caught the disease. He could call Dr. Adams—no, he might manage to interrupt Elliot's departure too, and if he caught the mountainpox as Dr. Barker had, then Xo would truly be out of options. It was too risky to contact anyone. Elliot was in check with nowhere safe to go, but forced to move.

Elliot took a clean handkerchief and wrapped it around a pen to jot a note to Xo. If she had contracted mountainpox, Dr. Adams was her only chance for recovery, and it was imperative that she act immediately. Still, he must hope and pray that she had not caught it. He had to make himself believe it was possible; this hope was the only thing keeping him going. It was doubtful that he could ever see her again, and as this thought took hold, his hand shook uncontrollably. He lifted the pen from the page—he couldn't write those words to her. He must leave her with something else instead. Hope. Faith. Whatever shred he had left, he would leave with her.

❖　　❖　　❖

Xo shifted the bag of groceries she was carrying from her knee back to her hip after unlocking the front door, and pushed it open. It had been a relief to finally make up the time she'd missed, even though she'd been pretty much useless at the coffee shop. She could only think of Elliot and replay the previous night in her mind with a silly grin on her face. If she closed her eyes, she could feel herself touching him, feel his fingertips following the contours of her body, his breath against her skin, his mouth on hers and everywhere else.

She shivered deliciously out of her imagination and back into the room. "Elliot?"

The silence that only came with an empty house told her he was out. Before too much disappointment succeeded her surprise at this discovery, she caught sight of a folded paper with her name on it taped to the counter, and picked it up, smiling.

She started to read it, and consequently missed the counter where she had been setting down the bag of groceries. The bag fell straight to the floor and eggs splattered everywhere while Xo stood in the midst of them, holding the note, paralyzed.

My Dear Xiomara,

I promised you I would not leave without telling you, so I am telling you. I also swear to you that I will come back if/when I am able. I cannot tell you in person because the mountainpox is back in its infectious state. As the virus is extremely contagious in this state, I am isolating myself until it passes. It is not supposed to be contagious before the rash appears, so I pray that you have not contracted it. If you show any signs of sickness, contact Dr. Adams immediately for treatment; do not waste time at that clinic.

I will always love you.

Yours Forever,

Elliot

The room spun around Xo. How could this be happening? How could he not tell her where he had gone? If the mountainpox could resurface, could he die from it?

Maybe it wasn't the same disease at all, but some other sickness he had caught, and he was taking undue precautions because he was so worried about her catching the mountainpox. She seized on this one positive idea. It had to be something else—she'd seen him that morning. He hadn't had a rash last night, or she would have noticed it. And he hadn't seemed sick, either.

She'd gotten up to go to work, Elliot lying there sleepily, hair curly and mussed, watching her get dressed in the dim light of the bedside lamp. *Don't go*, he had murmured, as she bent to kiss him goodbye. Had he ever asked anything else of her? And she had gone. That could not be her last memory of him. He could not have the mountainpox again. He must be mistaken. Xo realized she was hyperventilating and leaned against the counter to steady herself, taking deep breaths and letting them out slowly.

Though her body was now still, inside she was about to explode. Holding herself in place was making the tumult worse as her emotions careened around, colliding with every plan she tried to form. Pushing herself off the counter, she began searching through the house for any clue as to where or when Elliot had gone. The fire had not been remade in the woodstove that morning. The bed had been stripped.

Xo opened the silent washing machine. The wet sheets and blankets in it, smelling faintly of bleach, had gone cold. She tossed the soggy load into the dryer and started it. At least Elliot would appreciate that, wherever he was—there was no point in letting them sit there and mildew. Next to the dryer, her unfinished pictures for Sade sat on the easel. No time to think about that now. Returning to the kitchen, she scooped up the broken eggs and soggy grocery sack with a dustpan and dumped it all in the sink, running water to wash the liquid parts down, and then swabbed the worst of it off the floor. As she had hoped, applying her hands to the simple tasks gradually slowed her racing thoughts and helped her think more clearly.

She called Elliot's phone, but it rang from the nightstand. After the note, she hadn't been expecting to reach him this way, but it still called forth tears of frustration. She burst out the front door onto the step. Improbably, she'd pictured finding footprints where he had walked, but there had been no fresh snow that night. Numerous footprints from both of them ranged up and down the gravel path, and many more people had trampled holes in the snow on the sidewalk. His car at the curb had not moved. Up the street, the neighbor was out as usual on her porch. She was *always* there...

Xo cut across the street to the woman's house. The stairs to the porch creaked in the cold as she mounted them.

"I'm Xo. I recently moved in across the way," said Xo hesitantly.

The woman only smiled at her. She'd probably seen Xo come and go enough times to figure this out.

"Do you know Elliot? Of course you do…" Xo tried to net useful thoughts from the wave of panic rising again inside. "Did you see him leave this morning?"

Still smiling, the woman nodded assent. She patted the seat beside her, but Xo didn't want to sit down. The relaxed and silent responses were adding to Xo's agitation.

"Well, could you tell me which way he went?"

The woman raised her arm to point beyond Elliot's house. There were more rows of houses before the town turned into rocky sidehill, but there was no street at this point in the block leading in the direction she had pointed.

"What do you mean?" Xo said frantically. "Can't you please tell me? It's really important." Clearly she could understand. If she was deaf, she was reading Xo's lips.

The woman pointed again in the same direction.

Xo looked at Arin, blue and white against the sky. "Are you saying he went up there, or what?"

Isolating, yes, but where would he go? Maybe the woman had seen him leave for a walk, before he'd realized he had a rash and departed for somewhere else. Or he was staying some place near the edge of town. Unfortunately, the woman couldn't or wouldn't explain.

"Thanks," said Xo reluctantly. She was wasting time. Reaching the bottom of the porch steps, she stood uncertain for a moment. Alec had come into the coffee house before she'd left to go to the store, and if anybody would know where Elliot had gone, it was probably him. Hopefully, he was still there. She began to run, slipping on the snowy sidewalk.

When Xo came into the shop, Alec was sitting at his usual table with some of his friends. She hurried over without bothering to take off her coat, though the coffee house was excessively warm after her run there. Sweat was beading up on her face.

"Have you seen Elliot?" she demanded.

Alec looked up from his companions in surprise. "Hey, Xo!"

His smile faded in response to her expression, and he stood and walked away from the table to talk to her apart from the others.

"I haven't seen him today, why? What's the matter?"

"He thinks he's sick with that disease again, and he's gone off somewhere. Where could he have gone?" Xo pulled Elliot's note out of her pocket and handed it to Alec, who unfolded it and read.

"He didn't say anything to me." Alec frowned as he scanned the note. "How can this be? I thought we decided it didn't reactivate."

"I don't know! It was always a possibility, but...I didn't really think it would happen. Maybe he caught something else, and just thought it was the same thing. But it could be serious! Do you have any idea where he would have gone if he thought he was contagious?"

Alec bit his lip. "I'm thinking..."

"I asked this neighbor who's always sitting there and she wouldn't tell me anything, but she kept pointing up the mountain," said Xo in frustration. "But that doesn't make any sense."

"Aha," said Alec. "Mrs. Dupesh? She doesn't talk."

Xo groaned in despair. "That was her, then."

"It's been quite a few years now...throat cancer, I think, or was it mouth?" mused Alec. "Wasn't she in here the other day?"

"Will you please stay on track? Elliot...is...missing!"

Alec blinked. "Calm down."

"I am perfectly calm, and if I were not calm, you telling me to be calm would not make me more calm!" Xo's words left a wake of silence in the coffee shop. She closed her eyes and took a deep breath before looking at Alec again. "I am calm."

Alec raised his eyebrows. "Glad to hear it."

Xo closed her eyes again briefly in an attempt to retain her calmness. "Can you tell me," she said through gritted teeth, "If you have any idea where Elliot could be?"

Alec tapped the folded letter against his chin. "I wonder..."

"What? Tell me."

"There's an old fire lookout cabin on Arin that we stayed at a couple times while hiking," said Alec slowly. "It's certainly remote, and generally unoccupied. It's set up for people to overnight there."

"You mean he actually could have gone up the mountain? Where is this cabin? I'm going."

"Well now, hold on," said Alec. "If he really is contagious, he isolated himself for a reason. He'd kill me if I took you up there and you got infected."

"Alec!" Xo exploded. "He said '*if* slash *when* I come back!' IF. I am not letting him die alone up there regardless of what he has. He might not even have made it to the cabin—how far away is it? He could be sick with something else that is treatable. You have no idea how completely irrational Elliot is about this mountainpox business. It took me forever to convince him that I wasn't gonna catch it."

"Take it easy, Xo," said Alec. "I just think he probably knows what he's talking about."

"You obviously don't care what happens to him at all. I am going up there with or without you." Xo strode to the door and jerked it open. "If you won't tell me where it is, I'll find out another way!" she yelled over her shoulder.

42

The Search in the Snow

The icy air stung Xo's face after leaving the warm café, and she hunched against it, tucking her hands under her crossed arms as she walked up the sidewalk. There might be directions on how to get to the lookout cabin in one of the guidebooks at the visitor center.

Footsteps crunched on the sidewalk behind her.

"Can't even give a guy a chance to get his coat?" Alec caught up to her, still pulling the coat on.

Xo shook her head. Hot tears of relief burned her eyes.

"Let's stop by my house," Alec added in a subdued voice. "We're going to need gear to make it up there at this time of year, and the cabin's only stocked with emergency provisions." He handed Elliot's letter back to Xo. "He seems to think you could have caught it from him already. Do you have any symptoms?"

"No." Xo took a deep breath. "First, there's supposed to be a rash. Maybe he got a rash from something else and thought it reactivated."

"I don't know," said Alec. "If anybody's going to be able to recognize mountainpox, it's Elliot. He's certainly seen enough cases. It could be that he's right and just needs to wait it out. He might not even be very sick, since he's had it before."

"Or he could be dying," said Xo.

Alec didn't say anything.

They reached his house quickly, and Xo stood in the open garage entrance while Alec unearthed supplies from a large rack of equipment. He stood up a pair of skis next to her and then told her to strap them on her pack.

"We'll need them with this much snow." Alec set aside a pair for himself. "You know how to ski, right?"

"I've done it a couple times." Years ago, with a good deal of falling down. Better not to mention that. "How are we going to go uphill on skis?"

"Skins. They keep you from slipping back. Are you sure you've skied before?"

The skis were followed by boots and other gear which Alec instructed Xo either to pack or to put on while he gathered up other items and stuck them in or on the outside of his own pack. As he moved rapidly through the garage with occasional forays into the house, he seemed to know exactly what he was looking for and where to lay hands on each item. Despite his comments earlier discouraging her from trying to find Elliot, he looked worried—more worried than she had ever seen him.

"Let's get going." Alec squinted at the sky. "There's no way we're going to make the cabin before dark, but I'd rather spend the night there than out in the snow somewhere."

Xo trekked up the hillside after Alec, consumed with dread. She tried to concentrate on the possibility that Elliot was mistaken about whatever illness he'd come down with. What looked similar... chickenpox? No, too obvious, plus he'd already had it. Shingles could start on the stomach like mountainpox, but was one-sided, so he'd be able to tell the rash apart. Rocky mountain spotted fever started at the feet and hands, and measles started at the head, plus the rashes weren't blistery enough to confuse. Smallpox was eradicated. She should have done more research on similar diseases back when Elliot first got worried about it reactivating. There was no time, now.

Assessing herself, she felt worried sick, but not actually sick. Her legs ached from trying to keep up with Alec as he plowed ahead through the snow, and they weren't even very far up the mountainside. They were close enough to town that a few other people were out sledding and skiing.

"Put on your skis now. We should make better time across this side hill. Then we're going to have to cut up again, which will be slower going." Alec stopped and strapped on his skis and Xo did the same.

There wasn't much speed gained, if any, but the skis took less effort than wading through the snow. Xo still fell considerably behind Alec, though he waited for her occasionally without displaying much impatience. Unfortunately, it left her mostly alone with her worries about Elliot's welfare. Her sore muscles were beginning to take up more of her consciousness, though. They were a welcome distraction.

"I think we're following his tracks, now." Alec paused and Xo caught up with him. A line of footprints of approximately the right size chopped through the snow. By now, they had left behind all the people playing on the mountainside.

"Of course, it could be someone else," Alec continued as they followed the prints. "We don't even know for sure that he went up here at all."

Xo was more hopeful after seeing the tracks. They might even overtake Elliot along the way. "Why would anyone else hike up here at this time of year?"

"Some people do this for fun!" said Alec, as if it were perfectly reasonable.

Alec stopped at a large, smashed-down place in the snow. Xo didn't realize what it meant until he said, "Could be a normal fall."

It was too distressing to speculate about what this might mean in terms of Elliot's present condition. Xo could not help vividly recalling Alec's story of finding Elliot in the snow, bloody and unconscious. Shuddering, she tried to put the image out of her mind. What had possessed him to climb up here in the first place? It hardly seemed like the way to recover from an illness of any kind.

"I don't understand why he took off instead of just talking to me so we could come up with a sensible plan," Xo said. "We're supposed to handle things together. Did he expect me to sit at home and wait to see if he ever comes back? And he could be freaking out about something other than mountainpox. He could basically be killing himself for no reason by not treating it."

Alec digested this silently for a few moments before speaking. "Maybe he thought you wouldn't listen to him if he talked to you about it."

"Why? We talk about everything!"

"You mean *you* do…" muttered Alec.

Xo ignored this. "It's like he didn't trust me to be able to deal with this, so he didn't even give me the opportunity. He shouldn't be making unilateral decisions." She shook her head in frustration.

Alec snorted. "Well, you're not listening to him now, are you? You're doing the opposite. You're completely disregarding the possibility of contagion."

Xo gaped at him. "You're here too!" she countered.

Alec frowned and forged on ahead, leaving Xo to straggle along behind and mull over her uncomfortable thoughts herself.

At last, as it began to get dark, Alec stopped and pointed at a distant shape on an outcrop of rock. "That's the lookout cabin."

"Finally." Xo squinted through the gathering gloom, barely able to make it out. "I was beginning to think my legs were gonna give out. I don't think they've ever worked this hard in my life."

Alec looked concerned. "We've still got a couple hours to go, at least."

"How can that be? It doesn't look that far away," protested Xo.

"Not as the crow flies," said Alec. "But trust me, it'll take that long. Though I could do it in less time. Maybe you should have stayed in town and just let me go."

It was too late to take back her words about how sore she was, unfortunately. "Shouldn't there be lights on?" Xo asked instead. Already, the shape of the cabin was becoming obscured as darkness fell.

"There's no electricity up here."

"Right." Xo wished, for the first time ever, that Alec would joke around annoyingly again. His solemnity felt incredibly unnatural. It made her more frightened for Elliot.

"I think there's an oil lamp, and some candles," Alec conceded after waiting for her to catch up again. "But they might not be lit, or we might not be able to see them from here. Or the shutters might be down."

They removed their skis to climb a steep, rocky part of the trail. It was difficult to see Elliot's tracks anymore. The stark white patches of snow broken only by now-black rocks were disorienting in the dark. It seemed impossible that Alec should be able to find his way, and Xo would have been completely lost alone. It was now apparent that her earlier statement that she was going with or without him had been ridiculous, as Alec must have known then.

If only Elliot were holed up comfortably in the cabin with a book, waiting out whatever suspicious rash had made him think he was contagious again. Was he the one overreacting about this, or was she? Ideally, it would be both of them.

Xo had completely lost track of time when they finally dragged up to the lookout cabin. She ached all over, her body screaming complaints which she had long been ignoring. Alec still seemed brisk, already banging at the door.

Somehow, Xo summoned the energy to run the rest of the way.

"Well?" She reached Alec, panting.

Alec shook his head and folded his arms, while she knocked on the door in turn. There was not the slightest sound from inside.

"Someone's in there, or was." Alec indicated the thin stream of smoke curling up from the chimney. He turned the knob and pushed against the door experimentally. "Still is. It's barred. There's a wooden beam that can go across the inside."

"Please open up, Elliot! I just want to be sure you're okay." Xo knocked again.

"Elliot! There are people out here who love you. Open the door!" hollered Alec, leaning against the wall.

"Not a great argument, that's exactly why he won't let us in," pointed out Xo.

Alec tried a different tack. "We're going to freeze to death if you don't let us in!"

When there was still no answer, Xo slumped against the door and sank into a sitting position on the step. She was utterly exhausted. Her eyes flooded with tears, hot against her chilled skin.

"Why won't he even answer? What if—" Xo stopped, unable to voice her worst fears now that they were here.

Alec went to one of the windows. Although they looked to be on all sides of the building, there were large board shutters lowered down over each set like hinged awnings, closed and latched from the outside. They were higher than Xo could see into anyway. Propping one open, Alec chinned up on the windowsill and peered into the darkness inside. He dropped down again without reporting anything, and walked around the building. Xo got up and followed him.

A back window was more easily accessible from a snowbank that had piled up on the slope behind the building. Alec propped that window shutter open, took out a pocketknife, and started to pry on the edge of one of the window frames. A piece of wood popped off, part of the outside edge of the frame. He frowned, folding the knife again, and before Xo guessed what he was going to do, broke one of the panes of glass with the knife handle. She jumped at the sound of it shattering.

They both waited silently as small bits of glass tinkled on the floor inside, then Alec called again, "Elliot?"

There was no response. Alec broke the next pane over and picked out the loose pieces of glass from the frame, then grabbed the frame with both hands and pulled. With a loud creak, the entire frame came loose with the other panes of glass still in it. He put his hand on the windowsill, eyeing the gap experimentally.

"Let me," said Xo.

Alec made a stirrup out of his hands to boost her up. Xo took off her pack and stepped into his hands with one foot, and he lifted her until she could put her other knee on the sill. It was completely dark inside, though a faint warmth remained from the fire that had burned earlier in the stove.

"Go and unbar the door first thing. Mind the drop," said Alec.

Xo ducked under the top of the window frame and maneuvered herself into a crouch with both feet pointing forward, then jumped down to the floor, landing on her hands and feet. Glass crunched under her boots, and she stood up quickly, shaking off her mittens in case she had gotten glass on them. The first thing she wanted to do was look for Elliot, but she couldn't see anything in the dark. She crossed to where the door should be and felt for the bar, lifting it.

Alec pushed from the outside as she did so, freeing the bottom of the door that had frozen into the drifted snow. He dropped their two packs on the floor, took out a flashlight, and shone it around the room. Along the walls were low wooden slatted benches, as in a sauna. One held a shape wrapped in a blanket.

As Xo ran forward, Alec made as if to stop her, but she was faster. Filled with trepidation, she rolled the curled form towards her.

"Elliot?"

Elliot did not react. His eyes were closed, but he drew a labored breath. Xo's knees buckled and she collapsed by the bench. He was alive. Fighting to recover her own breath and slow her racing heart, she pulled off her mitten and felt his forehead, hot and drenched with sweat.

"Get me a thermometer," she said to Alec.

Alec pulled a medical kit out of his pack and passed the thermometer to her, along with a surgical mask and latex gloves.

"Put them on." When Xo hesitated, Alec went on, "Don't make me regret bringing you. You'd better not get sick."

Xo relented and put on the protective gear, as did Alec. As he located and lit the oil lamps from the cabin's cupboard, Xo put the thermometer in Elliot's mouth.

"105." Xo turned to Alec. "That's too high. What can we do? Take him outside?"

"No," said Alec. "Too cold." He wet some cloths with a bottle of water. "Put these on him. I'm going to have to get the fire going again." He moved about the cabin, putting a bucket of snow on the stove, and taping something over the broken window.

Xo unwrapped the blanket from around Elliot and opened his shirt, and her heart sank. The fresh rash of blisters looked like the pictures she'd seen, and they followed the path of the old scars, except they had not yet spread to cover his entire body. How could it be happening again, and why? She spread the damp cloths over Elliot's forehead and chest, feeling powerless. Elliot moved restlessly, but he did not appear to be aware of her at all, even when she took his hand

and spoke to him. Now that Xo had come, she had no idea what to do. Tears kept trickling from the corners of her eyes.

Alec ran out of chores to do and they both sat there in the dim light.

"Why won't he wake up?" asked Xo helplessly.

"I don't know," said Alec dully, looking Elliot over. "Maybe when his fever comes down…"

He convinced Xo they needed to eat something and they repaired to the other end of the room and disinfected. But when Alec passed her a sandwich, her stomach coiled up in rebellion.

"Is there anything else?" Xo felt ungrateful as soon as the words were out.

Alec dug around some more and produced a protein bar. She half-wished he'd tease her about eating birdseed again, but he was silent. The enormity of what faced them took away any possibility of appetite, but she had to eat, and had to somehow figure out something to do that would actually help Elliot. All she could remember about treating the mountainpox was that there was no treatment. The bar sat like a brick in her stomach, and the sports drink Alec gave her to wash it down tasted like plastic.

Xo moved to the bench near Elliot's head to check his temperature once more. It was minutely lower, but checking his temperature repeatedly wasn't going to pull him through this. She leaned back against the wall next to him, exhausted, and didn't realize when she fell asleep.

The sound of Elliot's voice woke Xo. The room was much lighter than before. Dawn, or close to it.

"Xiomara? What are you doing here?" Elliot's words were gravelly and confused. "Are you really here?"

"I'm here. Oh, Elliot, I thought you would never wake up!"

Elliot stared at her desperately. "No! You can't be!"

Alec, who had apparently also fallen asleep, woke with a start. He got to his feet and walked over.

Elliot turned wildly to Alec, pushing himself up. "Did you bring her here? How could you?" he cried, eyes watering.

Xo reached for him, but Elliot pulled away violently.

"Shh, take it easy," said Alec. "Drink this." He held a water bottle to Elliot's mouth. Elliot took it and drank, looking disoriented, then sat up the rest of the way. Alec gave him some aspirin, which Elliot swallowed with the rest of the water. He lowered the empty bottle and regarded Alec and Xo miserably.

"Why did you come here? I told you—" Elliot moaned.

Xo had planned for this question. "Because I love you and I'm not gonna let you die up here all alone."

"What is the point of dying up here with me?" Elliot pulled the blanket around himself like a shield where he sat, now shivering.

"We're taking precautions," said Alec. "Besides, how do you know it's the same disease? You could die up here for nothing."

Xo recognized her own argument that Alec had earlier dismissed, but after seeing Elliot, she was afraid she already knew the answer.

"It's the same. It looks the same. It feels the same," said Elliot. "Xiomara, you may have already caught it. And now you too, Alec." He groaned. "Will neither of you listen?"

"If I've already caught it, then I might as well be up here with you anyway," pointed out Xo reasonably.

Elliot shook his head. "No! I told you to go to Dr. Adams if you have any symptoms. Are you saying...you do?"

"I don't have any symptoms," Xo assured him. "But if I did, why go to Dr. Adams? If nothing can be done, I'd be just as well-off recovering here."

"No!" said Elliot again emphatically. "He has a treatment he can give you. Experimental. It might help."

Xo and Alec stared at each other and back to Elliot.

"What are you talking about?" said Xo.

"He told me. The last time I saw him for a blood draw," said Elliot. "It's something new."

"When did you—why didn't you tell me?" demanded Xo.

"I—I didn't want you to feel that I was…worrying, again." Elliot pressed his hands against his temples. "I should have told you. So you wouldn't come."

Xo frowned. "I would've come anyway."

"You have to go to Dr. Adams. You cannot be up here!"

"Why didn't he give this treatment to you?" asked Alec.

"He said it was for a new infection. If it reactivated…I would be fine." Elliot bent over, suppressing a grimace of pain. He seemed unable to sit still. "You have to go, now. Otherwise you probably won't live through this. It comes on…quickly."

Xo stood and pulled Alec aside, lowering her voice. "Does this make sense to you? Why can't this treatment be used for Elliot? He's obviously not 'fine.'"

"Is this Dr. Adams guy reliable?" asked Alec.

"He seemed to know what there is to know about the mountainpox," said Xo. "But Elliot is the one who needs treatment."

"We can't exactly take him with us in this condition," pointed out Alec.

"One of us should go to Dr. Adams," said Xo. "If he has some kind of treatment, Elliot needs it."

"You can't make it down and back by yourself," said Alec. "You'll get lost, or worse. I'll go, you stay."

"You both must go!" said Elliot from the bench, where he could apparently hear them after all. "Xiomara, Alec, you need to try that treatment while there's still time."

"We may have to bring this doctor back," whispered Alec to Xo. "If it's not the mountainpox, he should be able to tell. If it is—and I'm afraid it probably is—then maybe this treatment will do something for Elliot. And we might need it, too." He paused. "And Elliot's right…you might need it sooner. It's possible that you were infected before we left and it's not showing yet."

"What if Dr. Adams won't come up here?" whispered Xo.

"He'll come," said Alec darkly.

Xo knelt by the bench again. "Elliot, we're coming back. We'll bring whatever treatment Dr. Adams told you about. Maybe it can help you too." It had better do so. She turned to Alec. "Can we get down and back today?"

Alec nodded. "Down is faster."

"Promise me you won't die, Elliot," Xo whispered tearfully, touching Elliot's face with gloved fingers.

She wanted to kiss him, but he was sure to object over the chance of infection. And he would be right, she reproached herself, remembering all the times she'd brushed off his concerns about the virus. The chance of it being something else seemed remote now, and the chance of it being fatal, much more likely.

Elliot gazed back into her eyes. "You have my heart forever."

"But I need the rest of you to go with it." Xo bit her lip. "I will see you soon. I love you."

"I love you," said Elliot shakily.

Then the door was closing behind them.

"Alec, wait—" said Elliot.

43

THE BATTLE INSIDE

Alec's frame stiffened, silhouetted in the doorway. He closed the door, leaving Xo outside, and returned to Elliot with reluctance showing in every movement of his body.

"Elly," Alec said quietly, squatting loosely beside the bench.

"Alec…if I don't—"

Alec was shaking his head already. "I know what you're going to say, and I don't want you to say it."

Elliot swallowed. "Just…look after her. If I—"

"Don't have this conversation, man."

"What kind of man am I? I cannot even protect her from this—from myself. I bring disaster to anyone who comes in contact with me. I should never have—" Elliot choked. His entire existence, it seemed, was proven again to be a mistake.

"You want to know what kind of man?" said Alec. "*I* never would have come up here just to keep this virus away from her."

"You would," said Elliot.

"No." Alec shook his head again. "Only you would have. I'm a selfish guy—ask anyone. She needs you. You've got to hold on."

"Alec, listen," said Elliot. "Get to Dr. Adams. Then, you and Xiomara can't come here again."

"I'll make sure she gets the treatment," said Alec.

"You know it's too risky to come back," said Elliot. Alec shifted in his crouch, but didn't answer. "Give me your word."

Alec became still. "You can't ask me that."

"I am asking you." Elliot glared at him. If he could have shaken Alec into submission, he would have, but that was unlikely to be effective in his weakened state. If ever.

"You're asking the impossible." Alec looked away. After a few moments, he laid a hand on Elliot's shoulder in parting and rose to his feet.

Elliot allowed himself to relax. Alec would do the right thing. A weight had lifted from Elliot's shoulders, and now it bowed Alec's as he turned to go. He was sorry to burden his friend with such a request, but it couldn't be helped.

"Perhaps this is just things evening out, and I was always meant to die from this," said Elliot more quietly.

Alec spun to face Elliot again. He did not look comforted by Elliot's words—he looked angry.

"How did you feel when Lia died?" demanded Alec. "How did you feel when you were left to deal with things all alone after your parents died? Do you remember?"

Elliot twisted away as Alec's words cut him. Of course he remembered, but it was cruelty to uncover such wounds.

"Are you going to condemn Xo to that same suffering? Or are you going to try to beat this, and let us help you beat it?"

"It's not the same," protested Elliot.

"If you give up now, you're taking the easy way out," said Alec harshly. "And if you think it's good for Xo, well, you're just lying to yourself."

Now Alec was virtually kicking him when he was down. Elliot stared at him, speechless, as Alec turned abruptly towards the door. How could Alec leave this way? This could be the last time they spoke to each other. The lump in Elliot's throat would have choked any words he could have summoned, but he was in too much shock to speak anyway. With barely a parting glance, Alec went out, closing the door behind him.

As if Elliot had any choice in the matter once the mountainpox took hold. A chill shook Elliot's frame, the echo of Alec's words stabbing him. Even if he lived through this, it could reactivate and put Alec and Xo in danger again…and again.

He lay immobilized, the possible outcomes, all negative, seeming to swirl around him just outside the glow of the lamplight, pressing in. Alec and Xo were gone, their voices long since faded, but after Alec's outburst, he was no longer sure he could rely on him to stay away. And if either of them returned, they would have yet another chance to catch the mountainpox from him even if they hadn't already.

Unless Elliot wasn't here.

No matter what he did, he would lose, but if he was to have any further agency in the outcome he had to move now, before he was completely incapacitated. He could no longer even judge if it had been minutes or hours since they had left.

He pushed himself upright. His head swirled with dizziness and points of light sparkled before his eyes as the room darkened. After a few moments his vision cleared and he staggered, seemingly across a vast distance, to the door. It was only held closed now by the knob and its own weight, not that barring it had done any good earlier. He hauled on it, scraping it with difficulty across the floor. The fever had wrung out his strength to the point that he could barely stand.

The wind had packed a layer of snow against the threshold which collapsed inwards as he opened the door, and harsh light splintered the shadowy room. Alec and Xo's ski tracks led away down the hill, soft lines now mostly filled in by the drifting snow. Fear and confusion were inside the cabin, while outside was cool and clear and inviting.

Still, Elliot hesitated as he looked out, away from the tracks, his thoughts sharpening in the chill air that rushed through the opening. Leaving again in case they returned was no longer a sure way to protect Xo from catching the disease. It was now much more likely that she was already infected. But there was a real chance she could survive it if she reached Dr. Adams and his potential treatment. Xo's chances were better than Lia's had been. Elliot tried to dismiss what Alec had said: Xo was resilient, and logical. She would not blame herself if he died. It was not the same.

But if she lived, and returned to the cabin to find that Elliot had left, he would be making her live with the knowledge that he had given up because of her. Alec's biting words ricocheted around inside him. Alec was right. He was lying to himself, because it was too hard to face what he had done to her, and to face the fact that even if she lived, he could never be near her again. The icy mountainside he looked out on was easier to confront. But it was not only cowardly, it would hurt her even more than he already had.

He would have to stay and try to live through it, and if he lived, continue to do whatever he could to protect and support Xo—though always from a safe distance, a far distance, in case his disease recurred again. It might recur many times over until it killed him. Xo would not long remain voluntarily tied to such an awful life; she would see that the only reasonable course was for her to move on. But this would be better for her than tying her to his death—Alec had seen at once that would be a selfish route. In the cold, a fresh paroxysm shook Elliot at the thought of how close he had come to making a feverish choice that could scar Xo forever.

The door was still ajar. With a shudder, Elliot slammed his shoulder against the inside to close it. It didn't move. He shoved again, harder. It seemed impossible that the door should have become so heavy that he could not move it, but it would not budge, frozen to the snow that had fallen in over the threshold. It wasn't the door, then…it was him. His fingers were already going numb on the frame. Bracing his feet on the floor, he threw his weight against it again, and then darkness filled his vision.

44

DESCENT AND DECISION

"I hope we're doing the right thing." Xo caught up to Alec as he paused before skiing down another slope. Though she had no other ideas of how to help Elliot recover, leaving him in the cabin felt awful.

"There's nothing more we can do without that doctor," said Alec. "And I can't imagine Elliot pulling through this if you catch it and die. Or what he'd be like if he did," he added hollowly.

"What did he say to you?" She had felt so alone, standing outside the cabin, wondering why Elliot needed to talk to Alec again. Without her.

"Oh, nothing," said Alec quickly. "Telling me to keep you out of trouble and safe. You know Elliot."

"Hmph," said Xo.

"Here, you'd better take some of these too." Alec tossed her an aspirin bottle. "You're not used to this." He pushed off.

They were taking a different route down to allow more skiing. The descent was much faster, as Alec had predicted, though Xo still fell a few times. Unfortunately, it was a while before the aspirin kicked in. When they finally reached Lingen and unfastened their skis for the last time, her legs nearly buckled.

"I need to sit down for a minute. Are we back in reception?" Xo took out her phone. "I have to get ahold of Sade."

There was no telling how long it would be before she could finish the illustrations that were due for the newsletter. The fear that she might lose her job over this was like a vise on her lungs, but there was no choice.

"You don't have to go back up," broke in Alec as Xo was dialing.

Xo cancelled the call and stared up at him. "Yes, I do."

"You can stay here after the doctor gives you this treatment, and I'll go back up with him," Alec continued.

"No. What if Elliot's dying?"

"Then it's not going to make any difference if you're there or not," said Alec coldly.

"That's not true!" Xo's eyes filled with tears. "He needs me there. To give him hope."

"You know there's nothing you can do," said Alec quietly. "You saw that."

"Elliot and I are in this together. I'm going to do everything I can to help him get through this, and if nothing else, I'll be there anyway holding his hand. Maybe you're the one who should stay here!" Xo glared at Alec.

"You can't find your way back alone," countered Alec. "And what are you going to do if this doctor refuses to come? Talk at him?"

"Stop mocking me." The whole situation was unfair. Elliot could not die like this. He just couldn't. "I love him and I'm going."

"He doesn't want you to come back to the cabin. Okay?"

So that was what Elliot had told Alec. She could have guessed as much anyway. "I don't care. He doesn't want you to go back either, and yet you're going. And I'm going."

"I thought you were supposed to be the logical one." Despite his words, Alec's tone said he had relented.

"So did I," said Xo. "Good thing I'm learning not to be."

She stabbed Sade's number into the phone.

"Sade? I'm really sorry, but I'm not going to get this week's illustrations in on time."

The line was silent for a painful moment.

"Why is that?" crackled Sade's voice.

"It's…it's an emergency. It's Elliot." Xo had spoken quickly before, but now, it was hard to get the words out. Holding her breath, she waited for the reply. Her heartbeat was deafening in her ears, thanks to Alec riling her up.

"You do what you need to do," said Sade. "The pictures will keep."

"Thank you. Thank you." Xo hung up and stared at the phone in disbelief.

"Ready?" asked Alec.

Xo pulled herself together. "Almost. Now Megan."

"Let me guess," said Megan over the phone. "You need somebody to cover your shift today? What happened this time?"

"It's kind of a long story." Xo glanced at Alec, who looked impatient. "Elliot is sick, Megan. It's gonna be more than today. I'm sorry, I'll make it up later."

"That Elliot needs his own special insurance," said Megan. "Okay, I'll rearrange the schedule."

"She's flexible, I'll give her that," said Alec, when Xo hung up. "Come on. Let's go find this doctor of yours."

❖   ❖   ❖

Dr. Adams's office door at the college was standing open. Xo knocked on it, leaning inside. He was not there, but she recognized the folder from the Lingen outbreak lying on his desk.

Alec lingered at the door checking the posted office hours as Xo went in. She hesitated, then reached over and flipped open the folder. Lia's record was on top. Giving up any pretense, Xo walked around the desk and began going through the papers in the folder.

"He's supposed to be in now, so I guess we wait until he gets back," said Alec, stepping inside the office. His eyes fell on the open folder in Xo's hands and he raised his eyebrows.

Xo returned his glance defiantly and went back to flipping through the records. She stopped as one sheet caught her eye.

"Alec, take a look at this—" Xo raised her head and froze. Dr. Adams himself stood in the doorway.

"Xo, what a nice surprise!" Dr. Adams said, smiling. He held a steaming cup from an instant-espresso vending machine. The doctor nodded at Alec in a friendly way and extended a hand, which Alec shook in slow motion.

"You're the one the *Herald* interviewed for the mountainpox article," said Alec.

"Ah, yes, so I am," said Dr. Adams. "Glad to meet a fan." While Alec chewed this over, Dr. Adams turned back to Xo. "I take it Elliot must have told you about my experimental treatment. Are you showing symptoms?"

"No, but Elliot is." Xo was still standing behind the doctor's desk. She closed the folder. "You'd be able to tell if it's mountainpox, right?"

"Certainly, I can," said Dr. Adams. "Is he at home now?"

"No," said Alec. "He's in a cabin up on Arin."

"Well, that's rather inconvenient," said Dr. Adams. "Is he coming down?"

"No, he's very sick!" said Xo. "This treatment…could you use it to help him?"

"Elliot's immune system should recognize mountainpox and fight it off, as he's recovered from it before. Are you sure you're not showing any symptoms yourself, Xo?"

"I'm fine! Elliot's the one who's not fine!" Xo held up the folder, which Dr. Adams had been eyeing in her hand. "And why are there references to a vaccine in here? I thought there was no vaccine."

"Ah." Dr. Adams gently closed the office door. "I'm afraid that was just a trial," he said regretfully, taking the folder from Xo and tucking it in a cupboard.

"What do you mean?" Xo folded her arms. "Did the vaccine work or not?"

"It was never approved for distribution," said Dr. Adams carefully.

"But you know it works." Xo's eyes narrowed. "You took it yourself, didn't you? That's why you're not worried about catching anything from Elliot. You were ready to go see him a second ago!"

Dr. Adams spread his fingers wide and tamped down the air. "Now, let's all settle down. Have a seat."

Alec and Xo remained standing, Xo still occupying the desk. After a moment, Dr. Adams sat down in one of the guest chairs.

"You're correct. The vaccine did work, and I did take it myself. But, unfortunately…" Dr. Adams shook his head. "There were some… disagreements over the development process, and I was not allowed to do further human testing during the outbreak."

"I can't believe you didn't tell us there's a vaccine!" exclaimed Xo. "Elliot was worried sick about me catching this! We almost didn't get married. And think of all the people you could have saved before!"

"I do think about it!" said Dr. Adams. "That's why I'm still hoping to get both the vaccine and my new treatment put into general use! Unfortunately, as there haven't been many outbreaks, there've been limited opportunities to prove myself—after my research methods were slandered."

"There's an opportunity now," Alec cut in. "Xo and I both may have been exposed, and we're going back up."

"All right." Dr. Adams stood. "I'll test your blood, and if you haven't already caught it from Elliot, I'll give you the vaccine. But you'll need to sign this release."

"Fine, but let's make it quick." Alec rolled up his sleeve.

"If the test shows you have caught the mountainpox, I'll give you the new treatment."

Xo frowned, watching Alec sign the paper as the doctor passed her one as well. If Dr. Adams was able to administer the unapproved vaccine based on signing a release, why hadn't he done so when she and Elliot had gone to him before? Then Elliot might not have fled when he got sick. Still, it was more urgent right now to get on with helping Elliot. There would be time to extract further explanation from the doctor on the hike. She signed the form and let Dr. Adams draw some blood, as he'd done with Alec.

The doctor mixed her blood with a preparation from a small refrigerator behind his desk. Then he returned to Alec's sample, which he had already prepared, and examined it under a microscope.

"No signs of infection," Dr. Adams said to Alec. "Congratulations, you must have been very careful." Alec grunted impatiently and offered his arm again for the vaccine, and the doctor injected him.

Xo waited in the doctor's chair, rolling it back and forth. If she also hadn't caught it, maybe she didn't even need the vaccine. But Elliot would definitely want her to get it now that there was an opportunity.

A flicker of concern creased the doctor's forehead as he examined her sample. "You really ought to be showing signs of infection, Xo. Let's give it another minute."

"I guess I was careful, too," said Xo. "Why wasn't this vaccine approved for distribution?"

"I assure you my tests were quite definitive, my dear. Only, some people care more about methods and regulations than saving lives." Dr. Adams peered through the microscope again. "I should take another blood sample from you, Xo, to be sure."

"What for?" said Xo. "Just give me the vaccine already."

"If you've caught the mountainpox, you'll need the other treatment I've developed, not the vaccine. You have been in close contact with Elliot in the past few days, correct?"

Xo gritted her teeth. "Yes, but I already told you I don't have a rash. We don't have time for this. I don't want to give another blood sample—I want the vaccine, and for you to go help Elliot."

Dr. Adams sighed. "Very well."

Xo rolled up her sleeve, and the doctor swabbed her arm to prepare the injection site. He opened the refrigerator and removed a vial from which he filled a fresh syringe. Out of the corner of her eye, Xo saw Alec tense.

"Hang on," Alec said suddenly, starting forward.

The doctor's languid movements accelerated all at once, and he grabbed Xo's arm, stabbing the full syringe downward towards her shoulder.

"Hey!" Xo squirmed out of his grasp. The chair tipped sideways and Dr. Adams lost his grip on her arm. As she scrambled away backwards across the floor, Dr. Adams stepped back slowly with both hands raised, surrender-like, the still-full syringe in one.

Alec pointed at the syringe. "That's not what you gave me!"

Xo raised herself to a standing position against the wall, eyeing Dr. Adams with alarm. "Is that true?" Yes, it was different; the liquid administered to Alec had been pale pink, while this was translucent yellow. She'd been too focused on getting it over with and heading back to Elliot to notice.

"Don't trust anything he says!" Alec's eyes narrowed in suspicion. "I think it's time you and I get out of here, Xo, and report this guy. I'm beginning to understand what questionable research methods he got in trouble for."

Xo didn't move. Alec had a point, but first, she needed more info on what was going on.

"If you report me, I won't be able to help Elliot," said Dr. Adams, his voice rising.

"We know you have the cure," said Alec, one hand on the door. "We'll get the authorities to retrieve it. It's too risky to take you."

"I'll have to tell them I don't know what cure you're talking about." A shadow of a smile flickered in Dr. Adams's face. He had lowered his arms, still holding the syringe away from his body, like a knife.

Xo edged sideways and opened the refrigerator. There were several different vials of varying colors, labeled numerically. Someone might eventually be able to figure out what was what by analyzing the doctor's notes, but not in enough time to save Elliot. She caught Alec's eye and shook her head to try to signal him that they needed the doctor's cooperation. Alec seemed to get it—at least he took his hand off the door and folded his arms, watching the doctor suspiciously.

"What is that shot you tried to give me?" Xo gestured at the yellow syringe. "It's not the vaccine."

"No, it isn't," admitted Dr. Adams, his voice now calm. "Xo, you seem like a reasonable person. I know you want to do all you can to help Elliot."

"Yes," said Xo carefully, eyeing the syringe.

"I can treat him if you agree to work with me," Dr. Adams said.

"What is it you want?" asked Xo.

"I originally wanted to administer the treatment to you, so I could have documented proof that it worked."

"But you said I'm not infected."

"No, you don't appear to be," said Dr. Adams. He sounded disappointed. "I can't understand why not. Elliot was certain to have been shedding live virus well before he left. I was sure you would contract it."

"Now hold on…" said Alec.

"You said Elliot wasn't shedding any virus before," Xo broke in. "That's not supposed to happen until the rash develops."

"He wasn't. Initially." Dr. Adams stood to one side, his eyes flicking from Xo to Alec. "But he should have been, after I injected him with it."

His words echoed around the silent room.

"What?" shouted Xo. Alec swore incoherently.

"He thought I was doing another blood draw," said Dr. Adams matter-of-factly. "I'd thought he would become contagious the first time I injected him with the virus—you were there for that, Xo, it was when I first met you. I knew it might be my only chance, so I did it after I took his initial samples. He thought the second needle was because I missed a vein."

Xo stared at him in shock.

"But apparently, his prior immunity suppressed it too much, because he didn't become symptomatic and you didn't catch anything. On the plus side, I was able to perfect my treatment using his antibodies, just as I'd hoped. But you, Xo, were the key to proving it worked."

"Me?" said Xo.

"What do you mean she was the key?" demanded Alec angrily.

"I needed a test subject who would believably catch mountainpox and immediately come to me to be cured." Dr. Adams addressed Xo, not Alec. "Elliot was already convinced he could infect you, which made you the ideal candidate. It would have worked perfectly if you'd actually caught it.

"But you didn't, so I had to inject him again a few days ago, unbeknownst to him, when he came to donate more blood for research. I used much more of the virus that time, but his immune system must still have been suppressing it at first, since he didn't shed enough virus to infect you before he left. Unfortunately, I didn't count on him taking off."

Xo's head whirled. This meant Elliot definitely did have the mountainpox, potentially an even more severe infection than when he'd caught it the first time.

"You're going to jail!" she yelled. "You can't go around shooting my husband full of viruses! Elliot could be dying right now because of you!"

Dr. Adams appeared unfazed. "I wouldn't have done it if I didn't think he could handle it. It was the only way outside of an actual outbreak that I could make sure someone—in this case you, Xo— would catch it without suspicion, to give me the chance to prove my treatment works. And finally get recognition for my years of toil combating this disease."

"You put my friend's life in danger, not to mention myself and Xo." Alec spoke menacingly, blocking the door. "If you think you're getting out of here with accolades, you're much mistaken."

"Both my vaccine and treatment will save many lives, if I can overturn the unfair tarnish on my reputation," insisted Dr. Adams. "No one else ever has to die from this again!"

"What about Elliot?" wailed Xo. "He's not 'handling it' as you put it! He has an incredibly high fever and the rash is spreading. If you want to save lives, why don't you save his?"

"I could treat him, but since Elliot's immune system has fought off this virus before, it would not be a conclusive test," said Dr. Adams. "That's why I needed to test the cure on you."

"Well, that's not gonna work, since I didn't get infected."

"No." Dr. Adams sighed. "Meaning I still need a test subject." He gave Xo a significant look. "And you still need me to help Elliot. Which I will not be able to do if you have me arrested," he added, eyeing Alec's threatening expression.

Xo did still need the doctor, unfortunately. "Please help Elliot." She tried to moderate her voice. "He could die from this infection, and you wouldn't even have been able to make your treatment without his antibodies. Don't you think you owe him this?"

"That's a fine sentiment," said Dr. Adams. "But it doesn't do any good to have developed the treatment if I can't prove it works. I already went through this ten years ago when I perfected my vaccine for mountainpox. But do I have any recognition? No. Are manufacturers distributing it and allowing people to benefit? No."

He sighed again, shaking his head. "I trusted the wrong person and as a result was forced to conceal my work on the vaccine or lose my license altogether. I'm not willing to go through that again, not when I have this breakthrough. This medicine could help many people, Xo. It could save lives. Elliot's life."

Xo searched the doctor's face. He wanted something, but what could she bargain with besides appealing to his compassion?

"If I had caught the mountainpox, I'd be willing to let you test your cure in exchange for helping Elliot," said Xo finally. "But I didn't catch it."

Dr. Adams smiled slowly. "That can still be arranged."

A chill ran down Xo's back. Dr. Adams rolled the yellow syringe in his palm. "There's more than one way to get infected, Xo. It's just hard to make it subtle when one is not able to work with patients on a regular basis—though I did pretty well concealing it from Elliot. But there's no need for pretense, if you're willing…"

"Don't do it, Xo," interrupted Alec, loudly. "You can't possibly consider letting him infect you with a deadly disease! Who knows if his cure even works? This guy has already proven he's a nutcase." He rubbed his own shoulder where the vaccine had gone in.

"I have full confidence in my treatment," said Dr. Adams. "Elliot knew I didn't treat patients, and he still let me harvest his antibodies for research. He was willing to do anything to protect you, Xo. Are you willing to do the same for him?"

Xo was frozen in place. She tried to breathe steadily and quiet her mind, which was screaming in the background.

"He's trying to manipulate you," spat Alec. "Don't be stupid."

"I can't think." Xo crushed her hands to her forehead.

"Your friend here," Dr. Adams glanced coolly in Alec's direction and back to Xo, "Was willing to take the vaccine to save himself, but he doesn't want to take even the smallest risk to save Elliot. I'm sure you'd risk more than he would, to save your husband."

Deep down, Xo knew what he said about Alec was not true, and that there was no guarantee the doctor's cure did anything. She would be the first test subject, and Elliot the second. It was too dangerous, all of it. She could walk out now, turn the doctor in before he managed to inject anybody else with who-knew-what. Elliot *might* survive without the treatment…but…

But…

But he might not, especially with however much virus this guy had injected him with. She would still be alive and safe, with her dream career in hand, but that future seemed thin and empty without Elliot in it, containing only broken pieces of her. As Elliot had once said: without loving, what was the point of the other two things? What the doctor was asking was wrong, but every rational course of action she could take against it might end up with Elliot dying when she'd had this chance to save him. The idea made her feel like her heart was stopping. It didn't matter how many reasons she came up with against the plan. She might die trying, but she couldn't live with not trying.

She forced down the objections in her mind, pinning them under the weight of emotion. This was stronger than all the reasons, stronger than anything else, so strong it scared her. So strong that ever since it had begun to grow, as she'd realized how much Elliot meant to her, she'd kept it trapped, suppressed, to keep it from making all her decisions. When she'd seen Elliot lying in the cabin it had nearly crushed her. This time, it would work for her, to give her the strength to do what felt right, even if she couldn't force the decision to make sense.

"I'll do it," said Xo.

"Xo! Don't!" shouted Alec.

"Elliot would do it for me."

"Elliot's just—That doesn't mean it's a good idea!" Alec spluttered.

"I think he'd even do it for you." Xo was calm now that she had made her decision. Her feelings weren't so explosive when she wasn't suppressing them.

Alec held up his hands. "All right, maybe. But you know what else? He absolutely would *not* let you do it. He would stop you from taking that shot, don't tell me he wouldn't!"

"Oh? And how exactly would he stop me?" Xo asked, keeping her voice mild. For one flickering moment, at the look in his eyes, she wondered if Alec would grab her and physically drag her from the room. Then he'd raise the alarm, and there'd be no chance of figuring out the right vial in time to treat Elliot.

But Alec scowled and jammed his hands in his pockets. "If I knew that, I'd stop you myself."

"This is what I have to do," said Xo. She turned back to Dr. Adams. "Give me the virus and test the cure on me. But you have to go with us immediately to help Elliot. We've already wasted time."

"Of course." The doctor smiled and waved Xo back into the chair.

Her arm twitched in apprehension of the shot of mountainpox, but if the doctor actually could cure her, then he could probably cure Elliot too. She forced herself to remain still as the needle from the yellow syringe pierced her skin.

45

A Shot in the Dark

Xo held a cotton wad that Dr. Adams had given her over the injection site, while he packed medical equipment in a small case. Alec lurked by the door, backpack on and arms crossed.

"Are you going to give me the treatment before we leave?" asked Xo.

"That will have to wait until your rash appears and I can confirm you're infected," said Dr. Adams. "I need to have that on record. But don't worry, it should happen quite quickly. I gave you a nice large dose of virus, and unlike Elliot, you have no prior immunity to suppress it."

Xo pulled her coat back on, frowning as they left the office. "If you meant for me to catch this after the first time you injected Elliot, how did you know you'd be able to finish your treatment using Elliot's antibodies in time to cure me?"

"I didn't, technically. But there was a good chance that it would work," Dr. Adams added brightly, in response to Xo's scowl. "I'd long theorized that survivor immunity was key to developing a cure, but survivors are hard to find. Hector was uncooperative from the start, probably because he got wind of the rumors about the vaccine. But when I did that interview with the *Mountain Herald*"—Dr. Adams gestured at Alec—"with one of your colleagues, the reporter happened to mention that a survivor from an earlier epidemic still lived here. Someone who refused to give an interview himself, or even talk about it, apparently." He smiled as Alec glared at him.

"That turned out to be Elliot, naturally, the unnamed person who had recognized mountainpox in Lia. But I'd realized that even if I could get his antibodies and get the treatment working, I'd never secure approval for a trial study after what happened with the vaccine. It wasn't until I heard the gossip about how he might have infected Lia that it struck me: fear of reactivation offered a believable setting in which to prove my treatment worked. So I pumped up that idea when the college paper quoted me in their follow-up piece. I was surprised Elliot didn't come to me right after that—in the end it took Xo to tip the scales."

"That piece in the college paper was you, too? I might have known," snarled Alec. "Elliot didn't come to you then, because I made sure he didn't read it. It was blatant fearmongering."

"You didn't complain when I interviewed for *your* paper," countered Dr. Adams lightly. "And when you first came to my office today, you'd bought into the reactivation scare along with everyone else."

"I'm turning you in, once this is all over," said Alec. He seemed too disgusted to look at Xo since her decision to take the shot.

"I see I can't expect better from you," said Dr. Adams. "However, my successful cure will speak for itself at that point, and reasonable minds will see that my actions were justified."

Xo pulled Alec aside as they left the college campus. "Don't you think we'd better get him some proper gear from your house? He's not gonna do Elliot any good if he can't make it up the mountain."

Alec frowned. "I'd rather he froze." He turned to the doctor. "Come on. We're making a detour on the way."

At his garage, Alec silently doled out equipment for Dr. Adams, and sandwiches for lunch, which they ate while walking to save time. They fell into a line with Alec in front, then Dr. Adams, then Xo following in case the doctor attempted to desert them. But Dr. Adams seemed enthusiastic to accompany them, and not at all remorseful.

"Say, how long does it take to get to this place?" said Dr. Adams to Xo after they had been ascending the mountain for a while. He had stopped to catch his breath, so Xo stopped as well.

"Several more hours, from what I remember." Muscles Xo hadn't even known she possessed were aching. The aspirin she'd taken earlier must have worn off.

Dr. Adams gave a low whistle. "He really didn't want to infect anybody, did he?"

"You should have just told him about the vaccine from the beginning," said Xo angrily.

"But I didn't need to test that anymore. Besides, if I'd vaccinated you, I wouldn't have had a good test subject for the treatment."

"I'm surprised you didn't just jump Elliot in a dark alley and draw his blood," muttered Xo. Dr. Adams would have made an oddly cheerful vampire, but maybe those were the ones that caught you unawares.

Dr. Adams smiled a little too long, making Xo fear that he'd actually considered this idea.

At last he said, "You are wrong to imagine me as some sort of depraved lunatic, Xo. Alienating Elliot would have been detrimental to my research, especially if I'd needed multiple samples to get the treatment working. Also, until the concept of reactivation came up, I had no way of proving my cure short of unleashing another outbreak. That was a worst-case scenario if I didn't get to you, of course, but knowing how carefully Elliot handled Lia's infection I figured I'd be able to keep it contained."

He started forward again, at what looked like an easy pace, but Xo was so sore it was all she could do to keep up with him. "Did you ever really believe it could reactivate? Or was it all lies from the beginning?" she demanded.

"Considering how much live virus I had to inject Elliot with to get him symptomatic again, which still didn't cause him to infect you, I'm sure that the mountainpox wouldn't naturally re-occur in someone with immunity. All the evidence points to a non-human host for the virus, something that likes it up here. Sasquatch, maybe." He glanced around the snowy mountains with a smile.

Xo glowered at his back. "Then what about when people discovered later that it didn't reactivate after all?"

Dr. Adams chuckled. "Despite the lack of evidence, it would be hard to prove that it *doesn't* reactivate, without a lot of dicey tests that most people don't have the guts or interest to do. Years later when this became clear, Elliot's isolated case would be assumed to be a misunderstanding, where instead of reactivating, his immunity had worn off and he'd caught it again."

"But why not just publish your results and get proof next time there's a real outbreak, since Elliot willingly gave you the samples you needed to make the treatment?" It still stung Xo that Elliot hadn't told her about his continued participation with the doctor, when the idea of a cure must have been so important to him. "Surely creating the cure is enough. Why wouldn't that be accepted even after your stupid research methods with the vaccine?"

Dr. Adams smiled and shook his head, pausing to look back at her. "Your naivete is charming, Xo. I don't hold it against you; it really did help the process. I was like you, once. I thought people would simply accept a good thing for what it was." He started forward again, setting a pace that allowed him to talk. "I'd been developing the vaccine for years when the epidemic hit Lingen, and when I tested it on people here—subtly, of course—it worked even better than I'd hoped. I rushed to tell Dr. Barker what I'd made—ah, to think I used to hold him in such esteem. I trusted he would see the value, would understand there was no time to go through the proper channels and approvals with the rate at which mountainpox spread, but no: not only did he refuse my offer of the vaccine for himself, he had the gall to file a report against me for so-called 'unethical human testing' as well.

"That might have been the end of my career, but Dr. Barker died before he could prove anything against me. I was still discredited among my colleagues by the accusation. I couldn't even get another decent research post. The only chance to redeem myself was to develop something even better, with evidence that couldn't be ignored. With a proven cure to this previously untreatable and devastating virus, the accusations of a foolish bygone doctor would be forgotten and my abilities finally acknowledged."

A disturbing thought occurred to Xo. "Dr. Barker—Lia's doctor—he died after he threatened to turn you in…"

"Again, you misjudge me, Xo. Dr. Barker caught the mountainpox through his own carelessness, not through me. In fact, I would have been his salvation if he'd accepted the vaccine. Either he was envious of my achievement, or he simply could not grasp that my discovery was more important than following protocol. And as a result of his insinuations, I ended up having to accept a job in this microbiology department when I could have been out saving lives."

They both stopped again to catch their breath, and Xo saw gratefully that Alec was waiting a short distance ahead to allow them to catch up. Dr. Adams must be at least as sore as she'd been on the first hike yesterday, but she was achieving heretofore unknown levels of pain. Was this the mountainpox infection kicking in, or just exhaustion? Whatever it was, she had to fight through it to get back to Elliot. At least harnessing her anger at Dr. Adams seemed to be helping drive her forward.

"As you know, I didn't let my time at the college go to waste," Dr. Adams continued. "And I'd learned enough not to let anyone in on my experiments. It almost went off without a hitch." He shrugged. "You really shouldn't go through papers in other people's offices, Xo. It complicates things. But I think even this…stumbling block…will be judged worthwhile after what I've achieved, single-handedly taming a deadly virus. A glance at the history of medicine will find far greater crimes than mine with far less benefit to humanity."

"If Elliot dies, that won't matter," said Xo, with a catch in her voice. She tightened her grip on her pack straps and started climbing again, herding Dr. Adams on ahead.

"A single death can benefit many others," said Dr. Adams. "Take Lia, for instance: if she hadn't died, I'm not sure Elliot would have been worried enough about re-infecting you for anyone to convince him it was possible, even me."

Underneath her renewed fury at Dr. Adams, Xo felt a momentary flare of sympathy for Lia. She'd only ever condemned Lia after finding out how she'd betrayed Elliot, but Lia had never managed to follow the path she'd wanted, back to Francis. If she'd done that, she still would have hurt Elliot, but she wouldn't have left him saddled with the guilt of her death and so susceptible to the doctor's trap. Considering the lengths to which Elliot was willing to go, the damage was even deeper than Xo had guessed. Still, they had to be able to overcome it, if only he would live. She pressed forward, trying to move faster.

❖   ❖   ❖

As they gained altitude, Xo's path through the snow took on a mechanical quality. There was no more talk, to save breath and energy, and she was scarcely aware of telling her legs to move, or of anything she passed on the way. No fresh snow had fallen since their first ascent, so the ground ahead was broken by a combination of their old ski tracks and footprints, making a clear path to follow even as she found herself lagging farther and farther behind Alec and Dr. Adams. Dr. Adams—older than either of them, greying, and having lost his grip on reality to boot—must be more rugged than she'd realized. Or was Xo moving more slowly than usual? It was impossible to tell without passing any discernible natural features, just snow and snow-covered rocks, dimmer and dimmer as the day wore on.

It was the same path again, unlike what Machado's poem said. Or was it different this time? A cold chill shook her. Was Elliot still alive, or would they be too late? A drench of sweat replaced the chill. Her muscles burned and the inner layer of clothes clung to her uncomfortably, scraping her skin. Xo unzipped the front of her jacket to let in a little air. It was refreshing, but it didn't make her any less tired. Keep sliding one foot in front of the other. There were voices up ahead. Next thing, she was squinting at a bright light. Were they in the cabin? No, it didn't have ceiling lights. Alec's face appeared above her, and she gradually realized that the bright light was the sun, low in the sky. She was lying in the snow. She tuned in to Alec's words with difficulty.

"Why can't you give her that medicine now?"

"Let's see if there's any sign of a rash," Dr. Adams's voice replied. "She has to be symptomatic first." A glove loomed into her personal space.

Xo jerked back, folding her arms around herself. "Get away!" One of her feet was caught; she kicked the ski off. The other ski was already gone.

"Xo," said Alec. "Are you okay?"

"I'm fine," said Xo. "Give it to Elliot."

Above her, she saw Alec and the doctor exchange a look.

"We're not there yet," said Alec.

"Then what are we doing?" Xo lurched to her feet and staggered forward, but the snow impeded her. Alec retrieved her other ski and she managed to reattach both. The others walked closer to her, featureless dark shapes, moving unsteadily. The light was fading; that meant they needed to go faster. If only her shirt didn't cling to her so much. She plucked it away from her stomach and flinched, gasping, as her fingertips grazed her body. It felt as if she'd scraped her skin with a handful of razors.

Xo stopped, swaying, and tried to open her sweatshirt under her jacket, but gave up on the zipper after the third try and lifted her shirt. A blast of cooling air hit her stomach, where a few red blisters showed above her waistline. She poked one and the searing pain returned—marvelous how such a tiny spot could be so painful. Wait, this was when she was supposed to take the medicine. The doctor and Alec had pulled ahead. She took a step forward and dizziness overwhelmed her and she pitched into the snow again. The cold soothed the rash, once the physical contact with the snow had numbed her burning skin.

Now somebody was rolling her over. Alec argued with the doctor about something, couldn't they be quiet? She could barely understand them, they sounded both unpleasantly loud and far away.

Her coat and then her sweatshirt came off, delicious cool. A stabbing pain in her arm that she wrenched away from, but hands held her down.

"We need the sample to verify infection," said Dr. Adams.

"Hold still…now it's the treatment, Xo," said Alec.

"If Dr. Barker had been as reasonable as the two of you, he needn't have died at all," mused Dr. Adams as the needle went in again. "But he was quite a stubborn man."

"How long until we know if it works?" Alec sounded angry.

"Oh, it'll be evident very soon if it *doesn't* work." The doctor's voice was jocular as he released her arm. "Congratulations, by the way, Xo. You will likely be the first person cured by means of this treatment!"

Xo pushed herself up with difficulty to get away from Dr. Adams, and felt Alec steady her. "What happened to the other ones?" Xo said through gritted teeth.

"You're very droll. Don't worry, no one has died at my hands—well, no one who wouldn't have died anyway."

Xo's renewed loathing of Dr. Adams gave her a jolt of fresh energy. They reached the climbing part where she could take off her skis again. She struggled up the hill ahead of the others, but it had gotten steeper, and she kept tipping.

Alec pushed her upright again from behind. "Do I need to carry you?"

"You are not going to carry me." Xo shoved away from him, but not too hard. It helped her balance.

"Now, now, children," came the doctor's voice. "Don't forget, I need a living test subject, especially if you want me to treat Elliot when we get there."

"We have a deal," said Alec. "You treat him regardless, now."

"My deal is with Xo, not you," said Dr. Adams lightly.

"We're making a new deal," growled Alec. "You treat Elliot and I let you leave the cabin again."

Dr. Adams did not deign to respond to this, and Xo forced herself to move slowly up the rocks, almost wishing she'd taken Alec up on his offer to carry her.

The cabin loomed out of the dusk as they approached. Something was different. The lamp within had gone out, and a dark opening showed at the door. Alec quickly outdistanced Xo as he ran forward. She stumbled behind him to the threshold. The door was open a few inches and Elliot was lying on the floor inside, snow drifted against him.

"Elliot!" She tried to push through the crack.

Alec forced the door open the rest of the way. "I…I must not have shut the door all the way," he said, stumbling over his words. "And it blew open…"

Xo dropped to her knees beside the still form. "Elliot?"

His rash had spread, reconquering its former territory, red against a pallor unnatural even for Elliot. His skin was so cold as she felt for a pulse…faint, rapid, but present. A sob, part terror, part relief at finding him alive, choked out of her and she doubled over, burying her head against his unresponsive shoulder.

There they could have stayed, but Alec stepped over her where she had fallen to the floor and pulled Elliot from her exhausted arms, carrying him away despite her attempts to hold on. Her head spun as she tried to rise, and her body, burning in every limb, refused to cooperate. Then Alec was back and she was being lifted.

"I told you not to carry me." Her own words sounded muddled and far away. Before she'd managed to speak them all, she was being laid down again on one of those wooden benches, between the wall and Elliot's cold, now shivering body. She scooted against him, trying to warm him, as Alec draped a zipped-open sleeping bag over both of them.

Dr. Adams knelt beside them, checking Elliot's vitals. His formerly chipper demeanor had gone.

"Still think he can 'handle it?'" Alec's voice was harsh.

The doctor's forehead creased. "Be a shame if I did overdo it, after all," he muttered, half to himself.

Xo pushed herself up on one arm, watching Dr. Adams frown at the reading he had just taken of Elliot's blood pressure.

The doctor glanced at her. "The treatment might not help much at this stage, but it shouldn't make him any worse."

"Do whatever you can," whispered Xo.

The needle went into Elliot's arm, and Xo winced. Elliot's eyelids fluttered but he did not wake.

"Try to sleep, Xo" said Dr. Adams. "My cure is working for you or you'd be extremely ill by now. You wouldn't have even made it up here."

If this was working, what did not working feel like? But Xo had only to look at Elliot beside her to know.

"Go ahead. I'll keep an eye on the doctor," said Alec.

Xo brushed back the hair plastered on Elliot's forehead and took his hand. The ache in her heart made it hard to breathe as she gazed down over the slight form of this adoring man who loved her with his entire being and whom she loved with all of hers.

"Elliot? Please hang on."

She couldn't be sure, but she wanted to believe Elliot's hand gripped hers faintly, in reply.

46

Between Living and Dreaming

Elliot's eyes flickered open. He had a peculiar sense of clarity after a long period of confusion and restless sleep, half-dreams—hallucinations, perhaps. His thoughts were too calm now to be dreaming. He no longer felt hot, or cold, or even pain. Bright, grey, morning light streamed across his vision, making everything a haze of light and shadow. After the chaos that had reigned in his mind, the unfamiliar location was disorienting. Was he still alive? Was this what it was like not to feel anything, or just what it was like not to feel feverish anymore?

After a moment, he realized that his arms were numb because he was lying on top of them on a hard surface. He shifted one of them and a searing, tingling feeling shot down it, a burning ache that told him undeniably that his arm was still alive, and therefore so was he. Reaching down without thinking why, his hand touched his glasses immediately under the bench he was sleeping on, and soon the patches of light and shadow resolved into the interior of the lookout cabin. The night had passed…no, more than one night, it felt like many more. The shutters of two of the windows had been opened—

by someone other than Elliot. Three still figures lay in the room, one of them inches away.

Elliot pushed himself up on his other protesting arm as apprehension rushed back in. Xo had to be all right, she had to. Anything else would be more weight than the world could bear. He studied the sleeping face beside him that he had feared he might never see again. Her expression was peaceful and free of obvious signs of illness, but she was lying here right next to him…could she have really avoided catching the disease? He quietly lifted the edge of the sleeping bag to see the rest of her, and Xo's dark eyes flashed open.

"Elliot!" Xo breathed in a whisper. "You're awake!" She touched his face, staring at him in wonder, then sat up and crushed him against her, rocking back and forth.

"Wait! I could be—"

Xo pulled back slightly and shook her head. "It's okay, I can't catch it now anyway. Well, none of us can. But try to whisper, Alec only got to sleep a little while ago, and I think he was up most of the night."

"Is he…?" Elliot's heart leapt into his throat again as he turned to where Alec's sleeping bag lay in front of the stove. Only the top of his head was visible.

"No, he's fine too," Xo assured him, crawling back into his arms.

"Thank God you didn't catch it. You took such a risk." Elliot's voice caught in his throat as he wrapped his arms around her. The knife-like pain of his rash had faded into the soreness of healing. He had been given one more chance to see her, but it couldn't last. Reluctantly, he broke the embrace. "Xiomara…now that I know it can reactivate…" He swallowed hard.

"No, no, no," said Xo. "Elliot, it can't reactivate."

"But…" He stared at her.

Xo shook her head. "Elliot, the mountainpox isn't coming back again, I promise. I'll explain all about it, just…hold me, first."

He did, bewildered. The world had turned out to be quite a beautiful place again.

❖　　❖　　❖

After as much breakfast and fizzy electrolytes as Xo—and Alec once he awoke—could get Elliot to consume, he started to feel like himself again. Fresh air and sunshine from a brief and necessary foray outside also helped, though it revealed he was a little unsteady on his feet. New snow had fallen during the past day and night, of which Elliot had no recollection except in fractured dreams.

"Your fever went down some after Dr. Adams gave you the treatment, but you still wouldn't wake up the next day," explained Xo, biting her lip. "I'm so glad you're all right now."

"And you?" asked Elliot softly. "Are you truly recovered?"

Xo showed him where the drugs had arrested the spread of the rash on her stomach, and it wrenched his heart. Though she insisted her experience with the mountainpox had been next to nothing with the treatment, he guessed otherwise.

"Don't look so concerned," said Xo. "I never got too bad, and both our rashes are healing right up." She tugged Elliot over to join the others for a lunch of the last stale slices of Alec's seed bread, plus reconstituted soup heated on the woodstove.

They ate while Alec and Xo added details to what Xo had already told him about the course of events. Dr. Adams started to interject at one point, but Alec shut him down with surprising force and he shrugged and returned to eating silently, leaving Elliot confused. Then the rest of the story about the doctor came out.

As Elliot pieced together what had happened, the blissful joy of recovery in Xo's arms departed with the realization that it was his fault she'd contracted the mountainpox after all, even if he hadn't infected her directly. His stomach churned, unwilling to accept both food and guilt simultaneously.

"Please try to eat more, Elliot," said Xo. "You haven't had a proper meal in days, and you're gonna need fuel to get back down the mountain."

"Xo's right," said Alec. "I hate to say this when you're not fully recovered, Elliot, but if you're able, we should try to go down today. We're running pretty low on supplies."

"I can make it," said Elliot. He managed to choke some food down as Xo stood and began to pack.

She shook out Elliot's coat and a scrap of paper drifted down. "What's this, should I toss it?"

Elliot took it slowly; it was the other name and number Dr. Rotariu had given him before she referred him to Dr. Adams—as he'd foolishly insisted. He folded the paper in a small square and put it in his shirt pocket for safekeeping, then reluctantly turned to Dr. Adams, the only doctor currently available.

"Are you absolutely sure I won't infect anyone if I return to Lingen this soon?" Elliot tried to keep his voice steady.

"Never fear, you're not contagious anymore now that you've scabbed over, neither is Xo." Dr. Adams was eating heartily. "You're amazingly good at suppressing this virus. Though I might have overdone it a bit. You weren't doing too well when we first got up here. Another triumph for my cure, though!"

"I'm not certain that I should thank you, considering the circumstances," said Elliot to Dr. Adams. "But thank you—for at least keeping us alive."

"You shouldn't thank him." Alec sounded disgusted. "None of us would've needed to be kept alive if it hadn't been for him." He collected soup bowls and dunked them angrily in the bucket he was using to clean up.

"I'm afraid that burden is mine," said Elliot miserably. "I am the one who brought on all of this when I allowed Francis to plant the notion of contagion in my mind."

"Hold on," said Xo. "Dr. Adams manipulated you! Though I do wish you'd talked to me when you found out you were sick. Maybe we could have come up with a better plan."

Dr. Adams nodded vigorously, earning a scowl from Xo.

"Elliot almost died, why are you trying to make him feel worse?" retorted Alec. "He only came up here to protect you, Xo. He wouldn't have gone through any of this if it wasn't for you."

Xo glared at Alec, and before Elliot could say anything, tears coursed down her face. She turned abruptly and went outside, closing the door behind her.

"Alec…!" Elliot rose to go after her, a jolt of dizziness hitting him as he stood up too fast. "It's not Xiomara's fault at all. It's mine."

Alec sighed and shook his head. "We've just all been stuck in this cabin too long. It's time we get going. Elliot, hang on a sec." Alec stopped him on his way to the door and retrieved an extra pair of skis leaning against the wall. "Brought these for you."

"Thank you." The skis would help what Elliot predicted would be a shaky descent. "How did you know I'd be going back down?"

Alec gave him a look. "I didn't. You had us all pretty scared for a while there."

"I don't think I would be going down, if you hadn't come up here," said Elliot. "I...I think I yelled at you about it, before. I'm sorry."

"Don't mention it. You were delirious." Alec gave Elliot a rough one-armed hug. "I'm glad I came up here, too."

Elliot sighed, wishing he could think of something more appreciative to say to Alec. It was never enough.

Dr. Adams inserted himself into the conversation. "Now, Elliot, before we go: I know you want to protect the world from mountainpox as much as I do—I think you are the only one who truly grasps how important my achievements are. My vaccine and treatment can save many more people, but your friend here has the idea of having me locked up as soon as we get back to town. Doubtless it will all be straightened out soon enough, but in the meantime, can I count on you to make sure my research gets into the right hands? Just don't go letting anyone else take credit for my discoveries!"

"Uh...yes," said Elliot. Not that anyone would want to claim involvement with Dr. Adams's process, despite his ultimate success. It was sickening that the doctor saw him as an ally with a common goal. But was Elliot really any better than him? If it hadn't been for Elliot's attempt to protect her, Xo never would have been drawn into participating in the doctor's dangerous experiments.

Alec scowled and prodded the doctor towards the door, collecting his pack on the way. "People might be saved with your drugs, but you won't be the one to administer them. I've got those papers you made me and Xo sign, as evidence, and I've written a full report of what you did to Elliot as well. You're going to be in prison for a long time. And don't even think of giving me the slip; you're not getting out of my sight until I personally see the police lock you up."

"Or I have an 'accident' on the way down the hill, eh?" replied Dr. Adams.

Elliot's mouth went dry. "Alec…"

"Don't worry," said Alec. "Much as I'd like to see him ski off a cliff, I want him exposed. I'm going to get you justice."

"Maybe you just want a breaking story?" said the doctor derisively. "The *Mountain Herald* has never seen the like!"

"Shut up," said Alec harshly. "That's not what this is about." He frowned and turned back to Elliot, lowering his voice. "Look, I'll do my best to stop it—I know you don't want any more publicity—but this'll make the news one way or another. You know Lingen."

Elliot swallowed hard. "Alec, it's your article to write." It was the only thing he could say, the one thing he could do.

Alec straightened up, his face clearing. "You'd be okay with it?"

Elliot nodded. "Break the story."

Alec grinned and patted Elliot's shoulder. "I'm on it, then, Elliot. As for you," he said to Dr. Adams, "It's all over."

"I'll follow you down, with Xo," said Elliot, as Alec prodded the doctor out the door.

"See you at the bottom, then! The sooner I turn him in, the sooner I can get a decent coffee from Megan. That stuff I made on the stove here was truly awful," Alec added cheerfully.

The coffee had not been as bad as Alec claimed, but it was all gone now. After Alec and Dr. Adams left, Elliot found one tea bag left in the cupboard and took the travel mug from Xo's pack. As it brewed, he collected the remaining equipment he and Xo would carry, then went to join her.

Xo stood apart from the cabin, watching the figures of Alec and Dr. Adams dwindle into the distance. As Elliot approached, she took from her coat pocket the sack that had held the bread they'd eaten, and shook the seeds from the bottom of the bag onto the snow. A futile gesture—the snow-drifted mountainside was starkly bereft of life besides themselves.

"I know what you're thinking, but one never knows, right?" said Xo. Smiling now, she walked back to meet Elliot. "Today, with you well again, I feel like anything's possible."

Elliot pressed the warm cup of tea into her hand. "Xiomara...I am so sorry for what I put you through. Dr. Adams would never have been able to harm you with this disease if I had not given into my fears."

"Oh, he might have found a way." Xo wrapped both hands around the cup. "Please don't blame yourself. Alec said—" Xo stopped.

"He shouldn't have said that. It wasn't your fault," said Elliot.

Xo shook her head. "Before, I was mad that you'd left. He pointed out that I wouldn't have listened if you'd just told me you were sick, wouldn't have taken your fears seriously." She studied the tea. "I hated to admit it to Alec, but I think that's true. And I'm sorry."

"Xiomara..." Elliot touched her arm, gently, so as not to spill her cup.

"Alec's not that bad, really," said Xo. "I mean, annoying behavior aside, he can be handy to have around, sometimes."

"I'm glad you think so," said Elliot.

"I can't believe you climbed all the way up here to get away from me." Xo laughed. "I can't believe *I* climbed up here—twice! I didn't know I had it in me, to do that. To...feel that much. I knew that you loved me, but I didn't know you loved me like that. Although I don't know why I didn't see it before, it's...who you are. And I didn't know I loved you like that, but I do." She looked over at him at last.

"I only ended up putting you in more danger by trying to protect you. I was just so afraid you would die." Elliot's voice shook. "I...I don't know what I would have done..."

"Elliot, you're the bravest person I know. If a person isn't afraid, they don't have to be brave."

Giving him a smile, Xo drank her tea and tucked the cup back into her pack. Elliot swallowed the icy lump forming in his throat. Now that the current danger was over, the possibilities still seemed endless for repeating his folly. He had to stop imagining new dangers. Yet he encountered plenty of real hazards as well on a regular basis. He might have unwittingly drawn Xo into a life of one catastrophe after another.

"What if I do something foolish like this again?"

"You're not foolish. If you get worried about something again, I won't dismiss it." Xo's eyes were filling with tears once more. "I'll try to listen, like you always do for me, and we'll fight through whatever it is together, whether it's fear or anything else."

Elliot looked at her wordlessly. The fear of something, anything, happening to her was still there, but he couldn't put a name to it. It had not disappeared with the mountainpox as he'd hoped it would, because the mountainpox had just been one of its many forms, a mask lying around from his youth, made real through his very efforts at prevention. The fear had been there before, and it was still there. It had grown along with his love, inextricably tied together for as long as he could remember, as inseparable as its shadow.

And like a shadow, it was not going to go away—not altogether. But he wouldn't run from it again. As long as he knew what it was, the shadow was not a true threat to the love itself, strong and solid.

"I'm more durable than you seem to think." Xo laughed through her tears. "I'm still here, right? Try me, I'm not that breakable."

She caught the front of Elliot's coat and pulled him against her. She was definitely there, warm and soft and real. Elliot held her close and kissed her mouth. It felt like an eternity since he had last kissed her.

"Are you afraid the sun isn't going to rise again?" asked Xo, between kisses.

"No…" said Elliot.

"Are you afraid that I won't love you anymore?" she asked.

Elliot gazed into her eyes. "No," he said slowly. "Do you know that you are the most precious thing in the world to me?"

"Yes," said Xo. "Do you know we're bound to run into other difficulties? You don't have to handle them alone."

"I know. And I won't," Elliot promised.

"I still want to go through it all with you," said Xo.

Elliot pressed his face into her neck and breathed deeply, closing his eyes. With Xo in his arms, he could feel hope unfolding again inside him, like the first sign of spring. Right at this moment, all was well…perhaps not all of the future, and certainly not all of the past, but for this moment.

One moment at a time—and then the next moment.

Opening his eyes again, he saw over Xo's shoulder that a cluster of small birds had materialized out of the bleak mountainside to peck at the seeds she had scattered.

"Some birds found your seeds after all," Elliot said softly, so as not to startle them. He vaguely remembered seeing one before, but no name came to him from the reference books he'd studied. Their beaks were short and heavy, and oddly flattened, with prominent nostrils.

Xo turned her head and gasped. "Oh! Elliot, it's them: those are hog-nosed finches! Yes!" The birds were just feet away, hopping about on the snow. "I wish I had a camera," she whispered after a moment.

Elliot unwrapped his arms from around her and produced his camera from his pack.

"You were facing potential death and you brought your camera?"

"I always bring my camera." Elliot reflected for a moment. "And I suppose in a way, we're always facing potential death, aren't we?"

"Sometimes we're facing potential field guide subjects we may never see again," said Xo urgently. "Photos first, then philosophy."

Elliot carefully captured some photographs. Moments later, the birds finished the seeds and flew up in a sudden cloud of wings. They swooped away and were lost to view in the glare of the sun on the snow.

"I wonder where they go up here." Xo gazed after them, squinting in the sunlight. "They're so rarely seen."

"I don't know. But I think they come down to Lingen in the fall," said Elliot, remembering that long-ago day. The first Xo sighting.

"Really, you've seen one? That's amazing! Did you recognize it, before?"

Elliot shook his head, smiling at her. "I had no idea how rare it was, the first time I saw it."

Xo turned thoughtful. "You know, the mountainpox host is probably something elusory like these hog-nosed finches."

Elliot felt unexpectedly calm at the notion. "Perhaps."

"Once we get Dr. Adams's medicine into the hands of a proper doctor, maybe they could come up with a way to treat the host as well. Especially if it is one of these birds." Xo smiled. "Just don't mention the bird idea to Dr. Adams," she continued, putting on her pack and skis. "He'd want to dissect them all."

"I won't." Elliot strapped on the skis Alec had brought him. "And I do not think Dr. Adams will have access to hog-nosed finches or anyone else for a while. If ever." Alec would see to that.

Reaching out to clasp Xo's mittened hand, Elliot surveyed the vast expanse of peaks, and dark crags, and clouds, and blank white snow that they were poised above.

"Are you ready, Xiomara?"

Xo squeezed his hand and gave him a brilliant smile. "I'm ready for whatever's next."

A note to my readers:

Thank you, thank you. This book isn't truly a book without you.
I hope you enjoyed lingering in this corner of the world for a while.
If you did, please share it and write a review, so others will know if
they'd like it too!

Hope to see you online :)
—*Sirkka*

About the Author

Sirkka Smith lives in the Pacific Northwest, where she's spent a number of years in Lingen or stuck on Mount Arin somewhere.

Besides writing, common activities include puzzling over the peculiarities of human interaction, blurting out impromptu song lyrics, and getting robots to do her chores for her. She enjoys most caffeinated beverages.

See a picture of Sirkka and her biggest fan along with other bonus material for *The Third Thing* at **sirkkasmith.com**

www.ingramcontent.com/pod-product-compliance
Lightning Source LLC
Chambersburg PA
CBHW021845010726
47493CB00005B/1565